GEORGES PEREC (1936–1982) was the author of *Life A User's Manual*. His output is bewilderingly varied in form and style: it was his aim to write every kind of work that it is possible to write in the modern world without doing the same thing twice. He composed crossword puzzles and poetry, radio plays and a book on the game of Go, essays and palindromes, autobiography (*W or The Memory of Childhood*) and straight narrative, such as *Things*, his prize-winning first novel. After writing *La Disparition (A Void)*, he took all his unused e's and devoted them to a short text, *Les Revenentes*, in which e is the only vowel employed

GILBERT ADAIR lived and worked in France for more than ten years. In Great Britain his reputation as a writer is based on three novels, *The Holy Innocents*, *Love and Death on Long Island* and *The Death of the Author*, as also on two sequels to classics of children's literature, *Alice Through the Needle's Eye* and *Peter Pan and the Only Children*. He is a regular columnist on the *Sunday Times* in London and has published three books on aspects of contemporary culture.

Georges Perec

A VOID

Translated from the French
by Gilbert Adair

THE HARVILL PRESS
LONDON

First published in France with the title *La Disparition*
by Editions Denoël, Paris, 1969
First published in Great Britain in 1994
by Harvill
an imprint of HarperCollins*Publishers*

This edition published in 1995
by The Harvill Press,
84 Thornhill Road,
London N1 1RD
First impression

This translation has been published with
the financial support of the French Ministry
of Culture and Communications.

© Editions Denoël 1969
English translation © HarperCollinsPublishers 1994

A CIP catalogue record for this book
is available from the British Library.

ISBN 1 86046 098 4

Photoset in Linotron Galliard by
Rowland Phototypesetting Ltd,
Bury St Edmunds, Suffolk

Printed and bound in the United States by R. R. Donnelley,
Harrisonburg, Virginia, USA

SUMMARY

INTRODUCTION

In which, as you will soon find out, Damnation
has its origin

Today, by radio, and also on giant hoardings, a rabbi, an admiral
notorious for his links to Masonry, a trio of cardinals, a trio, too,
of insignificant politicians (bought and paid for by a rich and
corrupt Anglo-Canadian banking corporation), inform us all of
how our country now risks dying of starvation. A rumour, that's
my initial thought as I switch off my radio, a rumour or possibly
a hoax. Propaganda, I murmur anxiously – as though, just by
saying so, I might allay my doubts – typical politicians' propaganda. But public opinion gradually absorbs it as a fact. Individuals start strutting around with stout clubs. "Food, glorious
food!" is a common cry (occasionally sung to Bart's music), with
ordinary hard-working folk harassing officials, both local and
national, and cursing capitalists and captains of industry. Cops
shrink from going out on night shift. In Mâcon a mob storms a
municipal building. In Rocadamour ruffians rob a hangar full of
foodstuffs, pillaging tons of tuna fish, milk and cocoa, as also a
vast quantity of corn – all of it, alas, totally unfit for human
consumption. Without fuss or ado, and naturally without any
sort of trial, an indignant crowd hangs 26 solicitors on a hastily
built scaffold in front of Nancy's law courts (this Nancy is a
town, not a woman) and ransacks a local journal, a disgusting
right-wing rag that is siding against it. Up and down this land
of ours looting has brought docks, shops and farms to a virtual
standstill.

Arabs, blacks and, as you might say, non-goyim fall victim to racist attacks, with pogroms forming in such outlying Parisian suburbs as Drancy, Livry-Gargan, Saint-Paul, Villacoublay and Clignancourt. And stray acts of brutality abound: an anonymous tramp has his brains blown out just for a bit of moronic fun, and a sacristan is callously spat upon – in public, too – whilst giving absolution to a CRS man cut in half by a blow from a yataghan (a Hungarian slicing tool, if you must know).

You'd kill your own kith and kin for a chunk of salami, your cousin for a crust, your crony for a crouton and just about anybody at all for a crumb.

On 6 April, from Saturday night until Sunday morning, 25 Molotov cocktails go off around town. Pilots bomb Orly airport. Paris's most familiar landmarks burn down, and its inhabitants look on in horror at a still blazing Alhambra, an *Institut* that is nothing but a sad, smoking ruin, a Saint-Louis Hospital with all its windows alight and gaily flaming away. From Montsouris to Nation not a wall is intact.

Opposition MPs add insult to injury by baiting a now almost suicidal ruling party, which, though obviously hurt by such an affront to its dignity, has a fair stab at smoothing things out. But whilst assassins start liquidating a handful of junior Quai d'Orsay officials (23, or so it's said), a Dutch diplomat caught filching an anchovy from a tub of fish is soon put paid to by an impromptu stoning. And whilst an odiously smug and arrogant viscount in shocking pink spats (*sic*) is laid into by Wagram's hoi polloi until his skin is of a similarly shocking colour (his only fault, it turns out, was to qualify starvation, to a dying man who had put his hand out for a coin, as just too, too boring for words), in Raspail a tall, blond Scandinavian, of actual Viking stock, riding a palomino with blood pouring down its shanks and brandishing aloft a long bow, starts firing arrows off at any local not to his liking.

A poor, starving, half-mad corporal purloins a bazooka and mows down his battalion, commandant and all; and, on his instant promotion to admiral by public acclaim, is just as instantly slain by an adjutant with aspirations to match his own.

In Paris a young man, a bit of a wag, no doubt nostalgic for his country's military incursion into Indo-China, sprays napalm up and down Faubourg Saint-Martin. In Lyon, upwards of a million lost souls pass away, mostly martyrs to scurvy and typhus.

Acting without instructions, wholly on his own volition, an idiot of a city official puts all pubs and clubs, poolrooms and ballrooms, out of bounds – which prompts such a global craving for alcohol (in fact, for oral gratification of any sort), such a profound thirst for whisky or gin, vodka or rum, that it's just as painful as going hungry. To cap it all, this particular May is proving a scorchingly hot and sunny month: in Passy an omnibus combusts without warning; and practically 60% of our population go down with sunburn.

An Olympic oarsman climbs on to a rooftop and for an instant attracts a mob of volcanically frothing fanatics, a mob that abruptly crowns him king. Naturally, it asks him to adopt an alias fully worthy of his royal rank and vocation. His own wish is – wait for it – "Attila III"; what, by contrast, his champions insist on calling him, is "Fantômas XVIII". As that isn't at all to his fancy, his downfall is as dramatic as was his coronation. As for Fantômas XXIII (who follows him – don't ask why), think of a pompous ass sporting a top hat, a gaudy crimson sash, a walking-stick with a solid gold tip and a palanquin to transport him to Palais-Royal. With a crowd awaiting his arrival in triumph, though, our poor monarch-for-a-day has his throat slit by an assassin, a villain with a cold, malignant grin shouting, "Down with tyrants! Forward for Ravaillac!" You'll find his tomb (King Fantômas's, that is) in Paris's catacombs, which a commando of impious vandals soon took to profaning – without actually analysing why – and did so for six scandalous days and nights.

Following his burial our nation has had, in turn, a Frankish king, a hospodar, a maharajah, 3 Romuli, 8 Alarics, 6 Atatürks, 8 Mata-Haris, a Caius Gracchus, a Fabius Maximus Rullianus, a Danton, a Saint-Just, a Pompidou, a Johnson (Lyndon B.), a lot of Adolfs, a trio of Mussolinis, 5 Caroli Magni, a Washington, an Othon in opposition to a Hapsburg and a Timur Ling, who, for his own part, got rid of 18 Pasionarias, 20 Maos and 28 Marxists (1 Chicist, 3 Karlists, 6 Grouchists and 18 Harpists).

Although, on sanitary grounds, a *soi-disant* Marat bans all bath-taking, this sanctimonious fraud hoards a zinc tub for his own scrotal ablutions; but, I'm happy to say, a back-stabbing (or ball-stabbing, as word has it) from a Hitchcockian psychopath in drag soon puts paid to his hypocrisy.

Following this assassination, a mammoth tank lobs mortars at a tall municipal building into which Paris's administration has withdrawn as though for a last, forlorn stand against anarchy. Upright on its roof, a city councillor starts waving a flag of pacification, proclaiming to all and sundry that total and uncon-ditional abdication is at hand and assuring his public of his own solidarity in any totalitarian call for martial law. Alas, this oppor-tunistic U-turn is in vain: not caring to put any trust in his hollow vows, any faith in his word of honour, without bargaining with him or proposing any kind of ultimatum, his assailants forthwith launch an all-out assault, razing to its foundations this surviving bastion of authority.

God, what a world it is! Strung up for saying a word out of turn! Slain for a sigh! Go on, attack anything you want! A bus, a train, a taxi-cab, a postal van, a victoria! A baby in a pram, if such is your fancy! A body in a coffin, if such is your fantasy! Nobody will stop you. Nobody will know. You can go barging through a hospital ward, lashing out at this man writhing in agony or firing point-blank at that man with chronic arthritis and no right arm. You can crucify as many phony Christs as you wish. And nobody will mind if you drown an alcoholic in alcohol, a pharmacist in formol, a motorcyclist in lubricating oil.

Boil infants in cauldrons, burn politicians to a crisp, throw solicitors to lions, spill Christian blood to its last drop, gas all shorthand typists, chop all pastrycooks into tiny bits, and circus clowns, call girls, choirboys, sailors, actors, aristocrats, farm-hands, football hooligans and Boy Scouts.

You can loot shops or ravish shopgirls, maim or kill. Worst of all, nothing can stop you now from fabricating and propagating all sorts of vicious rumours. But stay on your guard, don't trust anybody – and watch out for your back.

I

ANTON VOWL

1

Which at first calls to mind a probably familiar story
of a drunk man waking up with his brain in a whirl

Incurably insomniac, Anton Vowl turns on a light. According to his watch it's only 12.20. With a loud and languorous sigh Vowl sits up, stuffs a pillow at his back, draws his quilt up around his chin, picks up his whodunit and idly scans a paragraph or two; but, judging its plot impossibly difficult to follow in his condition, its vocabulary too whimsically multisyllabic for comfort, throws it away in disgust.

Padding into his bathroom, Vowl dabs at his brow and throat with a damp cloth.

It's a soft, warm night and his blood is racing through his body. An indistinct murmur wafts up to his third-floor flat. Far off, a church clock starts chiming – a chiming as mournful as a last post, as an air-raid alarm, as an SOS signal from a sinking ship. And, in his own vicinity, a faint lapping sound informs him that a small craft is at that instant navigating a narrow canal.

Crawling across his windowsill is a tiny animal, indigo and saffron in colour, not a cockroach, not a blowfly, but a kind of wasp, laboriously dragging a sugar crumb along with it. Hoping to crush it with a casual blow, Vowl lifts up his right hand; but it abruptly flaps its wings, flying off without giving its assailant an opportunity to do it any harm.

Hand-tapping a military march on his thighs, Vowl now walks into his pantry, finds a carton of cold milk, pours it out into a bowl and drinks it down to its last drop. Mmmm . . . how scrumptious is milk at midnight. Now for a cosy armchair, a

3

Figaro to look at and a good Havana cigar, notwithstanding that its rich and smoky flavour is bound to sit oddly in his mouth with that of milk.

And music, too, radio music, but not this idiotic cha-cha-cha. (A casual fiddling of knobs.) Ah, a boston, and now a tango, and a foxtrot, and now a jazzy, harmonically spiky cotillion *à la* Stravinsky. Dutronc singing a ballad by Lanzmann, Barbara a madrigal by Aragon, Stich-Randall an aria from *Aida*.

Probably nodding off for an instant or two, Vowl abruptly sits up straight. "And now for a public announc–. . ." Damn that static! Vowl starts twiddling knobs again until his transistor radio booms out with clarity. But no particularly significant communication is forthcoming. In Valparaiso an inauguration of a viaduct kills 25; in Zurich a Cambodian diplomat "has it on good authority that Norodom Sihanouk is not planning to visit Richard Nixon in Washington"; in Paris Pompidou puts forward a non-partisan proposal for improving conditions in industry, but a majority of unionists outflank him with a radical (and frankly Marxist) social contract. Racial conflict in Biafra; rumours of a putsch in Conakry. A typhoon has hit Nagasaki, and a tornado (known to aficionados as Amanda) is about to lay Tristan da Cunha in ruins: its population is waiting for a squadron of Brazilian aircraft to fly it out *in toto*.

Finally, at Roland-Garros, in a Davis Cup match against Darmon, Santana has won 6–3, 1–6, 3–6, 10–8, 8–6.

Vowl turns off his radio, sits down on a rug in his living room, starts inhaling lustily and trying to do push-ups, but is atrociously out of form and all too soon, his back curving, his chin jutting out, curls up in a ball, and, staring raptly at his Aubusson, succumbs to a fascination with a labyrinth of curious and transitory motifs that swim into his vision and vanish again.

Thus, on occasion, a sort of parabola, not fully confocal in form and fanning out into a horizontal dash – akin to a capital G in a mirror.

Or, as achromatic as a swan in a snowstorm, and rising out of a diaphanous mist, an imposing portrait of a king brandishing a harpoon.

Or, just for an instant, an abstract motif without any form at all, but for two Kandinskian diagonals, along with a matching pair, half as long and slightly awry – its fuzzy contours trying, if in vain, to draw a cartoon hand, which is to say, a hand with four digits and no thumb. (If you should find that puzzling, look hard at Bugs Bunny's hands or Donald Duck's).

Or again, abruptly surfacing and just as abruptly fading, a wasp humming about, with, on its inky black thorax, a triangular rash of chalky markings.

His mind runs riot. Lost in thought, scrutinising his rug, Vowl starts imagining 5, 6, 26 distinct visual combinations, absorbing but also insubstantial, as though an artist's rough drafts but of what? – that, possibly, which a psychiatrist would call *Jungian* slips, an infinity of dark, mythic, anonymous portraits flitting through his brain, as it burrows for a solitary, global signal that might satisfy his natural human lust for signification both instant and lasting, a signal that might commandingly stand out from this chain of discontinuous links, this miasma of shadowy tracings, all of which, or so you would think, ought to knit up to form a kind of paradigmatic configuration, of which such partial motifs can furnish only anagrams and insipid approximations:

a body crumpling up, a hoodlum, a portrait of an artist as a young dog;

a bullock, a Bogartian falcon, a brooding blackbird;

an arthritic old man;

a sigh;

or a giant grampus, baiting Jonah, trapping Cain, haunting Ahab: all avatars of that vital quiddity which no ocular straining will pull into focus, all ambiguous substitutions for a Grail of wisdom and authority which is now lost – now and, alas, for always – but which, lost as it is, our protagonist will not abandon.

Staring at his rug in this way starts grating on Vowl, who, a victim of optical illusions, of sly tricks that his imagination is playing on him, starts to fancy that a focal point is at long last within his grasp, though just as it's about to solidify it sinks again into a void.

But Vowl insists, stubbornly hangs in, without trying to surmount his fascination, without struggling to kick his habit. It's almost as though, intrinsic to his rug, to its vitals, in a way, is a solitary strand looping around a vanishing point – Alpha, you might call it – as though, acting as a mirror to all unity and harmony, such a point might grant him a synoptic vision of cosmic infinity, a protological point of origin gradually maturing into a global panorama, an abysmal chasm discharging X-rays (which is to say, not a radiographical "X" but that, in maths, indicating an unknown quantity), a virgin tract of curving coastlands and circuitous contours which Vowl cannot stop tracing, as grimly and untiringly as a convict pacing back and forth along his prison wall, pacing, pacing, pacing, without any notion of scaling it . . .

For four days and nights Vowl works hard at his oblong rug, squatting and crouching on it, languishing and lying in ambush, straining at his imagination so as to catch sight of its missing strand, so as to construct an occult fiction around it, wilting, cracking up, pursuing an illusion of instant salvation in which it would all unfold in front of him.

It starts suffocating him. Not a hint nor an inkling drifts his way, nor again that kind of involuntary illumination that may on occasion turn out fruitful, but myriad combinations floating in and out of his brain, now amorphous, now polymorphous, now just within his grasp, now as far from it as it was within it, now a common, ordinary, almost banal thing, now dark, sly and cryptic, a faint and riddling murmur, an oracular form of mumbo jumbo. In a word, an imbroglio.

*   *   *

Notwithstanding a cup of hot cocoa and a cordial of allobarbital, opium or laudanum, a moist cloth on his brow and a slow countdown from 100 to 1, Vowl simply can't stop tossing and turning on his pillow.

Finally, oblivion – but only for a blissful half-hour or so. For, just as a church clock is chiming half-past two, Vowl sits up again with a start, his body twitching uncontrollably. Soon, too, his vision starts haunting him again, it brutally assails him, it swims into but also, sad to say, out of focus. For a capricious, all too capricious, instant light dawns on him.

At that point Vowl would hastily hunch down on his rug, but only to confront a conundrum: nothing, nothing at all, but irritation at an opportunity knocking so loudly and so vainly, nothing but frustration at a truth so dormant and frail that, on his approach, it sinks away into thin air.

So, now as vigilant as a man who has had an invigorating nap, abandoning his pillow, pacing up and down on his living-room floor, drinking, staring out of his window, taking down a book, switching his radio on and off, putting on his suit and coat, Vowl would go out, would stay out all night, in a bar, or at his club, or, climbing into his car (although driving was hardly his strong point), would motor off around Paris's suburbs on a whim, without having any particular goal in mind: to Chantilly or Aulnay-sous-Bois, Limours or Rancy, Dourdon or Orly, and as far as Saint-Malo – but to no avail.

Half out of his wits with insomnia, Vowl is willing to try almost anything that might assist him in dozing off – a pair of pyjamas with bright polka dots, a nightshirt, a body stocking, a warm shawl, a kimono, a cotton sari from a cousin in India, or simply curling up in his birthday suit, arranging his quilt this way and that, switching to a cot, to a crib, a foldaway, a divan, a sofa and a hammock, lying on his back, on his stomach, or with arms akimbo, casting off his quilt or placing a thick, hairy tartan rug on top of it, borrowing a plank of nails from a fakir or practising a yoga position taught him by a guru (and which consists of forcing an arm hard against your skull whilst taking hold of your foot with your hand) and finally paying for a room in lodgings – but without anything satisfactory to show for it.

It's all in vain. His subconscious vision starts buzzing around him again, buzzing around and within him, choking and suffocating him.

Sympathising with his unusual condition, a good Samaritan living two doors away opts to accompany him to a local hospital for a consultation. A young GP jots down his particulars and insists on his submitting to palpations, auscultations and X-rays, a diagnosis with which Vowl is happy to comply. "Is your condition painful?" this young GP asks him. "Sort of," Vowl blandly informs him. And what is its principal symptom? Chronic insomnia. What about taking a syrup last thing at night? Or a cordial? "I did," says Vowl, "but it had no impact." Conjunctivitis? No. A dry throat? Occasionally. An aching brow? And how! A humming sound in his auditory ducts? "No, but all last night, an odd kind of wasp was buzzing around my room." A wasp – or possibly an imaginary wasp? "Isn't it your job to find out," asks Vowl laconically.

At which point Vowl pays a visit to an otolaryngologist, Dr. Cochin, a jovial sort of chap, balding, with long auburn mutton-chops, bifocals dangling on a chain across his plump stomach, a salmon pink cravat with black polka dots, and, in his right hand, a cigar stinking of alcohol. Cochin asks him to cough and say "Ahhhh", puts a tiny circular mirror into his mouth, draws a blob of wax out of his auditory organs (as doctors say), starts poking at his tympanum and massaging his larynx, his naso-pharynx, his right sinus and his nasal partition. It's a good, thoroughgoing job and it's a pity that Cochin can't stop irritatingly whistling throughout.

"Ouch!" moans Anton. "That hurts . . ."

"Shhh," murmurs his doctor soothingly. "Now what do you say to our trotting downstairs for an itsy-bitsy X-ray?"

Laying Vowl flat on his back along a cold, shiny, clinical-looking couch, pushing a pair of buttons, flicking a switch down and turning off a lamp so that it's pitch dark, Cochin X-rays him and lights up his laboratory again. Vowl instantly shifts back to a sitting position.

"No, don't sit up!" says Cochin. "I'm not through with you, you know. I ought to look for hints of auto-intoxication."

Plugging in a circuit, Cochin brings out what a layman would call a small platinum pick, akin to nothing so much as a humdrum Biro, puts it against Vowl's skull and consults, on a print-out, an X and Y graph, its rhythmic rising and falling charting his blood circulation.

"It's too high, much too high," says Cochin at last, tapping his apparatus, noisily sucking on his cigar and rolling it around his mouth. "It shows a constriction of your frontal sinus. A surgical incision is our only solution."

"An incision!"

"'Fraid so, old boy. If not, don't you know, you'll finish up with a bad croup."

Although all of this is said so flippantly that Vowl starts to think Cochin is joking, such gallows humour in a doctor cannot fail to disturb him. Bringing his shirt-tail up to his lips and spitting blood on to it, our invalid snorts with disgust, "Fuck you, you . . . you quack! I ought to go to an ophthalmologist!"

"Now now," murmurs Cochin in a conciliatory mood. "With an immuno-transfusion or two I'll know what prognosis to adopt. But first things first – I must obtain an analysis."

Cochin rings for his assistant, who turns up clad in a crimson smock.

"Rastignac, go to Foch, Saint-Louis or Broca and bring back an anti-conglutinant vaccination. And I want it in my laboratory by noon!"

Now Cochin starts dictating his diagnosis to a shorthand typist.

"Anton Vowl. Consultation of 8 April: a common cold, an

auto-intoxication of his naso-pharynx, which could possibly put his olfactory circuit out of action, and a constriction of his frontal sinus with a hint of mucal inflammation right up to his sublingual barbs. As any inoculation of his larynx would bring about a croup, my proposal is an ablation of his sinus in such a way as to avoid damaging his vocal chords."

Vowl, according to Cochin, shouldn't worry too much, for if ablation of a sinus is still a ticklish proposition, it's had a long history dating as far back as Louis XVIII. It is, in short, an incision any physician worth his salt can carry out. Within 10 days, should Vowl hold firm, his throat won't hurt him at all.

So Vowl stays in hospital. His ward contains 26 cots, most of its occupants striking him as, frankly, mortuary carrion. To calm him down Cochin drugs him with such soporifics as Largactyl, Atarax and Procalmadiol. At 8 a.m. an important consultant starts doing his round, with a cohort of aspiring young doctors accompanying him, drinking in his words of wisdom, dutifully chuckling at his *bons mots*. This lofty individual would accost a visibly dying man and, airily tapping him on his arm, solicit from him a lugubrious smirk; would comfort anybody incurably ill with an amusing or a consoling word; would charm a sick child with a lollipop and his fond mama with a toothy grin; and, confronting a handful of almost moribund invalids, would propound an instant diagnosis: malaria, Parkinson's, bronchitis, a malignant tumour, a postnatal coma, syphilis, convulsions, palpitations and a torticollis.

Within two days or so Vowl, laid out flat, swallows a drug, a kind of liquid chloroform, that knocks him unconscious. Cochin slowly and cautiously installs a sharp nib up his right nostril. This incision in his olfactory tract producing a naso-dilation, Cochin profits from it by quickly scarifying Vowl's partition with a surgical pin, scraping it with a burin and closing it up with a tool thought up not long ago by a brilliant Scotsman. Now our otolaryngologist taps his sinus, cuts out a malign fungus and finally burns off his wound.

"Good," – this said to his assistant, who is almost numb with fright – "I think our oxydisation is going to work. Anyway, I can't find any sign of inflammation."

Cochin briskly starts swabbing Vowl's wound, stitching it up with catgut and bandaging it. For 24 hours a slight risk subsists of trauma or shock; but, promisingly, his scar knits up without complication.

Vowl has to stay in hospital for six days, until, at last, a grinning Cochin allows him to go. I might add, though, that his insomnia is still as chronically bad, if not now so agonisingly painful, as it always was.

2

*In which luck, God's alias and alibi, plays a callous
trick on a suitor cast away on an island*

Laid out languorously, all day long, on a couch or on a sofa, or
on occasion rocking to and fro in his rocking chair, stubbornly
trying to copy out on an old visiting-card that indistinct motif
that had sprung at him from his rug, as frail as an infant but not
now, thanks to Cochin's surgical skills, in all that much physical
pain, our protagonist starts hallucinating, blowing his mind.

As though in a slow-motion film, Vowl is walking down a corridor, its two high walls dwarfing him. To his right is a mahogany
stand on which sit 26 books – on which, I should say, 26 books
normally ought to sit, but, as always, a book is missing, a book
with an inscription, "5", on its flap. Nothing about this stand,
though, looks at all abnormal or out of proportion, no hint of a
missing publication, no filing card or "ghost", as librarians
quaintly call it, no conspicuous gap or blank. And, disturbingly,
it's as though nobody knows of such an omission: you had to
work your way through it all from start to finish, continually
subtracting (with 25 book-flaps carrying inscriptions from "1"
to "26", which is to say, $26 - 25 = 1$) to find out that any
book was missing; it was only by following a long and arduous
calculation that you'd know it was "5".
Vowl is avid to grasp a book, any book at all, in his hand, to
study its small print (with a possibility of chancing across an
important fact, a crucial tip) but in vain; his groping hand is,
alas, too far away for any physical contact. But what (his mind

runs on), what would such a book contain? Possibly a colossal, a cosmic dictionary? A Koran, a Talmud or a Torah? A magnum opus, a Black Book of black magic, cryptograms and occult mumbo jumbo . . .

A unit is lacking. An omission, a blank, a void that nobody but him knows about, thinks about, that, flagrantly, nobody wants to know or think about. A missing link.

Now, still hallucinating, Vowl scans his *Figaro* and finds it full of startling information, both significant and trivial:

BANNING OF CP
NOT A COMMUNIST IN PARIS!

*

If you wish to wrap anything up – no ribbon, no strings

BUY SCOTCH!

FINANCIAL SCANDAL IMPLICATING
A RING OF SPIVS

A vision now assails him: of a filthy sandwich-man, practically a tramp, his clothing in rags, handing out tracts with a myopic and haggard air, mumbling to nobody in particular and buttonholing any unlucky individual crossing his path with a rambling story of how consumption of fruit will cut down lust – a typical crank, in short, a madman, a pitiful laughing-stock. An urchin, warming to his cry of "A million, a billion birds will vanish from our sky!", pins a baby chick on to his mackintosh.

"Oh, how idiotic," murmurs Vowl. But just as idiotic, now, is his vision of a man going into a bar:

MAN, *sitting down and barking (with gruff and, as you might say, military incivility)*: Barman!

13

BARMAN *(who knows a thing or two)*: Morning, mon Commandant.

COMMANDANT *(calming down now that, although in mufti, his rank is plain to this barman)*: Ah, good morning to you, my boy, good morning!

BARMAN *(who has a slight but distinct hint of Oirishry about him)*: And what, pray, can I do for you, sir? Your wish is my command.

COMMANDANT *(licking his lips)*: You know what I fancy most of all – a port-flip.

BARMAN *(frowning)*: What? A port-flip!

COMMANDANT *(vigorously nodding)*: That's right, a port-flip! Any port-flip in a storm, what? Ha ha ha!

BARMAN *(as though in pain)*: I . . . don't . . . think . . . any . . . in . . . stock . . .

COMMANDANT *(jumping up off his stool)*: What, no port-flips! But only last month I had *(laboriously counting out)* 1, 2, no, 3 port-flips in this bar!

BARMAN *(almost inaudibly)*: But now . . . now . . . you can't . . .

COMMANDANT *(furiously pointing in front of him)*: Now look, that's port, isn't it?

BARMAN *(in agony)*: Uh huh . . . but . . .

COMMANDANT *(livid)*: So? So? And *(pointing again)* that's an . . .

BARMAN *(abruptly dying)*: Aaaaaaah! Shhhhhhh . . . *R.I.P.*

COMMANDANT *(about to go but first noticing his body)*: What a storm in a port-flip!

Which is what you might call adding insult to injury.

Vowl isn't always in such good humour, though (in so far as this vision of his can claim much humour at all), occasionally taking fright, starting up in panic, his blood curdling. For what if a crouching Sphinx is about to attack him?

14

Day in, day out, and month in, month out, his hallucination would go on distilling its poison – akin to an addiction, to opium having him in its thrall, to a suit of armour imprisoning him.

At night, his spotting an ant or a cockroach scrambling on top of his window crossbar only to fall back down again would, without his knowing why, instil within him a profound discomfort, as though so tiny an animal could function as a symbol of his own bad luck.

At night, too, just as dawn is rising, his habitual fantasy, *à la* Kafka, is of tossing and turning on his hot, damp pillow, without anything at all to hold on to, as though caught in a sort of iron cuirass and growing a carrion crow's claws, claws that would start writhing about to no avail. Nobody would rush to assist him. Not a sound would disturb his long nocturnal vigil – but, at most, for a monotonous drip-drip-drip from a tap running in his bathroom. For who would know of his plight? Who would find a solution to it, now and for always? Did any dictionary contain a word that, only by pronouncing it, would calm his morbid condition? Slowly asphyxiating, Vowl gasps for air. His lungs burn. His throat hurts as much as though sawn in half. Trying to call for aid, his lips, crinkly from a moribund grin that also starts wrinkling his brow, form only a dry, mournful cough. As panicky as a pig in an abattoir, sobbing, panting and suffocating, shaking, rattling and rolling about, his pupils dilating, a crippling load cracking his ribs, a flow of black blood oozing continuously from his tympanic cavity, a monstrous tumour bulging out of his right arm, from which a catarrhal pus would occasionally squirt, Vowl is visibly shrinking, losing from four to six pounds a day. His hand is now nothing but a stump. His physiognomy, ruddy, jowly, puffy and thick of lip, sways to and fro atop his tall, scrawny stalk of a throat. And as always, torturing him, throttling him, that clammy whiplash, as of a boa constrictor, as of a python, as of a python out of *Monty Python*, would coil and curl and crush his torso with a flick of its tail. His discs would

15

slip and his ribs would snap – with nary a word, nary a cry, issuing from his lips.

I'm dying, thinks Vowl. And with nobody to pour balm onto my wounds, nobody to accompany my last hours, no sacristan to grant absolution for my Original Sin, for nobody at all has an inkling of my plight.

Now Vowl looks upwards and sights a carrion crow watchfully circling him. In his room, all around him, sits a pack of animals – plump black rats, stoats, rabbits, frogs and toads, a solitary cockroach – as though on guard, lying in wait to ambush his stiff carcass, anticipating a Gargantuan picnic. A falcon swoops down on him. A jackal burrows out of Saharan sands to attack him.

On occasion Vowl finds his imaginings alarming, on occasion almost amusing: to finish up as a jackal's lunch, a snack for a rat or nourishing bait for a falcon (a notion that brings to his mind a book by Malcolm Lowry) has, as it had for Amphitryon, no slight attraction for him.

But it's his chronic attraction to anything sickly that is of utmost fascination to him. It's as though, for him, this is an unambiguous sign confronting him with, and initiating him into:

Not annihilation (though annihilation is still at hand), not damnation (though damnation is still at hand), but first of all omission: a "no", a non-admission, a missing link.

Things may look normal and natural and logical, but a word is but a *faux-naïf* talisman, a structurally unsound platform from which to sound off, as a world of total and horrifying chaos will soon start to show through its sonorous inanity. Things may look normal, things will go on looking normal, but in a day or two, in 7 days, or 31, or 365, all such things will rot. A gap will yawn, achingly, day by day, it will turn into a colossal pit, an abyss without foundation, a gradual invasion of words by margins, blank and insignificant, so that all of us, to a man, will find nothing to say.

Without knowing why such an association is popping into his

16

mind at just this instant, Vowl now thinks of a book that was bought by him in his youth, a book brought out by Gallimard in its imprint *La Croix du Sud*, a work of fiction by Isidro Parodi – or should I say Honorio Bustos Domaicq (if, to his compatriots, known simply as Bioy) – an account of an amazing, astonishing and also alarming calamity in which an outcast, a runaway pariah, is caught up.

Call him Ishmail, too. Having had to sustain many, almost inhuman hardships, this Ishmail drops anchor on an island that is, at first sight, totally without inhabitants. Initially, things go badly, with his almost dying of cold and starvation, burrowing into a sand pit, shaking, suffocating, coming down with malaria, curling up both day and night in a tight ball, simply waiting to pass away.

But six days go past, and his unusually robust constitution allows him finally to sit up and look around him. Our protagonist is now disturbingly skinny but can still, if with difficulty, climb out of his pit – a pit that was almost his tomb. So Ishmail starts living again by first luxuriantly slaking his thirst; now swallows an acorn but instantly spits it out in disgust; and soon works out which fruits and mushrooms won't do him any harm. A particular fruit (akin to an apricot) brings him out in a rash of itchy, purplish spots, but bananas, avocados, nuts and kiwi fruit abound.

At dusk, using a sharp rock, Ishmail cuts a notch on a stick (to tick off his first night as a castaway); and, with a total of 20 such cuts, constructs a hut, a sort of impromptu shack, with a door, four walls, and flooring and roofing built out of mud. With no matchsticks at hand, though, his food is invariably raw. Constant, too, is his panic that an animal might attack his camp; but, as it turns out (such, anyway, is his supposition), no lynx or puma, no jaguar, cougar or bison, stalks his island. At most, comfortably far off, and only at sundown, a solitary orang-utan prowling around but not caring (or daring?) to approach him.

17

And if it did, Ishmail had cut a stout club out of a mahogany branch that would firmly put paid to any assailant.

This lasts a month. At which point, his physical condition improving on an almost daily basis, our Robinson Ishmail (if I may so call him) starts making a tour of his unknown Tristan da Cunha, taking a full day to walk around it, his club in his hand, and by nightfall pitching camp on top of a hill that would allow him a panoramic command of his domain.

At dawn, cupping his hand to his brow and gazing about him, Ishmail looks northwards and sights a kind of canal swirling and foaming into marshland, and also, to his horror, not too far from his hut, a row of mounds (akin to that sort known as tumuli), six in all; cautiously slinks down towards this curious construction (possibly a sort of windpiping?); and hazards an assumption (and rightly so) that it's by a tidal flow that it functions.

Now, abruptly, as it dawns on him what it is and of what it consists, Ishmail starts noticing signs of habitation – a housing compound, a radio installation, an aquarium.

But it all looks forlorn and vacant, its fountain as dry as a structuralist monograph (and playing host to a trio of fat and languorous armadillos), its pool mouldy with fungus.

As for its housing compound, it was built, *circa* 1930, in a crypto-rococo fashion imitating, variously, a pink-icing casino in Monaco, a bungalow on a Malayan plantation, a colonialist villa, an ultra-chic condominium in Miami and Tara from *GWTW*.

Passing through a tall swing-door with slats and a mosquito guard, you would walk along a corridor, about four yards high and six yards long, taking you into a largish sitting room: on its floor is a vast Turkish rug and, all around, divans, sofas, armchairs, cushions and mirrors. A spiral stair winds up to a loggia. From its roof, built out of a wood that, though light in colour, is actually rock-hard (most probably sumac or sandalwood), a thin aluminium cord, from which hangs a shiny brass ring of outstanding craftsmanship, supports a colourful lamp no doubt brought back from a trip to Japan and which casts a dim but oddly milky light. Finally, via four bow windows inlaid with gold, you could go out on to a balcony surmounting a fabulous natural vista.

With a caution born of suspicion, Ishmail now pays this compound a visit from top to bottom, from ground floor to loggia, tapping its roof, its walls and its wainscoting, going through its cupboards, not missing any nook or cranny and noting, in particular, in a downstairs stock room, a labyrinthian circuit which, linking up an oscillograph, a prismatic mirror, a two-way radio, a hi-fi (with an apparatus to amplify its sound), a multi-track rack and a strobo-cycloidal rotator, probably has a global function unknown to him.

Not daring to pass a night in such unpromising surroundings, Ishmail simply "borrows" as many tools as his arms can carry, as also a big brass cauldron, a chopping board, a winnowing fan, a matchbox or two and a hip flask brimming with whisky, and quickly slips off to a clump of dark woodland not too far away, in which stands a run-down shack; starts doing it up, allowing not a day to go by without improving it; hunts, kills and cooks rabbits; and, on his most fruitful raid, actually corrals an agouti with his lasso, making bacon and ham, dripping and black pudding, out of its carcass.

Days and days of this. Days of monsoons, of a curdling sky, of ominous clouds amassing on its horizon, of a high, cold, gusty wind blowing up all about him, of tidal troughs and billows, of a foam-capp'd flood rushing inland, plashing and splashing, washing and sploshing, anything in its path. Days of rain, rain, rain.

Not long into his third month Ishmail sights a yacht putting into port and dropping anchor off his island. Six individuals now climb up to its casino, from which soon float out sounds of a jazz band playing a foxtrot, a 30s "standard" that's obviously still popular. At which point nothing again is as it was.

Though, initially, his instinct is to turn tail, to withdraw into his shack, Ishmail cannot but find this situation intriguing and crawls forward on all fours. What *is* going on? In a malodorous pool choking with fungus, and around a shabby, unglamorous casino, his visitors start swimming and dancing: a trio of guys, a matching trio of dolls, plus a sort of footman adroitly mincing back and forth with a tray of snacks, drinks and cigars. A tall, smiling, muscular man – in his mid-20s at most – is particularly conspicuous in a suit with a Mao collar and without any buttons down its front, a Cardin fashion of long, long ago. His companion, a man in his 30s with a tuft of bushy black hair on his chin, sporting a stylish morning suit, sips from a glass of whisky, adds a dash of soda and lazily hands it to a young woman – obviously his girl – snoozing in a hammock.

"This is for you, Faustina. May I kiss you for it?"

"Why, thank you," says Faustina, half in a laugh, half in a huff.

"Ah, Faustina, what bliss I'd know if only . . . if only I could . . . oh, you know what I'm trying to say . . ."

"Now now, I said no, no and no again. Why can't you and I stay just good chums?" adds Faustina, fondling his hand for an instant.

What a fascinating woman! thinks Ishmail, who now starts to follow Faustina around, though naturally, as a runaway convict, still afraid for his own skin. For who's to say that this group of upstarts isn't harbouring a cop or a grass? What am I but an outlaw, worth a king's ransom to any informant? As an outcast from my own country, having had to fly from a tyrant as corrupt as Caligula, as bad as any Borgia, how can I know that this insignificant-looking yacht isn't on a kidnapping mission? Alas, I don't know and I don't want to know; all I know is that, loving this woman as I do, I want to *know* Faustina – Biblically.

Caring not for company, Faustina strolls about this way and that, hips swinging lightly to and fro. Finally Ishmail accosts his inamorata, who is studying a book, Virginia Woolf's *Orlando*, as it turns out.

"Miss, oh Miss, I'm sorry, awfully sorry, I . . . I had to talk to you. It's just my hard luck if anybody spots us . . . I'm willing to risk it . . ."

Alas! ignoring all his sighs and supplications, Faustina looks straight through him.

At which point Ishmail falls victim to hallucinations, possibly from consuming a poisonous black mushroom or having had too much to drink; or, why not, from having shrunk so much as to vanish wholly from sight, so that Faustina is nothing but a vision, a vision passing right through his body; or, if not, from losing his mind, going crazy, moonstruck, stark, staring mad, as though still stagnating in his filthy marshland and simply conjuring this vision out of a bout of paranoia – casino, yacht, Faustina and all.

All right – but, if so, why, as though caught up in a warp in chronology, should Ishmail again catch sight of a party uncannily similar in both word and act to that of his first visit: dancing by moonlight, Louis Armstrong playing a foxtrot . . . ?

All right – but, if so, worst of all (for Ishmail's fiction now actually starts to nourish his own hallucinations, it's now that a comparison of his own situation with that of Bioy's book, a comparison that's possibly illusory and anyway naggingly hard to pin down, will occur to critics), why, occasionally, whilst walking along a corridor, should Ishmail abruptly find a door ajar in front of him and a footman coming out with a tray in his hand and why should this footman look glassily past him?

As though by instinct, Ishmail jumps out of his way, watching him put a book, say, on top of a trunk and approaching it in his turn to find out what's in it. But why is it so inhumanly hard and smooth to his touch? No Titan, no Goliath, could lift up such a book.

It's as though a cunning troll or hobgoblin has sought to *statufy* all that is solid within and around this casino, to spray it with poison gas or coat it with varnish, incrusting surfacings and suffusing grains, controlling atoms and ions, so that nothing stays for long as it was.

21

Things may look normal: if Ishmail looks at a thing or at an individual, it logically follows that that thing or individual is actually in front of him; a sound (a laugh, a cry, a jazzy riff) is just as loud in this world as in any normal world, an odour (of a blossom, of a woman's hair) just as fragrant to his nostrils. Now Faustina is lounging on a sofa among an array of silk cushions as soft and light and airy as balloons. Now his darling stands up and walks out, abandoning on a cushion (as a gift to him?) a bulky gold ring with a multi-carat diamond stud. Ishmail jumps up, taking this ring as a sign, a sign that Faustina is his, but is too afraid of that odious individual with his morning suit and his glass of whisky – a husband? a suitor? just a companion? – to admit it (for nobody could claim immunity from a Law making of Ishmail an outcast, a pariah: nobody could touch him or stop him from strolling back and forth; but nor was any human conscious of him at all).

Making contact with Faustina's cushion or ring for only an instant, though, a numb, downcast, haggard Ishmail withdraws his hand. What, again, occurs is that this cushion, say – a thing normally as soft and downy as a baby's bottom – is, to his touch, now a hard, cold, compact block, as rock-hard as a diamond, as though part of a shadowy twin world consubstantial with Ishmail's own but caught through a glass darkly, a living mirror of our own world and just as cold, shiny and insular as a mirror. A world, too, in which all that is human, or inhuman, maintains a capacity for motion and action: thus Faustina can unlock a door or charmingly languish on a sofa; thus that boorish individual (as Ishmail cannot stop thinking of him) has no difficulty at all pouring out a whisky-and-soda; nor, thus, has a jazz band any difficulty striking up a foxtrot, a yacht docking, a woman dropping a gold ring, a footman sashaying along a corridor holding a tray. For anybody, though, not part of it all (which was obviously Ishmail's plight), that world was nothing but a smooth, cyclical continuum, without a fold in it, without any form of articulation, as compact as stucco or staff, as putty or portland; an imbrication of nights without adjoining days, a total lapidification, a flat, hard, constant, monotonous uniformity in which all things, big or small, smooth or lumpish, living or not, form a solitary, global unit.

Though trying hard, straining with all his might, Ishmail cannot bunch up a small and dainty silk cushion, for it's a cushion of rock-solid silk; nor, though bringing his foot down hard on it, disturb a tuft of hair on a Turkish rug; nor, with his hand, turn a light-switch on and off. No, poor Ishmail is now an outcast from two worlds.

Ishmail (as it slowly, far too slowly, dawns on him) is living in a film, a film that was shot, wholly without his companions' authorisation or approval, by M., Faustina's suitor, on a short tour of his (Ishmail's) island in or about 1930.

Whilst a fatal malady attacks "his" island's baobabs, whilst a mould crawling with tiny, malignant bugs starts to run riot in its swimming pool, whilst its villa is rapidly going to wrack and ruin, a haphazard sprinkling of raindrops all too soon turns into a noisy downpour, a tropical monsoon, so that a concomitant tidal flow, rising and falling, flooding that coastal construction that Ishmail first saw from on top of a hill, activating its circuitry (circuitry which had initially struck him as totally baffling) and causing its dynamo to hum into motion, brings about a curious and oddly tragic situation in which, word for word, act for act, so many instants (instants long past but also immortal) visibly start to shrink into what you might call ions of chronology, just as, with an apparatus built from vitalium, Martial Cantaral would allow any ghostly carcass to act out, in a vast frigidarium, and again and again right up to doomsday, a crucial instant from its past.

Things look normal, but looks can play tricks on you. Things at first look normal, till, abruptly, abnormality, horrifying in its inhumanity, swallows you up and spits you out.

*   *   *

23

Anton Vowl's ambition is to find out just what brand of affinity links him with Bioy's book: on his rug, constantly assailing his imagination, is his intuition of a taboo, his vision of a cryptic sort of witchcraft, of a void, a thing unsaid: a vision, or loss of vision, a mission or an omission, both all-knowing and knowing nothing at all. Things may look normal, but. . .

But what?

Vowl simply cannot work it out.

3

Concluding with an immoral papacy's abolition and its claimant's contrition

Days pass. Trying to work this thing out to his own satisfaction, Vowl starts writing a diary, captioning it with just two words:

A VOID

and continuing:

> *A void. Void of whom? Of what?*
>
> *A curious motif runs (or ran or has run or might run) through my Aubusson, but it isn't only a motif, it's also a fount of wisdom and authority.*
>
> *An imago as snug as a bug in my rug.*
>
> *What, on occasion, it brings to mind is a painting by Arcimboldo, a portrait of its own artist, possibly an astonishing portrait of a haggard Dorian Gray, of a bilious albino: an Arcimboldian jigsaw, not of shrimps and crayfish, not of a cornucopia of fruit, nor of snaky, tortuous pistils twisting upwards to mimic a human brow or chin or nostril, but of a swarming mass of sinuous bacilli of so subtly skilful a combination that you know straightaway that such a portrait had a body at its origin, without its affording you at any instant a solitary distinguishing mark, so obvious is it that it was its artist's ambition to fashion a work which, by masking and unmasking, closing and disclosing, turn and turn about, or mayhap in unison, would hatch a plot but totally avoid giving it away.*

25

It's hard, initially, to spot any modification at all. You think at first that it's your own paranoia that's causing you to find anomaly, abnormality and ambiguity all around you. Abruptly, though, you know, or think you know, that not too far off is . . . a thing, an incarnation that distracts you, acts upon you and numbs you. Things rot around you. You panic, you sink into an unnatural sloth; you start losing your mind. A sharp – though not, alas, so short – shock chills you to your marrow. If this horror is only a hallucination, it's a hallucination that you can't simply throw off.

If only you had a word, a noun. If only you could shout out: Aha, at last, now I know what it was that I found so disturbing! If only you could jump for joy, jump up and down, find a way out of this linguistic labyrinth, this anagram of signification, this sixty-four-thousand-dollar conundrum. But you simply can't fall back on any such option: you must stubbornly go on, pursuing your vision to its logical conclusion.

If only, oh if only you could pin down its point of origin, that's all you ask. But it's all such a fog, it's all so distant . . .

This diary lasts about six months. Day by day, as twilight falls, Vowl jots down, in a typically finicky fashion, a host of insignificant notations: drank up all my provision of liquor, bought an LP for my cousin Julot for passing his *bac* with flying colours, took my Moroccan kaftan to a local laundry, said hullo to a man living down my road notwithstanding that Azor, his pug-dog, has a habit of shitting on my doormat, and so on; notations, too, on his books, on his chums, on a puzzling word or an intriguing fact (a QC at court who couldn't finish his oration; a hooligan firing blank shots at nobody in particular; a compositor at a printing plant wilfully vandalising his own typographic apparatus . . .).

Now and again, automatically clicking a Bic with his thumb, Vowl would pass on to his own autobiography, would submit his own past to psychological analysis, touching, most notably, on his hallucination and Ishmail's island.

A particular day dawns on which it's a synopsis of a book, a wholly imaginary book, that finds its way into his diary:

In a far country is found a small boy, Aignan, just two days away from his fifth birthday and living in an old mansion that's collapsing about him. This small boy has a nanny who, without any warning at all, ups and says to him, "As a child, Aignan, you had 25 cousins. Ah, what tranquil days – days without wars or riots! But, abruptly, your cousins would start to vanish – to this day nobody knows why. And, today, it's your turn to go away, to withdraw from our sight, for, if you don't, it is, as Wordsworth might put it – and you know, my darling," adds this palindromic matron, "almost all of Wordsworth is worth words of almost all – it is, I say, intimations of mortality for all of us."

So Aignan slinks away out of town. And in classic *Bildungsroman* fashion his story starts off with a short moral fabliau: barring his path, a Sphinx accosts him.

"Aha," says this fantastic (and not so dumb) animal, lustily licking its lips, "what a scrumptious sandwich for my lunch! How long ago it is I last saw such a plump and juicy human child in my vicinity!"

"Whoa, Sphinx, whoa! Just hold on a mo!" says Aignan, who knows his Lacan backwards. "You must first of all quiz my wits. Your famous conundrum, you know."

"My conundrum?" says his antagonist, caught short by this unusual invitation. "What for? You can't throw any light on its solution. Nobody can. So stop fooling about."

But, just a tad suspicious, it adds, "Or possibly you think you can?"

"Who knows?" says Aignan with a roguish grin.

"I must say you sound a bit of a show-off, you brattish boy, you, but I won't hold that against you. I'm willing to play fair,

I don't mind allowing your ambition to act as a cushion to your annihilation."

So saying, with harp in paw, it hums aloud for an instant and, making an airy harp-string glissando, starts to sing.

> *Which animal do you know*
> *That has a body as curving as a bow*
> *And draws back inwards as straight as an arrow?*

"*Moi! Moi!*" Aignan (no doubt a fan of Miss Piggy) shouts back at it.

A frown furrows its horridly bulging brow.

"You think so?"

"Why, naturally," says Aignan.

"I fancy you ought to know," says his inquisitor mournfully.

For an instant nobody says a word. A cold north wind cuts a blast through a cotton-cloud sky.

"I always said a kid would bring about my downfall," sighs a Sphinx so dolorous it looks almost as though it's about to burst into sobs.

"Now, now, Sphinx, no hamming it up, *s'il vous plaît*," says Aignan gruffly and with a faint hint of compassion for his victim – adding, though, "You must admit, had I got it wrong, you'd instantly claim what's owing you. I got it right, I won; and so, by law, it's curtains for you." And, raising an intimidating hand in front of him, adds, "So – what about taking a running jump off that cliff?"

"Oh no," it murmurs softly, "not that, oh God, not that . . ."

"*Si, si!*" Aignan roars back, without knowing why an Italian locution should pop into his brain at such a point of crisis and climax.

Picking up a thick, knobby stick, Aignan knocks it down – so hard, in fact, that it falls unconscious, spiralling downward out of control, spinning round and round in mid-air, down, down, down, into a profound abyss, into an aching Boschian void. A blood-curdling wail, a wail partaking of both a lion's roar and a cat's purr, of both a hawk's inhuman squawk and a hauntingly human, all too human, cry of pain, throbs on and on all around for fully thirty days . . .

With a fabliau of so obvious a moral, it's not too difficult to intuit what kind of fiction or plot must follow. Aignan tours his country, roaming back and forth, uphill and down again, arriving at sundown in unfamiliar and unknown townships, proposing a day's labour to local rustics and cartwrights and sacristans and taking for his pay just a thin, fatty cut of bacon or a dry crust with a scrap of garlic as its only garnish. Starvation gnaws at him, thirst too, but nothing can kill him.

Whilst approaching his maturity, Aignan would soon know how to adapt to almost any kind of situation confronting him, would soon grow cool and nonchalant, fortifying his worldly wisdom, magnifying his vision of his surroundings, his *Anschauung*, and crossing paths with many curious and intriguing individuals, all of whom would, in various ways, transform him, by giving him a job of work to do, or board and lodging, or by indicating a vocation to him. A con man would instruct him in his craft; a mason would show him how to build a small but cosy shack; a compositor would tutor him in printing a daily journal.

But that isn't all. What occurs now (as you'll find out) is a hotchpotch of cryptic plots and complications, simulating, word for word, action for action, its conclusion apart, that saga of profound roots, that amusing but also moral and poignant story that a troubadour, whom history knows as Hartmann, took for his inspiration, and whom Thomas Mann would follow in his turn, via a trio of short fictions.

Thus, to start with, Aignan is told that his papa was good King Willigis (or Willo for short) and his aunt was Sibylla. Sibylla, though, was so fond of Willigis, fond of him with a passion that sat oddly with kinship, that sororal adoration would gradually blossom into carnal lust (notwithstanding Willigis's faithful old

29

hound howling with horror and dying just as coition was about to occur). Within 8 months and 23 days Aignan was born.

Blushing with guilt at his iniquity, hoping that castigation in this world might guard him from damnation, Willigis (Willo for short but not now for long) fought a holy war against Saladin and was struck down, as was his wish, by an anonymous son of Allah.

As for his Dauphin, Aignan, with immoral blood coursing through his body, his mama, Sibylla, thought to abandon him on a raft so that it might float away northwards to an insalubrious district of filthy marshland, full of moronically drooling young cutthroats (for adult consumption of alcohol was said to attain as much as six gallons a month) and animals of unknown origin but of, no doubt, voraciously carnivorous habits: talk was of a dragon "stuffing guts wit' battalion, a' way down t' last drop o' last man", as a charming patois had it in an inn into which many locals would crowd for a warming drink on concluding a hard day's work outdoors. In addition to which, it was always dark and always drizzling – a cold, thin, stabbing, British sort of rain-fall. Thus you wouldn't go far wrong in supposing that only miraculous odds (I fancy a Christian would put it down to God working in mystical ways and is probably right to do so; but fiction has an intrinsic duty to contradict such an illusion of propitiatory fatality; for if not, what's its point?) – in supposing, as I say, that only miraculous odds could account for Aignan's surviving up to and including his 18th birthday. But I mustn't run on too quickly . . .

Anyway, on or about Aignan's 18th birthday, Sibylla, in a mansion fashionably got up *à la brabançon* or *flamand*, is still doting, if now posthumously, on poor Willigis (or Willo) and turning down all invitations to marry. A rich and rutting Burgundian aristocrat pays court. Sibylla simply says no. "What!" says this aristocrat in a purplish paroxysm of wrath, prior to razing half of Hainault and marching on Cambrai.

But wait . . . At this point in my story, to Cambrai, clippity-clop, clippity-clop, riding Sturmi, his black and bay brown Anglo-Norman stallion, clippity-clop, clippity-clop, gallops a knight-at-arms, with all you could ask for in youthful vigour and good looks. Brought to Sibylla's mansion, this dazzling young paladin charms his monarch, who commissions him to slay his Burgundian rival. "Your wish is my command," fair Sir Adonis says instantly, kissing his lady's hand and adding wittily, "And, may I say, your command is actually my wish."

Mounting Sturmi, with its saffron housing and its caparison of indigo, and illustrious in his own gold strappings inlaid with opal, his cloak, his broad cuirass and his coat of armour, Adonis gallops out into a sort of oblong paddock with paling all around it. A fish adorns his standard; and a long standing ovation from his Brabançon champions totally drowns out an irruption of scurrilous anti-Brabançon sloganising from a mob of Burgundian hooligans and paid agitators.

What a bloody clash of arms it is, with onslaught following onslaught, mortal blow confuting mortal blow, chain mail clashing clamorously against chain mail, attacks by harpoon and spontoon, hook and crook! In all it lasts a full day. Finally, though, by a cunning ploy, young Adonis dismounts his rival: victory is his.

Brabant and Burgundy mutually disarm. Joyful carillons ring out in both lands. Floors throb to dancing, walls to playing of hautboys, horns and drums, roofs to toasting of this artful young paladin – now, by a logical promotion, known as Grand Admiral of Brabant. And, complying with a royal summons, our Grand Admiral pays an additional visit to Sibylla's mansion. Boy looks at girl, girl looks at boy . . . imagining how it turns out is child's play (or, should I say, adult's play).

Oh you, browsing or scanning or skimming or dipping into my story, or actually studying it word for word, moving your lips as you go, I must now throw light on a startling twist in its tail, though you no doubt know without my having to inform

31

you who it is that Sturmi is carrying on its caparison – why, that's right, it's Aignan.

Aignan, though, still blissfully ignorant of Sibylla's kinship with him, falls into just that trap in which Oïdipos was caught. And Sibylla, ignorant of Aignan's analogous kinship, falls into just that trap in which Jocasta was caught. For Sibylla admits to an infatuation with Aignan. And Aignan admits in his turn to an infatuation with Sibylla. And, without a filial qualm, Aignan starts fornicating with Sibylla. And Sibylla, not surprisingly, starts fornicating back.

Luckily or unluckily – it's hard to know which – Aignan all too soon finds out what kind of filiation it is that links him with Sibylla.

Sibylla, praying daily, not to say hourly, for God's pardon, has a hospital built in which a crowd of filthy waifs and strays stay for nothing, with not a limb, not a dirty hand or a stinking foot or a gamily aromatic armpit, that its nursing staff will not lovingly wash.

Aignan, donning a ragamuffin's rags, a hairshirt worn out of mortification, with a stick in his hand, but without a vagrant's rucksack or tin can, slips away at dusk from a mansion in which an illusory and, alas, mortally sinful form of conjugal intimacy lay almost within his grasp – slips far, far away, going hungry and thirsty and living rough and tough, and pays for his infamous conduct by asking God to vilify him, to damn him outright.

So pass four long and hard days of wayfaring, culminating in his arrival at a poor woodman's hut. Aignan timidly knocks at its door. In an instant its occupant is standing inquiringly in front of him.

"Would you know," Aignan asks him, "of a *Locus Solus* not far off in which, till Doomsday, God might punish my Sin of Sins?"

"That I would, my lad, that I would," growls this doltish wood-man (who is in fact as thick as two of his own planks). "'Tis an island, no, no, I'm wrong, 'tain't that at all, 'tis just a rock, sort of a crag, look you, with an awful sharp drop down t' bottom o' loch. 'Tis just th' spot, I'd say, for a man with drink or damnation on his mind!"

"Oh woodman, do you own a boat?"

"That I do."

"And will you row it out to your island, your rock?" Aignan asks him imploringly. "For my salvation!"

Though caught short by this proposal, his saviour concurs at last, with a warning that Aignan will rot on such a solitary crag – rot till his dying day.

"I wish only for God's will," says Aignan piously.

At which his rustic Charon murmurs a (slightly incongruous) chorus: "And so say all of us!"

So our young pilgrim sails forth to this Island of Lost Souls on which his companion, almost throttling him, binds him to a rock with a hangman's tight collar. A nourishing mould or humus oozing by night out of a cavity in his rocky crucifix is his only form of nutrition; a storm or a cutting blast or an icy south wind or a burning simoon or a sirocco swirling about him his only roof; a typhoon or a tidal flood his only wall; and his only clothing (for his poor, worn, torn rags rot away as fast as crumbling old wood) is his birthday suit, soon just as poor and worn and torn as his rags. Not cold but glacial, not hot but roasting, Aignan stands thus, a living symbol of contrition, a human incarnation of purgatorial pain.

Now half-starving for want of food, now wholly fading away, notwithstanding that mouldy humus that God in all His wisdom and compassion has put his way, Aignan gradually grows thin, his body physically contracts from day to day, from hour to hour, it slims down and narrows out until unimaginably gaunt and scrawny, until as small and insignificant as that of a dwarf, a pygmy, a homunculus, until Aignan is nothing at last but a shrimp of a man, a Hop-o'-my-Thumb . . .

*   *   *

18 springs pass. In Roman Catholicism's sanctum sanctorum Paul VI is dying. Vatican City is in a tizzy: it must now swiftly appoint a Paul VII and affirm papal continuity. But six polls go by – and no Paul VII! This cardinal submits a proposal for an idiot and that cardinal for a glutton, a third opts for a psychopath and a fourth for an ignoramus. Corruption is rampant: anybody willing to put down a cool million in cash can practically buy his nomination as pontiff. Things look bad. Faith is vacillating. Nobody thinks to pray to his patron saint.

It's at this point that black clouds start forming in Abraham's bosom, bolts of numinous lightning shoot down from on high and Almighty God in all His wrath pays an unusual visit on a Cardinal – unusual in that His outward form is that of a lamb, a lamb with stigmata of blood on its flanks and a couch of fragrant blooms to accompany it.

"O hark my words, Monsignor," God booms out at His Cardinal. "Thou now hast that Vicar of Christ that thou sought in vain. I, thy all-knowing King of Kings, do appoint Aignan as My apostolic missionary – Aignan, who hast, in that corporal nudity and purity which was My birthday gift to him, for so long stood upright upon a rock and for just as long withstood without flinching My tidal attacks upon him."

"O Lamb of God, O Lamb That is God, O God That is Lamb," His adoring Cardinal croaks, words stumbling out any old how, "I will do as Thou commandst!"

Thus an official inquiry tracks down this Aignan who calls God's wrath upon him with truly Christian humility (and a hint, too, of pagan stoicism); and at long last, following many trials and tribulations, a commission of Cardinals stands in front of that woodman's hut from which Aignan, so long ago, was brought to his island prison. To start with, though, its occupant is in a slightly noncommittal mood, mumbling:

"Aignan, y'say? No . . . don't know any Aignan. Don't know any island. No island as I know of in this part of world."

Finally, with a tidy sum of gold coins to coax him out of his mutism, Aignan's oarsman talks. A boat sails forth chock-a-block with Cardinals who start laboriously climbing that rocky promontory on which, through thick and thin, Aignan is living out his martyrdom. On top of it, though, no martyr, no Aignan, nobody at all is found (proof that Our Lord is occasionally wrong, a notion that brings about a profound diminution of faith in His flock) – just thin air, nothing, a void. So God, too, alas, is only human.

Thomas Mann notwithstanding, such was my story's only conclusion, murmurs Anton Vowl, writing "finis" on his manuscript, his rough draft, I should say, or synopsis, as, with his chronically vivid imagination now running riot, Vowl simply cannot bring his task to what you might call authorial fruition, jotting down 25 or 26 random notations, amplifying 5 or 6 crucial points, drawing a portrait of Aignan that's both thorough and scrupulously fair, ditto for Aignan's Burgundian rival ("a tall thug of a man, with short hair and long auburn muttonchops": it's obvious that his inspiration was his own Dr Cochin, who had brought him back to tip-top physical condition), coining (though only in a short paragraph) an amusing nautical-cum-Scotch patois for that wily old bumpkin who was willing to row Aignan out to his island limbo ("Avast an' ahoy! All aboard who's going! Oh, but it's a braw, bricht, moonlicht nicht th'nicht, an' that's a fact!") and portraying his and Sibylla's tragicomic imbroglio with a touch so tactful that a Paul Morand, a Giraudoux or a Maupassant would not disown it.

But that's as far as it got: in his diary Vowl would try to justify his procrastination on slightly unusual grounds. If (is his *a priori* postulation) I could finish my story, I would; but if it truly had a conclusion, would it not contain a fund of wisdom of such cold hard purity, of such crystal clarity, that not any of us, just dipping into it, could think to go on living? For (Vowl scrawls away) it's a quality of fiction that it allows of only a solitary Aignan to rid us of a Sphinx. With Aignan put out of action, no triumphant

Word will again afford us consolation. Thus (signing off) no amount of prolix circumlocution, brilliant as it may sound, can abolish flip-of-a-coin fortuity. But again (adding a wistful postscript) it *is* our only option: all of us should know that a Sphinx might assail us at any instant; all of us should know that, at any instant, a word will do its utmost to thwart that Sphinx – a word, a sound, an if or a but. For – as Zarathustra might say – no Sphinx is living that inhabits not our human Mansion . . .

4

*Which, notwithstanding a kind of McGuffin, has no
ambition to rival Hitchcock*

It's on All Saints Day that Anton Vowl would first go missing
– as possibly an offshoot of his noticing, just two days prior to
this vanishing act, a most alarming story in his *Figaro*.

It was all about an unknown individual (a man, so rumour
had it, of such vast, almost occult authority that no journalist
had sought to crack his incognito), who had, at night, unlawfully
burst into a commissariat building that was said to contain many
important official manuscripts and got away with a particularly
hush-hush account of a major scandal implicating a trio of guards
at Poulaga Prison. Normalising such a situation was an awkward
task; convincing so diabolically crafty a burglar to hand back such
a compromising manuscript just as awkward; but it was crucial
to do so, for this kind of traitor usually has no difficulty in finding
a nation willing to buy his goods at any cost. But though it was
obvious that X . . . (for our burglar holds a high-ranking position
to this day and is, I am told, a notoriously litigious man) had
put it away out of sight in his flat, ransacking that flat again and
again had thrown up nothing significant.

Staking all on a hunch, a Commandant, Romain ("I just want
th' facts, ma'am") Didot, along with Garamond, his adjutant and
Man Friday, pays a visit to Dupin, known for his unfailing gift
for nosing things out.

"*A priori,*" Didot informs him, "it's not our constabulary's job
to worry about such a burglary. For anything . . . 'normal', shall
I say, in our filing library, for an *x* or *y*, nobody'd complain too

37

much. But this sort of McGuffin is, I'm afraid, just a tiny bit too significant to – "

"McGuffin? McGuffin?" Dupin, to whom this word's connotation is a total blank, savours it in his mouth for an instant or two.

Didot grins. "Pardon my film buff slang. Put simply, I want you to know that solving this burglary is vital to us, in that it'll ruin, it'll undo, what can I say, it'll play bloody havoc with our organisation. Why, it risks cutting our working capacity by up to 20%!"

"So," asks Dupin, "you say you shook down our burglar's flat, high and low, with a toothcomb? Is that right?"

"Uh huh," admits an unhappy Didot, "but I can't say I found anything incriminating. And I was as thorough as any of my rivals from Scotland Yard!"

"Hmm," grunts Dupin. "It's as plain as daylight. You hunt high and low, you tap walls and floors, but without any luck; for whilst you may think that your approach is obvious, it's ironically that which is truly obvious that it can't account for. Hasn't it struck you that your criminal had to find a hiding spot that a big, plodding flatfoot – it's you I'm alluding to, Didot – wouldn't think of looking at, and would probably not stash his loot away at all but simply stick it into an ordinary blotting pad, a blotting pad that you probably had your hand on again and again, without knowing what it was, without caring or trying to know that what it had on it was no casual scrawl but your own almighty McTavish!"

"McGuffin," says Didot sulkily, still smarting from Dupin's insults. "Anyway, I saw no such blotting pad."

"That's what you think," Dupin murmurs with ironic suavity.

Putting on his mackintosh, taking a big black brolly out of its stand and unlocking his front door, Dupin turns to Didot and says, "I'm off. In a twinkling I'll hand you back that manuscript of yours."

But – not that anybody could fault his logic – but our famous dick was, on this particular occasion, all wrong.

"I'm PO'd, truly PO'd" (PO was a contraction of "piss off"), sighs Dupin; who, at that point, as consolation, and allowing Didot and his constabulary to work it all out without his aid, starts tracking down a homicidal orang-utan with a grisly trio of victims.

If Dupin should fail, though having it all within his grasp from A to Z, how can I possibly look forward to my own salvation, to my own absolution? That's what Anton Vowl jots down in his diary – adding:

"I did so want to sink into an alcoholic coma. I did so want to finish my days in a softly intoxicating and long dying torpor. But, alas, I cannot avoid . . . a void! Who? What? That's for you to find out! 'It' is a void. It's today my turn to march towards mortality, towards that fatal hour, towards 'that good night' (as Dylan Thomas put it), that 'undiscov'r'd country from which bourn no man . . .' and so forth, towards omission and annihilation. *It's a must*. I'm sorry. I did so want to *know*. But a lancinating agony gnaws at my vitals. I can only talk now in a dry, throaty, painfully faint hum. O my mortality, a fair ransom for such a mad compulsion as that which has had my mind in its tight grip. Anton Vowl."

And to that Vowl adds a postscript, a postscript which shows him as having truly lost his mind: "I ask all 10 of you, with a glass of whisky in your hand – and not just any whisky but a top-notch brand – to drink to that solicitor who is so boorish as to light up his cigar in a zoo" – adds, finally, and almost as though initialling a last will, a trio of horizontal strips (No. 2, curiously, isn't as long as its two companions) with an ambiguously indistinct scrawl on top.

Was it a suicidal act? Did Vowl put an automatic to his brow? Or slit his wrists in a warm bath? Swallow a tall glass of aqua-toffana? Hurl his car into an abysmal chasm, a yawning pit, abysmal till Doomsday, yawning till Doomsnight? Turn on his flat's gas supply? Commit hara-kiri? Spray his body with napalm? Jump off Paris's Pont du Nord by night into a flowing black miasma?

Nobody knows, or can know, if his way of quitting this world was wholly of his own volition; nobody in fact knows if Vowl did quit this world at all.

But, four days on, a chum of his, who had found Anton's last writings alarming and had thought to support him through what was obviously a major crisis, was to knock at his flat's front door in vain. His car was still placidly sitting in its hangar. No stains of blood on floor or wall. No clothing, nor any trunk to carry it in, missing.

Anton Vowl, though, *was* missing.

ILLUSORY PARDONS FOR ANTON VOWL

a Japan without kimonos,
a smoking boa constrictor on a curling rink,
a flamboyant black man,
a shrill cry of nudity in a plain song,
a kindly scorpion,
10 bankrupt tycoons spitting on a stack of gold coins,
a gloating sorrow,.
a simoon in a long Finnish corridor,
a profound cotton hanky:
that's what could rid our world of Anton Vowl . . .

a hippy cardinal shouting out an anti-Catholic slogan,
a razor for citrus fruits,
a raid on a trio of British bandits by a Royal Mail train,
a straight compass,
a man's tummy-button from which a volcano spouts forth,
a land only natal by adoption,
a twilit balcony supporting a lunatic who has lost an arm,
a crucifix without a Christ,
a sisal pissing Chardonnay for magicians without cloaks;
that's what would function as a pardon for Anton Vowl . . .

a farrago without fustian,
a looking glass dull from a tiny, not spiny, fish,
autumnal grazing,
a myriad of billows rolling in from a promontory,
a faithful old hunting-gun,

a whitish burn, a body without body, a world without war,
an illusory omission,
that's what would stop Anton Vowl from dying . . .
but how to construct it all in just that instant in which is
born a Void?

6

*Which, following a compilation of a polymath's random
jottings, will finish with a visit to a zoo*

Anton Vowl's bosom companion is a man known as Amaury
Conson.

Conson has (or had) six sons. His firstborn, Aignan (odd,
that), did a vanishing act similar to Vowl's almost 30 springs
ago, in Oxford, during a symposium run by a *soi-disant* Martial
Cantaral Foundation and in which Lord Gadsby V. Wright,
Britain's most illustrious scholar and savant, was a participant.
Conson's following son, Adam, was to pass away in a sanatorium,
succumbing to inanition through wilful auto-starvation. And that
was only to start with: in Zanzibar a monstrous shark would
swallow Ivan, his third; in Milan his fourth, Odilon, Luchino
Visconti's right-hand man at La Scala, had a particularly bony
portion of turbot catch in his throat; and in Honolulu his fifth,
Urbain, was a victim of hirudination, slain by a gigantic worm
sucking his blood, totally draining him, so that as many as 20
transfusions would fail to bring him back. So Conson has a solitary surviving son, Yvon; but his liking for Yvon is gradually
diminishing, as Yvon, living so far away, now hardly visits his
poor old dad.

Conson ransacks Anton Vowl's flat from top to bottom; calls on
that Samaritan living two doors down who informs him about
Cochin ablating Vowl's sinus; and asks anybody who might assist
him in tracking down his companion.

Vowl's flat is in a most unpromising sort of building, wholly

44

without "standing": walls in a whitish stucco; filthy, poor-quality cotton rugs losing tufts of dank hair on an almost daily basis; a narrow drawing room; an untidy living room with a mouldy sofa jostling a cupboard that has a rancid oniony stink about it and a trio of horribly kitschy prints stuck on to its shaky doors with a Band-Aid; a bow window of milky-murky glass giving off a dark and turbid glow, a pallid photocopy of sunlight; a monkish cot to doss down on with torn pillows and a quilt full of scummy stains; and a dingy lavatory-cum-washroom with a jug, a pot, a bowl, a razor and a washcloth hanging all in rags, off which a tiny stowaway of an animal, a moth but just possibly a rat, had got fat.

Cautiously lifting down, from a flagrantly DIY-built rack, a stack of dusty old books with grubby bindings and torn stitchings and a lot of rambling, criss-crossing annotations and marginalia, Amaury is drawn to 5 or 6 works that Vowl was obviously studying with a particular goal in mind: Gombrich's *Art and Illusion*, Witold Gombrowicz's *Cosmos*, Monica Wittig's *L'Opoponax*, Thomas Mann's *Doctor Faustus*, Noam Chomsky, Roman Jakobson and, finally, Louis Aragon's *Blanc ou l'Oubli*.

Now Conson starts rummaging about a bulky cardboard box and finds a host of manuscripts proving to his satisfaction that his companion was thirsty for instruction, for Vowl, who was always an anal, finicky sort of chap, hadn't thrown out anything dating from his schooldays. Studying it raptly, practically word by word, Amaury could thus follow from its halting origins all of what you might call Anton's *curriculum studiorum*.

First, composition:

Là où nous vivions jadis, il n'y avait ni autos, ni taxis, ni autobus; nous allions parfois, mon cousin m'accompagnait, voir Linda qui habitait dans un canton voisin. Mais, n'ayant pas d'auto, il nous fallait courir tout au long du parcours; sinon nous arrivions trop tard: Linda avait disparu.

Un jour vint pourtant où Linda partit pour toujours. Nous aurions dû la bannir à jamais; mais voilà, nous l'aimions. Nous aimions tant son parfum, son air rayonnant, son blouson, son pantalon brun trop long; nous aimions tout.

Mais voilà, tout finit: trois ans plus tard, Linda mourut; nous l'avons appris par hasard, un soir, au cours d'un lunch.

Now philosophy:

Kant, analysing a priori *intuition, had for an instant a nagging doubt about his Cogito ("I think, thus I am") and its validity, knowing that it would fail to account for a situation in which God, musing on His own primacy in that Trinity on which Christianity was built, might boast (but to whom?) of constituting a holistic, all-including "I". "And so," said Kant, "Spinoza thought to accomplish a mutation that would abolish all godhood? Judaising Baruch? Bandaging 'Natura', suturing it (or, should I say, saturating it), closing up its gaps, by a Siv with aspirations to Infinity!" Thus, a Platonician by anticipation, but fallaciously so, Kant saw Spinoza as part of a long tradition of castrating cosmologists. For, many moons prior to that, Plato, killing off all archaists, saw that no participant having his origin in that cosmic "I" could bring it to a conclusion.*

That aboriginal Arc thus found its triangulation, drawing out its diagonal to its sinusoidal tip, casting a sharp point at Kant's brow, causing him to pass away from having thought for an instant of a Cogito without a God.

Maths:

On Groups.

(By Marshall Hall Jr LIT 28, folios 5 to 18 inclus.)

Who first had this particular notion, who brought it to its maturity, who found a solution to it? Was it Gauss or Galois? Nobody could say. Nowadays, though, all of us know. But it's said that, just prior to dying, at night, at about 4 or 5 a.m.,

46

Galois put in writing on his jotting pad (Marshall Hall Jr, op. cit, folio B) a long, continuous chain of factors in his own form of notation. To wit:

$$aa - 1 = bb - 1 = cc - 1 = dd - 1 = ff - 1 =$$
$$gg - 1 = hh - 1 = ii - 1 = jj - 1 = kk - 1 =$$
$$ll - 1 = mm - 1 = nn - 1 = oo - 1 = pp - 1 =$$
$$qq - 1 = rr - 1 = ss - 1 = tt - 1 = uu - 1 =$$
$$vv - 1 = ww - 1 = xx - 1 = yy - 1 = zz - 1 =$$

As part of his manuscript is missing, though, nobody knows to this day what conclusion Galois was hoping to draw from his calculations.

Cantor, Douady and Bourbaki thought, on many and various grounds (from algorithms to topoi, from Möbius strips to C-star, from Shih's K-functor to Thom's $\square$s, and including all sorts of distributions, involutions, convolutions, Schwartz, Koszul, Cartan and Giorgiutti) of following a hunch that would surmount such an abrupt hiatus. It was, alas, all in vain.

Though it took him from 1935 to 1955, working at it virtually nonstop, Pontryagin finally had to admit to accomplishing nothing.

Just 8 months ago, though, Kan, working on his own adjoint (cit, D. Kan Adjoint Functors Transactions, V, 3, 18) could, it was said, show by induction (his calculation – so Kan told Jaulin – had a major cardinal as its basis) this proposition: G or H or K ($H \subset G$, $G \supset K$), 3 magmas (following Kurosh) in which $a(bc) = (ab)c$; in which, if a is a constant, $x > xa$, $x > ax$ do not "vary", so that $G \approx H \times K$, if $G = H \cup K$; if H is as invariant as K; if H has with K a solitary unit in common $H \cap K = $ Alas! as Kan quit this world prior to bringing his work to fruition, a solution is not forthcoming.

Pastoral:

It is a story about a small town. It is not a gossipy yarn; nor is it a dry, monotonous account, full of such customary "fill-ins" as "romantic moonlight casting murky shadows down a long, winding country road". Nor will it say anything about tinkling, lulling, distant folds, robins carolling at twilight or any "warm glow of lamplight" from a cabin window. No . . .

Continuing his inquiry, Amaury Conson also finds out that Anton Vowl had a fascination with aboriginal customs:

In Gogni (Chad) a Sokoro, clad in his traditional tunic, a tunic as long as a raglan coat such as a snobbishly insular Parisian might sport whilst on safari, paid a visit to a son of his who was living in Mokulu as a willing victim of an unusual (and, until now, unknown) marital status constituting a paradoxical – or, as anthropologists say, "uxorilocal" – form of subjugation. It was no doubt wrong of him to furnish a youth to such mountain folk (or Diongors), thus forcing him out of his own tribal circuit, with its basic, lucid, rigorous – in a word, structural *– warp and woof of articulation.*

Sûñ or Margina, Uti or Kaakil, Longai or Zori – O almighty rain gods, grant us comfort in our sorrow. What I now pray for is oblivion, that soft, cradling balm of oblivion, for my solitary misdoing. If not, would you slay a man for simply, unmindfully, ignoring his duty?

Finally, avoiding both Scylla and Charybdis, our Sokoro saw a witch doctor who told him that what would pacify his Sûñ was sacrificing a goat kid – and, as an additional victim, a black cock, so as to find grain for a rainy day.

Zoology:

Ovibus, or musk-ox: an animal, half-lamb and half-bullock. Its natural habitat is that snowbound Arctic or Russian plain that is commonly known as a "tundra". Its skin, which turns soft if you pound it, has a sharp and piquantly liquorish flavour. To catch hold of such an animal, you must fix upon what you think is a propitious occasion, lying flat out as it runs towards you and pouncing on it just as its front hoof looms up in front of you, monstrous and intimidating.

As soon as you put your hands on its throat, surrounding it, it looks up at you, starts lowing and, in its turn, squats along by you and actually nods off.

At which point you will find that its body, with its aroma of acacia, alfa, alfilaria, onion, oxalis, origanum, upas and union, is oddly soft to your touch.

Urus, or aurochs: a wild ox living in our own country and not found in any zoo. It's said, though, that you may occasionally find, on a nocturnal trot, a urus casting its hunchback shadow. Not so: its back has no hump at all. Nor has it any dip. In fact, it's just a boringly normal sort of back. So why should anybody hold forth on a urus?

Social conflicts:

3 May 1968. "*Agitation on Boul'Mich*", *so would claim a* Figaro *photo-caption. Slavishly carrying out his boss's command, an adjutant had a battalion of cops attack a crowd of anarchists, communists and sundry radicals who, wanting only what was right and just, sought total and unconditional pardon for six companions rotting in jail. A giant slab of paving brought from a courtyard was thrown at a Black Maria crawling with vicious gun-toting gorillas. A mound of paving bricks was soon built up in front of it; and a wiry old poplar, its thick trunk sawn in half, lay diagonally across a chaotic, haphazard mass of burning cars. Worrying that this situation was about to turn against him, Grimaud did not balk at imposing a pogrom, and his thuggish minions would thrash, gas and harass many a half-moribund agitator.*

But public opinion wasn't for long in his favour. A crowd a million strong took Paris by storm, brandishing black flags and crimson flags and shouting out anti-dictatorial slogans:

"Down with Gaullism!", 'Charly is not our Darling!" and "CRS – SS!".

Grouping Paris's population according to job classification, a union got all work to stop, all production to shut down, and had sit-ins in public transport, coal basins, shops, workshops, schools, mills and dockyards. Gas-stations would soon start to go short . . .

And Sarrish patois:

Man sagt dir, komm doch mal ins Landhaus. Man sagt dir, Stadtvolk muss aufs Land, muss zurück zur Natur. Man sagt dir, komm bald, möglichst am Sonntag. Du brummst also los, nicht zu früh am Tag, das will man nicht. Am Nachmittag fährst du durchs Dorf, in Richtung Sportplatz. Vorm Sportplatz fährst du ab. Kurz darauf bist du da. Du hälst am Tor, durch das du nicht hindurchkannst, parkst das Auto und blickst dich um. Du glaubst, nun taucht vor dir das Haus auf, doch du irrst dich, da ist das Dach. Ringsum Wald, dickichtartig, Wildnis fast. Wald, wohin du schaust. Baum und Strauch sind stark im Wuchs. Am Pfad wächst Minzkraut auch Gras, frisch, saftig und grün. Ins Haus, wovon du nur das Dach sahst. Du träumst, dass das Haus, wovon du nur das Dach sahst, laubumrankt, gross und mächtig ist. Mit Komfort natürlich, Klo und Bad und Bild im Flur. Dazu Mann und Frau stoltz vorm Kamin. Träumst du, doch das Tor ist zu und ins Haus, wovon du nur das Dach sahst, kannst du nicht. Nachts, auch das träumst du noch, löscht man das Licht und dann glüht rot und idyllisch das Holz im Kamin. So träumst du vor dich hin, doch man macht das Tor nicht auf, obwohl Sonntag ist. Da sagt man dir also, komm doch mal ins Landhaus und dann kommst du wirklich zum Landhaus und bist vorm Landhaus und kommst doch nicht ins Landhaus und warst umsonst am Landhaus und fährst vom Landhaus aus zurück nach Haus . . .

At long last, on top of a writing pad of an ochrous gold similar to that of artificial chamois, Amaury Conson finds Anton Vowl's diary; unclasps it; sifts through it till night falls; and thoughtfully shuts it again. It's dark out. Conson hails a passing cab – "To our local commissariat, pronto" – and, worn out by his day's probing, flops down on its baggy back cushion.

Waiting for hours in this commissariat, having to hang about until past midnight, maniacally twiddling his thumbs, Conson slowly starts going crazy. Finally, a dispiritingly doltish-looking individual sits down in front of him, biting on, occasionally just sucking on, with a horrid slurping sound, a gigantic ham sandwich, washing it down with a low-quality *Pinot blanc* drunk out of a plastic cup and, whilst so doing, casually drawing blobs of moist wax from his auditory canal with a toothpick and scouring his flat, simian nostrils with his thumbs.

"Now now," says this typically stolid cop, through a mouthful of York ham, "what I think is this. Your pal vows to blow his brains out, and did blow his brains out. So that's that, isn't it? If not, why would anybody say such a thing? Am I right or am I right?"

Amaury stubbornly sticks to his guns. "But, you idiot, I saw his diary, I saw his flat! In addition to which, Anton did *not* vow to blow his brains out, it was imagining his brains blown out by an assassin that was making him shit his pants. You won't find his body, you know! It's a kidnapping, an abduction!"

"An abduction? So your . . . hunch, shall I say," (this said with an infuriatingly ironic smirk on his ugly mug) "is that it was an abduction? But why, pray? This isn't Chicago, you know . . ."

Conson, at a loss for words, aghast at such crass buck-passing, at last thinks to ring up a cousin of his, a Quai d'Orsay official, who in his turn consults with an admiral who has a word with a commandant who upbraids Conson's sandwich-munching ironist and pulls strings to put a cop at his disposal, a Corsican, Ottavio Ottaviani.

*　　*　　*

So Amaury calls on Ottaviani (who inhabits a top-floor maid's room in a dingy block of flats adjoining a subway station, Sablons, not far from Paris's Jardin d'Acclimatation) and finds him, a fat, slobbish layabout, rocking to and fro in a rococo rocking chair, lolling back on a cushion of soft kapok quilting around which loops a braid as snakily sinuous as that on a hussar's uniform, dunking a rollmop in a big bowl of dills and swallowing it with a noisy smacking of his lips.

"All right," says this Ottaviani with a burp, "I was put at your disposal. So what's it all about?"

"Just this," says Amaury: "Anton Vowl is missing. About 3 days ago I had a postcard from him announcing his flight. In my opinion, though, it's actually a kidnapping."

"Why a kidnapping?" asks a civil but doubtful Ottaviani.

"Anton Vowl was on to . . ." murmurs Amaury in ominous fashion.

"On to what?"

"Nobody knows what . . ."

"So?"

"In his diary I found 5 or 6 odd hints that you and I ought to follow up. In it, notably, Vowl claims both to know and not know; or, should I say, not know but also know . . ."

"If you want my opinion, this is all a bit of a –"

"His postcard," says Amaury, unflinching, "had a curious post-script. It said: 'I ask all 10 of you, with a glass of whisky in your hand – and not just any whisky but a top-notch brand – to drink to that solicitor who is so boorish as to light up his cigar in a zoo.' By that it was plainly his wish to tip us off and, in my opinion, you and I should look into it and also study his diary, which, mark my words, contains a lot of important information . . ."

"Uh huh," says Ottaviani, though with a total lack of conviction. "This affair is proving a tough nut to crack."

"First of all," submits Conson, ignoring his doubts, "you and I might go for a stroll around a zoo."

"A zoo?" Our Corsican's jaw drops. "Why go to a zoo with a Jardin d'Acclimatation just fifty yards away?"

"Think, Ottaviani! 'That solicitor so boorish as to light up his cigar in a zoo'!"

"Okay, okay," says Ottaviani with a compliant sigh, "you go to a zoo and I'll ask around at a handful of hospitals to find out if anybody has brought him in."

"Good thinking," says Amaury. "I'll join up with you tonight to discuss our findings. Midnight at Maxim's, what do you say?"

"Lipp isn't as pricy."

"Right. Lipp it is."

Thus Amaury trots off to Paris's world-famous zoo, photographs a Sahara lion and cautiously hands a candy bar to a chimp that has thrown a twig at him. Pumas, cougars, stags, muskrats and mountain goats. A lynx. A yak. And, without warning:

"You! Lord, what a small world it is!"

It's Olga, a distant cousin of a Canadian consul in Frankfurt, and a woman who has always had a passion for Anton.

Olga starts crying. "Oh, Amaury, darling Amaury, do you think Anton is . . . is . . ."

"No, Olga, I don't. Missing, I'm afraid so. But not . . . no, no, not that."

"Did you also obtain a postcard from him advising you of his going away for good?"

"I did. And did *your* postcard also contain a PS about a solicitor smoking in a zoo?"

"That's right. But you won't find any solicitor in this zoo."

"Who can say?" murmurs Amaury.

And, in fact, at that point, as if by magic, standing not far from a pool simulating, with uncanny naturalism, a mini-Kamchatka, a pool in which a host of birds, fish and mammals play as happily as infants in a sandpit – frogs, squids, cormorants, basilisks, dolphins, finbacks, cachalots, blackfish, lizards, dugongs and narwhals – Amaury spots, and naturally accosts, a man just about to light a cigar.

53

"Good morning," says this individual.

"Morning. Now, my good man,' Amaury asks him straight out, 'do you know of any solicitors in this zoo?"

"I do. I am such a solicitor." (This is said with blunt, oddly disarming candour.)

"Shhh," says Amaury, "not so loud. And did you know Anton Vowl?"

"I got him to do occasional odd jobs."

"Do you think Vowl is still living?"

"Who knows?"

"And you? I didn't catch your . . ."

"Hassan Ibn Abbou, High Court Solicitor, 28 Quai Branly, Alma 18–23."

"Did Anton also mail you a puzzling postcard similar to that which both of us got prior to his vanishing?" Amaury pompously asks him.

"I did."

"And do you know what its closing words signify?"

"I didn't at first. But now I think that Anton was making an allusion to yours truly by writing about a cigar-smoking solicitor. Which is why I instantly took a taxi to this zoo. As for his tots of whisky, I had no notion of what it was all about until noticing this morning in my *Figaro* that Longchamp's Grand Prix is just 3 days off."

"I don't follow."

"You will! For it has a trio of odds-on nominations: Scribouillard III, Whisky 10 and Capharnaüm."

"So your hunch is that Anton was subtly hinting at this Grand Prix?" says Olga, who, until that point, hadn't said a word.

Amaury cuts in. "Who can say? It's an indication worth following up, though. You, Hassan and I will go to Longchamp this coming Monday."

"Talking of which," says Hassan, "I got from Anton Vowl, a month or so ago, 26 cartons containing all his labours, all that hard, cryptic work that Vowl was carrying out in his flat. I know of no surviving kinfolk of his who can claim familial, suppositional, optional or subsidiary rights to this voluminous body of work. So I think it normal that you hold it in trust, particularly as it might contain all sorts of hints vital to our inquiry."

"How soon can Olga and I study it?"

"Not until Monday, I'm afraid, as I'm just about to go off to Aillant-sur-Tholon. But I'm coming back on Monday morning and I'll contact you both. At that point you should know what Anton Vowl was trying to say in his allusion to 'a glass of whisky'."

Amaury laughs. "I'm willing to go as far as to put 10 francs on that nag."

"So am I," adds Olga.

"Good," says Hassan, consulting his watch. "Gracious, I must run! My train's at 4.50. So long! Till Monday night!"

"God go with you," murmurs Olga piously.

"Ciao," says Amaury.

Striding away, Hassan is soon out of sight. With Olga following him, Amaury idly strolls from animal to animal; but, finding nothing of any import, asks Olga out to a charming lunch.

Whilst Amaury is at Paris's zoo, Ottavio Ottaviani is paying a visit to its hospitals, Broca, Foch, Saint-Louis and Rothschild; and inquiring in many of its commissariats. Nobody has any information for him about Anton Vowl.

At midnight, though, hurrying on towards Lipp, at that busy Vavin-Raspail roundabout, who should our Corsican run into but Amaury, who quickly grasps his arm and mouths at him in a vivid dumb-show, "Don't go in, Lipp is simply crawling with cops!"

"Not too far off," says Ottaviani, who occasionally had a habit of confiding information not normally for public consumption, "not too far off is an individual whom this country's top brass want, shall I say . . . to go missing."

"Missing?" Amaury, thinking to catch a whiff of his quarry, practically jumps out of his skin.

"Damn it!" says Ottaviani, cursing his stupidity at passing on such hush-hush information to a layman.

"Now, now, Ottaviani, out with it! Vowl is also missing!"

"This affair has nothing to do with him," affirms Ottaviani.

"How do you know?" says Amaury, adding, with an authority that allows no pussyfooting on Ottaviani's part, "Who is this individual?"

"A Moroccan," admits Ottaviani.

"A Moroccan!" shouts Amaury.

"Shhh," murmurs Ottaviani, looking around anxiously. "That's right, a Moroccan. A Moroccan solicitor . . ."

"Hassan Ibn Abbou!" Amaury proclaims in triumph.

7

*In which an unknown individual has it in for
Moroccan solicitors*

"No," says Ottaviani with his usual sang-froid, "it isn't Ibn Abbou
but Ibn Barka."

"Oh, thank God, that's a load off my mind," says Amaury with
a sigh, afraid, without knowing why, first for Hassan Ibn Abbou,
and, *a fortiori*, if almost subliminally, for his own skin. For if
Anton Vowl falls victim to an abductor (or abductors), who's to
say that this abductor (or abductors) won't now try to lay a hand
on his faithful companions, Olga, Hassan and so forth?

Conson, with Ottaviani dogging him, walks off to Harry's Bar,
sits down (in a dark ill-lit booth so as to avoid gossip), signals
to a barman and asks for a whisky, a Chivas, straight. Ottaviani's
fancy is for a Baron but without any thick, sudsy collar of froth
on top. Munich or stout? Our Corsican hums and haws for an
instant, saying at last "Oh, Munich'll do," simply as a way of
dismissing a barman who visibly cannot wait to chat up a pair
of young girls in an adjoining booth and is sarcastically, not to
say "smart-asstically", humming "Why am I waiting?".

Without choosing to go into all its various ins and outs,
Ottaviani sums up what was most scandalous about Ibn Barka's
kidnapping. It was a total cock-up from start to finish. *Paris-Soir*,
a right-wing rag that was normally of a rampantly colonialist
bias, sought to stir things up by publishing a lot of juicy, malicious rumours. Public indignation was at boiling point. Diplomats
would go to ground, politicians usually avid for publicity would

abruptly drop out of sight. Papon took an oath that it had nothing to do with him. Souchon, though, at last had to own up to it, as did Voitot. All Matignon took fright at a diary by Figon incriminating a high-court dignitary, which was finally, if not without difficulty, shown up as a fabrication. Oufkir had an alibi – if you could call so ridiculous a story an alibi! Nor, following Fugon's hara-kiri *à la* Mishima (in fact, so rumour had it, this was not a totally voluntary affair, for, calmly placing a sword in front of him, and saying only, in an odd transatlantic twang, that "a man's gotta do what a man's gotta do", his boss at Matignon had no doubt in his mind what would occur) – nor, I say, did any inquiry gain much ground. With an accumulation of damning data, opposition politicians saw an opportunity of indicting a form of tyranny guilty of an act so arrantly criminal as to go as far as confiscating a tract that sought to point up a shadowy conspiracy linking this abduction of Ibn Barka with that, six months prior to it, of Argoud in Zurich. Talk was of a contract going out to a commando of informants, outcasts of all kinds, all of whom had criminal pasts as long as your arm (mostly bank jobs) and who had also had payoffs from Matignon for having brought off 5 or 6 political "liquidations": an antagonist of Bourguiba shot down in Frankfurt, ditto an African militant in Saint-Moritz, Yazid in Louvain, Gabon's consul in Madrid! So, to maintain in his position a cowardly tyrant, his waning authority totally, and notoriously, in pawn to a major Parisian bank (Capital Français), Foccard had a rag-tag-and-bobtail gang of thugs, good-for-nothings, gold, contraband and drugs Mafiosi, join up with his battalion of bullyboys, all working hand in hand! It was a squalid affair all right. Discussions would go on out of sight in smoky back rooms. Though any small fry not up to scratch, any moron placing his organisation at risk, was instantly (in gangland lingo) "put out of harm's way", nothing and nobody could touch its instigators, its VIPs, its "big boys" . . .

"Ho hum," murmurs Ottaviani, gulping down his Munich and wiping its froth from his lips. "Talk of a can of worms . . ."

It's his last word. Amaury sighs and, though Anton Vowl's abduction has at first sight nothing at all to do with Ibn Barka's, informs Ottaviani of visiting a zoo, running into Olga, and Hassan Ibn Abbou, who was also trying to find his companion.

"Aha!" laughs Ottaviani. "So Vowl had a champion you didn't know about!"

"Why . . . that's right," says Amaury, curious as to why Ottaviani thought that important. Continuing, though: "Now look at what you and I know. This morning I saw Hassan Ibn Abbou in a zoo. But what was it that Anton Vowl said: 'A solicitor who lights up his cigar in a zoo". So I rush off to this city's only zoo. And what do I find? A solicitor lighting up a cigar. All right. But what if said solicitor thought to turn up at said zoo and light said cigar simply to conform to Anton's portrait of him, hoping by so doing that Olga or I would contact him?"

"So," Ottaviani succinctly sums up, "it was possibly not fortuitous?"

"Fortuitous or calculating, who can say? But what I plan to find out on Monday is what, if anything, was significant about Anton's allusion to 10 tots of whisky. First, though, it's worth studying a factor that's not as crucial but still apropos. To wit: do you know Karamazov?"

"Dmitri of Karamazov Bros Inc.?"

"No, his cousin Arnaud, who runs a taxi out of Clignancourt and who would occasionally do odd jobs for Vowl. You could find out for us if this Karamazov also knows of Anton's kidnapping. Do that on Monday morning, will you, whilst I'm at Longchamp."

"Just as you say, boss," grunts Ottaviani, snoozing into his glass.

It's suffocatingly cold. So cold, in fact, no duck would think of putting a foot outdoors, nor would a chimp (with brass balls or not). But Ottavio Ottaviani is robustly striding along, as though that night's thick, damp fog simply hasn't got through to him.

Arriving at Alma, Ottaviani mounts a bus that drops him at Paris's famous Quai d'Orsay, stops an instant to catch his wind and consult his watch. It's 11.40. Longchamp is still a long way off.

"Off I go," says Ottaviani, mumbling inaudibly to nobody in particular.

Not far from Orsay, only yards away from Iran's consular building, is a small snack bar with which our Corsican is familiar from having had an occasional ham or salami sandwich in it. Ottaviani walks in, dusty, haggard, worn out. A crowd of individuals is propping up its bar.

"Ciao," says Ottaviani.

"Hullo, hullo," says Romuald, a barman who, though always at work, is always smiling: "ain't a fit night out for man nor animal."

"You can say that again," murmurs Ottaviani, vigorously blowing into his hands. "Brrrr . . ."

"Only minus two, though," Romuald points out. "Not as cold as all that."

"P'raps so, but it's blowing up a fair old storm," says Ottaviani.

"Can I bring you a sandwich? Parma ham, York ham, Italian salami, Danish salami, bacon, black pudding, chipolata, cold roast, tuna fish, Stilton, Cantal, Port-Salut, Gorgonzola? Or what about a hot dog?"

"No thanks. A grog's all I want. I think I'm catching a cold."

"A grog for M. Ottaviani!" Romuald calls back to his assistant who is busy cooking a plat du jour of osso bucco with *artichauts au romarin*.

"Coming up!"

In an instant Ottaviani's drink plops down in front of him.

"A boiling hot grog," proclaims Romuald. "No cold can withstand it."

Ottaviani sips his grog.

"Mmmm, yummy."

"Not too sugary?"

"No, it's just right. Fit for a king."

"That's 23 francs 20 all told."

Ottaviani throws down a handful of coins, for which Romuald thanks him.

Noticing, half out of sight, his boss, Aloysius Swann, idly picking at a bowl of fruit, Ottaviani, cautiously balancing his grog in his hand, thrusts his way through a crowd of drunks and, still panting, sits down facing him.

"Hullo, boss."

"Hullo, Ottaviani," says Swann. "You okay?"

"Just so-so. I'm coming down with a cold."

"You want a yoghurt?"

"No, I'm not at all hungry."

"So?"

"So what?"

"Amaury Conson?"

"Conson still thinks it was a kidnapping."

"Sounds as if that's what it was," murmurs Swann.

"You think so too, but why?"

Without saying a word, Swann pulls a photocopy from his bag and hands it to his adjutant.

"Good Lord!" Ottaviani almost shouts, "this is straight from GHQ!"

And this is what it said:

Analysis of Consul Alain Gu. rin
to Royal G – P.R.C.

(Distribution SACLANT – "cosmic"
NATO – S AG – G/PRC – 3.28.23)

A month ago an analysis from Orrouy's GHQ-NATO Commandant, with corroboration from HCI Andilly, which midshipman 3/6.26 of Cp. Horn's straggling group thought to pass on to us for confirmation, told us what was about to occur to Anton

Vowl. That month's K. Count was instantly put in by Mission "NATO-cosmic" 5/28-Z.5. Anton Vowl was not on it. In addition, an anti-abduction plan, jointly drawn up by Mission "off days" 8/28-Z.5, instruction L 18, and by "cosmic 1A", was soon circulating to all GRCs, SR assistants, SM assistants, HCIs, ONIs, CICs, "G.3"s, BNDs, SIDs and "Prima 2"s – all, that is, saving MI5, but including stimuli to various unorthodox commando units.

Without wishing to imply that this information, of an A.3 or B.I rating, is not crucial, it is worth noting that, 18 days ago, our organisation got virtually nothing out of placing all its apparatus at point "3". Why was it such a thorough fiasco? HCI Arlington claims to know: CIA infiltrations? but also SIS in our staffs within NATO jurisdiction. It is said, in addition, that, by compromising a *soi-disant* Bushy Man from Ankara, an Albanian SR assistant had sought (and not, as it turns out, in vain) to gain total control of his group.

Thus, to sum up this difficult situation, our organisation may opt for (a) abandoning Anton Vowl to his doom or (b) instigating a *casus* – not a *casus violationis*, at most a *casus damni*: in my opinion, only our PM could find a solution to such an unusual affair. Which is why I submit this analysis (in flagrant violation of SR norms), advising you against consultation but in favour of a global opinion plus instructions.

"God, it's got so many ramifications!" says Swann. "What did Hassan Ibn Abbou say?"

"Oh, Hassan wasn't talking, but I'm going to confront him tonight at midnight; with a bit of luck I might just find out what's what. As for Olga, softly, softly. That's a young lady who knows a lot but isn't giving too much of it away."

"You think so?"

"I know so. Talking of which, I saw Karamazov."

"And?"

"Karamazov saw Vowl on 3 occasions a month ago: (1) taking him, by night, to a vacant, run-down bungalow in Aulnay-sous-Bois; (2) by day, to play whist at Augustin Lippmann's club (Karamazov won about 20 points off Vowl); and (3), most significantly, just 20 days ago, Vowl had Karamazov fit an anti-burglary contraption to his, that's to say to Vowl's, Fiat."

"Vowl had him fit an anti-burglary contraption to his Fiat?"

"Yup."

"You don't say! But why?"

Ottaviani has simply no notion why and is hoping that Swann, who has, it's said, a flair for a hunch worthy of a Sioux or an Iroquois, will furnish him with a motivation. His boss, though, lacking that crucial spark of inspiration, is not on form today.

"Why fit an anti-burglary contraption to his car?" murmurs Swann, adding grumpily, "And to think that you and I at first thought this affair was a cinch . . ."

A mutual sigh.

"It's all a ghastly hotchpotch, particularly as I still don't know who is hiding Anton Vowl."

With his hand Swann signals to Romuald, who says to him:

"A mocha? A cappuccino?"

"Thanks but no thanks. Just my bill, if you wouldn't mind."

"Righty-ho, I'll tot it up for you in a jiffy."

Scribbling on his pad with a Bic, Romuald murmurs:

"Tuna, plat du jour, Stilton, fruit, drink . . . that's 18 francs, including tip."

"18 francs!" complains Swann. "Isn't that a bit stiff for what I had?"

Romuald puts it down to VAT, whilst, for his part, Aloysius actually calls him a crook. It all risks coming to fisticuffs, but Ottaviani finally calms Swann, who, furious but compliant, if still not brought round to Romuald's way of thinking, pays up.

On his way out, though, Swann is caught in a draught, discharging a sonorous "Atishoooo!"

"Don't go looking for sympathy!" laughs a now jovial Romuald. "You had that coming to you. What a lark – catching your pal's cold!"

Vigorously shaking hands with Aloysius Swann, who has to rush off to his commissariat, Ottavio Ottaviani hails a taxi to go to Longchamp, which today, and Paris's ominous political situation notwithstanding, holds its annual Grand Prix du Touring-Club, an arduous handicap that will award its victor with not just a gold trophy but a million francs, or so it's said, a donation from a racing-mad nabob. And, with *tout-Paris* jostling Paris tout, all go parading through Longchamp's lavish paddocks.

Most conspicuous by far is Italy's top film star, Amanda von Comodoro-Rivadavia, soon to fly out to Hollywood to sign a six-million-dollar contract with Francis Ford Coppola for a trilogy of Mafia dramas with Marlon Brando and Al Pacino. Voluptuous Amanda is clad (*o sancta simplicitas*) in a pair of bouffant pink slacks as billowy as a Turkish Ottoman's, a coral polo shirt, a bright crimson cardigan, an ivory sash, a maroon scarf, a shocking pink mink coat, ruby stockings, a damask muff and purplish bootikins. Accompanying this lurid apparition is Urbain d'Agostino (inamorato or simply sugar daddy, who knows?), sporting a lacy jabot, an Ungaro tail coat with a Mao collar, a top hat and an ambassadorial gold chain. And milling around, with much aristocratic ado, is a host of Maharajahs and moguls, Kronprinz, Paladins and Hospodars, pillars all of *Who's Who*.

Grooms, spivs and turf officials stroll to and fro; at a kiosk a young lad is shouting "*Paris-Turf*! Git your *Paris-Turf*!"; touts offload dubious tips and long columns start forming in front of casinos and gambling halls.

Having sought him high and low among this cosmopolitan crowd, Ottaviani at last finds Amaury Conson sitting on a stairway with Olga, a vision of Pariso-colonial chic in a viridian Arab tunic.

Through a pair of binoculars, Amaury is scrutinising Longchamp's world-famous track lap by lap, practically inch by inch:

"I think that ground is just a bit too soft."

A boorish individual standing at his right affirms (though, in truth, nobody had sought his opinion) that Conson is a total ignoramus on track sports. Amaury starts blushing furiously but backs off from, so to say, standing his own ground. And, in actual fact, Longchamp had not known a track so icy and of such volatility: no rainfall for a month or so, no mist hanging about, but a hard, nippy frost all around.

"Why hasn't Whisky 10 shown up?" asks Olga, squinting through Amaury's binoculars.

"It's dropping out. It was just this instant broadcast on a Tannoy."

"Why?"

"Nobody knows."

"So why stay on?" murmurs a thoroughly downcast Ottaviani.

"Olga wants to know how it turns out."

"You said it!" laughs Olga. "I put 25 francs on Scribouillard."

Out of 26 original nominations, only 25 now stand at Long-champ's starting-post, Whisky 10 (No. 5) having withdrawn. Initially, Whisky 10 was thought a cinch to win, although, surprisingly, at official odds of 18 to 1. With it scratching, most touts had a good opinion of Scribouillard III; Schola Cantorum, a young Anglo-Norman colt out of Assurbanipal; Scapin, a roan that had won at Chantilly in March (Grand Prix Brillat-Savarin); Scarborough, a "dilly of a filly", as word had it, with all-black hair and a trio of gold cups at Ascot; Capharnaüm, a mount that was, though, slightly short in its forward limbs; and, finally, Divin Marquis, an occasionally moody kind of nag that wasn't tops in anybody's book but had a habit of starting slowly and rapidly gaining ground.

Riding Scribouillard, Saint-Martin – Paris's Sir Gordon Richards – gallops off to an ovation from his faithful public, only to fall flat on his back at Longchamp's notorious Mill Brook. So it's Capharnaüm that wins, just nosing out Divin Marquis.

"In my opinion," says Amaury, "Hassan Ibn Abbou is a bit of a fraud. Has today taught us anything at all?"

Abandoning Longchamp to its aficionados, its huntin', shootin', fishin' and racin' buffs, Amaury boards a Paris-bound bus along with his two companions. And it occurs to him that Whisky 10's withdrawal might still throw light on Vowl's abduction.

"Just 3 days ago you had 3 odds-on nominations; but, with Whisky scratching and Scribouillard stumbling, Capharnaüm won!"

"It sort of puts you in mind of a whodunit, don't you think," says Olga.

"No," says Amaury: "of an April Fool's Day hoax."

"No," says Ottaviani: "of a Dick Francis."

Our trio strolls into a bar, hoping to drown its frustration in a round or two of cocktails. Through this bar wafts a languorous aroma of amaryllis. Stirring a dry Martini, Olga starts painfully, almost inaudibly, confiding in Conson and Ottaviani:

"If only I'd known — but how could anybody know? Anton didn't look normal, but, whilst talking to him, it was hard to grasp what was wrong with him. On occasion my darling would pound his fists and cry out for . . . for just forty winks, that's all, forty winks of blissful oblivion. Anton hadn't had a nap in two months. Two months! His body was on a rack of pain, such pain, his brain simply wouldn't function, its tribal drums wouldn't stop pounding, pounding, pounding . . ."

Olga's soliloquy gradually sinks into a sigh as long and languid as an autumnal chord from a violin.

"*Mia carissima*," coos Amaury, fondling Olga's hand with an ardour that's slightly at odds with his usual avuncular joviality, "if Anton hasn't actually . . . hasn't . . . oh, you know what I'm trying to say, you'll probably find him in an alcoholic stupor!"

"*Lo giuro!*" says a martial (and cod Mozartian) Ottavio.

"Do you mind!" sniffs Olga, with a toss of auburn curls.

It's Ottaviani's turn to sigh. "What I do mind is almost four days of bloody hard graft with damn all to show for it."

"What about paying a call on Hassan Ibn Abbou now," is Amaury's proposal, "and finding out what information awaits us from him?"

Hassan Ibn Abbou owns a charming Louis XVIII villa on Paris's ultra-chic Quai Branly. Knocking at its door, Amaury finds, standing in front of him, a footman who fawningly asks him and Ottaviani (Olga, still low in spirits, had thought to turn in) into a spacious formal drawing room.

"My companion and I wish to talk to M. Ibn Abbou," says Amaury.

"If you wouldn't mind waiting, sirs, I shall inform him of your arrival."

A young man, slightly too good-looking for comfort, sporting that sort of oblong gold braid that is traditionally worn by a Parisian flunky, and sashaying towards Amaury with an insinuating swing of his slim hips, asks him:

"Cocktails for two?"

Amaury opts for a whisky-and-soda, Ottaviani a glass of Armagnac.

Just at that point, though, from an adjoining room, a clamorous din bursts forth. What confusion! What hubbub! A mirror smashing, a fist-fight, various dull thuds.

A bloodcurdling cry is drawn from Ibn Abbou: "No! No! Aaaaargh!"

Amaury jumps out of his chair (and also practically out of his skin). For a solitary instant, an agonisingly short instant, no sound at all. And, in an instant following that, crying out again, Ibn Abbou falls.

Amaury and Ottaviani quickly rush forward to assist him. But, with a last, dying moan from Hassan Ibn Abbou, it's all in vain.

Sticking in his back, and right up to its hilt, is a poniard with a tip containing a poison known to bring about instant (and fatal) paralysis.

What nobody could work out, though, was how Abbou's assassin got away . . .

Finding this situation alarming, to put it mildly, and without waiting for Ottaviani's authority, Amaury starts burrowing high and low through Ibn Abbou's villa, finally chancing across a vault that, as Abbou hadn't told anybody its combination, was got into with calculation, cunning and a dash of chutzpah, and finding in it that thick manuscript that Anton had thought to mail to him only a month ago. It ought to contain 26 folios. Amaury counts 1, 2, 3 . . . to 25; naturally, fatally, a folio is missing. That's right, you win! No. 5 it is!

So, complication piling on complication, a major conundrum unfolds: that famous "solicitor who is so boorish as to light up his cigar in a zoo" (but nobody had any proof that this particular solicitor was in fact a boor) has a poniard in his back and Anton Vowl is still missing.

That night, at about two o'clock, Amaury Conson strolls back to his studio flat, Quai d'Anjou – and, till dawn, till cockcrow, till first blush of morning, avid to find out just what's going on, dutifully ploughs through Vowl's diary . . .

8

*In which you will find a word or two about a burial
mound that brought glory to Trajan*

ANTON VOWL'S DIARY

A Monday.

Call him Ishmail, and him Ahab, and it Moby Dick.

*You, Ishmail, phthisic pawn, glutton for musty old manuscripts,
puny scribbling runt, martyr to a myriad of sulks, doldrums and
mulligrubs, you who lit out, packing just a smock, four shirts and a
cotton hanky in your bag, hurtling to salvation, to oblivion and to
mortality, you who saw, surging up in front of you by night, a Bassalian mammoth, a paradigm of pallor and purity, a shining symbol of
immaculation, a giant Grampus coming up for air!*

*Away four springs, abroad four springs, braving whirlwind, whirl-
pool and typhoon, from Labrador to Fiji, from Jamaica to Alaska,
from Hawaii to Kamchatka.*

*Midnight, aboard ship, with Pip playing on his harmonica, Star-
buck, Daggoo, Flask, Stubb and Doughboy would sing:*

> *Yo Ho Ho!*
> *And a flask of rum!*

*A Nantuckian sailor brought immortality to a titanic combat oppos-
ing, triply, Captain Ahab and that giant Grampus, Moby Dick.
Moby Dick! Two words to chill a strong man's blood, to stir a ship's
rigging with a frisson of horror. Moby Dick! O animal of Astaroth!
Animal of Satan! Its big, blank, brilliant trunk, with its court of*

birds flying noisily about it, now gulls, now cormorants, now a solitary, forlorn albatross, would sculpt, so to say, a gigantic, gaping pit, a curving concavity of nothing, a brimming bowl of air, from a rippling rut of billows and furrows, would crimp any horizon with its foamy, whitish dip, a fascinating, paralysing abyss, a milky chasm drawing you in, drawing you down, down, down, down, flashing at you from afar, flashing its virginal wrath, foaming at its mouth, a corridor sucking you in, in, in, in to oblivion, a wat'ry quarry, a plunging void drawing you forward, drawing you downward, drawing you dizzily down into a miasma of hallucination, into a Styx as dark as tar, a ghastly livid whirlpool, a Malström! Moby Dick! Only out of sight of Ahab would anybody talk about it; a bos'n would blanch and draw a pious cross in front of him; and many an ordinary sailor at his work would murmur a dominus vobiscum.

And now Ahab would limp forward, supporting his body on an artificial limb sawn out of wood but as shiny as ivory, an imposing stump that, many, many springs ago, his sailors had torn off a giant rorqual's jaw, Ahab, a long and zigzagging furrow tracing its path through his grizzly, stubbly hair, incising his brow and vanishing at his collar, a drawn and haggard Ahab now looming out and booming out, cursing that animal for having got away from him for nigh on 18 springs, cursing it and insulting it.

And now, to his ship's mainmast, Ahab would nail a gold doubloon, promising it to any sailor who was first to sight his arch-antagonist.

Night upon night, day upon day, at his ship's prow, numb with cold, stiff as a rod in his captain's coat, hard as a rock, straight as a mast, still as a post, and dumb too, not saying a word, not showing any hint of a human soul, cold as a carcass, but boiling inwardly with an inhuman wrath, Ahab would stand out, stark and gaunt, a rumbling volcano, an imploding storm, a still point in a turning world, against a dark, cloudy horizon, raptly scrutinising it for a sign, for any sign, of Moby Dick. Sirius would glow uncannily bright in a starry night sky; and, on top of that mainmast, and akin to nothing so much as a dot on an i, would glow, too, a livid halo infusing that diabolic doubloon and its gold with a wan chiaroscuro.

Ahab's circumnavigation would last four springs. For four long springs his valiant and foolhardy craft would roam, rolling uncontrollably, pitching and tossing, tacking from north to south, from south to north, combing Triton's wavy, curling hair, labouring now in August warmth, now in April chill.

It was Ahab who first saw Moby Dick. It was a bright, sunny morning, without wind or cloud, with an Atlantic as flat as a rug, as limpid as a looking-glass. Milky-whitish against a lapis-lazuli horizon, Moby Dick was puffing and blowing, its back forming a foggy, snowy mount for a flock of birds circling around it

But first a lull, an almost subliminal instant of tranquil immobility. Just six furlongs off from Ahab's ship Moby Dick lay: now drifting, a numinous animal, a symbol of calm awaiting its own storm, fragrant with a throat-catching aroma, an aroma of purity, of infinity; now, rising out of that cold, mirrory Atlantic, a lustral halo imbuing all around it with a virginal glow. Not a sound, not an angry word. Not a man stirring, as though brought to a standstill by all this calm and radiancy, as though swaying languidly in vapours of adoration rising up out of that glassy main, out of that dawning day.

O harmony, total unison, absolution! For an instant, oblivion holds back, draws back, as though waiting for this snowy Himalaya, this giant Grampus, to grant absolution to Starbuck, to Pip, to Ishmail and Ahab.

With burning brow and twisting, hunching, horrifying body, long did Ahab stand, staring into a void, saying nary a word, only sobbing – sobbing and shaking.

"Moby Dick! Moby Dick!" was his final, fulminating cry. "Now, all of you, into a boat!"

Daggoo found his crinkly buckskin chaps handy as a strop for his harpoon, honing its point till it was as sharp as a razor.

*   *   *

71

*It was an assault that was to last four days, four long days of appalling
conditions and appalling collisions, a furious tug of war with 26 sailors
putting up a prodigious fight, attacking that Bassalian titan, attacking it again and again, puncturing its invincibility, implanting in
it, again and again, a harpoon as sharp as a bistoury, thrusting that
harpoon in right up to its shaft, to its crossbar, whilst Moby Dick
would roar and flail about in pain; but also whilst (with razor-sharp
barbs slicing through its body, with hooks viciously clutching at its skin,
ripping it up into narrow, bloody strips, flaying it, raising its wrath
to a foaming pitch by scratching long furrows along its shiny back) it
unflinchingly stood up to its assailants, butting, upturning and sinking boat upon boat, till it too would sink in its turn, vanishing abruptly
into a turbid, now darkly crimson Atlantic.*

*But, that night, confronting Ahab aboard his ship, capsizing its
prow, Moby Dick split it in two with a solitary blow. Although, in a
last spasm of fury, Ahab slung his harpoon in midair, to his horror
its cord, twisting back, spun about his own body. Moby Dick, swirling
around, now swam straight for him.*

*"Till my dying day your blood is all I shall thirst for!" was Ahab's
cry. "From my Stygian limbo I shall assail you! In my abomination
I shall spit on you, spit on you, accurs'd Grampus, animal accurs'd
till Doomsday!"*

*His own giddily spinning harpoon snagging him, causing him to
thrash about in agony, Ahab's fall was nigh; and, soaring upwards,
Moby Dick caught him on its back and sank out of sight.*

*All around, yawning in mid-Atlantic, was a livid chasm, a colossal
canyon, a whirlpool sucking down into its foaming spiral, now a sailor's
body, now a harpoon cast in vain, now a capsizing boat, and now, at
last, Ahab's own forlorn ship which its captain's damnation was turning into a floating coffin . . .*

Apocalypsis cum figuris: *as always, though, a survivor will hold out,
a Jonah who will claim that, on that day, his damnation, his oblivion,*

was writ in plain sight in a Grampus's blank iris – blank, blank,
blank, as a tabula rasa, as a void!
  Ah, Moby Dick! Ah, moody Bic!

Almost all *tout-Paris* turns out to mourn Hassan Ibn Abbou's
passing and accompany his coffin to its burial ground – or so
you might think from a column of VIPs so long it holds up traffic
for two hours from Quai Branly to Faubourg Saint-Martin. As
conspicuous in this as in any crowd, Amanda von Comodoro-
Rivadavia stands apart, chatting to Baron Urbain d'Agostino.
Olga sobs unconsolably. Ottaviani is just as surly as usual.
Amaury Conson, still grasping at straws, still struggling to throw
an inkling of light on Anton's "Moby Dick", is lost in his
thoughts.
  Hassan Ibn Abbou's tomb is in a columbarium in Antony, a
suburb of Paris; and wholly charming it is, too, juxtaposing trans-
lucid quartz with onyx as blindingly brilliant as a South African
diamond, built up from a solid brass block with incrustations of
iridium and bristling with a galaxy of official cordons and chains,
of ribands, garlands and stars, posthumous honours by which
many a king, many a maharajah, sought publicly to display an
unconditional admiration for Ibn Abbou – Croix du Combattant,
Victoria Cross, Nichan Iftikhar, Ours Royal du Labrador and
Grand'Croix du Python Pontifical.
  Six orators in all hold forth. First, François-Armand d'Arson-
val, in his capacity as official administrator of a Civic Tribunal
that Hassan had thought out from A to Z; following him, and
acting for a major Anglo-Iranian bank, Victor, Baron d'Aiguillon
(no vulgar factotum, Hassan was for long his loyal right-hand
man); an Imam from Agadir who lauds his patriotism, his nation-
alistic passion for Morocco; Lord Gadsby V. Wright (Hassan
was his assistant at Oxford and by vigorous string-pulling would
obtain his nomination as Auctor Honoris Causa), who charms
his auditors with an account – so high-flown, so orotund, it's
almost Johnsonian – of his confidant's *curriculum studiorum*; and

Raymond Q. Knowall, who talks of Hassan's spasmodic though always cordial association with OuLiPo.

Finally it's Carcopino's turn, Carcopino, a luminary of *l'Institut*, that mortuary of Immortals on Paris's Quai Conti, who starts:

"Six springs ago Hassan Ibn Abbou won a uninominal 3-ballot poll by 25 out of 26, a poll that was to stir up a commotion for a day or two – but, as I say, voting in favour of Hassan Ibn Abbou was practically unanimous, so our organisation thought to appoint him to a subcommission of PC-IMAM (Patrimonial Corpus of Inscriptions in Morocco's Atlas Mountains), a fairly lowly position but which had its own distinction, won by Hassan on account of his polymathic study of an almost unknown tumulus (and nobody who did know it could work out its import) from an *oppidum civium romanorum* which a scholar from Munich, a Judaist in flight from Austria's *Anschluss*, had found in diggings at Thugga (or, as it's nowadays known, Dougga). It's said that it withstood many attacks by Jugurtha, it's said that Juba Africanus 'did pass a night by it' (*Titus Livius dixit*) and that Trajan had a villa built on it for Adrianus, his son by adoption."

Carcopino, though, citing Piganiol's biography, affirms that this is only a rumour.

Notwithstanding that Trajan has nothing much to do with Hassan Ibn Abbou, a handful of his auditors warmly applaud. For, although talking in a low, unsonorous, almost soporific murmur, our Immortal knows how to grip his public with his oratory.

Now, totally impromptu, Carcopino starts painting a vivid word-portrait of his companion. "Hassan Ibn Abbou was tragically cut down in his maturity, and his passing is a loss not only to that *Institut* for which I am proud to talk today but also, most profoundly, to our Nation – and it's a loss not only of a man, of a scholar, but also of his vast scholarship and, which is just as important, his unfailing practical know-how. For nobody could match Hassan's capacity for conciliating romanisation and barbarisation, for coming to grips with an ambiguous if highly significant association linking two outwardly opposing notions, so constituting, so instituting, an insight out of which, poor orphan as it is on this tragic day of days, will unfold, by that important, nay, by that paramount, innovation of Hassan Ibn Abbou's, will unfold, I say, a truly dazzling tomorrow. Faith – that is what all of us now must put our trust in, faith in that lowly grain that Hassan Ibn Abbou was first to plant, that acorn of thought that will grow into an oak and thus grant us, and for always, immunity from hardship," Carcopino says in conclusion, his vocal chords almost cracking, his auditors sympathising with him, sobbing along with him, sharing his pain, won round by his oratorical skills and not daring to applaud.

To Amaury Conson's disgust, though, a man standing not far off is actually smiling. But this individual, tall, of stocky build and sporting a chic raglan coat, cut as only British tailors know how, has a candid, jovial and, in a word, chummy look about him, oozing "warmth and charmth" (to borrow a famous Goldwynism), that soon disarms him. Amaury walks up to him and asks point-blank:

"Pardon my intrusion, but may I know what's amusing you?"

"If you must know, I'm smiling at an omission in his oration that I find most significant."

"An omission?" gasps Amaury, who cannot mask his agitation.

"About six months ago, for his CNRS Commission Ph.D., Hassan Ibn Abbou was author of a succinct but, in my own opinion, slipshod monograph on *jus latinum*, which is to say, Latin law, a topic that our Moroccan, notwithstanding his lack of rigour on this occasion, could claim to know backwards. This monograph of his sought to focus on a particular point, a point so baffling it had thrown all you highbrows into a tizzy: to wit, what obligation, if any, bound a city, a town or a rural district to allow its population (rustics, occasionally shopfolk) a status abjuring any kind of distinction that had, ipso facto, a Roman outrank a Saharan nomad? Although not wholly satisfactory, notably in its conclusions, his work, confirming Marc Bloch's intuition vis-à-vis Donjon-Vassal's study, Mauss's on

Chaman-Tribu unification and also Chomsky's on that famous Insignificant-Significant junction, was ironclad proof that no such obligation was binding (it was at most an option among many), thus proving in its turn that any analysis (from a *soi-disant* dogmatic notion of Law) of a substratum which would contain colonisation, romanisation or barbarisation was automatically illusory. It was, thus, important to avoid any sort of *a priori* thinking and, most of all, to distinguish what about it was truly infrastructural. It was a paradoxical situation: Karl Marx an Immortal! Nobody thought to find such a day coming to pass. But a majority of jurors had no difficulty swallowing it, and it was only Carcopino (known at Quai Conti as Cola Pinada or Copacabana) who was said to cry out 'Idiot! Idiot! Idiot!'"

"But what about that oration?" murmurs Amaury.

"I know. I admit I found that surprising. I must say I thought our Immortal would slip in a handful of cryptic allusions to it. But not at all!"

"Shhh!" says Olga, who has stood apart from this discussion. "It's winding up now."

This man formally doffs his panama, that man his shako, a third his homburg. An old fogy of an admiral, obviously gaga, starts saluting nobody in particular. Ottaviani bashfully sniffs into his cotton hanky. Olga sobs again. Paparazzi rush about, snapping away at Amanda von Comodoro-Rivadavia who, with pinpoint timing, falls into a swoon in Urbain d'Agostino's awaiting arms.

Now, first, a sacristan in a bright canary *cappa magna* and waving a solid gold thingamajig . . . um, you know, that sprinkling thing, walks forward; following him, a trio of chaplains brandishing a slightly shopworn crucifix with its kitschy canopy of swishily rustling frills; finally six human caryatids hoisting up a mahogany coffin by its shiny brass knobs.

A clumsy pratfall – and Hassan's coffin slips, falls, its lid swings up. Holy Christmas! No Hassan Ibn Abbou!

* * *

Talk of kicking up a row! What with diplomats accusing cops, cops accusing Matignon, Matignon accusing Maison Roblot, Maison Roblot accusing Maison Borniol, Maison Borniol accusing – try to work this out if you can – Foch Hospital, Foch Hospital accusing Carcopino, Carcopino accusing Baron d'Aiguillon's Anglo-Iranian Bank and that bank accusing Pompidou, Pompidou compromising Giscard, Giscard blaming Papon, Papon in his turn lodging a strong complaint against Foccard . . . it's a daisy-chain that could go on ad infinitum!

"I can't stand it!" says Ottavio Ottaviani. "First Ibn Barka, now Ibn Hassan. Ibn forbid a third such calamity!"

It's a difficult job hushing up such a murky affair, but within days a curtain of fog and iron, as Winston Churchill would say, is drawn down tight. Nobody claims to know anything at all of Anton Vowl's abduction – if abduction it was. And now, similarly, nobody claims to know anything at all of Hassan Ibn Abbou's body-snatching.

III

DOUGLAS HAIG
CLIFFORD

9

In which an amazing thing occurs to an unwary basso profundo

A day or two on – with, for company, that curious individual who had had such an illuminating talk with him at Hassan Ibn Abbou's burial – Amaury Conson pays a call on Olga who, laid low with both a sniffly cold and a crippling bout of lumbago, is vacationing in a small family manor at Azincourt.

It's by train that our two protagonists go first to Arras.

"In days of old," says Amaury's companion in a nostalgic drawl, "if you had an inclination, say, or an obligation, to go to Dinard or Pornic, Arras or Cambrai, your only option was to climb into a mail coach, usually a wobbly old jalopy. As your trip would last from four to six days, you would try to ward off monotony by chatting to your coachman, taking an occasional sip of brandy from a flask, skimming through a radical tract, airing your opinion on this, that and virtually anything you could think of, talking shop, narrating an amusing play by Sardou and holding forth on a cutthroat's trial that had all Paris in its grip (notwithstanding his prodigious oratorical skills, you'd attack this cutthroat's QC, who, disparaging all his antagonist's accusations, alibis and affidavits as a put-up job, sought to disclaim, in toto, what was almost cast-iron proof of guilt and also vilify a poor, law-abiding pharmacist from whom our assassin had bought his poison, laudanum; you'd find fault with this or that juror; nor had that shifty procurator struck you as wholly trustworthy). You would gratify your company with ironic *bon mots* on political topics, wittily puncturing Du Paty du Clam's corruption, as also

Cassagnac's, Drumont's and Mac-Mahon's. You would sing that "Chanson du Tourlouru" that Paulin or Bach was immortalising in Paris's most modish nightclubs and music halls. You would vigorously affirm your unconditional admiration for Rostand's *Cyrano* or Sarah as *l'Aiglon*. Finally, you'd trot out a dirty story or two, about a maharajah and a cancan girl, or a vicar and a choirboy, giving your auditors a good laugh whilst your mail coach would roll on and on till dusk. At nightfall you would sup in a charming rural inn. For a paltry six francs you'd tuck into fish or crab, lamb or mutton, washing it all down with a good strong Burgundy or a Latour-Marcillac, a Musigny or a Pommard, gorging and carousing away till you'd had a skinful! Upon which you would go for a long walk or, as you'd no doubt call it in your hoity-toity fashion, a postprandial constitutional, through a public park with stout oaks and spindly acacias and tall, thin pawlonias, with marbly malls and lush and languid lawns. You'd sip a curaçao, a maraschino or a boiling hot toddy. You'd play a hand of whist or pharaoh. Or you might play a round of billiards and win a franc or two from a local rustic. And, gradually, you'd yawn and start to think about shambling upstairs to your room. First, though, you'd drift into a chintzy front room, in which you might obtain, gratis, a *chocolat au kirsch*, a dainty bit of ribbon or a tiny flask of Armagnac. You'd find a buxom maid to carry off with you up to your room and, having had your filthy fun with this bit of crackling, you'd nod off at last, all in."

"Uh huh," sighs Amaury, "nowadays you go by train. It's rapid, but totally lacking in chic."

Concurring with this opinion, his companion draws out of a bag on his lap a curious cardboard box full of oblong cigars.

"A brazza?"

"I won't say no," says Amaury. "*A propos*, I still don't know what I'm to call you."

"Arthur Wilburg Savorgnan," says his companion.

"Is that so?" murmurs Amaury, caught short, but instantly adding, "I'm Amaury Conson."

"Amaury Conson! Hadn't you a son who . . ."

Amaury abruptly cuts in. "I had six sons. All now, alas, food for worms. All, that is, but – "

"Yvon!"

"That's right! But how do you know?"

Savorgnan grins. "Don't worry. You'll soon know my story. What you should know now is that I too was a confidant of Anton Vowl. But as I'm British, living at Oakwood, not far from Oxford, I hardly saw him from month to month. That said, though, Vowl was willing to talk about his condition, claiming, as all of you know, that his dying day was at hand. Nobody took him at his word – no, not Olga, not Hassan, not you, and not, I'm sorry to say, yours truly. But, six days ago, Hassan rang up and I said I'd discuss it all with him. As soon as I got to Paris, alas, I was told of his dying . . ."

"But did you work out what that postscript of his was trying to say to us?"

"No, but in my opinion it's wrong of us to try construing it word for word. Was 'a solicitor so boorish as to light up his cigar in a zoo' alluding to Hassan Ibn Abbou? I don't think so, and you know why? (a) Vowl didn't know Hassan was a solicitor; (b) that word 'boorish' didn't apply to him at all; and (c) you'd catch him smoking at most two Havanas in six months."

"Hmm. What you say has a ring of truth about it, particularly," adds Amaury, "as Hassan, with that addiction of his to margaritas, had no strong liking for whisky."

"That's right. In addition, Hassan was much too fond of his local Jardin d'Acclimatation to think of going to a zoo."

"So why that odd postscript?"

"I thought at first it was a phony. My hunch, now, is that it was his only option: Anton had to go out on a full stop, so to say. Possibly, his wish was to transmit a signal to us that wasn't so ambiguous; but, not having such a pithy communication at his disposal . . ."

"Nothing is as cryptic as a void," murmurs Amaury.

Arthur Wilburg Savorgnan starts. "Why do you say that?"

"I saw it in his diary. I should say, I finally got it through my skull that Hassan had always said that. Which is why," Amaury adds, "I'm taking you to Azincourt to visit Olga."

Not a word is said from that point onwards. Savorgnan puffs on his brazza and Amaury, burrowing into a book bought at a station kiosk, a long and circuitous saga about an association of major con artists, its liquidation, gradual slump, crash and bankruptcy, wholly fails to grasp that staring at him, in print, is a solution to that conundrum that is haunting him, consuming him . . .

His train briskly chugs on, making its dining-car chairs rock to and fro. An undulating rural panorama, with a solitary plough-man raking his patch of land from a shiny tractor, bowls along backwards as if on its way back to Paris. Now both train and panorama start grinding to a halt, giving way to a drab, slummy suburb, a draughty platform, an array of hangars, a bus stop and a roundabout.

Amaury and Savorgnan go by coach from Arras to Aubigny – a slowcoach of a coach crawling along at 20 mph maximum – and on foot to Azincourt (or, archaically, Agincourt, that ignominious blot and bloodstain on our military history).

A hillock, curving as unassumingly as in a child's drawing and smiling at visitors with an aroma so piquant, so vividly autumnal, it cannot but charm a discriminating nostril, an intoxicating cock-tail of aromas, in fact, both cordial and miasmal, of *myosotis palustris*, damp wood, wild mushrooms and rotting humus – this hillock, I say, stands just in front of Olga's sanctuary, a charming old manor that François Daunou had built for his family *circa* 1800.

Whilst sycophantically traditionalist masons sought to copy

Hardouin-Mansard's Grand Trianon, constituting as it did a summit, a paragon, of crypto-classicism, Soufflot, wading across a flock of Rubicons with that nonchalant aplomb, that faintly lunatic audacity, that was to bring him such popular acclaim, thought to submit to his august patron a ground plan of rococo inspiration: which is to say, portals with flying ramparts, mock-Tudor moldings, tympanums and astragals, plus (this was what was truly innovatory) a floridly imposing wing flanking it with its own gothic quad.

It was, alas, a Rubicon too far. For four days Daunou would squint this way and that at Soufflot's rough drafts, finally murmuring, "I'll say this for it, it's . . . original" and giving him, for his pains, a kick in his hind parts. To avoid a fatal scalping from M. Guillotin's sharp razor, Soufflot had to fly to Lyon clad as a pastrycook.

A downcast Daunou saw Chalgrin, Vignon, Potain and Hittorf, all of whom said no, and at last struck gold with an unknown quantity, François Tilman Suys, a Dutchman. Placing abundant funds at Suys's disposal, Daunou told him to follow nobody's inspiration but his own. And, as nobody is as rascally as a Dutchman, so much hard cash was thrown away on this folly – a colonial pavilion with a rhomboid roof, its supporting arch inlaid with ugly (or, if not ugly, vulgar) frostwork – that, with its finishing touch, Daunou was without a brass farthing. With just two months of occupation, it was put up for auction. A shady individual from Audruicq bought it for a song, installing first of all a stud farm and, during that short outburst of optimism brought about by victory at Wagram, a casino in which you could find McDonald, Soult, Duroc, Caulaincourt, Savary, Junot and Oudinot playing whist and baccarat. (This crook, it's said, got away with a cool million.) At that point it was won off him at cards by a Louis-Philippard cop, who was fond of playing host to an unsavoury crowd of drunks, thugs and informants, until succumbing to a fatal stab wound during a notably riotous orgy. As this cop had no offspring to hand it on to in his will, his manor, soon going to wrack and ruin from casual looting, would turn into a lair of tramps, criminals, vagrants and ruffians.

In April 1918 a British major, Augustus B. Clifford, advancing with his battalion towards no-man's-land and putting his troops up in it for a night, took a liking to this quaint, rundown manor. In 1924, now of Canadian nationality and occupying a post as a consular administrator in Frankfurt, Clifford bought Azincourt for his family, living in it on and off whilst pursuing his diplomatic obligations. Through his caring disposition as an occupant, along with his polish and discrimination as a man, its roof, which was caving in, was gradually brought back to mint condition; its walls had a thorough scrubbing down; oil, and not coal, was burnt; and a spacious parkland was laid out.

Augustus B. Clifford had a son, naming him Douglas Haig in honour of that grand old warrior, his victorious commandant at Douaumont.
    A charming child, Douglas Haig (or Haig *tout court*, for that was how his doting papa always thought of him) had an idyllic infancy at Azincourt, filling it with his boyish whoops, playing blind man's buff on its soft, cottony lawn, climbing its acacias, giving food to a fish, a young carp, that swam about in a small pond, taming it not without difficulty, baiting it with crumbs, worms, wasps, moths, a gadfly or two and an occasional crocus. It would swarm up at his approach, at his whistling or murmuring call of "Jonah! Jonah!".
    Haig had a lot of chums, most living in town and mad about sport – football and rugby, mainly, but also organising amusing trials by bow-and-arrow and going on long cross-country walking tours. Coming back from such jaunts, his companions would find his nanny waiting with a tray of muffins and fruit tarts and cups of hot cocoa. So Augustus's manor was an oasis of calm and good humour, of high jinks and high spirits. It was, in short, a kind of Arcadia.

At 18, having sat his school finals, Augustus's son found his vocation: basso profundo. Haig, though not what you would call a prodigy, had a natural vocal gift; and, unconscionably fond of singing, was willing to work long and hard at honing his skills, studying composition at Paris's Schola Cantorum. Fricsay taught him plain song, Solti canon, von Karajan tutti and Krips harmony. Sir Adrian Boult sat in on his first public audition, at 19, in Turin's Carignano Hall. Haig sang "Unto Us a Child Is Born", a madrigal by Ottavio Rinucinni and, to finish with, a trio of arias from *Aida*. Boult was wholly won round, writing a word of introduction to Karl Böhm, who was staging *Il dissoluto punito ossia Il Don Giovanni* at Urbino's "Musical May". Böhm had Haig sing for him, found him vocally convincing if occasionally shrill in a high pitch and, handing him a copy of Mozart's composition, told him to study it for a forthcoming production.

Placing his gifts in Karl Böhm's firm but faithful hands, Haig was soon gaining ground. "Your fortissimo is possibly too languid," Böhm would admonish him on occasion, or "You should attack *Altra brama quaggiù* with total rigour and accuracy. Don't distort it by howling or roaring. It has to flow forth without any vibrato." Mostly, though, his pupil brought him satisfaction.

That spring, on a boiling hot day, strolling along a corridor in Urbino's ducal *palazzo* (visitors to which would habitually find him practising sol-fa of a morning just as his idol, Caruso, had), Haig ran into Olga Mavrokhordatos, a soprano whom Böhm had cast as Donna Anna, and took an instant liking (I should say, loving) to that world-famous diva. Nor did his passion fall on stony ground: it took him just two days to obtain Olga's blushing accord and to marry his inamorata in San Marino. A municipal official, vainly stifling a yawn, for it was going on midnight, saw it as his duty to trot out a string of hoary old truisms on conjugal rights and obligations. As a consolation, though, on that indigo night, from an imposing rampart on San Marino's main plaza, and all night through until first faint flush of dawn, soft strains and paradisiacal chords would drift down, music from *I Virtuosi di Roma*, rigadoons and madrigals, arias, rondos and sinfonias, music to charm an animal with two backs.

O blissful instant! O Calm! A nocturnal violin singing a song as candid and natural as a lark's, and an alto, and an organist's sonorous clarion – and Haig advancing slowly, his hand tightly clasping Olga's.

I know that you too, you, my ghostly collaborator, hanging on my words, would wish it all to work out satisfactorily, with Douglas Haig Clifford marrying Olga Mavrokhordatos, with both Douglas and his Olga knowing only harmony and connubial bliss, "a spiritual coupling of two souls" (as Jonson put it), and with Olga giving birth to 26 sons, all surviving into full maturity.

Alas, no, that's asking too much! I cannot hold out any such possibility of absolution. Nor will God grant Douglas Haig a pardon. Infusing, always and infallibly, that cryptic signal that I am trying, and will go on trying, ad infinitum if I must, to clarify, Damnation will do with Haig what it has to do – with just four days to go till that swan song of his which, sung in Urbino, would link up, 20 springs on, with Anton Vowl's kidnapping and Hassan Ibn Abbou's assassination . . .

To transform him into an apparition, into that ghoulish Commandant who, *Uomo di sasso, Uomo bianco*, brings Mozart's *dramma giocoso* to its climax, Karl Böhm actually thought to wrap Haig in a sculptor's mould with an iron collar, almost causing him to swoon. A broad slit was cut through this mould, giving his singing a rich bass intonation without in any way muffling it. Böhm, happy with such an acoustical idiosyncrasy, told him, "In fact, it's akin to having a rotting carcass posthumously cursing us from within his coffin." Böhm was right; alas, nobody could know just how right. For (and how such a thing could occur, nobody would say), as a pallid Haig was put into his mould, and it was shut tight, and laid on thick with stucco, totally confining him, Böhm, aghast, saw that nobody had put slits in for him to look through. But Böhm also saw no point in panicking, for it was just at that instant that Don Juan commands his flunky to ask Haig (in his capacity, naturally, as Mozart's Commandant) to lunch with him.

First, Haig was drawn up on a sling. So far, so good. From that point on, though, bad luck would dog his path.

All of you know *Don Giovanni*'s closing bars of music:

Giovanni sings: "... *Grido indiavolato* ..."

And his flunky (who, in this production, was sung by van Dam): "*Ah signor ... L'uom di sasso ... L'uomo bianco ... Ah padron ... Tum-ti-tum ...*"

This was Haig's prompt and van Dam was waiting for him to walk forward, coming into sight as Böhm had his violinists play a closing, fading chord; and, advancing again to allow his public to savour his imposing physical proportions, to launch into his famous "*Don Giovanni ... m'invitasti*".

But Haig was to wait an instant too long. On his approaching Don Juan, van Dam haltingly sang "*Ah Padron ... Siam tutti morti*" ... Haig, looking around him in confusion, as though slowly going adrift, took fright, turning crazily this way and that, spinning about as a robot or a mutant might run amok and loudly crying out "*mi mi mi mi mi*" ... At which point our basso lost all control, stubbing his foot on a column, tripping up, swaying and falling – falling as straight and stiff as a mast, as a baobab adroitly cut in half. With his fall making a loud thud, its shock so startling that, as though imitating Humpty Dumpty tumbling off his wall, Haig's mould split from top to bottom, a cry of horror shook that auditorium to its foundations, from its balcony to its stalls, and from its gods to its royal box. A long furrow, ashy in colour, zigzagging from his foot to his skull, ran through that mould, that stucco trap in which poor Haig was caught, fissuring it with tiny sharp cracks, through which, as in a crumbling dam, purplish blood would start to spurt and spout till, finally, stomach-turningly, gushing forth.

Using a blowtorch, a jack and an automatic drill, unhitching him as you might pluck a rotting pit, say, from an inhuman fruit,

Böhm's assistants got Haig out and saw, first of all, on his body, a grisly, ashy furrow similar to that on his mould, also running from top to bottom and zigzagging down his torso as a bolt of lightning from Thor might flash across a lurid Nordic sky. And though Haig's own doctor would insist on carrying out an autopsy, nobody could work out any natural grounds for his dying in this way . . .

Why, nobody could say, but Augustus B. Clifford was also at Urbino's "Musical May". And, that night, following his son's tragic mishap, Clifford slunk into a local hospital – in which Haig's body was laid out – took it away with him by swaddling it in a shroud and carrying it out by a back door, bought a Hispano-Suiza sports car and, driving all night, all day and all night again, as frantically as a madman, as fast and furious as a champion at Indianapolis or Brands Hatch, got to Azincourt. A local myth has it that Clifford actually had his son's body burnt; probably, though, Haig is now lying in his coffin, possibly in that shady nook of parkland on which, as it's also said, grass grows in particularly thick clumps and in a particularly intriguing form, almost as though a topiarist had had a hand in shaping it: that of a harpoon with 3 prongs or a hand with 3 digits, Satan's diabolical sign such as might initial a Faustian contract.

Augustus, whom many local townsfolk thought raving mad, would go for months and months without quitting his mansion at Azincourt and would hurl rocks at any infant straying into his domain, any busybody hawking goods or any tramp asking for alms at his door. A high wall was built around its grounds, which, at night, it was said, would turn it into a prison, a sort of Spandau, with its solitary, voluntary convict, who would now stay indoors for good. You might, at most, find his maid in town buying a ham or a pair of fatty lamb chops. But if you sought to chat up this maid, who, of part-Iroquois origin, was known as "Squaw", if you said, "So, Squaw, your boss, still off his nut?", Squaw

would shout back at you, "Sonofabitch!" and "Scumbag!",
two traditional Iroquois oaths.

And, as Squaw was an old judo pro, it wasn't politic to
insist.

Occasionally, too, with an ugly gap-tooth grin, Squaw would
add: "If boss good to Jonah, boss good man."

For it was known that Augustus, conscious of his son's mission,
would approach his pond at noon sharp, murmuring "Jonah,
Jonah!" Though Jonah was grown-up now, it always swam
upwards at his call; and Augustus would throw crumbs at it that
it would gulp down with obvious satisfaction.

It took Olga six springs to track down Augustus, who had only
caught sight of his gracious in-law for an instant. On Olga's initial
arrival at Azincourt, Squaw had instructions not to unlock its
door to this prima donna for whom Augustus's son had had such
a strong passion. But as things would work out, Augustus, taking
pity on Olga and also itching to satisfy a natural curiosity, would
start to thaw and gradually warm to this fascinating woman who
told him about holy matrimony with a man as romantic as his son,
a union brought, alas, to a tragically swift and abrupt conclusion.
Augustus in his turn would talk of Haig in his childhood,
giving scraps to Jonah, climbing acacias and playing blind
man's buff.

Taking a fancy to Azincourt, finding in it a tranquillity missing
in Paris – in which it was work, work, work all day long! – Olga
was soon paying it four visits a month, going for long walks
through its grounds, drinking fruit cocktails in a formal drawing
room from which Augustus had dustcloths vanish in honour of
his charming visitor. Following a light lunch, consisting of cold
cuts, salad and fruit, Olga, slumping on to a ravishing mahogany
sofa (still giving off vibrations from a torrid affair that La Grisi
had had on it with a Boyar and for which a youthful Augustus
had paid a tidy sum at an auction), Olga, I say, would stitch a
dainty rustic motif on a patchwork quilt, whilst Augustus, sitting

upright at his grand piano, would play a sonata by Albinoni, Haydn or Auric. Occasionally, too, Olga sang a song by Brahms or Schumann that would float out into a starry night sky.

10

Which will, I trust, gratify fanatics of Pindaric lyricism

Whilst, far off, a dog, an Alsatian or an Afghan hound, starts howling mournfully, Amaury knocks at Olga's front door and Clifford's maid soon unbolts it.

"Morning, Squaw," says a smiling Amaury, visibly savouring such an unusual alias.

"Good day to you, Sir Amaury," says Squaw; "and good day to you too, Sir Savorgnan."

Amaury, caught short, looks squintingly at Savorgnan.

"What's this? Do you also know Squaw?"

"Didn't it occur to you I might?"

"Why . . . no," admits Amaury.

"I told you, didn't I, and not all that long ago, whilst our train was drawing into Arras, I told you that you'd soon know my story in its totality. So now you know just how similar my *curriculum*, so to say, is to yours: an unfailing aspiration uniting us now as it always has and always will. Your information is my information, your informants my informants, your companions my companions – so it's not surprising, is it, that our paths should finally cross as both of us scurry about on this cryptic pursuit of ours . . ."

"*Similia similibus curantur*," a witty Amaury sums up.

"*Contraria contrariis curantur*," a sardonic Savorgnan snaps back.

Pointing indoors, Squaw buts in. "Lady Olga is waiting for you."

Amaury and Savorgnan stroll into a stylish living room: two nylon rugs of a lilyish purity, oval armchairs, a lamp (from China) of such formal sophistication that, by comparison, Noguchi's work would look almost naïf, a divan as long as a bar in a Hawaiian nightclub with big shiny vinyl cushions in Day-Glo colours and, filling a wall from top to bottom, an Op Art church window by Sartinuloc.

Olga is dozing in a hammock, a hand trailing daintily floorwards. Amaury stoops to kiss it, and Savorgnan follows suit.

"*Cari amici*," murmurs Olga with a languorous yawn, "I know I can always count on you, both of you. Augustus wants to say a word or two. Sound that gong, Amaury, will you."

Picking up a small aluminium gong, Amaury whacks it, producing a sound which, if a bit "off", has an oddly long-drawn-out vibration.

Abruptly, as though by magic, Augustus B. Clifford is standing in his own doorway. Clifford, a frail old fossil, wrinkly of brow, frosty of hair, and having to cup his hand to catch what is said to him, plods up to Savorgnan and puts his arms around him:

"Wilburg, old chap, how do you do?"

"How do you do?" says Savorgnan with typical urbanity.

"How was your trip?"

"Oh, it wasn't too bad."

"No, not bad at all," adds Amaury, who, as usual, has to put in his two bits' worth.

"Good, good," says Clifford, rubbing his hands. "Now sit down, sit down, both of you."

Olga hands round a tray of fruit and fruit cocktails and fruit crystals: fruit, only fruit, which our visitors dutifully swallow without a word. In fact, nobody says anything at all. Savorgnan coughs. Olga sighs.

94

"What all of you must do now," says Olga at last, "is pool what you know about this quicksand that risks sucking us in as though along a giant straw. It's my opinion, and yours too, I know, that during this past month (which will finish today) just too much damn bad luck – or, as Augustus would put it, a disturbingly high ratio of affliction – has struck down two of our companions. Now, apart from a handful of scraps, you still lack information on Anton's abduction and Hassan's . . . passing away." (Prim Olga was always loath to say that basic D-word that for many in our civilisation is still a major taboo.) "But what you do know, or think you know, is that at its crux is a conundrum worthy of a Sphinx and it is its signification that you must try to grasp. Which is why, as I say, Augustus and I want to join up with you by pooling our information and coordinating our actions!"

"Your proposition is worth its avoirdupois in gold," says Augustus.

"You can say that again!" says Savorgnan (no doubt in a malicious allusion to Augustus's linguistic pomposity). "Probably you, Olga, or you, Amaury, know a thing or two that I don't and probably I know a thing or two that you don't and it's by closing ranks that our horizons will roll back and a communal intuition spring forth!"

Arthur Wilburg Savorgnan is a hard act to follow. Amaury simply shouts, "Bravo!" And Squaw, approaching with a tray of drinks, caps this with "Hip hip hooray!"

A toast.

Proposing to submit his contribution first, Amaury maintains that it is, *a priori*, of particular import. This was a slightly surprising tack for him to adopt, but it gains him his right to hold forth first.

Amaury starts straight in without any banal small talk. "I'm now familiar with most if not all of Anton Vowl's diary, in which I found 5 or 6 allusions to a book, a work of fiction, which, it claims, contains a solution to our conundrum. Anyway, I found indications in it of why this book was so crucial for him, without Anton actually giving anything away."

"That's right," says Savorgnan, "you might say our chum had a gift for both showing and masking, both giving and taking away."

"*Larvati ibant obscuri sola sub nocta*," murmurs Olga, who was, as is obvious, no classical scholar.

"Thus," adds Amaury, tactfully ignoring Olga's Latin, "on occasion it's *Moby Dick* or a postwar work by Thomas Mann or a fiction by Isidro Parodi initially brought out in 1950 or so by *La Croix du Sud*. But Vowl's diary also contains a quotation from Kafka, an allusion to a 'McGuffin', to a King and on occasion to Rimbaud. I found, in all of that, a point in common: an apparition (if you'll allow my using such an oxymoron) of a blank, a Void."

"A Void!" shouts Augustus B. Clifford, dropping his crystal glass and spilling aquavit on his rug.

"A Void!" moans Olga, smashing a lamp in agitation.

"A Void!" roars Arthur Wilburg Savorgnan, swallowing half his cigar.

"A Void!" brays Squaw in a shrill and jangling whinny, atomising a trio of matching mirrors.

"A Void, right, that's what I said," affirms Amaury: "it all turns on a Void. But, by constantly writing about 'a Void', what do you think Anton was alluding to?"

From a cupboard Augustus pulls out an album in foolscap format bound in sharkskin.

"This is what our postman brought us from Anton a month ago day for day."

Doing a rapid calculation, Amaury says:

"In short, just two days prior to his abduction."

"That's right. You won't find a word in it, though, but for what I think you call a 'small ad' which Anton probably cut out of his *Figaro* and stuck in."

Olga, Clifford and Savorgnan form a group around Amaury,

who starts scrutinising Anton's album. It consists of 26 folios, all blank but for a solitary column, without any sort of illustration, stuck on to folio No. 5, a column that Amaury runs through in a faint murmur:

DOWN WITH OBSCURITY

(Homo w*sh*s wh*t*r th*n P*rs*l)
ANYTHING can look virginal, for It will wash
ANYTHING AT ALL: your pants, stockings, T-shirts,
your shifts, smocks and cardigans,
your saris and Arab burnous.
ANYTHING AT ALL: your cotton pillowslips and cotton
  sailor suits,
but also your woodwork, your black puddings, your raisins,
your spirits, your hands, your pains
your worms, your swords
your big fish in small ponds, your small fish in big ponds
your hair, your coal
your nights without 40 winks, your connubials without 69
your savings put away for a rainy day,
your billows, your too famous flaws, your fabrics without a scar
your omissions, your gaps, your lapsus
your manuscripts
your aims and ambitions, your months in a shopping plaza,
your notations for hautboy, your abominations for Tarzan,
your bars and bistros, ad infinitum, a Void, a Void, a Void!

DOWN WITH OBSCURITY

"Alas, only a Champollion would know how to clarify that," murmurs a downcast Amaury.

"It's my turn now," says Savorgnan, who can hardly wait to add his contribution. "A month ago I too got mail from Anton

Vowl. It had on it no distinguishing marks indicating who it was from, but it was obvious that it had to do with our missing companion" – adding, "although I still can't work out why Vowl was so stubborn about maintaining his incognito . . ."

"What was in yours?" asks Amaury, as jumpy as a cat on a hot tin roof.

"I'm coming to that. Look."

Unzipping his holdall, and rummaging through it, Savorgnan pulls out a card and holds it up in front of his trio of companions.

"It's a 'kaolin' card (kaolin is a kind of clay found in China), black as tar from a coating of Indian ink, at which a skilful local craftsman ground away with a sharp scraping tool (or possibly a vaccination pin), his inspiration for such a cunning notion no doubt arising from a contraption thought up by Jarjack, who was imitating that sad circus clown, that 'August', to whom (prior to him) Oudry's arch-rival had brought immortality. And this craftsman, by judiciously stripping off parts of its black background, finally had a diagram of a high-quality finish akin to bamboo inscriptions such as you'll occasionally find on wash-drawings from Japan."

"Is it from Japan?" Olga wants to know.

"Yup, it's from Japan all right. I instantly shot off for a talk about it with my boss," says Savorgnan, "to wit, Gadsby V. Wright. And with him I took a train to Oxford to show its inscription to Parsifal Ogdan. This is a transcription of it:

> *Kuraki yori*
> *Kuraki michi ni zo*
> *Usuzumi ni*
> *Kaku tamazusa to*
> *Kari miyura kana*

"Sounds charming," says Augustus.

"It's a haïkaï," says Savorgnan, "or should I say a tanka, but not, as you might think, by Narihira. No, it's by Izumi Shikibu (scholars, in fact, claim that it's probably his final work, his swan song); or, if not, by Tsumori Kunimoto who, though just as important, isn't as famous. Its initial publication was in *Go shu i shu*, a compilation drawn up in honour of Japan's Mikado. Parsifal Ogdan's word-for-word translation of this tanka is, in my opinion, of an astonishing purity and proportion, particularly as I was told by a chap from Tokyo's National Library, a man Anton Vowl had known during his sojourn in Japan, that a tanka always has 3, 5, 6, on occasion as many as 8, distinct connotations. But, as Parsifal was to show us, such ambiguity, though crucial to Japan, to its quaint way of thinking about things, has, for an inhabitant of Paris or London, no charm at all about it, with our traditional antipathy to all notions of obscurity, incongruity, approximation and intangibility. A tanka must boast clarity, concision, incision, candour, vivacity and unity of thought: in translation, that's worth any amount of arguably major omissions. So this is just a translation among many that Ogdan thought up:

> *Out of tar-black*
> *In a black tracing*
> *By a point so sharp*
> *Inscribing a sign which isn't black:*
> *O look! an albatross in flight*

"Too, too charming," sighs Amaury, "if not too, too illuminating."

"I'm afraid my own contribution risks not advancing us much in our task," says Olga, following an instant during which, as though in growing discomfort, nobody says a word. "I say I'm afraid, for if, in your diary, card and tanka, you found allusions to a common point, a Void, my manuscript is as lucid, limpid and unambiguous as yours, Amaury, or yours, Augustus, or yours, Arthur, was cryptic, allusory and hard to grasp . . ."

"But," says Amaury, "that sounds as if it has a solution for us . . ."

Olga won't allow him to finish. "No, no, you don't follow. In what I'm about to show you, you'll find no sign, no allusion of any kind. For it's not an original work but a sort of anthology comprising 5 or 6 works by various hands – various famous hands, I might add – but containing nothing of any import to us . . ."

Now it's Augustus's turn to cut in. "Olga, my darling, has nobody told you about cutting a long story short? Why don't you just stick to facts?"

"All right, all right, I'm coming to that. Six days prior to that odd postcard with its fascinatingly ominous postscript, I too got mail from Anton – a bulging jiffy bag. And what I found in it was:

a) a short story by a *soi-disant* Arago, 'An intriguing tour of our country'. I was full of admiration for such a charming octavo with its Arabic motifs and its morocco binding inlaid with gold. Strictly as a work of fiction, though, it didn't, in my opinion, amount to much;

b) six highly familiar madrigals, which most of us had to study at school in our childhood: Anton's painstaking transcription, word for word, without any annotations, any marginalia at all, of:

- William Shakspar's 'Living, or not living' soliloquy
- PBS's *Ozymandias*
- John Milton's *On His Glaucoma*
- Thomas Hood's *No*
- Arthur Gordon Pym's *Black Bird*
- Arthur Rimbaud's *Vocalisations*.

"Now and again, in an odd stanza or two, you'll find an illusion to Anton's hang-ups: obscurity, immaculation, vanishing and damnation. But I was struck most of all by how random it was . . ."

100

"Possibly," says Amaury, "and, again, possibly not! For, if Anton thought fit to copy it all out so laboriously, it's now our job to find an indication in it as to his motivation."

Mumbling about proofs and puddings, it's Savorgnan's proposal that only by a thorough study of Anton's transcriptions will anybody hit upon such a motivation. "And who knows – you, Amaury, or you, Augustus, or I may spot a crucial missing link?"

Thus:

LIVING, OR NOT LIVING

Living, or not living: that is what I ask:
If 'tis a stamp of honour to submit
To slings and arrows waft'd us by ill winds,
Or brandish arms against a flood of afflictions,
Which by our opposition is subdu'd? Dying, drowsing;
Waking not? And by drowsing thus to thwart
An aching soul and all th' natural shocks
Humanity sustains. 'T is a consummation
So piously wish'd for. Dying, drowsing;
Drowsing; and, what say, conjuring visions: ay, that's th' rub;
For in that drowsy faint what visions may disturb
Our shuffling off of mortal coil,
Do prompt us think again. Of that calamity, to wit,
That is our living for so long;
For who would brook duration's whips and scorns,
A tyrant's wrong, a haughty man's disdain,
Pangs of dispriz'd ardour and sloth of law,
Th' incivility of rank and all th' insults
That goodly worth from its contrary draws,
If such a man might his own last affirm
With a bald bodkin? Who would such ballast carry,
To grunt and wilt along his stooping path,

But that his horror of th' unknown,
That vast and unmapp'd land to which
No living man pays visit, is puzzling to his will,
Making him shrug off what now assails him
And shrink from posthumous ills?
Compunction thus turns all of us to cowards;
And thus our natural trait of fixity
Is sickli'd through with ashy rumination,
And missions of much pith and import
With this in mind soon turn awry,
And from all thoughts of action go astray.

WILLIAM SHAKSPAR

OZYMANDIAS

I know a pilgrim from a distant land
Who said: Two vast and sawn-off limbs of quartz
Stand on an arid plain. Not far, in sand
Half sunk, I found a facial stump, drawn warts
And all; its curling lips of cold command
Show that its sculptor passions could portray
Which still outlast, stamp'd on unliving things,
A mocking hand that no constraint would sway:
And on its plinth this lordly boast is shown:
"Lo, I am Ozymandias, king of kings:
Look on my works, O Mighty, and bow down!"
'Tis all that is intact. Around that crust
Of a colossal ruin, now windblown,
A sandstorm swirls and grinds it into dust.

PBS

102

ON HIS GLAUCOMA

Whilst I do think on how my world is bound,
  Now half my days, by this unwinking night,
  My solitary gift, for want of sight,
  Lain fallow, though within my soul abound
Urgings to laud th' Almighty, and propound
  My own account, that God my faith not slight,
  Doth God day-labour claim, proscribing light,
  I ask; but calming spirits, to confound
Such murmurings, affirm, God doth not dun
  Man for his work or his own gifts, who will
  But kiss his chains, is dutiful, his gait
Is kingly. Thousands to his bidding run
  And post on land and bounding main and hill:
  Your duty do who only stand and wait.

JOHN MILTON

NO!

No sun – no moon!
  No morn – no noon!
No dawn – no dusk – no hour of night or day –
  No sky – no bird in sight –
  No distant bluish light –
No road – no path – no "'tis your right o' way" –
  No turn to any Row –
  No flying indications for a Crow –
  No roof to any institution –
No nodding "Morning!"'s on our constitution –
  No gallantry for showing us –
  No knowing us! –
No walking out at all – no locomotion,
No inkling of our way – no notion –
  "No go" – thus no commotion –

No mail – no post –
No word from any far-flung coast –
No Park – no Ring – no door-to-door civility –
No company – no nobility –
No warmth, no mirth, no jocularity,
No joyful tintinnabula to ring –
No church, no hymns, no faith, no charity,
No books, no words, no thoughts, no clarity –.
No thing!   THOMAS HOOD

BLACK BIRD

'Twas upon a midnight tristful I sat poring, wan and wistful,
Through many a quaint and curious list full of my consorts slain –
I sat nodding, almost napping, till I caught a sound of tapping,
As of spirits softly rapping, rapping at my door in vain.
"'Tis a visitor," I murmur'd, "tapping at my door in vain –
                    Tapping soft as falling rain."

Ah, I know, I know that this was on a holy night of Christmas;
But that quaint and curious list was forming phantoms all in
    train.
How I wish'd it was tomorrow; vainly had I sought to borrow
From my books a stay of sorrow – sorrow for my unjoin'd chain –
For that pictographic symbol missing from my unjoin'd chain –
                    And that would not join again.

Rustling faintly through my drapings was a ghostly, ghastly
    scraping
Sound that with fantastic shapings fill'd my fulminating brain;
And for now, to still its roaring, I stood back as if ignoring
That a spirit was imploring his admission to obtain –
"'Tis a spirit now imploring his admission to obtain –"
                    Murmur'd I, "– but all in vain."

104

But, my soul maturing duly and my brain not so unruly,
"Sir," said I, "or Madam, truly your acquittal would I gain;
For I was in fact caught napping, so soft-sounding was your
    rapping,
So faint-sounding was your tapping that you tapp'd my door in
    vain –
Hardly did I know you tapp'd it" – I unlock'd it but in vain –
                        For 'twas dark without and plain.

Staring at that dark phantasm as if shrinking from a chasm,
I stood quaking with a spasm fracturing my soul in twain;
But my study door was still as untowardly hush'd and chill as,
Oh, a crypt in which a still aspiring body is just lain –
As a dank, dark crypt in which a still suspiring man is lain –
                        Barr'd from rising up again.

All around my study flapping till my sanity was snapping,
I distinctly caught a tapping that was starting up again.
"Truly," said I, "truly this is turning now into a crisis;
I must find out what amiss is, and tranquillity obtain –
I must still my soul an instant and tranquillity obtain –
                        For 'tis truly not just rain!"

So, my study door unlocking to confound that awful knocking,
In I saw a Black Bird stalking with a gait of proud disdain;
I at first thought I was raving, but it stalk'd across my paving
And with broad black wings a-waving did my study door attain –
Did a pallid bust of Pallas on my study door attain –
                        Just as if 'twas its domain.

105

Now, that night-wing'd fowl placating my sad fancy into waiting
On its oddly fascinating air of arrogant disdain,
"Though thy tuft is shorn and awkward, thou," I said, "art not
    so backward
Coming forward, ghastly Black Bird wand'ring far from thy
    domain,
Not to say what thou art known as in thy own dusk-down
    domain!"
                            Quoth that Black Bird, "Not Again".

Wondrous was it this ungainly fowl could thus hold forth so
    plainly,
Though, alas, it discours'd vainly – as its point was far from plain;
And I think it worth admitting that, whilst in my study sitting,
I shall stop Black Birds from flitting thusly through my door
    again –
Black or not, I'll stop birds flitting through my study door again –
                            What I'll say is, "Not Again!"

But that Black Bird, posing grimly on its placid bust, said primly
"Not Again", and I thought dimly what purport it might contain.
Not a third word did it throw off – not a third word did it know
    of –
Till, afraid that it would go off, I thought only to complain –
"By tomorrow it will go off," did I tristfully complain.
                            It again said, "Not Again".

Now, my sanity displaying stark and staring signs of swaying,
"No doubt," murmur'd I, "it's saying all it has within its brain;
That it copy'd from a nomad whom Affliction caus'd to go mad,
From an outcast who was so mad as this ghastly bird to train –
Who, as with a talking parrot, did this ghastly Black Bird train
                            To say only, 'Not Again.' "

106

But that Black Bird still placating my sad fancy into waiting
For a word forthcoming, straight into my chair I sank again;
And, upon its cushion sinking, I soon found my spirit linking
Fancy unto fancy, thinking what this ominous bird of Cain –
What this grim, ungainly, ghastly, gaunt, and ominous bird of
    Cain
                        Sought by croaking "Not Again."

On all this I sat surmising, whilst with morbid caution sizing
Up that fowl; its tantalising look burn'd right into my brain;
This for l'ng I sat divining, with my pain-rack'd back inclining
On my cushion's satin lining with its ghastly crimson stain,
On that shiny satin lining with its sanguinary stain
                        Shrilly shouting, "Not Again!"

Now my room was growing fragrant, its aroma almost flagrant,
As from spirits wafting vagrant through my dolorous domain.
"Good-for-naught," I said, "God sought you – from Plutonian
    strands
    God brought you –
And, I know not why, God taught you all about my unjoin'd
    chain,
All about that linking symbol missing from my unjoin'd
    chain!"
                        Quoth that Black Bird, "Not Again."

"Sybil!" said I, "thing of loathing – sybil, fury in bird's clothing!
If by Satan brought, or frothing storm did toss you on its main,
Cast away, but all unblinking, on this arid island sinking –
On this room of Horror stinking – say it truly, or abstain –
Shall I – shall I find that symbol? – say it – say it, or abstain
                        From your croaking, 'Not Again'."

107

"Sybil!" said I, "thing of loathing – sybil, fury in bird's clothing!
By God's radiant kingdom soothing all man's purgatorial pain,
Inform this soul laid low with sorrow if upon a distant morrow
It shall find that symbol for – oh, for its too long unjoin'd
   chain –
Find that pictographic symbol missing from its unjoin'd chain."
                    Quoth that Black Bird, "Not Again."

"If that word's our sign of parting, Satan's bird," I said,
   upstarting,
"Fly away, wings blackly parting, to thy Night's Plutonian
   plain!
For, mistrustful, I would scorn to mind that untruth thou hast
   sworn to,
And I ask that thou by morn tomorrow quit my sad domain!
Draw thy night-nibb'd bill from out my soul and quit my sad
   domain!"
                    Quoth that Black Bird, "Not Again."

And my Black Bird, still not quitting, still is sitting, still is sitting
On that pallid bust – still flitting through my dolorous domain;
But it cannot stop from gazing for it truly finds amazing
That, by artful paraphrasing, I such rhyming can sustain –
Notwithstanding my lost symbol I such rhyming still sustain –
                    Though I shan't try it again!

ARTHUR GORDON PYM

108

VOCALISATIONS

A noir (Un blanc), I roux, U safran, O azur:
Nous saurons au jour dit ta vocalisation:
A, noir carcan poilu d'un scintillant morpion
Qui bombinait autour d'un nidoral impur,

Caps obscurs; qui, cristal du brouillard ou du Khan,
Harpons du fjord hautain, Rois Blancs, frissons d'anis?
I, carmins, sang vomi, riant ainsi qu'un lis
Dans un courroux ou dans un alcool mortifiant;

U, scintillations, ronds divins du flot marin,
Paix du pâtis tissu d'animaux, paix du fin
Sillon qu'un fol savoir aux grands fronts imprima;

O, finitif clairon aux accords d'aiguisoir,
Soupirs ahurissant Nadir ou Nirvâna:
O l'omicron, rayon violin dans son Voir!

ARTHUR RIMBAUD

11

Which will finish by arousing pity in a big shot

Having painstakingly run through it, glancing at Amaury, Savorgnan, Augustus and Squaw in turn, striving to find an obvious bait, a solid anchor to hold on to, a hook to catch on to, a hint as to what such-and-such a locution might signify, Olga sighs, a loud, long, profound sigh of frustration.

"I said just an instant ago that only Champollion would know how to crack such a conundrum," says Augustus sadly. "But now I doubt if Champollion could pull it off. A Chomsky might in a pinch, though."

"Or possibly a Roman Jakobson, who could submit a structuralist's opinion of *Ozymandias!*"

"Why not Malcolm Bradbury!"

"And why not OuLiPo!"

"Baffling, just too, too baffling," Amaury stubbornly murmurs as though in a world of his own.

"What is?" asks Arthur Wilburg Savorgnan.

"Rimbaud's 'Black A (a blank), ruby I, viridian U, cobalt O': it's obvious to you, is it not, that it's trying to point us towards a solution!"

"Why not? If I know anything about Olga's anthology, it's that not a word in it, not a comma, was put down at random. But that's Anton Vowl's doing, not Arthur Rimbaud's!"

"Who can say?"

His mind a total blank, his imagination a tabula rasa, Augustus starts to talk – if almost inaudibly. Rapt in thought, his companions hang on to his words, which, though at first bristling with abstractions, blown up out of all proportion, soon glow with an aura of inspiration:

"Black A (a blank). An ambiguity, such as this is, is a major factor in any *a contrario*; advancing from that *signifiant*, which signals ipso facto how important it is first to pinpoint, by chronologically listing, all rival sounds (such actualisation, paradoxically, proving virtualisation by outwardly confuting it, it's crucial, if absorbing such a blank in its immaculation, first to affirm its distinction, its original particularity, its opposition to black, to ruby, to viridian and cobalt), this 'a blank' thus unfolds *motu proprio* out of its own contradiction, a vacant signal of that which isn't in fact vacant, a blank such as you might find in a book across which its author's hand inks in an inscription implicating its own abolition: O, vain papyrus drawn back, unavoidably back, into its own blank womb; a tract of a non-tract, a nihilistic tract localising that oblivion huddling, crouching, within a word, gnawing away at its own root, a rotting pip, a scission, a distraction, an omission both boasting and disguising its invincibility, a canyon of Non-Colorado, a doorway that nobody would cross, a corridor along which no foot would pad, a no-man's-land in which all oral communication would instantly find, brought to light, a gaping pit consuming any possibility of a praxis, a bright, blazing conflagration that would turn anybody approaching it into a human torch, a spring run dry, a blank word put out of bounds, a word now null and void, always just out of sight, always contriving to avoid scrutiny, a word no mispronunciation can satisfy, a castrating word, a flaccid word, a vacant word connoting an insultingly obvious signification, in which suspicion, privation and illusion all triumph, a lacunary furrow, a vacant canal, a Lacanian chasm, a cast-off vacuum thirstily sucking us into this thing unsaid, into this vain sting of a cry arousing us, this fold wrinkling, on its margin, a mystificatory logic that still confounds us, tricks us, inhibiting our instincts, our natural impulsions, our options, damning us to oblivion, to an illusory

111

dawn, to rationality, to cold study, to distortion and untruth, but also a mad authority, a craving for a purity which would synchronously affirm passion, starvation, adoration, a substruction of unfactitious wisdom, of not-so-vain rumours, a human articulation at its most psychically profound point, as of a particularly clairvoyant spiritualist, or a saint, or any man not as moribund as most of mankind. This is what I think. Within a Logos, in its marrow, so to say, lurks a domain that for us is off-limits, a zonal injunction that nobody can broach and to which no suspicion can attach: a Void, a Blank, a missing sign prohibiting us on a daily basis from talking, from writing, from using words with any thrust or point, mixing up our diction and abolishing our capacity for rigorous vocal articulation in favour of a gurgling mumbo jumbo. A Blank that, for good and all, will dumbfound us if accosting a Sphinx, a Blank akin to that giant Grampus sought for many a moon by Ahab, a Blank into which all of us will go missing in our turn . . ."

Augustus sits down, with a downcast air about him, totally worn out . . . His companions start ruminating on what was said.

"Just what I was going to say," murmurs Amaury in conclusion, as though intimating that Augustus took such obvious words out of his own mouth. "Anton Vowl is missing."

"Hassan Ibn Abbou is missing," says Savorgnan.

"Douglas Haig Clifford did his vanishing act all of 20 springs ago, an ashy furrow dividing his body in two," says Augustus.

"Douglas had on a sculptor's mould," sobs Olga, "to sing Mozart's Commandant in *Don Giovanni*."

"Now now," says Savorgnan, "why so gloomy? Think of that good old song by François Danican Philidor: 'All of us must act in unison, notwithstanding our individual sorrows'. What all of us must do right now is stop brooding about our missing companions and try to grasp what's going on, so as to ward off any damnation lying in wait for *us*, so as to rid us all of this frightful albatross!"

"How will that occur," sighs Olga, "with this conundrum baffling us, making us all limp and shaky, in proportion to our burrowing into it, burrowing down, down to its inmost marrow, as Augustus put it? Why rush at full tilt towards your own annihilation? Why actually court that ignominious oblivion that was Anton's lot and Hassan's and Haig's?"

Unanimously finding fault with this outpouring, judging it just too compliant and timorous, Amaury, Savorgnan and Squaw try to shout poor Olga down.

But with it soon looking as though it might turn into a full-blown row, Augustus holds up his hand and, in a flat, monotonous drawl that cannot mask his low spirits, says:

"Calm down, amigos, calm down. Do try to control your sorrow, your anguish, your wrath and your misgivings. You should try taking to its logical conclusion Arthur Wilburg Savorgnan's proposition, for, as Malcolm Lowry was wont to say, 'You cannot catch up with a man who outruns his rivals'." Consulting his watch, Augustus adds, "Look, it's almost midnight, I'm hungry and thirsty. I submit calling it quits, if only for an hour or so, and rustling up a snack worthy of gustatory buds as fastidious and discriminating as ours."

"Yum yum," murmurs a gluttonous Savorgnan.

"Unzip a banana," quips a waggish Amaury.

"In fact, a collation awaits you all in our dining room," says Squaw, whom nobody saw go.

Augustus lightly claps his hands in anticipation, whilst Olga, with intrinsic, *natural* sophistication (if that is not an oxymoron), insists on changing into a formal outfit.

As Olga's will is paramount, our protagonists rush off, arriving back in a flash, glamorous in glad rags.

Olga (who was, as I say, practically born "in") is a dazzling vision in a formal Christian Dior pyjama suit of a filmy rainbow satin, with a billowy flow of charming Victorian knick-knacks, ribbons and bows, frills and braids, hoods and cuffs, to cushion its diaphanous opacity. A chunky solid-gold Arab brooch, portraying an asp, insinuatingly coils its capital S around a wrist as slight and narrow as an orchid stalk.

Amaury foppishly sports a classic tail coat.

Savorgnan, a dandy, infallibly "with it", has put on a charcoal tux, a saffron jabot and a fawn cravat. Amaury chirps at him in grudging admiration.

"My tailor is rich," says Savorgnan in franglais, and with a slightly smug grin of satisfaction.

As for Augustus, who as a Consul was known for his ultra-modish but unshowy chic, his outfit is of a sort which calls to mind a British major informing Victoria of how wily Johnny Pathan was drawn into an ambush at a mountain pass in colonial India.

With "Ooohs" and "Ahhhs" and murmurs of mutual appro-bation, Olga, Amaury and Savorgnan now walk arm in arm into Augustus's dining room, which is laid out, thanks to Squaw, as lavishly as though for a king and his court. A Louis X tallboy prompts gasps of admiration all round, as also a Burgundy bow-back chair with Hugo Sambin's stamp on it, a sofa of a floral motif unmistakably by Ruhlmann and, most notably, a divan with its own vast, airy canopy. Its attribution to Grinling Gibbons was thought highly dubious, not to say downright scandalous, by scholars and buffs, although it did carry his hallmark.

"Did you know," says Augustus to Savorgnan, "that, sus-picious of this attribution, and in my opinion rightly so, *Warburg and Courtauld* would publish an important monograph of Gib-bons by Gombrich that was also – though, naturally, only by implication – a vicious attack on Panofsky?"

"You don't say?" snorts Savorgnan.

"Oh but I do! In fact, I don't mind adding that I actually thought it would finish in a bout of fisticuffs. Gombrich, though, who didn't want to fall out with his rival, would admit, in a tactful Parthian shot, to having found in his slanging match with Panofsky six major points on which, in an adroit combination, to ground his first draft of *Art and Illusion*."

"Now it's that kind of information that will maintain your divan's worth at any auction, Gibbons or not!"

On which prognosis all sit down.

It's no frugal cold-cut lunch that Augustus puts in front of his trio of companions but a Lucullan orgy of gastronomic, gustatory and, so to say, Augustatory glory. Its first dish is a *chaud-froid* of ortolans *à la Souvaroff*. No fish, but an *homard au cumin* for which nothing short of a '28 Mouton-Rothschild is thought apt. To follow, a roast gigot in onion gravy, its flavour subtly brought out by a soupçon of basil; and, to accompany that, in conformity with a tradition at La Maison Clifford (as Azincourt is jocularly known among Augustus's visitors), a tasty if not too spicy curry. And whilst this curry is still making its impact, a paprika salad is brought in, bristling with scallions, cardoons and mushrooms, zucchini and bamboo shoots. To fill that famous *trou normand*, a glass of calvados, naturally, of first-class quality; and, in fitting conclusion, a scrumptious *parfait au cassis* with which is drunk a fruity Sigalas-Rabaud of a sort to bring a sigh of swooning bliss from Curnonsky.

Proposing a toast, Augustus puts into tripping, flowing words his vow that "from all our communal labour a solution to this conundrum that's still baffling us, a way out of this circuitous labyrinth of which nobody among us has found a ground plan, will, and in fact *must*, soon turn up."

Glass clinks against glass. Glass upon glass is drunk. Naturally, it's all just what you might call *social* drinking: as soon as Augustus says, "I'm going to top up my glass", Amaury says, "*So shall* I." And Olga. And Savorgnan. And back to Augustus.

It's now long past midnight. Amaury, in a tipsily flirtatious mood, starts kissing Olga's hand (which, if timid and shaking slightly, is not withdrawn from his lips, lips moist and crimson from a fabulous Armagnac drunk out of a glass of a strikingly rainbowy irisation) and mumbling soft amorous nothings of a burbling baby-talk intimacy.

Night is slowly fading into dawn. Far off a cock crows. A mound of Iranian caviar is brought in.

Languidly snuggling up against Amaury, Olga nods off. Augustus, for his part, informs Savorgnan of his participation in a local rowing championship. Rowing was a sport wholly unknown at Azincourt, but Clifford sounds anxious to back it, founding an official Club, actually going as far as making this Club a baptismal gift of a skiff with which to start things moving, and togging out a trio of young locals in dark bluish suits boasting coats-of-arms according to a good old Oxford tradition (at which 'varsity, in his youth, Augustus had won acclaim as a first-class cox).

It's almost morning as Amaury and his companions finally call it a day.

Noon rings out. A wasp, making an ominous sound, a sound akin to a klaxon or a tocsin, flits about. Augustus, who has had a bad night, sits up blinking and purblind. Oh what was that word (is his thought) that ran through my brain all night, that idiotic word that, hard as I'd try to pin it down, was always just an inch or two out of my grasp – fowl or foul or Vow or Voyal? – a word which, by association, brought into play an incongruous mass and magma of nouns, idioms, slogans and sayings, a confusing, amorphous outpouring which I sought in vain to control or turn off but which wound around my mind a whirlwind of a cord, a whiplash of a cord, a cord that would split again and again, would knit again and again, of words without communication or any possibility of combination, words without pronunciation, signification or transcription but out of which, notwithstanding, was brought forth a flux, a continuous, compact and lucid flow: an intuition, a vacillating frisson of illumination as if caught in a flash of lightning or in a mist abruptly rising to unshroud an obvious sign – but a sign, alas, that would last an instant only to vanish for good.

116

"How was it?" Augustus now murmurs calmly. "It was. Was it? It was." It was a solution (or a pardon, or possibly just a form of compassion) that was flittingly within his grasp but which no word, no affirmation, of his could magnify into what is known, simply, as wisdom.

At which point, although not knowing why so insignificant a fact is having such an impact on him, it abruptly occurs to him that Jonah, his carp, hasn't had its food – a trivial omission on his part but also so haunting that, without waiting an instant, Augustus puts his clothing on whilst mumbling an indistinct incantation.

Nobody is stirring abroad. Augustus walks to a pantry cupboard, picks up a handful of grain, of a kind that Jonah is particularly partial to, and abruptly stops, having, in an unlit nook of his drawing room, on top of an upright piano, caught sight of that curious black clay box (black from a light coating of Indian ink) on which, according to Savorgnan, Vowl had paid a first-class artisan from Japan to paint a tanka. Drawn to it by an almost morbid fascination, Augustus picks it up and holds it flat in his hand, staring at Vowl's tanka, a pictographic symbol of an incomparably finicky calligraphy, and tracing out with a long almondy thumbnail its insinuatingly squiggly contours.

At which, and totally without warning, a horrifying, inhuman cry is thrust out of him:

"Ai! Ai! A Zahir! Look, look, a Zahir!"

With his flailing hand caught in mid-air, Augustus falls down in a fatal swoon.

As it turns out, his cry is so loud, shrill and blood-curdling that all of his company start up, quickly slip on nightgowns and rush downstairs, panicking and paling, aghast and cowardly, colliding with a chair and spilling a goldfish bowl, groping for a doorknob and finally locating a light switch – Amaury, as usual, arriving first, with Olga, Savorgnan and Squaw in tow.

Augustus is lying on a giant octagonal rug with Russian motifs.

117

A ghastly rictus contorts his lips. In its last, dying spasm, his hand had split Vowl's clay box in half. Around his body is a random sprinkling of grain.

"Why grain?" asks a dumbstruck Amaury.

"It was for his carp," says Olga, who knows all of Augustus's funny habits and quirks.

"Uh huh," adds Squaw, "Jonah hasn't had any food for two days. It was a daily obligation of ours that both of us had lost track of, what with all that was going on."

"And my hunch is," says Olga thoughtfully, "that, whilst choosing grain for his carp, Augustus was struck down by a malady as abrupt as it was mortal, a trauma, a shock, a coronary thrombosis – who can say?"

"All right," says Savorgnan, "but how do you link his attack with this box that our poor host was crumpling in his hand during his final agony?"

"His last word was that . . . that frightful cry," says Amaury in his turn, "but what was it trying to say? Could any of you work it out?"

"To my mind it was 'Traitor, traitor!'" says Olga.

"I thought I could distinguish 'Samar' or 'Zair'," says Savorgnan.

"No," says Squaw, "what it was in fact was 'A Zahir! Look, look, a Zahir!'"

"A Zahir?" Olga, Amaury and Savorgnan cry out in chorus. "Just what *is* a Zahir???"

"Oh, it's a long, long story," Squaw languidly murmurs.

"But it's our right to know!"

"Okay, if you must know . . ." says Squaw. "But first, why don't you try to ring up Aloysius Swann or Ottavio Ottaviani, for only two days ago Augustus had a radiogram from Swann that said: 'I'm following your situation. It looks bad. What I'm most afraid of now is foul play. All my suspicions focus on Azincourt, so both of us must stay on our guard. I must know a.s.a.p. if your inquiry brings anything to light, as it's only by knowing what's going on that I can act.' Aloysius Swann has – I should say, had – known Clifford for many a moon," Squaw adds, "known, too, about this Zahir affair. So his collaboration is crucial to us."

Amaury calls up Aloysius Swann; but, informing him that Swann isn't at his station, HQ puts him through to Ottaviani.

"Hallo hallo?" says Ottavio Ottaviani. "This is Ottavio Ottaviani."

"Hallo hallo?" says Amaury Conson. "This is Amaury Conson."

"Amaury? How's tricks?"

"Not so hot."

"Why, what's up?"

"Only an instant ago Augustus B. Clifford 'shuffl'd off his mortal coil', as our national Bard, our Swan of Avon, put it!"

"Crocus and plum pudding!" growls Ottavio (it's an old Corsican oath popular among Parisian cops). "Kaput?"

"You said it!"

"A killing?"

"No, no, probably a coronary – but that's only a layman's opinion."

"Good Lord!" roars Ottaviani. "Okay, now, don't touch anything – I'm on my way. Ciao!"

Ottaviani hangs up. Amaury ditto, saying to Olga, who was not *au fait* with this discussion, "Ottavio's coming round. Pronto."

Augustus Clifford's body is brought into an adjoining drawing room and laid out on a low divan, with a thin cloak for its shroud.

Upon which Squaw asks his companions to crouch around it on an oval Iroquois rug and starts to cast a hypnotic old Indian charm.

"Squaw," Olga murmurs almost inaudibly to Amaury, "cannot hold forth without first warding off God's wrath by a singsong chant that no Grand Manitou would sanctify if it didn't go in association with an imploration and an invocation of, I may say, a most rigorous liturgy, its ritualisation laid down, on his Clan's foundation, all of 784 springs ago, by its original Grand Satchmo (from which word a famous black jazz musician, Louis Armstrong, took his alias), so formulating a sort of oral canon which, passing down from clan to clan, from family to family, ad infinitum, is now part of our cultural patrimony."

"You don't say?"

Thus, in an outlandishly occult jargon that no noncommunicant could follow, Squaw proclaims Grand Satchmo's oral canon, announcing, to start with, a total submission to its instructions and, matching action to words, actually carrying out such instructions, from first to last in turn, with an assiduity that was a joy to watch.

"O Grand Satchmo, 784 springs ago, you taught us a mystical art, that of warding off Grand Manitou's horrifying wrath. Today I shall act just as you did. First, you did go into a dark wigwam. You did put down a pouch, unhitch it and draw out a black tomahawk. Now, on an oval rug, you did lay out six stalks of buffalo grass, as black as night from a touch of a tarbrush, four tiny clay pots, out of which you took a light sprinkling of tobacco, a strip of touchwood and a long, hollow roll of piping. Now, you did undo a truss of arrows, which was lying diagonally aslant your rug, honing arrow against arrow until its point was as sharp as a dart's. Now you did swap your clothing for a pair of buckskins and carry out your ablutions. At which, squatting not far from your rug, a profound tranquillity now filling your soul, you found that you could pacify Grand Manitou with soothing words: O Grand Manitou, thou art blind, but thou know'st all that is to know. I know thy might – as do both hippopotamus and tapir, gnu and urial, falcon and Vizsla, duckbill platypus and wapiti, cougar and xiphidon, bison and yak, low-flying albatross and furry African zorilla with its skin that, curiously, has no flavour. Today, with my companions, I am about to go forth in

120

my turn – go forth to absorb an occult and now, alas, outworn fount of wisdom, to construct, in my skin and in my soul, that original cry out of which our clans will spring full grown. Grand Manitou, O archaic Artisan, mount guard, today and always!"

12

In which an umbilical ruby avails a bastard's anglicisation

Falling on all fours, arms stiffly akimbo, brow touching floor, Squaw abruptly jumps up again and spins round and round and round.

"Voilà," says Olga. "That was Squaw's invocation. Our mission has found favour with Grand Manitou. Now to find out what this 'Zahir' is all about."

In Masulipatam (Squaw starts) Zahir was a jaguar; in Java, in a Surakarta hospital, it was an albino fakir at whom that city's population had had fun casting rocks; in Shiraz it was an octant which Ibnadir Shah had thrown into Iran's tidal flow; in a prison in Istanbul it was a compass found in a pariah's rags, a pariah whom Oswald Carl von Slatim had thought to touch for good luck; in Abdou Abdallah's Alhambra in Granada it was, according to Zotanburg, a stratum of onyx in a moulding; in Hammam-Lif's Casbah, it was lying in a pit; in Bahia Bianca it was a tiny notch on a coin.

To know about Zahir, you must apply your mind to an imposing doorstop of a book that Iulius Barlach brought out, in Danzig, just as Otto von Bismarck's Kulturkampf was at last drawing to its conclusion, a book containing a mass of information, including Arthur Philip Taylor's introductory study in its original manuscript. Faith in Zahir was born in Islam as Austria's war with its Ottoman antagonists was winding down. "Zahir", in vulgar Arabic slang, stood for "limpid" or "distinct"; it was also said that Muslims had as many as 26 ways of praising Allah – notably, naming him "Zahir".

At first sight a Zahir looks normal, almost banal: a slightly wan individual, possibly, or a common, humdrum thing such as a rock, a doubloon, a wasp or a clock dial. But, in any form it adopts, it has a truly horrifying impact: who looks upon a Zahir will not again know Nirvana, blissful oblivion, and will turn into a haggard raving lunatic.

Alluding first to Zahirs was a fakir from Ispahan, who told how, many, many moons ago, in a souk in Shiraz, a brass octant was found "of such craftsmanship that it cast an undying charm on anybody who saw it". As for Arthur Philip Taylor's long and thorough monograph, it informs us that, at Bhuj, in a suburb of Hydarabad, its author was taught a curious local saying, "Having known a Jaguar . . .", which, if it should apply to an individual, stood for madman or saint. Taylor was told, too, that Zahir is common to all kinds of civilisation; in a distant and idolatrous past, it was a talisman, Yaùq; but also a visionary from Irraouaddi sporting a crown of lapis lazuli and a mask spun out of a ribbon of gold. Taylor also said: nobody can wholly fathom Allah.

In Azincourt Zahir was an ovoid crystal of opaloid corundum, as tiny as a lotus, with a trio of distinct markings on it: on top a stamp akin to an Astaroth's 3-digit hand; at its midway point a horizontal 8, traditionally signifying Infinity; at bottom an arc gaping slightly ajar, so to say, and finishing in a short, fairly straight inward strip.

Accompanying Zahir's apparition was a disturbing fact (says Squaw, continuing). On a spring morning (28 April) a man rang at our door – squat, swarthy, a bit of a thug, in a whitish grubby smock, which was, if you want my opinion, a sum total of his clothing.

"I bin walking all day long," was what this insalubrious individual said first. "I'm hungry and thirsty."

"Fuck off, you sonofabitch!" said I, as, frankly, I didn't know him from Adam.

For an instant all I got from him was a long, hard, hurt look. Abruptly, though, as I was about to pick up a club to brain him with:

"No. I brought a . . . a gift for Clifford."

"What sort of gift?"

"I'm not saying – it's for him to find out, not for you to know."

"Okay, okay," I said, playing it cool, "walk this way. I'll find out if Mr Clifford's willing to talk to you."

I took him towards a small drawing room in which Augustus was just finishing his lunch with a satsuma and a slab of Stilton.

"Who is it, Squaw?"

"A vagrant – wants a word – has a sort of gift for you."

"A gift? Is it anybody I know?"

"I doubt it."

"A ruffian, would you say?"

"No, just a down-and-out."

"Knows who I am?"

"Uh huh."

"All right. Show him in."

As I was announcing him, our visitor was standing half in and half out, hopping from foot to foot, scrutinising Augustus with an air that wasn't so much uncivil as almost aghast.

"Augustus B. Clifford?"

"That's right. And might I know who . . . ?"

"I'm nobody at all, not having had any baptism in my infancy. But I do admit to an alias – an alias that'll charm you, I think, though you may find it just a tad outlandish: Tryphiodorus. What do you think of that?"

"Tryphiodorus? It's . . . most original," said Augustus, not knowing what this was all about.

"Thank you kindly, sir. Now," said Tryphiodorus, calmly going on as if nothing was untoward, "four days ago, in Arras, a cardinal – with a blush on his fat mug, I must say, as crimson as his cloak

124

– said that I should 'go instantly to Augustus B. Clifford at Azincourt and inform him that a son of his was in our city's public hospital, wailing away as if his –'"

"A son!" Augustus cut him short, almost falling down on his rump (his bottom, his buttocks, his bum, his ass or his BT – call it what you will). "But, for crying out loud, who brought him in?"

"Alas!" was Tryphiodorus's sigh. "His mama was also dying whilst giving birth to him, a poor, totally unknown woman. But a solicitor's affidavit was found in a handbag –"

"A *handbag*!"

"That's right. With confirmation that this (um, how shall I put it?) this fruit of a transitory affair uniting on a night of passion, 8 months ago, at Saint-Agil, Augustus B. Clifford and his mama, was officially your son."

"What's . . . what's that you say?" Augustus was practically choking. "A night of passion? But I . . . I insist . . . it's . . . not . . . not a word of truth in that farrago!"

"Shut up!" said a now intimidating Tryphiodorus, "and look at this court ruling, instructing you, ipso facto, to bring up your child."

"A bastard!" was all Augustus could cry.

"But also a Brit," said Tryphiodorus.

Although his initial instinct was to consult his solicitor, Tryphiodorus was so insistant that Augustus finally took off for Arras, compliant if still dubious. In Arras's hospital a plump, rubicund matron put in his grudging arms a baby clad in a cotton outfit that was a bit too big for his tiny body. So, making a trip that would occur again in 20 springs, almost without distinction, saving that his load would consist not of a baby in swaddling but a body in a shroud, Augustus sat his offspring down in his Hispano-Suiza sports car and, driving all night, was back in Azincourt by dawn.

Starting up at a furious knocking on our door, I ran downstairs to unlock it. Augustus, carrying his child in his arms, was hopping mad, an ugly rictus distorting his lips, a wild, spasmatic tic causing his chin to twitch up and down.

"I'll kill him, I'll kill him!" – that was his shrill cry. Why, my blood ran cold!

"This way, Squaw," Augustus said, briskly now, striding into his drawing room, brutally hurling his poor, worn-out infant on to a billiard board, drawing off his swaddling garb, picking up a poniard and approaching his victim, as Abraham to his son Isaac, his arm high and fatal. I couldn't stand to watch it. But it was just as Augustus was about to carry out this inhuman act that an abrupt transformation was to occur in him. With a look of profound anguish, this murmur:

"Oh! Oh!"

Approaching, I saw in my turn an oval ruby, as tiny as buckshot, with a trio of inscriptions, incrusting his infant's tummy-button, as if it was a bloody stump of his umbilical cord.

Unmindful of his child's continuing sobs, Augustus took that oval ruby (not without difficulty) out of its tummy-button, gazing at it for an instant without saying a word. A thick, suffocating gurgling sound shook his torso.

"Right," was his first word. "I am willing to confront public scorn. As this brat truly is my son, what can I do but adopt him? I'll call him Douglas Haig, thus immortalising that bold and cunning Commandant with whom I fought at Douaumont. I'll maintain a constant watch so that nobody will inform him of his status as a natural child, a bastard. His adoration for his guardian will stay unambiguously filial."

So Augustus B. Clifford found his Zahir on his own son, who was to find in him a worthy papa, magnanimous, solicitous and sagacious. As for that Zahir, it was to form an incrustation on a gold ring which Augustus would always insist on sporting on his right hand.

Douglas Haig would soon attain boyhood. Not a day at Azincourt would go by that wasn't calm and harmonious; not a day, for six long springs, that wasn't full of joy and good humour.

And, among Azincourt's shrubs, in its plush, lush, luxuriant grounds, a glowing, coruscating, autumnally purplish crimson would turn into a warm brown finish a sparkling bluish sky, across which would blow (God's own natural air-conditioning) a bracing north wind . . .

13

On a fantastic charm that a choral work by Anton Dvořák starts to cast on a billiard board

So that (says Squaw) you'll grasp how all our bad luck was born and out of what it's grown, I'm going to start again from scratch with a long flashback.

In his youth, Augustus had had (but why? To this day nobody knows but him) what you might call a moral crisis, a crisis so alarming that a cousin of his, a naval man, in fact an Admiral, afraid of his blowing his brains out in a fit of anguish, distraction or illumination, got him to do a six-month stint on his sloop "Flying Dutchman", aboard which young Augustus was taught a harsh but invigorating job, that of cabin boy.

On coming out of his psychological convulsion, which was in truth so profound that his circumnavigation didn't totally fulfil its function of curing him, Augustus was to fall for a charlatan (or quasi-charlatan), Othon Lippmann, who had, as a *soi-disant* yogi, a charismatic gift that would transform many of his faithful into fanatics.

With Augustus pinning his faith on this dubious guru, trusting him implicitly, worshipping him as a fount of occult wisdom, a holy pathway to oblivion, to Nirvana, sly Othon Lippmann, without wasting an instant, sought to act on his minion's child-ishly candid imagination by forcing him into a total abjuration of his Christianity, by inculcating him in his own cult, a schis-matic olla podrida that took as its immortal gods not only Vishnu and Brahma but Buddha and Adonai, by obliging him, in its

128

initiation ritual, to study as many as six "holy" books, actually an unholy mishmash, a ludicrous hocus-pocus drawn up from Vasavadatta, from Mantic Uttair, Kalpasutra, Gîta-Govinda, Tso-Tchouan and Zohar, and in which you could also find, thrown in any old how, Saint Mark, Saint Justin, Montanus, Arius, Gottschalk, Valdo, William Booth, John Darby, Haggada, a significant chunk of Shulhan Azukh, Sunna, Ghôlan Ahmad, Çruti, four Upanishads, two Purânas, Tao-to-King, Catapathabrahmana and thirty of Li-Po's songs.

An important factor in Othon's cult was its draconian Canon, imposing on his faithful a host of implorations, invocations, orisons and unctions.

It also had four purifications a day (at cockcrow, noon, six o'clock and midnight) and Augustus would carry out his morning purification in a particularly original fashion. This would consist of his taking a lustral bath of morning damp – damp which I had to scoop up from 25 tanks laid out in various locations around Azincourt's grounds and which an outlandish apparatus would start canalising into a low, long tub built out of a raw block of *antico rosato*, a crystal quartz so hard only an uncut diamond could polish it.

So that a surplus of irroration harmful to his constitution wouldn't afflict Augustus, this admission of damp was conditional upon a circuit of automatisation stabilising both its flow and its constant fluctuations, and calibrating that flow by a hydro-hoist of communicating airlocks, its oscillation provoking (by a narrow conduit, that of a cog-rotating piston on a fulcrum controlling an input-output transistor circuit and its induction) his apparatus's constriction.

Thus, day by day, dozily crawling from his futon, Augustus would find a lustral bath of a total, unvarying constancy.

For it, though, to conform to his faith and its laws, Augustus had to buy a trio of products with which Othon Lippmann would furnish him at an absurdly high cost:

first, a drop or two of starch, as, containing too much

ammonia, morning damp might risk an obstruction in his throat, thus making it obligatory to add a soothing lubricant;

also, six grains of albumin, strong in radioactivity, which Othon would claim had a vigorous purifying capacity (it was in actual fact a shampoo for phthiriasis, a dubious concoction from a notoriously unorthodox stomatologist in Avignon who'd sought to inflict it on that city's public hospital; a prohibitory injunction was almost instantly brought against it, though, as it was found to contain far too much *aconita*; and so it was said that Othon, coming by this surplus in his usual shady fashion, found it politic to fly to Tirana – only, on chancing across a pack of local bandits, to apply his skills to a flourishing traffic in opium);

finally, day in, day out, Augustus would add to his bath 26 or 25 carats of a product of unknown composition, a product that was most probably its principal factor, its gist.

Was its impact soporific? or hallucinatory? or hypnotic? To this day nobody knows. What I can say, though, is that it would transport him into a condition, a stupor, of almost voluptuous bliss. As soon as his lustral bath was just right, not too hot, not too cold, as soon as, in that hairy pink birthday suit of his, Augustus slowly sank into it for his morning purification, a monstrous frisson would run through his body. Knotting a tight caparison around his brow so that his nostrils would stay dry, thus avoiding any risk of suffocating in his tub, Augustus would, in a twinkling, go limp, sluggish, and fall into a coma.

On occasion, as soon as this coma of his would pass, Augustus was willing to talk about it, about his Nirvana, his fainting fit, his blissful swoon, his vision of an All-Surpassing Guru, his visitation by an All-Knowing Divinity, his introduction to a profound and original Fount of Wisdom, to a God Almighty and His holy Will, his fascination with total Sublimity – in a word, his Illumination. Numb and catatonic, but – and I'm quoting him word for word – soaking in Oblivion, bathing in Purity, wallowing in Infinity.

Until his son's, and thus his Zahir's, irruption into his daily round, Augustus took his morning lustral bath without fail, ritually, and also took profound satisfaction, both physical and spiritual, from it.

But if his Zahir was on his pinky (which, in truth, it always was, so allowing him constantly to gloat on it, allowing him, too, to inform anybody willing to pay mind to him that nothing was as alluring to him as his own mortality), Augustus found that dunking it, so to say, in his bath would straightaway bring about an agonising pain in his body, a constantly throbbing itch, a chafing inflammation, so sharp, stinging and prickly that, notwithstanding a will of iron, it was soon impossibly difficult for him to stand it – aching, tingling, vomiting and, in addition, losing sight of that swooning bliss that was his bath's vital, capital, cardinal alibi, its primary motivation, its basic goal.

So, racking his brains, Augustus thought up an apparatus which, akin to that harnass that would maintain his nostrils dry, would allow him, without too much pain, to sport his Zahir in his bath; and built a spool-hoist, fitting it out with a jack to control a maulstick that would float on top.

For fully six springs, by thus avoiding both Scylla and Charybdis, his morning ritual would go off without a hitch. From his lustral bath Augustus would draw an invigorating comfort as unfailing as it was abundant.

But a day would dawn on which, climbing out of his tub, languid, clumsy, awkward, still stagnating in his morning Nirvana, Augustus, noticing that his Zahir was now *not* on his pinky and that a clot of blood, about as big as a ruby, was coagulating on it, forming a pallid, oval stigma, as if marking his Zahir's incrustation – a day on which Augustus, I say, crying out in a truly inhuman fashion, his wits in total disarray, would start pacing back and forth, back and forth, for four days and four nights, turning this way and that, haggard and drawn, frantically unlocking tallboys and cupboards, looking high and low, rummaging Azincourt from top to bottom, from rooftops to floorboards, ransacking its outbuildings, its barns, its courtyard and its hayloft, raking all its shingly paths.

Four ghastly days, which a brutal fifth was to cap: Othon Lippmann's arrival at Azincourt.

Othon, obviously all in, his body giving off a strong musky odour, his raglan practically in rags, instantly ran towards Augustus with a foul outpouring of profanity, vilifying him, shouting a long string of disgusting cuss-words at him, almost physically abusing him.

His command of insults might rival Captain Haddock's in *Tintin* – "Oaf! Pinbrain! Numbskull! Big fat ninny! Nincompoop! Halfwit! Schmuck! Moron! Lazy good-for-nothing! Stupid old fart!"

At which point, Othon hit him hard on his jaw.

With amazing sang-froid, Augustus, thrown for a loop by Othon's fulmination, put up a good fight, landing a knockout blow, a right swing, which had his assailant on his back, groggy, out cold.

Watching this bout of fisticuffs, Augustus's son, who at that point was a typically naughty kid of six, had a lot of fun counting 1 . . . 2 . . . 3 . . . up to 10 and finally proclaiming his papa champion.

But Othon Lippmann was still unconscious. Abruptly triumph was turning to alarm.

I saw that Augustus was now frantically wringing his hands and asking in a low, gruff murmur, "What's wrong with him? Oh, what's wrong with him?"

For his part, Haig, too young to know that a tornado was just about to hit him, was frolicking around Othon's limp body, laughing so loudly that Augustus, in a fury, judging his son's antics unfitting in such a situation, curtly told him to go away.

"Off with you! Scram!" was his cry, a cry so loud that Haig, who, until that instant, had found his papa an unfailingly kind man, took off with a halting, blushing apology. An involuntary convulsion shook his childish body, causing him not only to burst into sobs but soil his pants.

So, whilst Haig ran off, trying to pluck up his spirits by sprinkling grain into his carp's pond, a task that would always amus–

"Hang on a mo," Olga cuts Squaw off in mid-word. "I forgot about Jonah. Poor thing, it's probably starving."

"Shhh! Shhh!" cry Amaury and Savorgnan. "First, Squaw has to finish this gripping, fascinating story!"

"Thank you," says Squaw.

So, as I was saying (says Squaw), whilst Haig was nourishing his carp, I took Othon into an adjoining drawing room, laid him out on a sofa and got him to swallow a tonic. Augustus and I took off his raglan and (oh, abomination of abominations!) had a vision causing us both to panic, causing our blood to run cold, our hair to stand up in tufts, our skin to go all pimply – a vision of Othon Lippmann bathing in his own blood. It was as if a monstrous hawk had flown again and again down on to his torso, flaying him, ripping off his skin, poking into his lungs, drawing out his innards, digging into his thorax with its anvil blows. What I saw in his body was a tiny zoo of vomit-making animals – gadfly, blowfly, wasp, worm, cockroach, moth – buzzing, humming, squirming, as gluttonous as carrion crows, on a bloody, slimy, gassy, putrid magma that stank a yard away!

"Ugh!" says Olga.

"Yuk!" says Amaury.

You said it (says Squaw). In an agony lasting all of six days Othon would slip into a profound coma, surfacing from it on occasion only to shout insults at us, accusing us, God only knows why, of conspiring to kill him, calling damnation down upon us. I did all I could for him and so did Augustus – hoping that his dying days wouldn't incur too much fuss or strain. And Othon did finally pass away, hurling hair-raising oaths at us and, with his last, rasping gasp, drawing from out of his lungs a cry so horrifying I instantly had to throw up.

This was, at his burial, Augustus's orison:

"Othon Lippmann – you, my Guru – go straight to God's kingdom, to that Holy City in which a Houri, a gift to you from Allah in all His compassion, now awaits you. I was a daily communicant in that faith that you brought us and taught us so long ago. Today I am abjuring it, today, tomorrow and for always. For, with your passing on, what can I do with your faith but abolish it? And so, with touchwood, will you and I go forth at midnight."

With that Parthian shot did his orison finish. It was, was it not, a curious thing to say and, for my part, only his action that night was to clarify it. Drawing his inspiration from Othon's own apostolic Canon, amassing and binding up six thick faggots, Augustus put a torch to his (which is to say, Othon's) body. It burnt for a day and a half, producing a whitish ash that a whistling north wind would sow all around us . . .

Nobody, not any of you, can know what anguish and affliction struck us down at that point. Totally caught up in his sorrow, his prostration, his apathy, mounting his Golgotha with a Cross on his back, carrying, too, a giant, flapping albatross of guilt and mortification, Augustus B. Clifford sank into a torpor.

It was frightful to watch him pacing up and down, all day and all night, in suicidally low spirits – to watch this man who, as you know, was a *bon vivant*, not to say a bit of a *gourmand*, just nibbling at his food, just picking at his lunch. Notwithstanding that I would lovingly cook for him all my most subtly scrumptious culinary concoctions – *aloyau aux oignons confits, turbot au court-bouillon*, a London broil, *boudin au raifort*, scampi – Augustus got down, at most, an anchovy, a shaving of Cantal, a dash of Izard, a drop of amontillado, half an apricot or a solitary walnut – and that was on a good day.

Starting to grow disturbingly thin, occasionally withdrawing to his donjon, locking its door, not surfacing from it for six days, although, from within, without warning, and invariably at midnight, giving out an alarming howl, Augustus would abruptly turn up again, as if in a stupor, his brow moist and sticky, his good looks haggard and drawn. In just 12 months his auburn hair had lost all its colour, transforming him into a grizzly old fogy.

Haig, a pallid, sickly, timorous boy, an unwitting victim of all that gloom and doom, was psychologically unfit for this cold, harsh world of ours, a world in which, if you want to function, you simply cannot show any pity. Gradually coming to know his son, snapping out of his nihilistic sloth at long last, disparaging his past duplicity, his misconduct, his casual abandoning of his offspring, Augustus finally got down to pray for moral stamina, so that no guilt, no stigma, should attach to his son for a sin that was his – which is to say, his own – and nobody's but his.

"I had what you might call an anti-Midas touch," is how Augustus put it, milking his propitiation for all it was worth. "I would spoil all that was truly important in my world, and what I couldn't spoil, what I couldn't corrupt, I would simply forbid. I know now that I'm going to rot, I'm going to go to pot, in my insignificant vacuum, in my void – but I will insist that my son, that fruit of my unruly loins, for whom I affirm, in front of all that is holy, an undying passion from this day forth – I insist, I say, that my son's schooling will start right away, from today, and it's I who will tutor him. In addition," Augustus finally said with a sigh, "may I find in this daily obligation my own harsh but vital salvation."

So Augustus took in hand his son's instruction – an arduous task as his mind was almost a tabula rasa. It was soon obvious that his tuition at Azincourt's local grammar school had had practically no impact on him. Haig, who had an amazingly poor vocabulary for a lad of 12, had no grasp of orthography at all;

was totally lacking in imagination; could do subtraction but not addition, division but not multiplication; was blissfully ignorant of Avogadro's Law or, should I say, mistook it for an axiom of Arago that had nothing at all to do with it; and would gladly inform you that Louis X was familiarly known at court as Hutin but had no notion why. As for Latin, although a thick manual was put at his disposal, it had childishly strict limits: "*Animula vagula blanda*", "*Aquila non capit muscas*", "*Sic transit gloria mundi*" or "*O fortunatos nimium sua si bona norint agricolas*".

Inculcating a satisfying command of basics in his son took a lot out of Augustus, who, although working hard at it, at all hours, did, as both tutor and adjudicator, inflict on his ignorant child a form of schooling that was far too high in its standards, incongruously abstract in its quality and mostly much ado about nothing. Poor Haig would swallow all this waffling, compliant, smiling and without any sulky ill will; but it was also obvious, within a month, that such tuition on its own could not, would not, bring about automatic intuition. To Augustus's dismay, his son was null in anything touching on maths, philosophy and Latin, and had, at most, only a faint inkling of Italian and Spanish. As for linguistics, Haig truly put in a lot of hard work, contriving to grasp, *grosso modo*, a host of grammatical, syntactical and phonic quirks, managing to distinguish – in, say, four words out of six – a glottal from a labial, a noun from a pronoun, an ordinary auxiliary from a modal auxiliary, a past from a conditional, a root from a suffix, a comma from a colon, a surd from a sonant, a chiasmus from an oxymoron, sarcasm from irony and, finally, pathos from bathos (and both from Porthos and Athos).

It was frustrating for Augustus (on whom it would quickly dawn that his original plan to turn Haig into a brilliant physicist was all in vain) that his own input vis-à-vis his son's vocation was practically minimal. At which point, forgoing all such ambitions, it struck him as a surprising but also charming fact that it was for music that Haig – whom Augustus had caught on two occasions puffing into a tuba and producing from it a sound that wasn't wholly discordant – had both a passion and a gift. Haig had, too, a natural instinct for harmony, a distinct vocal ability and could sing a song, any song, if it was sung to him first.

So Augustus, whom Iturbi had taught in his youth, bought a grand piano (it was a Graf with a slightly nasal tonal quality but miraculous pitch, built for Brahms, who would tap out on it, so it was said, his Impromptu Opus 28) and had it put in a drawing room in which also stood a billiard board (that billiard board on which, as I told you, Augustus almost took a poniard to Douglas as a baby).

Day by day, *do mi fah soh*, from morning till night, *soh fah mi do*, Augustus would drill his son in that gracious art that is singing, both accompanying and inspiring him. Abandoning his Latin, his Italian and Spanish, Haig thought only of his passion for classical music, finding total satisfaction in Mozart, Bach, Schumann and Hugo Wolf. In truth, not so much Apollo as Marsyas, his susurration was too squally, his sonority too soft, his modulation too shaky, his sharps flat, and his pitch simply off. Augustus's son, in short, sang badly – but was to know, notwithstanding, a joy in singing that no plummy vibrato could diminish.

As you all know, at 18, and not without difficulty, Haig sat his *bac*; and, making his mind up at last, taking an autonomous stand as to his aspirations, stood up to Augustus, accosting him in that forthright way of his:

"Now that I'm all grown-up, this is what I want to do – sing at La Scala. It's my vocation!"

"It's a long way from Arras to Milan," said Augustus, smiling.

"*Labor omnia vincit improbus*," said Haig, who was a stubborn young man on occasion.

"That's what you think, you big bag of wind," said Augustus.

Haig, who had no gift for humour, got angry at this, stamping his foot and crying:

137

"Oh, shut up!"

"Now now, my boy," said Augustus, trying to calm him. "I was just admiring your obstinacy. First things first, though. You know, don't you, that if you want to triumph against your rivals you must put in a lot of hard, slogging work? What kind of world would you call it if just anybody thought to turn up at La Scala and ask for a major part in a production?"

"But my plan is to go forward and upward rung by rung."

"If that's so, work hard and I'll assist you as much as I can," said Augustus in conclusion.

So, from that day forward, his son did nothing but work at his vocation – practising sol-fa from cockcrow to dusk.

Now, it was a warm, sunny April morning with spring on its way. Haig, who was taking particular pains with an oratorio by Haydn, sat down, flagging, worn out, on that billiard board – or, should I say, on its rim – that sat stagnating not far from his piano, stagnating, as I put it, for nobody now had any inclination to play on it.

Idly, as if simply twiddling his thumbs, Augustus was improvising on a choral work by Anton Dvořák.

Chancing just at that instant, who knows why, to look at Augustus's billiard board, Haig saw that part of its dust-cloth, about a third all told, was going mouldy. All along its margin was a rash of baffling points, whitish in colour and pica-high (as in typography), abnormal and anamorphous grains, small, flaky dots, almost circular and almost uniform. A handful had tiny incrustations, additions or variations, but all had this quality in common: a structural organisation that struck Haig as arising organically out of a conscious plan, a goal that was as obvious as it was blatant: not a random but a *signifying* sign (using that word in its structuralist connotation), partially if not wholly akin to a manuscript or possibly a quipos (a nodal ribbon, of Incan origin, that functions as an aid to communication).

But that wasn't all. What was most disturbing was that, as

Augustus was happily tinkling away at his Dvořák improvisation, Haig saw this inscription – which had, by his count, 25 points to start with – actually, fantastically, almost as if in a vision, micron by micron, angstrom by angstrom, *start to grow*. Ignorant of what his son was up to, Augustus was still playing and would go on doing so till nightfall; but not for an instant did Haig abandon his scrutiny of that fascinating dust-cloth, staring at it, or at a portion of it, as if in a condition of hypnosis; and noting, as soon as Augustus, running out of inspiration at last, brought his Dvořákiana to a conclusion with a jarringly atonal chord, that it now had, not 25, but 26 blank points, an additional point having burst forth, first as an aura, not so much a point as a hint of a point, and finally as a rash of whitish grains.

"Papa!" says Haig in a cry of anguish.

"Why, what is it, my boy?" asks Augustus, staring at him.

"Look! Look at that, will you! A Blank inscription on a Billiard Board!"

"What?" Augustus jumps off his stool. "A Blank on a Billboard?"

"No, no! A billiard board, on its rim – look, that inscription!"

Crouching to focus on it, his brow knotting, Augustus murmurs, softly, dully, "Again! Again! Again!"

"What's wrong?" asks Haig, starting to worry at how livid his papa is turning.

"You and I must fly, my boy, both of us, right now, straight-away – pronto!"

14

*In which you will find a carp scornfully turning down
a halva fit for a king*

Augustus finally thought to acquaint his son of his curious situation. I was on hand during this discussion.

"Till now I said nothing at all to you about a puzzling conundrum accompanying your apparition at Azincourt. Today, if only I could, I would inform you of just what kind of a Damnation it is that has both of us now in its claws. But a Law (a Law, my boy, unfamiliar to you) would punish any such injudicious admission on my part. Nobody, not I, not anybody, would wish to broadcast that flimsy truth, that X, that minimal unknown quantity, that total taboo, that is transforming – *ab ovo*, so to say – all our talk into poppycock and driving all our actions to distraction. All of us know of this anonymous abomination that acts upon us without any of us knowing just how it acts upon us, all of us know, alas, that, by continually barring our path, continually obliging us to adopt unidiomatic circumlocutions, roundabout ways of saying things and dubiously woolly abstractions, continually damning us to a bogus philosophy and its just as bogus spiritual comfort, a 'comfort' stifling all our crying and sighing, sobbing and blubbing – all of us know, as I say, that a wall far too high for any of us to surmount is now imprisoning us for good and a malignant wrath is thwarting all our approximations of that missing sign – quixotic approximations born out of a natural wish to grasp such an amorphous immaculation in our hands. So, Haig, my boy, you must know that, from this day on, as in a not too distant past, Thanatos is in our midst, prowling all around Azincourt.

"To start with," said Augustus, "I was optimistic about saving you from that inhuman fatality to which I was bound hand and foot. But I know now that I can do nothing for you, nothing. Thus you must go – for what a miscalculation you would commit, and I would commit, if, risking your all, you had a notion of staying on in Azincourt. No, my boy, go you must, and by nightfall!"

Instantly dismissing this proposition as absurd, and unworthy of a Clifford, Haig said that his "motivation" was unconvincing and most probably phony and that Augustus was simply trying to do away with his son!

Oh, poor Douglas was in a sorry condition, almost touchingly so. "What! You, too, my own blood! Don't think I don't know what you want – you want to find my body in a ditch, don't you? God, I was so trusting, I put my faith in you, I would look up to you with a truly filial admiration – and now I find you hatching a plot against your own son – a plot as brutal as it's stupid! And so goddamn obvious it wouldn't fool a child! Don't you know what candour is? If you truly want to abandon your own offspring, cry, shout, pull his hair out if you must, but don't try to justify your cowardly act with such an idiotic alibi!"

"My boy," said Augustus with a groan, profoundly hurt by such an insulting slight on his honour and probity. But his words got lost in an uncontrollably loud burst of sobbing.

That night I found out from him that it was his wish to blurt it all out – that Augustus, in short, if only for an instant, was willing to inform Haig of his status as a bastard, inform him of Zahir, of Othon Lippmann, and of Tryphiodorus in his grubby smock, and of his lustral baths, and so on, and on. But that took guts, and his valour would finally fail him.

Without saying a word, Haig took a long, last look at his papa; and, making an abrupt U-turn, ran off out of his sight.

I had to know if Augustus, who stood stock still through all of this, was going to call him back – or if I should.

"No." It was almost his last word on this unusual family drama. "Drop it, Squaw. Haig *must* go – thus Haig *will* go."

"And if Haig won't go?"

"Too bad – it's curtains for all of us!"

All that night Haig would go pacing upstairs and downstairs, along this corridor and that, into this room and out of that, through library and study, attic and pantry. Till, finally, at dawn, Augustus and I (spying on him, I admit) saw him go out, sporting a woolly cardigan and a thick parka and carrying a small bag in his hand.

First strolling around Azincourt's grounds, Haig found his way at last to Jonah's pond, stood thoughtfully for an instant on its rim and got down on all fours, whistling as follows

which was obviously a signal, as Jonah instantly swam up to join him. Haig had a long talk with his carp, if I may put it that way, whilst flipping an occasional pudding crumb at it – crumbs idly ground up in his hand just as you might grind flour.

And at that point, noisily slamming Azincourt's wrought-iron portals, and without so much as a last backward look at his papa, or at yours truly, Haig slowly shrank out of sight . . .

Not out of mind, though. Not knowing his son's location or situation was driving Augustus crazy. Nor did Haig's carp swim up if any of us thought to approach its pool, murmuring, "Jonah . . . Jonah . . ." Augustus and I had hit rock bottom.

Until, that August (this was in March), a postman, knocking at our door, brought us a most curious communication. Slicing its top with a pair of scissors, Augustus's initial instinct was to find out who it was from.

"Hmm. Anton Vowl? Do you know of any such individual?"

"No . . . I can't say as I do."

"Nor I. But this Vowl claims to know all about us. Look at this."

> *My Lord,*
>
> *In April I ran into Douglas Haig Clifford on about six occasions. Having found out, fortuitously, about his taking flight from Azincourt, giving you no hint as to his comings and goings, I thought it my duty to furnish you with a handful of indications which – such, anyway, is my wish – may aid in mitigating your all too natural anguish.*
>
> *On his initial arrival in Paris, Douglas's conduct wasn't at all, I'm afraid, what you would call morally uplifting: crawling from bar to bar, from clip joint to clip joint, usually hanging out with a trio of individuals from a notoriously slummy, insalubrious part of town – infamous blackguards, outlaws as unafraid of man as of God, with a long and bloody history of criminal activity. As if finding an almost diabolic fascination, a sort of kinky charm, in corruption, your son took part in hold-ups from which all profits would go to his unscrupulous pals. It almost brought about his downfall: caught with his hand rummaging in a lady's bag, Douglas's boss, his Fagin, if you wish, was run in and would languish for many months in prison.*
>
> *A poltroon if not a coward, anyway a bit of a milksop, your son saw a distinct possibility of his also rotting in jail, a possibility that wasn't at all to his liking. So, moving out of that casbah of corrupt cops and cutthroat crooks, Douglas took a maid's room on Boul'Mich. It didn't boast all mod. cons. but it had a kind of comfort that was, shall I say, succinct. I don't know what his bank account was at this point or just how such a capital had grown. Douglas didn't own a car, but ran up a colossal bill at his tailor's. His famous sports shirt – which had, as its "mascot", not an alligator but a tiny portrait of*

*Djougachvili – was, as soon as worn, familiar and
ultra-familiar from Paris's Quai Conti to its Club 13, from
Pont Sully to Lipp. In addition, Douglas would follow fashions
maniacally, going to talks by McLuhan on sociology, Lacan on
psychoanalysis and Foucault on philosophy, going to films by
Godard, Truffaut and Chabrol, plays by Anouilh, Giraudoux
and Duras.*

*All this was to last a month at most, until Douglas,
without a sou, saw that things had got out of hand, that his
riotous high-living was taking its toll, that his physical
constitution was going to pot and that his companions thought
of him as a promiscuous good-for-nothing.*

*It was at that point that, with his customary brio, your
son took as a political goal – a goal just as transitory as it was
radical – that of transforming his country's social status quo
by abolishing Capital and outlawing Profit. Douglas was a
militant in an "ultra-Albanian" (sic) party which, drawing
practically all of its inspiration from a talk by Hoxha in
Shkodra (or, traditionally, Scutari) about four months ago,
would attack, without discrimination, official Communist
policy and unofficial Maoist ravings. This ultra-Albanian
party, though, didn't last too long. To his chagrin, it took
only six days for it to split up.*

*At that junction it would dawn on him that, in his
childhood, his papa – you, in short – had casually said to him,
"You know, Albinoni's adagio was so comforting to us at cousin
Gaston's burial", and that a basic motivation for having sown
so many wild oats was to damp down what you might call his
subliminal ambition, his truly instinctual goal, in this world –
singing!*

*And, my, did your son work hard at music from that
point on! It took him just a month to sign up for a class at
Paris's famous Schola Cantorum, which, I must say, was
mightily struck by his gifts.*

Today Douglas is living, if you can call it living, in a

*tiny, spartan studio flat, six rond-point du Commandant
Nobody.*

   *Thus, straying but an instant from a straight-and-
narrow path, your son is now assiduously pursuing his
vocation.*

   *This information will aid, I trust, in taking a load off
your mind, a load which, from that day on which Douglas took
to flight, has lain so painfully hard upon you.*

   Yours truly,
   Anton Vowl

Without waiting, Augustus thought to forward to his son a substantial cash sum, dispatching with it a long communication – a
saga of sorts – that would amply justify his conduct. But nobody
would pick up his cash; and, wishing to find out why, both
anxious and suspicious, Augustus paid a visit not only to Paris's
main postal administration, which told him that no Douglas Haig
Clifford was living at six, rond-point du Commandant Nobody,
but also, naturally, to that Schola Cantorum at which Anton
Vowl had said Haig was studying, inquiring at *its* administration
if it had a Clifford in any class. On this occasion his luck was in:
Augustus was told that his son *was* on its list; but was also told
that, coming top of his class in unison singing, Haig had just
flown off to Manhattan's Juilliard School of Music, to study
composition.

Six months go by. Things finally start to calm down. From a
criticism in his *Figaro* Augustus saw that Douglas had won round
Carignano's intimidating public. Longchamp, a famous musi-
cologist, had him "bound for instant stardom", whilst Gavoty,
his rival, thought of him as "tomorrow's Tito Gobbi". And that
was just in Paris: Hugh Canning, an important British critic, was
to call him a "Gigli with Kim Borg's vocal gifts, Ruffo's passion
and Souzay's intuition".

*   *   *

Now – it was on a Friday, if I'm not wrong – having bought that day's provisions and arriving from town with, in tow, an urchin whom I paid a franc or two, to carry a particularly voluminous shopping bag – I saw, strolling nonchalantly around our pond, a man with an air about him that I found just a bit disturbing as, for an instant, I actually took him for Haig. In fact, as you probably now know, it was Anton Vowl.

Vowl, tall, as straight as a capital I, as slim as a strand of hair, clad in a panama hat and a drab plastic mac with a tartan collar, carrying a stick and looking about 20 at most, was, at first sight, nothing but a normal, charming youth, but a faint hint of – oh, how shall I put it? – a slightly indistinct, out-of-focus quality about him instantly put you on your guard. His curious skin colouring, giving his bulging brow a sickly cast, his languid gait, half-lurching, half-undulating, his shifty look, his rabbity lash-bound iris so limpidly bluish I thought I was looking at an albino – all in all, I saw a kind of twitchy agitation in him which I found highly anxious-making, as if this poor man was carrying a cumbrous physical or psychological cargo within him.

I stood in his way, haranguing him according to a traditional old tribal custom.

"How! Ugh! Man of whitish skin! May your wigwam know only harmony, may you bury your martial tomahawk, as I shall bury my own, and may you not talk in fork'd words, for nor shall I! Now you and I must powwow."

"Ahiyohu," said Vowl, touching his brow with his right thumb and flicking it against my brow just as a Mohican would, thus showing his familiarity with our customs. "May a fat and juicy caribou sit roasting in your cauldron!"

I brought him in, inviting him to sit down and ringing a gong. In an instant Augustus stood in front of us, saying, "What is it?"

"Anton Vowl," said our visitor with a curt bow. "Last autumn . . ."

Augustus gruffly cut him short. "I know. Last autumn you told us all about my son's dissipation, his crazy 'political' activism

146

and, thank God, his finally choosing a vocation and sticking to it. Haig, or so I'm told, is at last making his way in this harsh world of ours, and in Turin, just four days ago, got a standing ovation in *Tristan*. It was my wish, you know, to thank you for your aid, but I had no notion at all as to how I might contact you. I found no information of that kind on your communication to us."

A sigh from Anton. "Alas, Mr Clifford, I simply forgot to add it – a thousand pardons. But, fortuitously passing through this district, not far from Azincourt, I thought I'd drop by and say hullo."

"By gad, I'm mightily glad you did!" said Augustus. "If you don't mind, though, I'll call you Anton from now on – and you, I trust, will drop that formal 'Mr Clifford'. Just Augustus, all right? That should simplify things, don't you think?"

"As you wish . . . Augustus."

"Good. Now can I talk you into joining us in a light but satisfying collation tonight?"

"Hmm, I won't say no."

First putting down his stick, Vowl took off his panama hat and his mackintosh.

"Now," said Augustus, "why don't you and I pop into my smoking room for a drink, a cigar and a chat. What do you say, Anton?"

Coming out into a dark hallway, walking down a narrow corridor and climbing up six stairs, Augustus brought Vowl into a room with a pair of cosy armchairs in black Morocco and shiny mahogany, giving him a thick Havana, and not a phony but a first-class product, as I can vouch, of Cuba's tobacco plants.

Vowl took a long puff on it, luxuriously savouring its odour.

Proudly showing off all his barman's apparatus, Augustus put it to him: "A whisky? Scotch? Irish? Bourbon?"

"Hmm . . ." Vowl said doubtfully.

"A gin and tonic? A cocktail? A Bloody Mary? Or possibly just a Virgin Mary? That's without any vodka, you know. No? A Bull Shot? A Tom Collins? A dry martini?"

"Actually, you know what I fancy? A blackcurrant drink."

"A kir? Naturally."

Clink-clink.

"Bottoms up."

"Skoal."

"Chin-chin."

At which point, having drunk his kir, Vowl said:

"Now, what you want to find out most of all is how I got to know your son. Voilà. It was a day on which I was idly strolling around an aquarium – you know, in Paris's Jardin d'Acclimatation. A youth clad in a black cloak, low in spirits, visibly downcast, a youth whom you might think of as my own kith and kin, stood with a curiously languid air, not far off, gazing down into a pool in which a shoal of carp was swimming about. Out of a plastic shopping bag this lad brought a funny-looking foodstuff, part-halva, part-loukoum, that sat crumbling in his hand until it was thrown to any fish daring to snatch it, notwithstanding constant complaints from a guardian who, on four occasions, would approach him, yapping at him and snapping at him and pointing with a shaky, nicotiny hand to a signboard prohibiting visitors from giving any food to animals, birds or fish.

"It was almost as if this poor boy was waiting in actual anticipation of a carp rising up and hopping out of its liquid habitat, just as would a dolphin, to grab a crumb in mid-air. But no carp did hop out, a fact that cast a pall on his spirits.

"I finally thought to accost him, talking to him of his poignant but, from what I could work out, totally solitary passion for fish, carps in particular, which brought from him a frank admission that in his past, among many casual companions, his only bosom buddy, so to say, was Jonah his carp, which would swim up on his murmuring 'Jonah . . . Jonah . . .' or his whistling a complicitous fishy signal. Not a day would pass, so I was told, without his carp catching a crumb or two out of his hand, without Douglas,

148

if at all downcast, taking Jonah as his confidant – Jonah, who wouldn't fail to wink back at him amicably.

"Today, said Douglas, lost in his thoughts, too candid for his own good and, frankly, just a tiny bit crazy (but his almost suicidal mood was an obvious product of his affliction), it was his *naïf* conviction that a carp from this Jardin d'Acclimatation would swim up and (why not?) flick its tail at him in a cordial salutation. And so, with his last franc, your son had bought a pound of halva, a sticky concoction for which Jonah had always had a gluttonous passion, particularly so if it was, as now, royal halva, Shah's halva, as Iranians call it – of a quality found only in first-class shops, Fauchon in Paris and Fortnum & Mason in London.

"Brought low in my turn by his sorrowful mood, I stood him a drink and a ham sandwich in a local snack bar. Douglas was hungry all right: watching him gulp his food and wash it down with a Coca-Cola, I thought of a Muslim coming out of Ramadan, a Ramadan just a tad too long and drawn-out for comfort.

"Whilst sipping my cappuccino, I was told by your son all I was avid to know about his work, about his vocation, about you, Mr Clifford – oh pardon, I should say Augustus – and about Squaw . . ."

Augustus, his brow moist with anticipation, cut him off. "What did Haig say? Was my poor boy conscious of that curious taboo surrounding his birth?"

"I'm afraid so, old man. Unknown to you, as a child of six, Douglas – or Haig, as you call him – had caught you on a fatal morning in his childhood in that soothing, drowsy-making caldarium in which you lay flat out, cut off from all human contact, in your lustral bath, sinking into Nirvana, murmuring, only half-consciously, a rambling glossolalia so intriguing to a child's imagination that, approaching you, Douglas stuck his auditory organ against that harnass, or its clasp, that you'd put on to hold you in position, a clasp that, according to him, had a strong amplifying capacity . . ."

149

A groan from Augustus: "*Ah capisco! capisco!*"

"That's right, Augustus, now you know. You unwittingly told your son all about it. You told him about Zahir, about that mystical scab in his umbilical cord. And, his wrath against you brought to its boiling point, a wrath making him as strong and vicious and unforgiving as a lion – what am I saying? a wrath driving him almost out of his mind – it was Douglas who would pull his Zahir off your pinky!"

"So provoking that damnation that's pursuing us to this day!"

"Right again," said Anton Vowl. "Douglas, as I say, was six at most, but it had all sunk in. Cursing you with all his childish brio, from now on your son would rancorously hound you, rapturous to find you falling, to find things going badly for you, and in agony, by contrast, if your luck was starting to turn. His loathing of you was constant – nay, undying!"

"My God! Oh my God!" Augustus was now loudly sobbing, as if in convulsions, and twitchily crumpling a hanky in his hand.

"Your son's fulmination against you, bastard as Douglas is, British as Douglas was, is intact to this day. What your son did, all of it, including his vocation, was part of a monstrous plot thought up by him to bring about your doom!"

"His vocation?" said Augustus in an anxious murmur. "I'm afraid I don't follow . . ."

"Which is why," said Vowl chillingly, "I was in such a hurry to catch up with you."

From his black chamois-bound bag Vowl took a charcoal drawing, not unskilful in its way, of that *Uomo di Sasso*, clad in an oval plastron of pallid stucco, who would punish Don Juan not so much for having slain him as for going so far, committing an act so sick, as to ask him to lunch. Think, if you will, of a gigantic Humpty Dumpty.

On its back, in Douglas's handwriting, was a disturbing prognosis: "Augustus, too, is in for it at *my* apparition, for my blood is a blot on his honour!"

"This," said Anton Vowl, "is what Douglas would hand in at

150

my club four days ago. With it was a card announcing that your son was living in Urbino, singing you-know-who in *Don Giovanni* and planning to marry Olga Mavrokhordatos . . ."

I saw Augustus jump up, as if stung by a wasp.

"No! No!" was his cry. "Haig is hurtling to his own damnation!"

IV

OLGA
MAVROKHORDATOS

15

In which, untying a long string of fabrications and falsifications, you will find out at last what sank that imposing Titanic

"No! No!" was Augustus's cry, as I say. "Haig is hurtling to his own damnation!"

"*Abyssus abyssum invocat!*" was Anton Vowl's gloomy conclusion.

But as Olga, in a turmoil, is sobbing, almost fainting, Arthur Wilburg Savorgnan cuts short (as abruptly, in truth, as with a pair of scissors) Squaw's rich, insinuating narration.

"Ah, such trials and tribulations," says Savorgnan, "and no solution in sight. Douglas Haig 20 springs ago, Anton Vowl a month ago, and now Augustus – kaput, struck down by a cunning form of malignancy that's still prowling around us, a malignancy which also struck at (for why not? who knows?) Hassan Ibn Abbou, Othon Lippmann and that poor, unknown woman who brought Douglas into this world . . ."

"All our sons, saving only Yvon," sighs Amaury Conson.

"But," adds Savorgnan, "isn't it so that all of us now approach our goal? Can't all of us now grasp its principal factors? What Squaw has just told us, omitting nothing, not a word, not a fact – didn't it contain a prodigious opportunity for us to find a way out of this abomination that's pursuing us?"

"But Douglas didn't know my family background!" Olga abruptly affirms.

"Douglas didn't know it, that's right," says Squaw, continuing, "nor did you. But Augustus did know it and instantly saw how important it was:

Of Turkish origin, mainly from Istanbul, living in a palatial mansion giving out on Thanatogramma and Ailippopolis, this Mavrokhordatos family (or Mavrocordato or occasionally Maurocordato: its connotation, in a Balkan patois so unknown it's thought by Saussurian linguists to contain an occult anagrammatic capacity, is "clad in black armour" or "skilful in black magic"), this Mavrokhordatos family, I say, would initially furnish its nation's Sultan with a host of loyal icoglans (or vassals). Thus Stanislas Mavrokhordatos's job was shaving Suliman. Constantin was Ibrahim's doctor. Nicholas was a tardjouman (or dragoman, as is said nowadays) who, for his particular patron, Abdul-Aziz, would amass a million or so manuscripts, most bought at a discount and all glorifying Islam. And his son, Nicholas junior, was Hospodar of Banat. In fact, it was said that Abd-ul-Hamid would hold nothing back from him, for Nicholas had a truly amazing gift for linguistic obfuscation and would turn an innocuous communication into such hocus pocus that nobody could follow it, notwithstanding many signs proving that his calculations or translations had sprung from an old and aboriginal canon.

Nicholas, who took as his coat-of-arms a burning Sphinx, was his patron's right-hand man and had a vision of rising at court to a rank of Vizir or Mamamouchi. All too soon, though, Mahmoud III, furious at his Hospodar for usurping so much authority, and mortally afraid of his laying down his law as far as Stamboul, summarily got rid of him, whilst commanding his troops to round up Nicholas's family and submit it to mass crucifixion.

But, sustaining many hardships, that family of yours, Olga, would cunningly slip through Mahmoud's hands. Arriving at Durazzo, Augustin, your grandpapa from way, way back, all in from so much roaming about, thought it a good town in which to start up as a notary and was soon publishing a monthly journal notorious for promoting insubordination vis-à-vis his nation's Sultan. "Albanians," ran his most famous proclamation, "a victorious day will dawn! Kill all tyrants! Hold high a flag dripping with Ottoman blood! Plough your furrows in it! And march, march, march!"

Such agitation shook Durazzo to its foundations. Six oustachis lay slain. "Down with Turks!" or "Down with Islam!" – this cry was ubiquitous. Its flag was a gonfalon of whitish organdy with, on its right-hand canton, just that flaming Sphinx that Nicholas had had as his coat-of-arms. A national political party, Whiggish in inspiration but anarchistic in its vocation, got busy mobilising public opinion in its favour; and a man, Arthur Gordon, a distant cousin of Byron, so it was said (and, as Byron was, both British and a hunchback), would start galvanising an opposition to it, composing a National Hymn that was sung by anybody willing to stand up to a yataghan.

It took thirty-six months to rid Albania of its Ottoman monarchs: signing a pact at Corfu, it was to gain its autonomy at last. Instantly arguing with Cavour about submitting this budding nation to a quasi-tutorial form of authority, Victoria would appoint as Consul to Tirana Lord Vanish, a brilliant alumnus of Oxford for whom Richard Vassall-Fox, third Lord Holland, was an unofficial sponsor, introducing him at court and fully supporting him in his nomination. This Lord Vanish slyly sold Augustin Mavrokhordatos, who had nothing but admiration for Victoria, an official British policy of a colonial or half-colonial status as most apt for Albania, worn out by Turkish domination and totally unfit for "automancipation"; adding that it was thus important to allow Britain to act quickly, whilst holding out, to any local political faction suspicious of its assuming a quasi-dictatorial authority, a possibility of participating in its civil administration, and so gradually making Albania a dominion. But it all had to go quickly, for, if not, it was obvious that Abyssinia or

Austro-Hungary or untrustworthy Italy would jump at such an opportunity. Won round by Vanish's sophistry, Augustin put into action a fairly crafty plot. British gold would flow into Albania. Collaborationists would occupy crucial positions. Third columnists would go foraging for information, or frankly digging for dirt, in bistros and poolhalls. A plan of attack of an astonishing sophistication was drawn up. But, with just two days to go to D-Day, with a battalion of hussars loyal to Britain languishing in an army camp in Brindisi, awaiting a signal announcing a total invasion, *manu militari*, of Albanian national soil, Augustin was caught out as a conspirator. A slip-up? A partisan talking off-guard? A turncoat changing his mind? Or a traitor, a Judas, informing on his companions-at-arms for thirty coins? Who knows? It was all so long ago. What I can say, though, is that it was to prompt an unholy commotion, for nobody in this world is as chauvinistic as an Albanian. Furious crowds brought thirty-six public officials to a kangaroo trial, found all thirty-six guilty, rightly or wrongly, of participating in Augustin's coup, and strung all thirty-six up on a gigantic scaffold.

As for Augustin, it would finish badly for him: first, a tanning from a cat-o'-9-tails; following this, two days stuck in a pillory, with half of Tirana's population cursing him, mocking him, hurling rotting fruit at him and urinating on him; now an iron clamp was put around his throat; his skin was cut up in a thousand ways; a gag was stuck into his mouth right down to his larynx; finally, surviving asphyxiation, immolation and dowsing with alcohol, his body was put alight.

Thanks (although "thanks" is hardly an apt word for so atrocious a plight) to his outstandingly robust constitution, Augustin took about a month to succumb. His carcass was thrown to a pack of wild dogs; but by that point it was so putrid no animal would touch it.

In Durazzo, things would go almost as badly for all 26 survivors of Augustin's family. A hunt was on, with rabid nationalists out for its blood, looting its mansion on four hair-raising

occasions, gang-raping Augustin's poor old granny and mass-
acring his sobbing infants.

It took such fanatics just six months to track down and kill all
but a solitary Mavrokhordatos, a Mavrokhordatos, though, so
significant to Albania as a living symbol of his family's past insubordination that his antagonists would go so far as to award a
million hrivnas to his captor. For this survivor was a first fruit
of Augustin's own vigorous loins: his son Albin (ironically, naming his son so patriotically was Augustin's own wish!).

Miraculously, though, Albin got out of Tirana by night and,
hiding out in a thick, dark, almost fairy-story wood, would languish in it for all of six springs and six autumns, a half-moribund
survivor, stoking up his loathing for that Albanian tyrant who
had slain his family but also, possibly primarily, for that British
aristocrat who, to his way of thinking, had drawn his poor papa
into a fatal trap.

But a day was to dawn on which, in a forlorn marabout, its
only, and occasional, visitor a farm boy with four mangy goats,
Albin dug up a stash of diamonds, gold doubloons and ingots.
And, in an unwitting imitation of Mathias Sandorf, using this
colossal capital to obtain satisfaction from his family's assassin,
Augustin's son would round up a gang of outlaws, which was
lavishly paid, as much as fifty-fifty a job, so that its loyalty to him
was total.

For his principal lair a rocky fjord was found that his gang
would punningly call "Fillbag Fjord", as Fra Diavolo, a Franciscan bandit who would hold up landaus and mail wagons and
fill his voluminous bags with booty, had had occasion to pass a
night or two on its banks.

Initiating a conscript into his gang, Albin first brought him to
his fjord, commanding him to drink six straight vodkas in a row.
Having drunk his fill, this conscript took an oath on a crucifix,
promising to do Albin's bidding right up to his final hour in this
world. At which point Albin would tattoo on his right wrist –
with a scratchy gold nib that would imprint a narrow whitish

striation along a man's skin, not drawing blood but so sharp that no amount of chafing could rub it out – an occult symbol that, as it turns out, an Albanian cop got a look at during a raid, although his drawing of it was so clumsy that nobody could work it out. It was in fact circular in form with a dash running horizontally across it; or, putting it simply, it wasn't dissimilar to that signpost stopping cars from going along a particular road.

On occasion an outlaw was caught; and his captors had no doubt at all, notwithstanding that our Albanian cop's drawing was fuzzy and indistinct, that a curious whitish symbol on his wrist was proof of his links with Augustin's diabolic son. In six springs, though, a trio of his companions, at most, was caught in this way, whilst Albin had around thirty outlaws, on and off, at his disposal!

His cohorts would mainly attack official visitors from Britain. That nation's consul in Tirana saw his mansion blown up again and again, and any yacht flying a Union Jack in Durazzo harbour ran a risk of rotting in it for good.

As for Cunard's famous Titanic, if it sank – or, should I say, *was* sunk – it was on account, not of any ghastly glacial collision by night, but (and this is no myth but a fact I'm willing to vouch for) of Albin's misdoing, for on board ship, discussing a possibility of constructing a gigantic rolling mill in a suburb of Tirana, was an important Anglo-Albanian consortium with capital from Barclays Bank.

A busy train colliding with a coach, in Quintinshill, a town not far from Hamilton, halfway from Huntingdon to Oakham, on 6 August 1918, was proof for Scotland Yard (which instantly got into a panic) that Albin could actually, if such was his fancy, attack his rival within his own country. But it was not known at first that his motivation in carrying out such acts was just for a bit of fun, or, in his own words, "for a holiday", as, for all his banditry, it was his custom to insist on a month off in six, going to Britain, a country that was an abomination to him, for its rain – soft, drizzly rain that was soothing to his unhappy soul.

160

His action finally driving his British antagonists out of Albania, in 1919 Albin would turn on his compatriots, making raids on shops and banks; but, in a country still without any form of industrialisation, his pickings would usually amount to a handful of scrawny, hungry lambs for which nobody would pay a ransom. His capital was dramatically low and his day-to-day bankroll was now starting to contract.

Not far from Fillbag Fjord, though, was a canyon in which . would grow in profusion a strain of poppy found only in Albania. Noting it instantly, and rightly too, as an opportunity for making colossal profits, Albin found out from a compliant pharmacist how to turn it into laudanum and, by fumigating that, would obtain a satisfying form of opium.

Now, as anybody who knows will inform you, opium isn't worth a brass farthing if you can't control its distribution. And though such a circuit of distribution was in position, starting from Ankara, going on, Balkanwards, via Kotor, Dubrovnik or Split, to Rimini, and from Rimini to Milan, a major crossroads for all this flourishing traffic, it was a multinational or possibly supranational organisation (consisting of thirty "big shots" who would appoint its Mafia, its Cosa Nostra, including Lucky Luciano, Jack "Dancing Kid" Diamond, Big Italy, Bunny "Gunfight" Salvatori and so on, plus six minor affiliations of various rankings) which had total control of it.

Albin, who was no fool, saw how stupid it was to try and horn in on such a tightly knit association; and, with all his usual cunning and daring, took a risk on finding his own dumping ground, contacting an unsavoury individual who ran a carnival stall in Milan and who was, so rumour had it, a small fish in that big Mafia pond, and proposing his opium to him at a discount.

Six months passing in this fashion, and his traffic growing almost daily, Albin thought it important to appoint in Durazzo an assistant to run transportation liaison, with opium arriving from Fillbag Fjord by car, moving to Chiogga on a dinghy and Milan on a Po canal boat.

161

So, in Tirana, Albin got to know a man of whom much was said (notwithstanding that his total rascality was a byword among Albania's criminal class) of his unfailing loyalty, tact, intuition, imagination and lightning-quick wits. This man was (and if you holding this book in your hands don't know by now, all I can say is you ought to), this man was, I say, our old chum Othon Lippmann!

Augustus got it all instantly: that Olga's papa – Olga, whom his son Haig was hoping and actually planning to marry – was a crony of his own old antagonist, a crony who, in addition, had an animosity, a rancorous loathing, towards anything British!

"But if so," Anton Vowl had to know, "who was Olga's mama?"

16

Which will furnish a probationary boost to a not always almighty dollar ($)

Ah (said Augustus, continuing his narration), it took fully 12 months for us to find that out.

It would so turn out that, whilst amassing a tidy sum from a traffic in opium that was now running without any major hiccoughs, and whilst living it up in his fjord as sumptuously as d'Annunzio in his *palazzo*, information was brought him that a famous Hollywood star, Anastasia, was shooting a film in his vicinity. Albin, thus, who was still looking for an opportunity of attacking his British rival, and who had an almost irrational loathing of *all* Anglo-Saxons, including Yanks, laid plans for a punitory raid on a barbican in which Paramount, Anastasia's studio, had thought to pitch its main camp.

In a blind fury Albin took a shotgun, a bazooka, napalm, TNT and as many rounds of ammunition as it was practical to carry; and with a salivating bulldog as his own guard, and six of his companions in tow, of a sort that you'd want with you in a tight spot, grimly struck out to satisfy his thirst for Anglo-Saxon blood.

On his arrival night was falling, a blazing spring night, with a hot day slowly fading into dusk.

What Albin saw first was that Paramount had built a trio of small studios, facing north, on a mountain (in fact, on its foothills), that its production staff was bivouacking not far from a local tarn and that its cast was living in six gigantic caravans – four to a caravan, saving Anastasia, who wasn't sharing with any supporting actor. Noticing a flurry of activity in a studio – with nobody too minor to muck in, from a stuntman to a storyboard artist, from a continuity girl to a grip, all proposing fanciful solutions to a tricky shot that just wouldn't work, consisting as it did of a group of four walk-on actors who, for want of room, had to stand so far back that only two at most would stay continually in focus – Albin told his gang to put a torch to it, to ravish and kill anybody found in it, man, woman and child, and to bring it all crashing down, whilst, on his own, approaching a caravan, a particularly luxurious caravan with a star on its door, obviously that in which Anastasia was dozing.

Slinking into a snug and inviting boudoir, with a romantic aura about it making it a fitting spot for an amorous tryst, Albin saw, in profusion and confusion, low divans, soft, furry rugs and mirrors all of a dull opacity, as a sign not of sanctimony but of sophistication. Its air was rich with a lascivious aroma and a lamp was giving off a faint, soporific glow.

Albin took a turn around this intoxicating room, and, noticing a thick canopy of rich, grainy damask, hid within it. An instant was to pass, with Albin imbibing, and almost swooning from, a fragrant odour that was wafting all about him.

And at last – Anastasia. What an apparition! Slipping off a kimono of whitish organdy with black polka dots, slowly, tantalisingly, unfurling, from waist to foot, a pair of clinging, cavity-hugging black tarlatan tights, Hollywood's First Lady, now with nothing on at all but a chunky gold ring with a ruby stud, languidly slunk down across an ottoman (a sofa, not a Turk), giving out, whilst doing so, a profound sigh of physical satisfaction – not so much a sigh, in fact, as a purr.

For a long instant Albin stood stock still, this ravishing panorama totally transfixing him, its sinuous undulation inspiring part of his own torso, at first against his will, to start curving outward and upward.

As for Anastasia's drowsy body, now clad only in its birthday suit, with skin of a milky purity, glossy and glowing, it was all

164

unwittingly displaying its charms to him, a chiaroscuro tattooing its voluptuous forms with a shadowy striation.

Almost foaming at his mouth, his body brimming with lust, Albin burst forth from out of hiding, crying, "Oh, Anastasia, I am but a pincushion for Cupid's arrows!"

Instantly, in a flash of inspiration, adapting Solomon's Song of Songs, Albin thought up an impromptu hymn to glorify Anastasia's luminous and numinous physical form:

Thy body is a glorious yacht aboard which I will sail to distant lands, a sloop, a brig rolling and pitching, tossing as I do turn upon it,

Thy brow is a fort against which I will launch an attack, a bastion, a rampart which my amorous transports, unruly as a north wind, will bring tumbling down, a triumphal arch through which it is I who will march in triumph,

Thy soft auditory conch, a spiral, a convolvulus, a morning glory abounding in twists and turns about which I so look forward to losing my way,

Thy lash, a vibration of a wink and twinkling of a blink,

Thy mouth, an atoll of crimson coral into which, willingly risking, all but asking for, suffocation, I will swim down, down, down,

Thy throat, a pallid prison, a paragon of a caparison, a tight collar for my strangulation,

Thy arm, a guard, a hoist, a staff of passion, a loop of a lasso with which to corral my carnality,

Thy hand, an animal with four digits and a thumb, a sampan and a skiff, a dory and a catamaran, floating, tacking, drifting at random on my languorous body and on thy own,

Thy back, a coast, an alluvial plain, a salt marsh, a smooth couch, a rolling vista, an arc curving with bliss's sting and spur,

   Thy skin, O thy skin, a chamois soft as swan's-down without which I cannot go on living, a downy buff upon which I will go to my tomb writing that holy word "Anastasic"

   Thy flank, a rippling rill, an inconstant link in thy carnal chain, a bodily boundary which I will accost first of all, a primary port of call for that cockboat sailing forth from its harbour in my lap,

   Thy tummy-button, a kaolin always out-of-joint, a tiny jug which I will fill up with my loving libations,

   Thy loins, a coat-of-arms of an unknown armorial, a dark, humid umbilicus, a door which I will unlock with my tumid rod,

   Thy buttocks, two round and rosy apricots, a plump pod, a fruit containing a pip worth shaking out,

   Thy bush, thy Burning Bush which I must know how to confront, as did Christ, with valour and without timidity, thy bush, holy pubis, tufts of passion, soft pinions, soft piping, soft quills, soft fair hairs, as of a stork or a flamingo, Shangri-la of physical and spiritual ardour,

   Thy furrow, thy lotus furrow, furrow of oblivion, along which all but my passion will vanish, which will swallow up all but my lust, thy furrow of Nirvana, thy moist furrow in which I will pass along, pass out and pass away, into which I will go, born, ailing, dying, again and again, of a human, all too human, bliss,

   Thy bud, in which all will pass away, thy bud, that final bastion in which I will confront my own total absorption, my own abolition, my own annihilation, in that passion that will last for always, in that last spasm that you and I will know all too soon, our souls singing in total unison, in bliss or oblivion, in that night that is a void, that instant of infinity in which you and I will turn into an animal with two backs!

Thus sang Albin who, now baring his own body, hastily casting off all his clothing, sprang, gluttonously, as if starving, as if dying of thirst, on top of Anastasia.

"What!" said an indignant Anton Vowl. "It was against Anastasia's will!" (But, you know, Vowl was still a callow youth, in his first flush of manhood, who, in addition, had grown up in a puritanical Catholic family, had had his first communion and his confirmation and had, on occasion, thought of joining a Franciscan community.)

"Oh no," said Augustus, smiling, "hardly that."

For, in fact, Anastasia, looking up at him, instantly took a fancy to this charming rascal, willingly giving in to him and, whilst Albin was slowly broaching *ad limina apostolorum*, murmuring:

"Ohhh – I long had an itch for a brigand, a bandit, an outlaw!"

Was Albin still in hiding from his country's cops?

"You can say that again," said Albin.

"A substantial sum, I fancy, for bringing you into custody?"

"And how!" said Albin.

"How much?"

"A million hrivnas."

"How much is that in dollars?"

As a dollar was worth about thirty-two hrivnas, Albin briskly ran up a rough calculation, taking inflation into account, and said, just a bit boastfully, "Thirty-six thousand."

"That *is* a lot," said an admiring Anastasia, who, succumbing to his approach, winking at him flirtatiously if not actually salaciously, was to add, murmuring as if in a swoon: "Now go to it, my Don Juan, my Casanova, my Valmont, my Lothario!"

It was as if Virginia Mayo was succumbing to Richard Widmark, Rita Hayworth to Frank Sinatra, Joan Crawford to Cary Grant, Kim Novak to Kirk Douglas, Gina Lollobrigida to Randolph Scott, Anna Magnani to Marlon Brando, Liz Taylor to Richard Burton, or Ingrid Thulin to Omar Sharif.

Was Anastasia, though, truthful to Albin or simply trotting out an old Hollywood film script, word for word?

Why ask? With such wanton tickling, cuddling, fondling, licking and kissing going on, it was hard to think of as lubricious a mating, as *galant* a coupling, as libidinal a mutual loving.

But whilst a goatishly rutting Albin was ravishing Anastasia just as (if you know your classical mythology) Apollo had had his way with Iris, Adonis with Calypso, and Antinous with Aurora, his gang, complying with his wish, was attacking that studio adjoining Anastasia's caravan, blowing it sky-high with a ton of TNT, illuminating a pitch-dark night with its conflagration and making an almighty Doomsday din. It was a sort of Walpurgisnacht. Its poor occupants, working hard at adjusting a shot or simply hanging about, as you do in film studios, ran this way and that, shouting and howling in panic. Most got it instantly, struck by a burning plank, by a scorching whirlwind, by a boiling rock torn out of its soil, by a spray of stinging-hot, skin-riddling coals, or by a smoking brand whooshing up as if from out of a volcano.

Notwithstanding all that was going on about him, notwithstanding his gang's act of criminal arson and its nightmarishly grisly impact on a group of Hollywood artists on location, nothing could distract Albin from a form of amatory arson that was just as hot if, naturally, not as homicidal.

So it was that, whilst his troop of outlaws, faithfully carrying out his instructions, was riding back to its fjord, with an inward glow of satisfaction at a job brought off without a hitch, Albin was still billing and cooing, still spooning and smooching, in pursuit of his passion.

It would last four days, all in all. At which point, it would abruptly occur to Anastasia, shying back from Albin's lips and warding off his warm, clinging arms, that, to fulfil a contract drawn up by Paramount (which was paying its most popular star a cool fifty thousand dollars) and William Morris (which would naturally want its customary 10%), it was vital to finish shooting its forthcoming film.

Alas, it was all an illusion! Not a survivor, in production or cast! As for Paramount's filmic apparatus – totally kaput! Not a Nagra, not a truck! A Paillard? Fit only for a junkyard! A pair of sound booms? Nothing but a stack of scrap iron, twisting innards, burnt-out casings, piping hot piping! A Dolly? It was now, in its way, a work of art, a work of art by an avant-gardist sculptor, a David Smith, say, drawing his inspiration from Naum Gabo or Baldaccini!

Anastasia was thus out of a job, and was so distraught that Albin, who was not a confrontational sort of chap and didn't know how to go about consoling anybody in such a situation, simply took off, abandoning, you might almost say marooning, his inamorata, first saying, though, with an intimidating frown:

"God willing, it may not occur, but if a baby *is* born to us, a fruit of our loins, a product of our passion, you must call it Albin," adding, "for, if not, I, Albin Mavrokhordatos, last of my clan, will pass away – and my Damnation will pass away too!"

17

In which you will know what Vladimir Ilich thought of Hollywood

So Albin took off, and would find out, from a postcard arriving at his fjord, that Anastasia had got as far as Cattaro in Italy, instantly making contact with an ambassador from Washington. But, having caught 'flu during what was by all accounts a long and arduous trip, our star's right lung was now ailing from catarrhal inflammation.

On studying a thick batch of X-rays, a local consultant finally said that Anastasia would pull through only by giving up film-making for good and all. In truth, notwithstanding "Actors Studio" histrionics and faintly Stanislavskian tics, it was now common gossip in Hollywood that Anastasia probably hadn't much affinity with sound-film acting. (All of this was occurring round about 1928 and it took a solitary film, an "all talking, all singing, all dancing" musical with Al Jolson, for Fox, MGM, Columbia and Anastasia's own studio, Paramount, instantly to opt for this most radical transformation in film history.)

Thus Anastasia, a vamp who had got Farouk to slim down and Baudouin to plump up, a vamp who had had Taft sighing, Wilson crying and Ramsay MacDonald lying, a vamp for whom Winston Churchill had bought a gigantic box of Havana cigars and of whom, in a radio broadcast from Moscow, Vladimir Ilich Ulianov had said no opium was as fatally noxious, brought to its abrupt conclusion a filmography so uniformly brilliant, so fantastically lustrous, it was absurd that it should finish in this way. Six Oscars! Four *Lions d'or*! Ah, *sic transit Gloria Mundi*!

It was a traumatic shock for thousands of film buffs. A fan club in Iron Mountain, in Wisconsin, not far from Michigan, took poison to a man, a young Kabuki actor in Tokyo would commit ritual hara-kiri in Anastasia's honour and a Jamaican sailor took it into his mind to jump off Radio City Music Hall, in midtown Manhattan.

Anastasia was to languish for six months in a sanatorium in Davos. Rumour has it that Thomas Mann, catching sight of this still ravishing wraith of a woman strolling about its grounds, said, "If only I'd known Anastasia whilst writing my *Magic Mountain* . . . What a companion for Hans Castorp! How pallid Clawdia Chauchat is by comparison!"

Finally Anastasia would go into labour but, by now fatally ill with TB, would pass away in childbirth, saying, in a last painful gasp, "You must call my baby Olga . . . Olga Mavrokhordatos . . . To Olga I assign a substantial patrimony . . . all of what I own, but for a donation of fifty thousand dollars to this sanatorium and its administration . . . And you, for your part, must contract to bring up my only child until . . . until its majority . . ."

Thus Olga would grow up in Davos, knowing nothing of Albin, in a chic sanatorium with only counts and viscounts, maharajahs and maharanis, lordships and ladyships, for company . . .

Anton Vowl cut in. "But what about Albin?"

"It was in 1931 that Albin found out that Olga was living at Davos; and, avid to contact this unknown offspring of his, took off in a flash, forcing Othon Lippmann, who was now his right-hand man, to follow him. Though it had to zigzag through lots of mountainous twists and turns, Albin had his Bugatti bowling along flat out, full blast . . . but actually didn't turn up at Davos."

"Why not?" said a dumbstruck Anton.

"I was told by Othon that, at about two-thirds of his way to Davos, not far from Innsbrück, Albin, virtually abandoning him, told him to stay put in his Bugatti, informing him of his own obligation to call on a man in that vicinity. Spying on Albin, watching him go into a vacant-looking hangar, Othon hung about all day and, that night, paid a visit to it in his turn . . . and found nobody in it but Albin, who was lying, all but bathing, in his own blood, now fit only as food for worms."

"Ho hum," said Anton with a sardonic grin. "A bit of a tall story, if you want my opinion."

"That's just what I said. In fact, I'd put my bottom dollar on it that it was Othon who'd slain him for his loot."

"But did Othon go on to Davos to join up with Olga?"

"Natch. And no doubt with a kidnapping job bubbling in his mind. A kidnapping from a sanatorium – that was typical of such a villain! Othon did in fact talk to its administration, but had no luck with Olga. In fact, a strong hint was thrown out that his 'rights' in this affair had no basis in Swiss law and that any insisting or importuning on his part would land him in jail – without passing Go, as *Monopoly* would put it."

"And so," said Vowl, summing up, "Olga still didn't know what this 'Mavrokhordatos affair' was all about?"

A sigh from Augustus.

"That's right. What's important to grasp, though, is that nobody at all was conscious that a form of Damnation was clinging to that family and always would do. Olga was to grow up without having an inkling of what an infamous and horrifying jinx it was."

On Othon finally giving up his own malignant ghost (and naturally told by him of this ghastly Law that clung to our family and sworn at by him for unwittingly allowing my Zahir to vanish), I would go to Davos in my turn, on four occasions, hoping to do away with Olga by my own hand, as an act of human charity. But, by now, Olga was too old to go on living in a sanatorium. An informant told of a woman conforming to Olga's physiognomy living in Locarno. I took a train to Locarno. A phony alarm! I was told, again, that Olga had flown off to London to buy a flat in Mayfair. So I instantly got going, my train arriving

172

at Victoria Station just as Olga's was pulling out, bound for Frankfurt. I rang up a diplomat in Frankfurt to whom I was known, asking him to shadow Olga until my arrival. But, ironically, my diplomat pal, an idiot whom I had thrown out of his job as quickly as you could say 'Jack Robinson', saw fit to stamp Olga's passport with a visa for Stockholm, in which city, worn out, I simply quit looking.

"And that," said Augustus in conclusion, "is why I said Haig hadn't got it. My poor son thought, with all his oaths and insults, to damn his papa. But, in wishing to marry Olga, it's actually Haig who's going towards that Damnation, not I, it's Haig who's sinking fast into that machination that is afoot all around us! Now, his first night is on . . . ?"

"Monday," said Anton Vowl, consulting an almanac.

"Four days . . ." said Augustus doubtfully. "Still, I think my Hispano-Suiza is up to it. But only by starting now, this instant. To Urbino! You and I must draw my son back from that void that's yawning insidiously on his horizon! So hurry up! Put a sock in it! Chop chop! *Andiamo!*"

18

For which many will no doubt claim that it adds much that is crucial to our story

"All right, all right," said Anton with conviction. "You and I will go to Urbino, driving all day and all night, you driving whilst I catch forty winks, and so on. But I think it important to put our trip off for a day or so, till tomorrow morning, say, for our first priority is to find out what Douglas was clumsily trying to say by 'a blank inscription on a billiard board'."

"But why, for crying out loud? What has my billiard board got to do with all of this?" said Augustus, who was itching to start off.

"It was, was it not, in your billiard room that that Damnation now stalking your son was born. And a crucial point subsists in this affair, a point on which, to this day, nobody has any information. You know that Douglas took your Zahir, right?"

"Right."

"What you don't know is what Douglas did with it!"

"But you . . . that inscription . . ." said Augustus, blanching.

"You may think I'm crazy, but that inscription will finally inform us — such, I should add, is my wish, not a fact — why such a Damnation clings to your Zahir."

"But who's going to work it all out?"

"I am!" said Vowl triumphantly. "Long ago I got Douglas to draw a rough diagram and I'd study it for hours and hours at a sitting, only stopping to consult with a famous cryptologist in Paris. Today, if I can hardly claim to know what it's all about, I'm willing to say that I harbour a suspicion or two that ought to furnish us with a solution, total or partial – or, at worst, iron out most of its complications."

"Okay, you win."

So, grudgingly going along with him, Augustus took Vowl into his billiard room.

Approaching Augustus's billiard board, running his hand along its inscription and applying a magnifying glass to it, Vowl took stock of its rash of curious whitish dots.

"Aha," said Vowl at last in a murmur, "I was right. It's a Katoun."

"A Katoun?"

"Katoun, or Katun – a noun indicating a scrap of graffiti common to various Mayan civilisations, principally that in Yucatan. It's a fairly basic *modus significandi*, particularly practical in transcribing sayings, myths, almanacs, liturgical writings and inscriptions found on tombs or on triumphal archways.

"It consists mostly of odd bits of information (invariably spanning a rigorous chronology of thirty springs), information about months, lunar months, canicular days, royal birthdays, migrations, cardinal points and so on. On occasion, though, you'll find, not a book, but, say, a tiny chunk of narration surpassing its strict transitivity and actually aspiring to what you and I might think of as an artistic quality . . ."

"So, knowing that it's a Katoun, you can automatically work out its signification?" said Augustus, who was dying to find a solution.

"Good Lord, no," said Vowl, smiling, "our work is cut out for us – till tomorrow morning, anyhow." (It was now approaching midnight.) "Its signification will only show up – *if it shows up at all* – as soon as I can fathom by what path of action, by what cryptological algorithm, I can transform it from a subscript (which is to say, this inscription as it now stands) via a transcript into a final translation.

"But what I must first try to grasp is what kind of axiomatisation such a transcription is bound up in. For, you know," said

175

Vowl, smoothly going on, "most of its complications will spring from this plain fact: that you and I cannot, obligatorily, work it all out. Today, at most, I can grasp, oh, about a fifth of it – and, by dawn tomorrow, you'll know, giving or taking a word, only as much as a third."

"All right, but do you think, notwithstanding so major an unknown factor, that you can unlock what signal it holds for us?"

"Why not? Cryptology is not a myth. It's not a form of witch-craft. Think of Champollion or of Laranda, Arago, Alcala, Riga, Riccoboni, von Schönthan and Wright. In truth, a signification will show up, but, I must say to you, distantly, in a slightly cloudy futurity, in a slightly vacillating cloud. I'll grasp it by association.

"Actually, I would count on a trio of distinct strata of clarifi-cations:

"First, you and I look at it casually and think of it as just confusing poppycock, foolish mumbo jumbo – noticing, though, that, as a signal, it's obviously not random or chaotic, that it's an affirmation of sorts, a product of a codifying authority, submit-ting to a public that's willing to admit it. It's a social tool assuring communication, promulgating it without any violation, accord-ing it its canon, its law, its rights.

"Who knows what it is? A bylaw? A Koran? A court summons? A bailiff's logbook? A contract for purchasing land? An invitation to a birthday party? A poll tax form? A work of fiction? A crucial fact is that, my work advancing, what I'll find rising in priority isn't its initial point of application but its ongoing articulation for, if you think of it, communication (I might almost say 'com-munion') is ubiquitous, a signal coursing from this individual to that, from so-and-so to such-and-such, a two-way traffic in an idiom of transitivity or narrativity, fiction or imagination, affabul-ation or approbation, saga or song.

"Thus, first of all, is Logos and its primacy, that talking 'it' of our inscription: putting it baldly, you and I know that it's talking to us but still don't know what it's saying. Now, assuming that it's a fictional work, or part of a fictional work, what I must look for is a group of banal, common, familiar signs surrounding it, by which I can start assuming, unambiguously, that a work of fiction is in fact what it is: a handful of individuals in conflict, in confrontation with a curious sort of fatality, imagining, right up to its last paragraph, that this fatality is actually a fortuity, a product of nothing but downright bad luck. An individual is slain, now two, now four, and now all six, with a haunting strand of plot working its way through a mosaic of motifs so confusing that you and I can't possibly summon up a vision of its totality from A to Z, its organic unity, so confusing that our wish to find a significant sign in it is simply an illusion.

"But, gradually, with our starting to grasp that a law is structuring its composition, this initial confusion of ours will turn to admiration – admiration at how, with such a niggardly grammatical, syntactical and punctuational construction, with a vocabulary cut down to a minimum by so many constraints of scission, omission and approximation, such an inscription can still contain so much information.

"Dumbstruck by this amazing capacity that it has – whilst outwardly avoiding a signification which it knows is taboo – to affirm it anyway, articulating it by a cunning bias, shouting it out as if from a rooftop, formulating it by association, by allusion, by saturation – dumbstruck, as I say, you and I, although still not totally grasping at this point what it's saying to us, can at last boast of proving its validity as a signal, as a communication.

"From which point it's but a hop, skip and a jump to grasping why so much was built on so rigorous a constraint, so tyrannical a curb. It was born out of a mad and morbid whim: that of wholly satisfying a fascination with linguistic gratuity, with proscription and subtraction, that of avoiding any word striking its author as too obvious, too arrogant or too common, of according its *signifiant* just a gap, a slit, a loop, so narrow, so slim and so sharp, that you instantly grasp its justification.

"Thus, as though by transmuting a quality into its contrary, from omission is born affirmation, from constraint is born autonomy, from obscurity is born light!"

"I would applaud your diagnosis," said Augustus, "if I had any faith in its conclusion. But now you must hurry. My watch is ticking away, night is falling fast, and from Azincourt to Urbino it's about 28 Indian kadams, which is to say, 8 nagis or 18 kuppoduturams!"

"I know," Vowl said simply. "Don't worry, I'll go to it, plunging up to my waist into all this murky arcana."

At first, though, Vowl said to yours truly, "Squaw, go into Augustus's atrium. In my bag you'll find a stack of six books. Bring it to us, will you, it's vital for our work."

So I did as I was told and brought Vowl back his stack of books. It was an amazing anthology of all things Mayan: a translation of Popol-Vuh by Villacorta-Rodas, R. P. Sahagun's transcription, in its totality, of Machu-Pichu and, most particularly, a trio of Chilam-Balam – Ixil, Oaxaca and Uaxactun.

Transcribing it took right until dawn. His armpits growing moist and malodorous, Vowl soon had his cardigan off and was busy working in his shirt, whilst, to cool him down, I'd bring him, variously, a glass of Chardonnay, a tomato sandwich, a cappuccino and a whisky-and-soda. I would pick my way through a mass of rough drafts and scorings-out, which Vowl, chain-smoking, sucking cigar upon cigar, coughing fit to bust his guts, spitting up saliva and pulling his hair out, had thrown away in dissatisfaction.

It was painfully slow going. Vowl would blow his top, coming out with disgusting cuss-words, boiling, almost frothing, with irritation at his own stupidity, gnashing his fangs in fury, turning a bright crimson colour and on occasion murmuring a word so inaudibly I just couldn't catch what it was, an odd sort of mantra that was said again and again, monotonously. It was all a bit alarming – *and* a load of codswallop, in my opinion.

But, finally, at cockcrow:

"Ouf!" said a hot and sticky Vowl, obviously worn out but glowing with satisfaction and giving Augustus (who had to put on a lorgnon to study it) a scrap of cardboard with 25 curious graffiti on it, adding, "I thought for an instant I wasn't going to crack it."

"What do you know," said Augustus cursorily glancing at it, "it's just as baffling as it was to start with!"

"Oh, do calm down, will you," said Vowl. "You'll grasp it in just an instant. Look, Katouns usually draw from a pool of six local patois. In this particular inscription it's a Chiapas patois, known as 'Lacandon', which, so tradition has it, was brought into play mostly in soothsaying Katouns. Its transcription is known, but not its pronunciation, for, as a morphology fit only for anticipation, divulgation or vaticination, it's invariably full of ambiguous locutions and syntactical shortcuts of a kind that only clairvoyants or shamans can unlock . . ."

Augustus anxiously cut in.

"But if that's . . . What will you . . . ?"

"I'm coming to that, Augustus, so just shut up, will you. I know of a handful of ad hoc solutions that will assist us:

"Its complication arising principally from its 'a-vocal' quality as a jargon (that's to say, it's a jargon with no history of vocalisation), and thus from an implicit contradiction with any notion of pronunciation, by choosing, in imitation of that which I do know:

Ba va sa ka ma sar pa ta par da
Bi vi si ki mi sir pi ti pir di
Bo vo so ko mo sor po to por do . . .

a matrix simulating transcription, I think that I can, by logic, intuition or imagination, polish up my original rough draft."

Vowl instantly got busy, chalking up his 25 signs on a blackboard and coming up with this:

Ja Gra Va Sa La Dâ La Ma Tâñ
A Ma Va Jaŝ ’A Ta Krat’ Dâ
La Pa Sa Ya Ra Da Ra Cha

This didn't calm Augustus, who couldn't fathom a word of it and who said in a fury, "For all I know, it's in Afrikaans or Sanskrit. What I do know, though, is that it isn't in any way stimulating my imagination!"

But, trying to mollify him, Vowl told him that his goal was at last in sight and that by noon Augustus could count on having a translation of his Katoun.

Chasing us both out of our own billiard room, Vowl also said that nobody should disturb him now, at any cost, for four hours or so. So, whilst Augustus got busy polishing his Hispano-Suiza, oiling it, filling it up with gas, fixing it up for its forthcoming dash down to Urbino, I was hard at work rustling up a filling lunch for all of us.

And Anton Vowl was as good as his word, surfacing punctually at midday and approaching Augustus with a scrap of cardboard in his hand.

"You want to know what that blank signal on a billiard board is all about? Voilà."

"Oh, you talk us through it," said Augustus, subsiding into a sort of ghastly languor. "I'm in a total funk about it all."

Thinking of that instant now, I call to mind a sky that was luridly clouding up, a horizon that was almost totally in shadow, a build-up of alarming nimbostratus, as if a storm was about to burst, and a gust of wind abruptly rising, smashing a fanlight window and causing us all to jump.

I think I said, if inaudibly, "Oh, God, I'm so afraid," and I saw that Augustus was mumbling, stumbling, possibly praying.

At which point Augustus and I finally, and *in toto*, got to know that inscription that was so damning to us. Vowl's articulation was horribly icy and cutting, chopping up what was said into small hard chunks of information and talking so distinctly I almost thought Vowl wasn't talking at all but spitting a host of razor-sharp darts at poor Augustus – darts that would sting him and prick him, drill him and nail him down, that, in short, would crucify him.

It was all long, long ago, my hair is now gray and straggly, but his words still haunt my soul:

I POLISH MY LAW ON A CLIFF,
IMPRINTING "AN I FOR AN I"
IN A ROCK'S TRITURATION

An instant – an instant as long as an infinity – was to pass. Nobody said anything. A gigantic wasp was buzzing around that scrap of cardboard that Vowl was brandishing.

"Now do you know what it's all about?" said Vowl softly.

"Actually," said Augustus just as softly, "what it calls to mind is *Arthur Gordon Pym*. In particular, its closing paragraph."

"I must say I hadn't thought of it," said Vowl, "but I'd go along with that."

"And my principal misgiving in this affair," Augustus would go on, "is that this inscription, too, is bristling with bad luck."

"But can any of us do anything about it?"

"That's what I found so alarming. What I saw in this 'rock's trituration' was a mould of stucco which, on Monday, my poor son will wrap about his body. Thus will this Law of 'an I for an I' kill him! Can't you grasp it – Haig is lost as soon as Karl Böhm, his conductor, pours him into that monstrous dicky. That's why you and I must fly to Urbino, arriving at its *palazzo* by Monday night!"

So, with Vowl in tow, Augustus quickly got into his Hispano-Suiza and took off in a flash.

Alas, as you know, notwithstanding Augustus's driving night and day, without pausing for a snack, or a drink, or forty winks, his throbbing brow practically stuck to his car's front window, such

181

was his fixation on arriving in Urbino by dusk, it was all in vain. Bad luck was to dog his path in a trio of small towns. At Aillant-sur-Thonon six cogs would jam, blocking up a joint; at Isonzo his dynamo would burn out, ruining an accumulation circuit; and, to cap it all, at San Laranda, his ignition was to grow so hot it would actually fall apart in his hands!

Arriving at Urbino's ducal *palazzo*, and told that Haig had put on what you might call his iron, or stucco, lung, Augustus's plan was to go to his son's changing room and instantly cut him out of it; but a doorman wouldn't allow him in and sat him down on a foldaway chair in a back row upstairs. (It was standing room only.) Augustus had to stay put on that chair throughout *Don Giovanni*, downcast, sobbing, oblivious of Mozart's ravishing music.

Finally, a spotlight would focus on Haig, transforming him into a pallid, marmorial monolith of light. Ah! but you all know what was to occur at that fatal instant: Augustus's son would stub his foot, trip up and fall . . . and his mould would split from top to bottom . . .

"No!" Olga has coldly cut in. "A fact is missing from your account, an important, a vital fact. You told us of Douglas's doom just as Augustus told us of it on his arrival at Azincourt, whilst transporting his son in a shroud.

"But, in informing you, Augustus was to omit a crucial point. Was it from a lack of information? Or a psychological blackout? Or did Augustus act unwittingly, assuming such a load of guilt for his conduct as to wish to block it at all costs from his conscious mind? I couldn't say. But Anton Vowl also saw Douglas's apparition, Vowl saw it all and got it all!"

"But saw what . . . ? got what . . . ? if not that Haig lost his footing, falling down as hard as a baobab cut in half?" asks Squaw, who may truly want to know or is simply trying to show Olga up.

Olga laughs harshly, unsmilingly. "Saw that Augustus, worn

out by his long trip down through Italy, full of misgivings and hardly in command of his own actions – Augustus, as I say, watching Douglas, abruptly stood up, giving out such a loud, fortissimo cry that it brought about his son's collision with a column and his final fatal fall!"

19

On running a risk by asking for a fish farci

"My God!" Squaw shouts out, visibly aghast at such an accusation and instantly going into attack against Olga.

"Who told you such a foul bit of dirt? It was a mishap, I know it. Blood will out! It's natural that you, a Mavrokhordatos, should spout such filth! Why, it was your papa who put a jinx on us all! All of us, facing damnation from your family!"

"Oh, do stop your squawking, Squaw!" says Olga. "It's just shock that's making you blurt out such stupid things."

But, stubbornly continuing, Squaw adds with a sly, shifty grin, "So why was it Augustus who had to cry out? Who knows if it wasn't you? That's right, how do I know – how do any of us know – it wasn't your cry that was so loud and sharp as to kill poor Haig? Couldn't you too claim a similarity with a protagonist in *Don Giovanni*? And didn't you too go to Urbino to watch it?"

"You know, Squaw has a point," sighs Savorgnan. "Anybody at all, Augustus as much as Olga, Anton Vowl as much as a woman, say, sitting in front of him, had an opportunity of throwing Douglas off his guard with an untoward cry, thus provoking that tragic fall of his. So how do you know, Olga, that it was in fact Augustus who did it?"

"I was told all about it by Anton Vowl," says Olga calmly. "Vowl saw it occur. And, talking about it, Vowl would actually claim to know by intuition that, in that stucco mantrap of his, Douglas was such a startling, such a disturbing, apparition that, as though in imitation of a dying lion or an albatross brought down and slain by a drunk sailor, Augustus was bound to cry out. As soon as Douglas was spotlit, Vowl saw Augustus turn livid, his lips shaking; actually saw a roar forming in his throat. Vowl's plan was to jump up and try to stop him from airing it, but Augustus's cry would halt him in his tracks, for it was a truly inhuman cry, a cry of Astaroth, of a Sphinx flapping its wings on a clifftop, a *grido indiavolato* roaring up from his lungs. Douglas lost his footing, collapsing as though struck down by a tumultuous gust of wind. And all that confusion and commotion that was naturally to follow, all that hubbub and din, would drown out Augustus's initial cry."

I, too, said Olga (continuing this dramatic account) would almost pass away as Douglas did. I was watching it all . . . As I saw him fall, a long furrow zigzagging across his mould, I sank swooning into a profound coma. I was put on a couch, on which I lay, practically dying, for six days. At which point a doctor brought to my nostrils a product with a strong odour of ammonia. Finally coming to, I found Vowl sitting in my room, clasping my hand in his. And it was by him that I was told, bit by bit, in dribs and drabs, what was going on. Having snuck into a local hospital, in which his son was laid out, Augustus took his body away without obtaining any authority to do so. I just *had* to go to Azincourt.

"No," I was told by Vowl, "you, too, can claim no authority in this sordid affair. Augustus would kill you as quickly and as unthinkingly as a wild animal, a jaguar, say – Augustus would kill anybody of your family, for it is, in his opinion, a Mavrokhordatos who was his son's assassin!"

So I was told all about my family, all about that Damnation with which its history is bound up. But, instantly contradicting him, I said with a sob in my throat:

"It was Augustus who brought about his son's doom by giving out such a horrifying cry. Thus will I now carry out that Dam-

185

nation that I carry within my soul, for it was that man's fault, and only his fault, that I am now a widow!"

For six springs, Anton would constantly tag along, faithfully following in my trail. I didn't ask him to. I didn't want him to. What I did want, in fact, was to catch a train to Azincourt and kill Augustus by my own hand. But I was starting to find that Anton had a curious aura about him – a sort of charisma, you might say. I found I simply couldn't do without his kindly disposition and his unfailing affability. I was about to lay down my arms, capitulating unambiguously to his natural gift for consolation. I found him awfully amusing and found, too, in his company, that I wasn't now thinking so much of Douglas's charms or, I must admit, of his killing. If, as would occasionally occur, I was in a sorrowful mood, Anton always had a comforting word. And if I abruptly had that old craving to do away with Augustus, Anton would know just how to calm my ardour.

I had quit my vocation for good: I wouldn't sing for anybody. All that capital (substantial capital, too) that I'd got from Anastasia had grown annually, by compound accumulation, into a bank account that would allow as gracious and luxurious a living as anybody could wish for. Nor was Anton in what you might call financial straits: as with a Larbaud, or should I say a Barnabooth, his capital was almost without limit, hinging as it did, so rumour had it, on a mining supply that just wouldn't dry up, so profound was it, containing zinc, strontium, platinum and cobalt.

Anton and I took lots of trips. With him I was to know how oddly wistful is cruising on a transatlantic ship, how chillingly cold it is to camp out at night, how fascinating to stand in front of an unknown vista, how afflicting to cut short a visit that's only just starting . . .

At long last, during a ball, and whilst I was indulging my passion for mazurkas, Anton was to admit to a passion of his own. I took him in my arms, giving way, informing him that I too had a soft spot for him. I'd had a handful of ungainly suitors, but Anton was a courtly kind of swain, gallant and good-looking, making his play with charm and assiduity, buying diamonds for my hand, diamonds for my wrist, a sparkling diamond collar for my throat, all vying for my approval, and, at lunch, invariably choosing such pricy tidbits as Scotch woodcock, *ortolans farcis* and Iranian caviar . . .

"Was that black or gray caviar?" asks Amaury, with his almost pathological fixation on food.

"Oh, can't you think about anything but your stomach, you big fat glutton!" a furious Savorgnan shouts at him.

Olga, continuing, anxiously scrunching a hanky up in a ball, looks about to burst into sobs.

"I had Anton's staff, a maid, a groom and so forth, at my disposal. Mornings, in my boudoir, I'd find a mountain of mimosas or orchids which Anton would grow in tropical conditions – this was in mid-March – and instantly forward to my Paris flat by air."

As our liaison was growing strong, though, as Douglas was gradually turning into a fond but fading ghost from my past, as, far from him, far from Urbino, far from Azincourt and Augustus, I was starting to blossom into an ordinary happy young woman, as if, having known so much crying and sobbing, an Atlantic of sobbing, I was finally coming into port, into dry dock, Anton was, by contrast, growing proportionally downcast. I had no notion why this was so, but, day by day, I found his conduct most alarming – his constant, nail-biting agitation, as if falling victim to an unknown pain or malignancy, his constantly grimacing and also, curiously, his constantly touching with his hand a talisman bound around his right foot by an invisibly slim gold cord. Chancing to catch sight of it – it was an ugly thing, clumsy-looking, inartistic, a bit puny, calling to mind nothing so much as a scrap of typography, a shaving off a compositor's floor – I

187

was avid to know why Anton thought that such an unsightly brooch (if that's what in fact it was) might bring him luck. But my darling abruptly lost his cool, boiling up with a fury that was as stormy as it was without foundation, shouting foul, scathing insults and unjust accusations and, as I thought, spoiling for a fight. I ran away.

For four days I had no word from him – until, on a warm autumn night, I was brought up short by a soft tapping at my door and, in an instant, with nary a hint of an apology, I saw him approaching and smiling but also saying things that I found profoundly disturbing.

"It was just six autumns ago today," said Anton, "that you and I took off on our world tour, roaming around this country and that, visiting all sorts of famous landmarks, from St Paul's in London to Agra's Taj Mahal. Now your mourning of Douglas is past, it's had its day. You hardly think of your loathing for Augustus. So what I say to you is that you must go to Azincourt with a word of consolation for him. Having lost his son, allow Augustus to gain an in-law!"

Controlling an instinct to cry, I said, "Augustus isn't important – I totally wash my hands of him – but for you, Anton, my passion grows daily. It's thanks to you, my darling, that I got my sanity back. If you abandon your Olga now, I think I'll go crazy again!"

"No," said Anton, coldly oblivious of my supplication. "It's only at Azincourt that you can go on living calmly and happily, in harmony with your soul. As for yours truly, I must go away, far from this city and, in particular, far from you. For that Damnation that struck Haig is now on my trail!"

"But why?"

"I'm just coming to that. Augustus was Haig's kin only by adoption – on a tramp's instructions, a tramp known as Tryphiodorus. Douglas didn't know who his natural papa was; nor, in fact, did Augustus. But I found out about six months ago, totally haphazardly, that – wait for it! – it was actually Tryphiodorus!"

"But what's that got to do with you?" I said, dumbstruck.

"This! I also found out, within four days of that information, by a card which a man, I don't know who, was to slip into my tux whilst I was at a nightclub in Albi watching Lolita Van Paraboom – you know, that star of Paul Raymond's shows in Soho – I found out, I say, that just as dark a shadow was cast on my own origins as on Haig's. I had always thought that I was a son of an Irish tycoon, who, dying of a coronary on my fifth birthday, had a tutor control my upbringing, a tutor who, a bit of a Catholic bigot, thought nothing of simply packing his ward off to a Franciscan school for his indoctrination. Not a bit of it – my natural papa, I was told, was also known as Tryphiodorus!"

"What!!!"

"That's what I said!"

"But . . . but if what you say is so . . . !!!"

"Uh huh. You got it. Douglas was my sibling!"

Half-choking, Amaury Conson can hardly say a word.

"What? Douglas was Anton's sibling? What do you know about that! It's . . . it's a gag!"

"You don't think Anton was having you on?" Squaw asks.

But Savorgnan, showing no sign of this story surprising him, says "Shhhh . . ." adding, "Shut up, all of you, and allow Olga to finish. And if I don't look too aghast, it's simply that I'm afraid, I'm much afraid, that, from now until nightfall, I'm going to find out many things just as astonishing, many facts just as confusing, and many plot points just as paradoxical."

So it all starts again, notwithstanding that Olga's public, as you might call it, lying flat out on a sofa, or lolling back in an arm-chair, would occasionally almost nod off, for this discussion, which had got going that morning, was proving long and tiring. In addition, it was hard to work out what its implication was, though nobody had any doubt at all that, at worst, chock-full of action, rising and falling, twisting and turning, it would follow an old, old tradition, that of fiction not fact.

Now (says Olga), if this fact, that Anton was a sibling of Douglas, was disturbing, if it was, to put it mildly, simply astonishing, still, it didn't imply, ipso facto, that it was any kind of nail in Anton's coffin. I had to ask what was prompting my inamorato to abandon his Olga, and all Anton could talk about was of living in constant panic of that Damnation that struck down his sibling striking him down in his turn.

"Douglas was slain," was how Anton put it, "and now it's my turn. If that law of 'an I for an I' that I found on Augustus's billiard board at Azincourt contains any truth, if, similarly, I should put any faith in your papa's abomination of us all – your papa, Albin, a man with a gift not only for loathing humanity but for acting on his misanthropy – if all of that is fact and not fancy, my only option is to abandon you, to fly as far away from you as I possibly can, splitting that chain of passion, that chain of mutual fascination, uniting us."

"But, my darling, I didn't draw poor Douglas to his doom! It was Augustus's cry, not my hand, that struck him down!"

"No!" said Anton. "As soon as Douglas got into that stucco mould of his, his Damnation was all but automatic. You can't say that any of us sought his doom. Douglas was simply a victim of that law that's punishing us all. Augustus, though, will guard you from harm; as for yours truly, an old hand at this sort of conundrum, I plan to go just as far as I can, to try and work out to my own satisfaction what's going on, what's causing this shadowy malignancy to cling to our family!"

So saying, softly kissing my hand, trying to calm a loud fit of sobs that was shaking my bosom and again advising my instant withdrawal to Azincourt, Anton took flight.

Anton would join a firm of solicitors in Aubusson, but nothing was to run smoothly for him. I don't know why it was so, but I found out that it took him just four months to pack it in and start practising common law at Issoudin. So from Issoudin to Ornans; luckily, I got to know a fact or two about his situation in that town. Anton would scoot about in a BMW, with lots of local girls swooning in admiration for him. In his bag was a thick manuscript consisting, it was said, of an important monograph on a tricky point of grammar, a monograph that Anton was working on and was about to finish. Nobody found him anything but gracious and civil, most particularly during a local symposium on Lhomond in which Anton took a major part, giving a stimulating talk on grammatical subjunctivity. But his, how shall I put it, his romantic companion was a tart working in a shop that sold various goods for sadomasochists; and, following criticism at court for a confusing affidavit, Anton had to quit Ornans for good.

I soon got a postcard saying that Anton was working at Ursins and (from what I could work out) living in lodgings. I took down an atlas and saw that this Ursins was a small, charming country town not too far from Oyonnax (Jura). Finally, I found out that Anton was living at Yvazoulay, just a tiny dot on a map, also not far from Ursins, and about which nothing was known. That, alas, was all of 20 springs ago – 20 springs without knowing in which town my darling was living, without knowing if Anton was living at all or . . . or not . . .

"Voilà," says Olga, summing up. "For my own part, bowing to Anton's ultimatum, I caught a train for Azincourt. Augustus, who was at first against unlocking his doors to a Mavrokhordatos, was in fact adamant about it, did finally back down and admit his son's consort.

"And so now you know my story, from start to finish . . ."

"It's almost nightfall," says Squaw, sounding all in. "I'm thirsty and I'm hungry – all of you, too, I don't doubt. And Jonah in particular – poor Jonah hasn't had its rations now for four days.

191

If you don't want to kill it by starvation, you must nourish it now – instantly."

"Squaw is right," says Olga. "Our first priority is food for Jonah."

It's a mild, almost sultry night that's just about to fall. A soft wind blows, rocking a tall acacia and swaying its fronds. Olga, Savorgnan, Squaw and Amaury all look down into Jonah's pool, whistling a song, that song that usually had Haig's carp swimming up in a flash, and crying out: "Jonah! Jonah!"

No Jonah.

"Now that's what I call abnormal," Squaw murmurs anxiously, "not to say a tiny bit alarming. Jonah's had 20 springs, as Olga would say, to adapt to us, to distinguish our vocal chords and to put its childhood companion – I'm alluding, naturally, to Haig – out of its mind."

Soon a torchlit hunt is on for Jonah, probing its pool, dragging it with toils and catching six goldfish, an anchovy, a turbot, a tuna fish and about thirty minnows.

And at last Jonah turns up – or should I say, Jonah's carcass. Poor Haig's baby carp had grown. It was about a yard long, if not a full fathom, its whitish crop scintillating in a pallid halo of torchlight.

Oh God, what a chilling sight! Oh what profound sorrow! Olga knows, almost by instinct, that Albin's damnation is still intact! What a black horizon looming up! Oh what a fatal sign! What a malignant warning!

Wiping away a drop of salty liquid that is dripping from his chin, Amaury talks wistfully of his liking for Jonah, that charming, cordial carp that would swim up out of its pool as if about to hum its song in unison with you. And Savorgnan is just as sad about it, and Olga, and Squaw. With Jonas's passing away, it's almost as if Azincourt is going to pass away soon, for it was a living symbol of Augustus's mansion.

192

Savorgnan puts forward an initially startling proposal: to swallow Jonah, thus according it, as Papuan Indians do, and as a last salutation to an animal inspiring such loving, to a fish inspiring such adulation, to a carp inspiring such adoration, a form of transubstantiation.

This proposal is put to a show of hands and wins, so to say, hands down.

"Stuff it," Squaw says abruptly.

"What th . . . !!!" says Savorgnan, aghast at such incivility.

"No, no," says Squaw, calming him, "it isn't what you think. What I'm proposing is that you stuff Jonah," adding, "You know, I had a pal in San Francisco, Abraham Baruch. Now, notwithstanding that, as his family had a loathing of circumcision, his . . . his thing, you know, was still intact, Abraham, practising his faith almost as much by whim as by conviction, had had his Bar Mitzvah as a boy and would always visit his rabbi on Shabuoth, Purim, Hanukkah, Sukkoth, Yom Kippur and Rosh Hashanah – a good pal was this Abraham, from whom I got to know a cunning art, that of making Gäfilt-Fisch."

So, whilst Olga soaks Jonah in a sink, trying to wash out that awful sour flavour typical of carps brought up in captivity, Squaw starts dicing a pound of Spanish onions to boil in a pot along with a light potpourri of garlic, tarragon, paprika, cumin and saffron, sprinkling it all with salt, mustard and just a hint of basil, mashing into it a sprout or two, lupin, rutabaga, asparagus and lots of juicy stock, finally blanching it, marinating it, trussing it and sifting it out.

Taking a small carving ax, Olga puts Jonah on a chopping board and splits it in two with a solitary blow, abruptly giving out a horrifying cry.

Amaury, Savorgnan and Squaw rush forward to find out what's going on. With a haggard look, Olga points at Augustus's chopping board – on it, intact, still fascinating, brought out of Jonah's stomach, glows that original Zahir!

Haig, it was now obvious, had, so long ago, out of a childish passion for his carp, got Jonah to swallow that Zahir that Augustus had worn on his pinky.

Quaking, mumbling inaudibly, frantically tugging a strand of hair with a shaking hand, a hand now almost crimson from Jonah's blood, lurching forward without any prior warning, Olga falls – and falls hard!

Taking Olga's limp body in his arms, Amaury cautiously lifts it up and lays it out on a couch, shouting wildly, "Olga's back is out of joint – call a doctor and, if you can't find a doctor, call a pharmacist and, if you can't find a pharmacist, call – oh, I don't know – call a Boy Scout – call anybody at all – anybody who can apply a cataplasm or a splint, a transfusion or a suturation, an ablation or an adduction!"

But it's all in vain.

Olga now starts raving. Loud palpitations . . . a gradual clouding of vision . . . a croaking lung giving out a sibilant whistling rasp . . . and a final spasm coinciding with a wish, an almost fanatical craving, to say a last dying word. An astonishing sound bursts forth and spurts forth, finishing in a gargling snort.

"What? What is it?" asks Amaury.

Now, crouching down on all fours, Amaury positions his auditory organ against Olga's lips, as a Huron or a Mohican would apply his to a railway track to find out if a train was rumbling far off.

Straining at first to grunt out a word, a word that for Amaury is nothing but an indistinct grunt, Olga abruptly falls back, as limp as a rag.

Vanity, all is vanity! So it is that Olga mounts that upward path to God's Holy City, uniting for all infinity with Douglas, with Augustus and with Jonah.

"Did you grasp anything at all of what Olga was struggling to say to us in that last gasp?" Savorgnan asks Amaury.

"I got a word, I think, but only a word, and a word, I must

admit, that I couldn't work out at all: Maldiction! Maldiction! Maldiction! At which point Olga's articulation was so faint, so fatally pianissimo, it brought all communication to a full stop."

20

Which, notwithstanding two paragraphs full of brio
and inspiration, will draw to an ominous conclusion

"Maldiction?" asks Squaw dubiously.

"Now that isn't too hard to grasp," Savorgnan instantly affirms.

"Oh, you think so?" says Amaury.

"I don't think so, I know so. For my part, I'd say that it all has to do with a malign trauma, a tumour, a condition, anyhow, blanking out Olga's vocal chords, thus implying a constriction or an inflammation inhibiting or, at worst, actually prohibiting any possibility of diction – so 'Maldiction'."

"Hmm . . ." says Amaury, who hasn't got that at all. "But why, at so crucial an instant, opt for such an ambiguous word?"

"Why? To inform us that, during that last ghastly gasp, a frightful constraint was muzzling, was actually strangulating, Olga: a thirst for a Taboo that could only find satisfaction in a fit of frustration, a fit, if you wish, of incapacity, harping on as it did, as it had to do, again and again, ad infinitum (not attaining a point of saturation but always in a limbo of dissatisfaction, which is to say, always conscious that any full and final form of illumination is blinking at us, winking at us, just out of our sight, just out of our grasp) – harping on, I say, at this solitary Malignancy, a Malignancy assailing all of us, a Malignancy proving a cross that all of us must carry, that Malignancy of which Haig was a victim, its first victim, but which also did for Anton Vowl, Hassan Ibn Abbou, Augustus and now Olga, a Malignancy causing us agony primarily by dint of our chronic inability to call it anything, to put a word to it, our chronic inability to do anything but sail around it, again and again, without any of us knowing how, or on which spot, to alight upon it, circumnavigating its coast, magnifying its jurisdiction, its attribution, constantly having to confront its total, global authority, without for an instant hoping that, out of that Taboo that it's imposing on us, a word might abruptly light up, a noun, a *sound*, which, saying to us, 'This is your Mortality, this your Damnation', would also say, word for word, that this Damnation *has* a limit and thus a possibility of Salvation.

"Alas, this insidious circuit to which I'm alluding has no Salvation. I thought, as did all of you, that Anton or Augustus was slain trying in vain to grasp what this horror was that had struck him down. No, not at all! Anton was slain, Augustus was slain, for not managing to grasp it, for not howling out a tiny, insignificant sound that would, for good and all, bring to an abrupt conclusion this Saga in which all of us must play our part. It is, I say to you, by our saying nothing, by our playing dumb, that this Law of 'an I for an I' that's pursuing us today is still so strong, so invincibly strong. Nobody's willing to talk about it, to put a word to it, so causing us all to fall victim to a form of damnation of which nothing is known. What awaits us all is a fatality from which no man or woman in this room has any sort of immunity, a fatality which will carry us off in our turn without our knowing why any of us is dying, for, up against this Taboo, going round and round it without coming out and simply naming it (which is in fact a wholly vain ambition, for, if it actually was said, if it actually got into print, it would abolish this narration in which all of us, as I say, play our part, abolish, notably, a curious anomaly distinguishing it from outwardly similar narrations), nobody among us will talk about this Law that controls us, forcing us to wallow in our own prostration, forcing us, at last, to pass away still ignorant of that Conundrum that sustains its propagation . . ."

"I am talking for all of us, I know," nods Amaury in approval, "if I say that your brilliant diagnosis of our plight has had an

197

impact – I fancy a lasting impact – on us. But so many circuitous paths! For a start, how could any of us know that that vanishing man, that dying Anton Vowl, dying by his own hand, possibly, or still living but in hiding – who can say? – would afflict us in so frightful a fashion? But though I now know, as you do, that this Law holds against us that which all of us do, that which all of us say, that not any word of ours is what you might call fortuitous, for it instantly and invariably has its own justification, and thus its own signification, I can't stop thinking that I'm in a sort of *roman à tiroirs*, a thick, Gothic work of fiction with lots of plot twists and a Russian doll construction, such as Mathurin's *Monk*, Jan Potocki's *Manuscript Found at Saragossa* and just about any story by Hoffmann or Balzac (Balzac, that is, prior to Vautrin, Goriot, Pons or Rastignac) – a work in which an author's imagination, functioning without limits and without strain, an author, mind you, making a mighty poor living by today's standards, having to cough up a thousand words an hour for virtually instant publication, churning out paragraph upon paragraph, writing his daily ration of incongruous scribblings till it's coming out of his nostrils – a work, as I say, in which an author's imagination runs so wild, in which his writing is so stylistically outlandish, his plotting so absurd, of an inspiration so capricious and inconstant, so gratuitous and instinctual, you'd think his brain was going soft!"

"That's right," says Savorgnan in his turn. "Now you might say, 'Why, that's all just a paradox!', but I, for my own part, was so struck by its accuracy that I would actually put it forward as not a paradox but a paradigm, a matrix, if you wish, for all works of fiction of today. To intuit an imagination without limits, an imagination aspiring to infinity, adding (or possibly subtracting) to (or from) its quasi-cosmic ambition a crucial factor, an astoundingly innovatory kind of linguistic originality running through it from start to finish, as a word, 'Brighton', say, might run through a stick of rock, what you imply is that such a work of fiction could not allow a solitary lazy or random or fortuitous word, no approximation, no padding and no nodding; that, contrarily, its author has rigorously to sift all his words – I say, *all*, from nouns down to lowly conjunctions – as if totally bound by a rigid, cast-iron law!"

"Thus," murmurs Amaury, waxing almost lyrical, "oblivious of this inhibition that's thinning out our capacity to talk, is born Imagination – as a chain of many, of so uncountably many, links; and thus too is born Inspiration, born out of a twisting path that all of us must follow if any of us is to ink in, to stain with black, if only for an instant, and with a solitary word, any word at all, our own Manuscript's immaculation!"

Squaw, finding it a bit alarming that Amaury should hold forth in such an abstract fashion, abruptly says, "Now just hold on! I pity you, Amaury. How can you talk about books and such with Olga's body still warm!"

"Oh, God, you must think I'm a callous lout, Squaw! I'm sorry, so awfully sorry," says Amaury, blushing with mortification.

"It's this room that's doing it," says Savorgnan, looking around him in mild agitation. "It's got a sort of morbid quality, don't you think? Is anybody for moving out?"

"No," says Squaw, "you can't go. Think – Aloysius Swann is now on his way to Azincourt and his contribution will assist us all in working out just what's going on. And if, as I think, Aloysius took his car, you can count on his turning up by nightfall. My proposal is that you wait for his arrival whilst dining, for, what with all our discussions, nobody's had anything all day to put in his stomach."

What Squaw cooks is suitably light and frugal, for, although naturally hungry, Savorgnan's low spirits won't allow him to think of gorging on what is laid out in front of him. Amaury is similarly downcast, simply picking at his food, nibbling it without any of his usual gusto.

"I know how hard it is for you to stop thinking of poor Olga," says Squaw at last, "but I insist that you both try this first-class gorgonzola, a gorgonzola of which Augustus was so fond, I occasionally had to go out at night to buy it from our local dairy if our supply had run out . . ."

But nobody lays a hand on Augustus's gorgonzola, or on Squaw's cold roast ham or *chaussons farcis à la Chantilly*.

As Savorgnan complains of an aching brow, as if his brain had a thick lining of cotton wool, Squaw starts making him an infusion and has him swallow an aspirin. At which point, lying down on a couch, Savorgnan tactfully asks if Amaury wouldn't mind slipping out, informing him of his wish to catch forty winks.

Amaury, for his part, avid to find out if, at Azincourt, a copy or a manuscript or a rough draft isn't lying around, anything that might furnish additional information, ransacks Augustus's library, unloading boxfuls of books and spilling out in disarray hardbacks and softbacks, works of fact and works of fiction, biography and autobiography.

His scrutiny proving all in vain, Amaury finally thinks of taking a turn around Azincourt's lush grounds. It's a starry, scintillating night, not too hot, not too cold – in fact, just right. Amaury lights up a long, luxuriously aromatic cigar, a Havana found whilst casually rummaging in Augustus's smoking room, and idly strolls about, along this pathway and that, inhaling a lungful of virginal night air that adds a faint whiff of opopanax to his cigar.

Who would think – who, truly, would think – that in such a halcyon spot, in such a park, with all its occupants, its plants as much as its animals and birds, living in total, natural harmony, so many atrocious killings could occur? Who would think to find damnation lurking in such an Arcadia?

Far off, an owl hoots. Without his knowing why, but probably through a chain of unconscious associations, this owl, Pallas's bird, so it's said, calls to his mind a book from long, long ago, no doubt from his youth, a work of fiction that also had an allusion to a park in which Damnation would triumph, a public park that it would finally claim as its own.

But, goddammit, what book was it? In his mind, its infiltrator was at last thrust out, with no kindly Good Samaritan rushing to assist him, and his carcass thrown into a gaping pit.

Amaury sits for about a half-hour in a mossy arbour, not far from that tall acacia with its swaying fronds producing a dull but continuous sound, a murmur soft and low, a humming sigh that's both sibilant and soporific.

His inability to grasp just what it is that insidiously links a book out of his past with his situation now is driving him crazy. Was it in fact a work of fiction? And didn't Anton Vowl claim long ago that a work of fiction would contain a solution to his plight? An amorphous mass of books and authors bombards his brain. *Moby Dick*? Malcolm Lowry? Van Vogt's *Saga of Non-A*? Or that work by Roubaud that Gallimard brought out, with a logo, so to say, of a 3 as shown in a mirror? Aragon's *Blanc ou l'Oubli*? *Un Grand Cri Vain*? *La Disparition*? Or Adair's translation of it?

Amaury starts, conscious of a chill night wind.

Standing up, taking a last puff on his cigar and idly throwing away its butt, a tiny glow-worm that wanly lights up Azincourt for a passing instant, Amaury, abruptly struck, during just that instant, by a *frisson* of unfamiliarity with his surroundings (no swaying acacia in sight, no stony path to assist him in finding his way back, but a soft plush lawn), fumblingly lights a match (but its spark burns out too soon to do much good), consults his watch (which says 11.40 but, alas, isn't ticking as it should) and, now a bit jumpy, with palpitations causing a slight pain in his ribs, starts cursing.

Groping blindly, Amaury walks forward, not only bumping into a wall but also falling into a shallow pit (in which, as is instantly obvious to him, Augustus caught all that morning damp with which Squaw would fill his lustral baths) and, totally lost, stumbling into a clump of shrubs that has a strong aroma of blackcurrant commingling with that, as strong if hardly as fragrant, of thuja, shrubs that scratch his arms in his frantic strivings to stop a rash of thorns from snagging his clothing.

Just as Amaury, in a now almost paranoid condition, is starting to think of its park as a sadistic labyrinth laid out as it is to imprison him, Augustus's mansion at last looms mistily up. It's pitch-black, with not a light burning in any window, on any floor at all, so that it has an oddly forlorn, almost ghostly look about it, as though not housing a living soul.

"Now, now, nothing at all to worry about. Probably just a short-circuit," murmurs Amaury, groping along a dark corridor until finally arriving in a small drawing room and lying down on a divan, shaking, worn out, numb with shock.

Not a sound around him.

An alarm, faint at first but soon disturbingly loud, starts ringing in Amaury's brain. "What's going on? What's Savorgnan up to? And Squaw? And Aloysius Swann – didn't Squaw say Swann would turn up tonight?"

A wholly irrational panic now grips him by his throat, causing a wild, stabbing pain in his back and making his brow go hot and cold in turn.

A moan. "I know – I know – it's food poisoning! It was that ham I had tonight – or Augustus's bloody gorgonzola – it was off. I thought it was a bit gamy – I thought it had a funny, rancid odour – only I didn't want to say anything to Squaw!"

Whilst rushing into Augustus's bathroom to look in its first-aid kit for a cordial or a syrup, anything to bring on instant vomiting, a suspicion abruptly assails him: what if a drop of poison was put in his whisky?

"Now that I think of it, it had a flavour of . . . a flavour of . . . oh God, I just know it was burnt almonds! It's my turn! Why, naturally, that's it! I'm going to . . . it's going to . . ."

If Amaury is mumbling and bumbling and crying out in this awful fashion, it is, alas, simply for want of knowing against whom or what to bring an accusation.

Such is his anguish, his mind is continually at risk of sinking into a coma. But, dragging his limp body forward with a strain that's almost inhuman, gasping, choking, sobbing, sobbing as an infant might sob, and cursing his long, stubborn opposition to submitting his body to mithridatisation, as his chums constantly told him to do, Amaury finally crawls out again into a dark corridor.

Is this it? Is this his last gasp? A fortissimo No!!! – that is his oath. By hook or by crook, by drinking gallons of milk or by taking an antibiotic, Amaury still trusts in his own survival. And in a flash it occurs to him that, upstairs, in a boxroom adjoining a studio that Augustus had put at Savorgnan's disposal, is a flask of Homatropini hydrobromidum

$$H_3C - CH - CH_3$$
$$N - CH_3 \; CHO-CO-CHOH-C_6H_5, \; BrH$$
$$H_3C - CH - CH_3$$

that will pull him through this crisis.

So, still groping, still in pain, grimly clinging to its rail, Amaury climbs, rung by rung, that dark and narrow stairway that spirals up to Azincourt's top floor . . .

V

AMAURY CONSON

21

In which, following a pithy summary of our plot so far,
a fourth fatality will occur, that of a man who has had
a significant part to play in this book

Around midnight, having brought Ottavio Ottaviani along for
moral support, Aloysius Swann finally draws up at Azincourt.
Having, that morning, quit his commissariat, Faubourg Saint-
Martin (which has a vault containing all official information
involving Anton Vowl and his vanishing act), and driving his
Ford Mustang as quickly as Fangio, as Stirling Moss, Jim Clark
or Brabham, Swann was hoping to park it in front of Augustus's
mansion by dusk. But it was almost as if a playful hobgoblin was
trying to bar his path with what you might call avatars (*avatars*,
naturally, signifying *mishaps* or, in fiction, *plot twists* [viz. Bloch
and Wartburg, Dauzat and Thomas], for no Hindu communicant
with Vishnu would think of applying to a man as pragmatic as
Swann notions as holy as incarnation, transformation and transubstantiation). On as many as six occasions his car was to stall,
forcing poor Ottaviani to labour long and arduously to put things
right again, that labour consisting in his scrutinising it in its
totality, point by point, from its chassis to its piston, from its
hood to its transmission.

On top of which, it would skid into a ditch, a ditch that, luckily
for both, was fairly shallow.

And, to cap that, it had collisions with, in turn, a chick (which
was crossing a road, but don't ask why), a cat, a puppy with
short, frizzy hair and a soulful look and, worst of all, a child of

six, a casualty that would prompt such a scandal that for an instant Swann was afraid of a lynching party.

"Ouf!" says Ottaviani, whilst Swann pulls to a halt in a billow of hot air. "Azincourt at last! And not an hour too soon!"

"For my own part," says his companion, looking around dubiously, "I can't stop thinking it's possibly a bit too tardy. Look – not a glint of light on any floor. It all looks so dark, as if totally vacant."

"Now now," says Ottaviani, assuring his boss, "it's just that nobody's up and about, that's all."

"Rubbish! What an odd hour to turn in! I told Savorgnan I was on my way – was it too much to ask him to stay up for my arrival?"

"Knock anyway, why don't you," says Ottaviani, trying to stay cool.

Swann raps his fist hard on Augustus's front door and waits . . . and waits . . . and waits. But nobody unlocks it.

"I told you so. Not a living soul," says Swann, blanching in horror; but, almost instantly taking that back, and squinting ambiguously at his companion, adds, "No, I was wrong. Living in this mansion is a solitary individual, but an individual, in my opinion, as dozy and as drunk as a Polack."

Obviously unfamiliar with Swann's allusion, Ottaviani says, "Don't panic now"; and, applying all his physical might to a thick partition in front of him, forcing a bolt in its clamp and, with his stick, a stick with a razor-sharp point, shoving Augustus's door, and in particular its flap, as far back as its doorstop will allow, finally wins through.

"That's that! Why don't you and I just go in?" says a triumphant if slightly jumpy Ottaviani, who starts cautiously inching forward, whilst a quailing Swann, still visibly in a condition of shock, timorously follows him. Abruptly, though, Squaw looms up, carrying a small oil-lamp that glows with a dim and dusky half-light.

"So wasn't I right?" says Ottaviani to his boss. "It was

unworthy of you to flip your lid as you did! Good old faithful Squaw!"

"Hallo," says Squaw, not putting much warmth into it. "You know, I had to hang about for you two all night!"

"You don't sound in high spirits, Squaw," says Swann. "What's up?"

"Augustus cashing in his chips, that's what's up!"

"But I know all about that!"

"Uh huh, but Olga too!"

Ottaviani's jaw drops. "Olga!!"

"That's right, Olga, and not only Olga but Jonah!!"

"Jonah too!" shouts Ottaviani, "Why, that's – that's awful! I – Hold on, who's Jonah? I don't know any Jonah."

"You do too," Swann cuts in a bit childishly. "Jonah is – that's to say, Jonah was – Augustus's carp."

"Oh . . . is that a fact?" murmurs Ottaviani thickly, not grasping why anybody would think of naming a fish as insignificant as a carp.

"But who? And what? And how?" says Swann, harassing Squaw, who has hardly got a word in up to now.

"You'll find out all about it in an instant," Squaw finally gasps, "but first," unlocking a door, "why don't you sit down in this drawing room and I'll pour you out a hot drink, for this wintry morning air is going to chill you through and through."

It's as dark in Azincourt as in a tomb.

"It was a short-circuit," says Squaw to Ottaviani. "I think a plug has blown but, for all that I sought to work out which was faulty, I'm afraid I still don't know. In addition, Azincourt has no such thing as a torch or a gas-lamp or a flashlight or a Davy lamp – nothing, in fact, but this poor apology for a light that I'm holding up in front of you."

"Oh, not to worry, Squaw," says Ottaviani with his usual affability. "Aloysius and I can follow what you say just as comfortably by night – I don't think dawn's too far off now, anyway."

*   *   *

As if blindly, Swann and Ottaviani accompany Squaw into Augustus's smoking room. And it's in that room, with its oil-lamp giving off both a sickly halo and a suffocating aroma, that Squaw finally fills our two cops in on that salvo of mortal blows that has struck down Augustus and his companions.

Amaury Conson's arrival, along with Arthur Wilbur Savorgnan;

A mass of information involving Anton Vowl's vanishing;

Anton's diary;

Augustus's album;

Savorgnan's virginal tanka on its black "kaolin" card;

Anton's transcription, for Olga, of six oddly familiar madrigals, all of which Augustus thinks of paraphrasing in a disturbing fashion;

Augustus dying that ominous morning, abruptly crying out "A Zahir!" whilst going out to drop grain into Jonah's pool;

Augustus's Zahir and its Saga;

Haig's apparition following Tryphiodorus's arrival;

Othon Lippmann's faith;

Augustus's morning purification in his lustral bath;

His Zahir vanishing;

Othon Lippmann dying;

Haig's vocation;

His blank inscription on Augustus's billiard board;

Haig running away from Azincourt;

Anton Vowl's apparition;

Haig's damnation;

Albin's family and its stock;

His passion for Anastasia;

Anastasia dying whilst giving birth to Olga;

Albin slain by Othon;

Anton both transcribing and translating that inscription, that "Katoun", found on Augustus's billiard board;

Haig dying in Urbino, for which a handful of motivations
  is put forward;
Olga's affair with Anton;
Anton vanishing on finding out that Tryphiodorus is his
  papa and thus Haig his kin;
Jonah, Haig's carp, dying of starvation;
Cooking a Gäfilt-Fisch;
Olga slitting Jonah in two, finding that horrifying Zahir;
Olga's fatal fall and dying murmur of "Maldiction!"

"And that," says Squaw in conclusion, "is a straightforward
chronology of a jinx which is clinging to us all and which, only
today, has struck again and again and again!"

"Hmm," says Swann, "that was an admirably succinct summary, I must say. But, now I think of it, why isn't my old buddy
Amaury with us? And Arthur?"

"Savorgnan was complaining of a stabbing pain in his brow
and lay down; as for Amaury, I saw him taking a long stroll
around Azincourt – around its grounds, I should say – and I
think his plan was to turn in on finishing it. I don't doubt you'll
find both upstairs, snoring away."

"But you'd think my knocking would bring both downstairs
again. God knows, I was making an uproar!"

"In my opinion," says Squaw, "Savorgnan is just too numb,
as is Amaury, for any sound to snap him out of his stupor – I
doubt that a witch's bacchanalia on a Sabbath night would do it."

"It's most important, though, that both Amaury and Savorgnan join us right now," murmurs Swann. "Do you know if, in
Azincourt, I can put my hands on a tuba or a sax, a bassoon or
a pair of cymbals, a tom-tom or a bongo drum?"

"No, but you might try this horn," says Squaw, picking up off
a tall stand a hunting horn, a paragon of a horn, a horn to kill
for, half of it in ivory, half in brass, dating from about AD 1000.

(It's said, although it's probably just a folk-myth, that a paladin
known as Alaric, a vassal of Clodion, who had such an abundant

crop of hair that his companions-at-arms would call him Samson, was willing, at a council of local barons, and whilst in his cups, was willing, as I say, to assign his own position at Clodion's court, along with all its rights and favours, to any man who could draw a satisfying roar out of his horn [all of this occurring, naturally, in a dark fairy-story wood]. Taking him at his word, an urchin, a skinny ragamuffin, a poor rustic, a common bondsman, stood forward, took Alaric's horn in his own horny hands and, blowing into it with as much might as a Tyrolian blowing into a horn to call his cows in, got from it a sound of an astonishing purity, a sound, though, so sharp that it split Alaric's tympanum in two. This was profoundly gratifying to Alaric's lord [Clodion, so rumour had it, was afraid of Alaric and thought of him not as a vassal but as an out-and-out rival], who, instantly, and pooh-poohing this word of warning from his bodyguard:

A bondsman crown'd will down you,
A bondsman down'd will crown you!

had his unwitting champion brought to him, making him his minion, knighting him, giving him his own fair cousin's hand in matrimony, along with a mansion, a stronghold in Gascony and six high-ranking positions at court, and publicly proclaiming that, just as Roland would always accompany Carolus Magnus, so would his young knight always accompany him.

Alas and alack for Alaric and his lass! Within just four days it would turn out that Hilarion, as Alaric's darling was known, if indubitably skilful at blowing horns, was totally ignorant of tilting and jousting, drawing an arrow across a longbow and training a hawk or a falcon. Caught in a skirmish with a dwarfish but surprisingly spry Arab, who was attacking him with a scimitar, Hilarion, a bit of a show-off, had a wild stab at knocking him down with a solitary mortal blow, but his swordsmanship was so clumsy that it was his own body that was run through!)

*   *   *

212

Squinting as doubtfully at Augustus's horn as a conscript at an Amati or a Stradivarius, and giving out a profound sigh, Swann blows into its brassy spiral of piping but, obtaining only a croaky, slightly mournful hiss, shouts out a furious "Shitr!", a notorious oath from Jarry's *Ubu Roi* that's still fairly common, from Aurillac to Saint-Flour, from Puy Mary to Mauriac, in Cantal – in which district Swann was born and in which his family is ubiquitous.

Bragging a bit, blowing his own horn, so to say, Ottaviani asks for a turn, saying that, in his youth, hunting stags, wild boar, aurochs and izards around Niolo, in its dark woods and along its scrubby hills, had taught him to how to play it. Cockily taking hold of Augustus's horn, twirling it around his hand as though it was as light as a baton thrown up by a drum-major in a dazzling rotating motion, and producing from it, with an amazing lack of huffing and puffing, a sonorous, wholly satisfying sound, Ottaviani actually starts improvising, and not without aplomb, a potpourri of military music.

Squaw wildly applauds him. "Bravo! Bravo! Bravissimo!"

"All right, all right, that'll do," says Swann, who, visibly grudging Ottaviani his triumph, put out at having his own mortifying incapacity shown up, is hoping to play down his assistant's skill, communicating to him by a dirty look how untactful it was of him, not to say suspicious, as an adjutant, a right-hand man, to flaunt his gift for music whilst all his boss could obtain was a sound as musical as a duck's fart!

"Okay, boss, okay," Ottaviani sighs, compliant but inwardly raging.

"Anyhow, what's important is our two companions. I did all I could – you too, Ottavio," adds Swann, now in a conciliatory mood, "– to stir up Arthur and Amaury. But, I'm afraid, to no avail."

In truth, nothing at all occurs for a long instant. Gradually, though, a sound floats down as if from a distant attic, a dragging sound as of a ghost laboriously pulling his chains, slowly, pain-fully, making his way downstairs, flip-flop, clip-clop.

And now Arthur Wilburg Savorgnan turns up, limp, numb, puffy, clumsy, haggard, sluggish, not at all on form.

"Good Lord," says Savorgnan, mumbling thickly, "Ottavio! What th' fuck you doing in this joint?"

"Now now, Arthur," says Swann, "don't talk rot. I told you all I was coming with Ottaviani."

Without saying a word, looking practically punch-drunk, Savorgnan rubs his cranium, blows out two big gobs of snot by holding his thumb against his nostrils and, spying a divan, drags his body to it, lays it out across it and starts noisily snoring.

"Oh, grant him his catnap," says Swann. "It's Amaury I'm most anxious about – for, without wishing to alarm you with a ghastly prognosis, all my information adds up to his dying tonight!"

A cry from Squaw. "Amaury dying! But why?"

"Why! Why! Always why!" groans Swann. "Oh God, why always this wish to find a motivation in mortality? Amaury is out of it, that's all I know! His bio won't turn up in any Who's Who!"

"But how can anybody know such a thing? How did you find out?"

It was soon obvious (says Swann) that Amaury was about to fall victim in his turn.

This is how it was. Ottaviani and I got to Noyon, all in. Our first stop was its commissariat, to find out if it had a communication for us from Paris. I got a radiogram from a man on duty and quickly took it in:

PARIS. SIXTH MAY. MIDDAY. FOUND OUT
ABOUT PASSING AWAY OF YVON CONSON IN
PAROS. STOP. CONFIRMATION POINT BY
POINT AT YOUR DISPOSAL IN ARRAS. STOP.

I got into my car and took off for Arras, arriving only at nightfall, as my road was oddly full of mishaps of all kinds. I ran to, I almost burst into, its local station, so avid was I for information, but all I found on duty was a lisping nincompoop who wouldn't stop talking, who didn't know what *I* was talking about and who was actually angling for a tip, a commission, a payoff! For a tip, all I was willing to accord him was a crack across his jaw with my walking-stick, but it took us two hours to obtain our radiogram confirming Yvon's passing away, a radiogram stuck away in a vault that was horribly difficult to unlock.

I found out thus that Amaury's son, sailing from Harwich on board a catamaran flying an Irish flag, plying along Istanbul's Adriatic coast, had cast anchor off Naxos, and finally off Paros, on which island it was his aim to stay all autumn, passing his nights on board, going into Paros by day and roving around. About six nights ago, in his usual fashion, Yvon thought to pop into a dingy local bar, a honky-tonk saloon for dockhands and sailors. Its barman, a man known only as Cock, got his kicks from watching his patrons slip into a coma, giving a gut-rotting glass of hooch to a sailor who was asking for a raki, a glass of bathtub gin to a dockhand who thought it was hock, and not plonking down a Chianti without first lacing it with a soporific drug.

Almost as soon as Yvon sat down, a unknown man was standing in front of him, daring him to play backgammon for his catamaran.

"If you want," said Yvon, "but not backgammon."

"All right," said his companion, "what do you want to play?"

Proposing, in turn, pontoon, blackjack, Tarot, gin rummy, canasta, pairs, brag and old maid, Yvon finally took him up on a round or two of zanzi, a quaint local variation on crap shooting.

An initial roll had him throwing a four against a King.

"Okay," said his antagonist, grimacing, "you won that round."

"I did?" said Yvon, dumbstruck. "But I had a four whilst you had a King!"

215

"That's right . . . But don't you know our local saying? A King first round is out of bounds."

"I'm sorry," said Yvon calmly but firmly, "nothing doing. That was yours or it's all off!"

"As you wish, it's your hard luck," said this curious individual with a harsh, rasping laugh, whilst picking up, touching, stroking, kissing, clicking, blowing on, rattling and finally rolling his craps – coming up on this occasion with a trio of Kings!

"Confound it!" said Yvon out loud but thinking inwardly: This guy's obviously a bit of a con man, but his is a trick that two can play!

So, in his turn, stroking, kissing, rattling and so on, Yvon also cast a trio of Kings!

"Rampot!" (which is what you cry at a draw in zanzi).

Not a man in that room but that didn't approach to watch what was going on.

"Shiiiit!" said Yvon's antagonist, an ugly rictus disfiguring his lips. "It's a rampot. How do you want to play it? On points? On pairs? On all-for-nothing?"

"On all-for-nothing," said Yvon coldly.

An icy, spooky, malignant aura was wafting about him and causing a chill to run up and down his back.

Nobody is drinking now! Nobody is saying a word! Not a pin drops!

As though unconscious of having brought all activity to a standstill, Yvon lit up a cigar with his usual sang-froid, drank down his glass of aquavit and said, "It's your go, I think."

Inhaling profoundly, his antagonist slowly, warily, shook his craps in his fist and, again producing a King, said with a loud guffaw, "Okay, laughing boy, match that if you can."

Yvon, whistling nonchalantly, cast his any old how, but Lady Luck was smiling on him and also brought him a King.

"A draw." This said by Yvon calmly and softly.

"A draw?!! No way! It's a rampot! You and I gotta rampot!"

216

"Oh, fuck off, will you," said Yvon, "that's it for now!"

But, a blind fury consuming him, Yvon's antagonist caught him by his throat and, pulling out a Spanish poniard, stuck it up to its hilt into his stomach, causing Yvon, who fought against it but in vain, instantly to succumb!

"Awful as it is," says Squaw, "to think of so charming a young man dying in that fashion, I must . . ."

Swann butts in. "Yvon? A charming young man? A thorough-going rascal, I'd say!"

"Okay, Aloysius, just as you wish," says Squaw. "But what I want to know is why Amaury has to fall victim along with his son?"

"You'll soon find out," says Swann, "for it's a most important point in this affair, a point on which, although I'm not totally ignorant, my grasp is still, alas, much too patchy, with too many missing links. Now, though, what if you and I and Ottavio go and find out what Amaury's up to?"

Abandoning poor old Savorgnan to his forty (or fifty or sixty) winks, Swann, Ottavio and Squaw start going through Azincourt with a toothcomb. But on no cot, no bunk, no divan, no sofa and no armchair is Amaury found, living or not. As for Augustus's imposing baldaquin, which Squaw had put at his disposal, it looks as trim and tidy as if nobody had got into it that night. In fact, it's almost as if Amaury hadn't put a foot in Azincourt at all.

But what Squaw finds, on a partition wall of a boxroom adjoining that studio that Amaury was put into four nights ago to rally from his alcoholic stupor, is a whitish Bristol board stuck up with four tintacks – a board displaying 25 or 26 portrait photographs, photographs most probably cut out of a tabloid journal, a *Paris-Jour* or a *Daily Mirror* or a *Historia* or a *Tit-Bits*.

Coming out of this boxroom, Squaw instantly calls to Swann, who is busily rummaging through a cupboard.

"Just look at this, Aloysius! 25 or possibly 26 photos which might put a hint or two our way!"

Always on duty, always, so to say, at his post, Swann joins Squaw to study this intriguing board.

"Hmm. But, say, Squaw, how do you know Amaury put this up?"

"Nobody but Amaury had any opportunity of doing so," affirms Squaw. "Four days ago I had to find accommodation at Azincourt for Amaury and Arthur, with both of whom Olga was avid to discuss our affairs, and I brought four pillows from this room, four matching pillowslips, two quilts, a handful of wash-cloths, that sort of thing. But I must say – and you know I'm not a liar – I saw no board, no photographs, on this partition."

"I could," says Swann thoughtfully, "point to a host of individuals in this display whom I know to look at, but I'm struck by four – no, six – with whom I'm totally unfamiliar, and this guy in particular I want to find out about."

So saying, Swann points at a portrait of a skinny man with long, curly, slightly wispy hair, thick hairy brows, a dark, bushy chin and an ugly, narrow gash scarring his lips. Sporting a woolly cardigan with four buttons on top of an Oxford smock without a collar, our man has a faintly folksy look about him, calling to mind a *zingaro* or a gypsy, a carny or a Mongol, but also (switching to a wholly distinct mythology and iconography) a hippy strumming his guitar in a barroom in Haight-Ashbury or at Big Sur or in Katmandu.

Swann calls out to Ottaviani, who's nosing about at random not far off. It's said, among cops, that Ottaviani, a bit of a robot but unfailingly loyal and hardworking, could fix in his brain for good any individual crossing his path.

"Ottavio," says Swann, jabbing at his snapshot with his thumb. "This put you in mind of anybody you know?"

"No, sir!" says Ottaviani instantly and unambiguously. "Anyway, it looks as if it was shot long ago."

"Hmm, that's a point," Swann admits. "I'm going back down

218

to ask Arthur, as I'm obviously drawing a blank with you and Squaw."

Swann quickly rips off Amaury's photo, which was stuck on with a tack, and, following Squaw, with Ottaviani in tow, taps on Savorgnan's door, looks in without making a sound, confirms that his chum is still snoring away and murmurs:

"Shhh! Our Arthur's dozing so soundly I don't want to knock him up. Actually, I fancy a mug of cocoa and possibly a fruit or – I don't know – bacon on toast? Can you do that for us, Squaw, for our work's cut out for us tonight?"

So Squaw brings in two mugs of hot cocoa which Swann and Ottaviani soon gulp down with lots of noisy lip-smacking. Swann dunks almost half of a crusty, oblong loaf into his mug, whilst Ottaviani puts a thick coating of apricot jam on his croissant.

Night is gradually fading at last. A cloudy, misty day is dawning, giving Azincourt's dining room a dispiritingly wan and pallid look. It stinks of cold tobacco.

"Good God!" says Ottaviani in disgust. "This room is suffocating!"

"What you want," says Squaw, unlocking a window, "is a lungful of cold air."

Swann and Ottaviani start, caught in a gust of sharp if invigorating morning air. Savorgnan, for his part, abruptly waking up and rubbing his palms with a loud "Brrrr . . .", jumps up off his divan, puffy, groggy, his hair all tously, his clothing in disarray, his look still as haggard as it was, and groans, "What? It isn't morning, is it?"

Although sniffing hungrily at Swann's mug of cocoa, Savorgnan insists first of all on having his morning bath. So Squaw shows him to Augustus's own sumptuous, marbly bathroom, from which Savorgnan almost instantly struts out again, grinning, having had his bath and put on a crisp pair of slacks, a stylish polo shirt and a playboy's polka-dot scarf.

Swann instantly, and anxiously, confronts him.

219

"What do you know about Amaury?"

"Amaury Conson,' says Savorgnan bluntly, drawing his hand across his chin, "is kaput."

22

*In which you will find an old family custom obliging
a brainy youth to finish his* Gradus ad Parnassum
with six killings

"Amaury Conson is kaput," says Savorgnan again. "If you want
to find his body, it's in a stockroom, floating in a gigantic basin
of oil."

"You saw him?" asks Swann.

"No – thanks to that damn short-circuit. But what I was conscious of was his dying cry – a long-drawn-out cry that'll haunt
my mind till my own dying day, particularly as it was blown up
by acoustics that would amplify a dropping pin into practically
atomic proportions – right up to a final splash. At that point I
had no doubt at all as to his lot!"

"But how? Or, should I say, why did Amaury fall? You didn't
push him, did you?"

"Oh, I was willing to if I had to," admits Savorgnan, vainly
trying to mask his pain, "but, jumping at my throat, Amaury
found his foot skidding, swung back and forth for an instant and
finally lost his foothold. I saw him falling right in. It was as
though I was actually watching gravity at work!"

"But why would Amaury think of attacking you?"

Savorgnan sighs but, almost as though sulking, as though at
a loss for words, says nothing to this.

Swann now pulls out his photograph and, holding it up in
front of Savorgnan, says to him, with an intimidating scowl,
"This is why, isn't it? It was this photo that brought him to such
a pass! You got him to look at it, didn't you?"

No (says Savorgnan), it was totally fortuitous that Amaury found it, in a cupboard in my room. This is how it was. Last night Amaury took a turn around Azincourt but, in doing so, got lost, finally making his way back indoors by about midnight. Squaw didn't stay up for him and nor did I. It was pitch-black. Amaury, his brow throbbing madly, lay down on a sofa, possibly nodding off but almost instantly jumping up again, suffocating, panicking without knowing why, and in pain, in ghastly pain, thinking wild, crazy, paranoid thoughts about individuals trying to kill him, lacing his drink with poison, thinking, too, that I had a flask of Homatropini hydrobromidum in my room that might pick him up and pull him through. So Amaury, going upstairs without waking anybody, bursting into that boxroom that, as you know, adjoins my room and rummaging through it, found this photograph and, as if throwing off his pain, and giving out an agonising cry, roaring, "That photograph!", caught my throat in his two clammy hands.

At that point Amaury quickly took off again, mumbling and grumbling inaudibly, to his own room; but, still running, was back in a flash, holding a Bristol board in his hand, a board with 26 subdivisions, 26 units, all of which had a portrait photograph – all, that is, but for a solitary blank unit.

"It wasn't blank till now," said Amaury. "That photograph that you hold in your hand was stuck," – pointing at it – "in this fifth unit that's now vacant. A burglar took it from my flat, almost thirty springs ago this April. Although I was both sad and angry at such a stupid act of criminality, I admit I thought it at first fairly trivial and hardly worth worrying about. But, within just four days of my loss, my son Aignan lay dying in Oxford!"

A sob rising uncontrollably to his throat brought his accusation to a halt.

"Amaury," I said in my turn, as kindly as I could, "that photograph that you found in my boxroom isn't yours. It's my own, and it always was. You must trust your old pal."

"But . . . but what's this all about?" said Amaury, now visibly brought up short.

"Isn't it obvious?" said I. "My photograph's a copy of yours!"

"You had this man's photograph, too?"

"That's right."

"But why?"

"Just cast your mind back to as many as four occasions on which I'd drop hints as to how oddly similar my biography, so to say, was to yours. Two of a kind, branching off from a common trunk – our pasts not simply similar but matching up point by point – that's you and I, Amaury!"

Amaury cut in. "I do call to mind your dropping such hints. And it was always on my mind to ask you about it all, in privacy. In fact, I was counting on you to pass on any such information that you had on our kinship, or on that conundrum which is my past and about which, alas, I know almost nothing. But our discussion was so long I couldn't find an opportunity to talk to you about it. Past midnight as it is, I don't think it's right for you now to hold off laying all your cards out, without flinching, without holding anything back . . ."

I took this on board, although adding:

"As you wish. But not in this room. It's too dark and it's too cold. Why don't you and I pop down to Augustus's cosy smoking room? A stiff drink might warm us up."

"Okay," said Amaury. "You go downstairs. I'll follow you in just a tick."

At which point, our companion hastily ran off, his hand clasping his Bristol board of photographs.

So I was first in Augustus's smoking room. I hung around for almost half-an-hour, drinking a glass of first-class aquavit.

Abruptly, I was struck by a loud din coming from downstairs. I ran as fast as I could but I still had to go fairly slowly, gropingly, as it was as black as tar. I got downstairs, though, without stumbling too much, and saw, in a sort of gloomy, glowing chiaroscuro, Amaury stuffing a substantial manuscript into a gigantic kiln – substantial, that is, by dint of how thick it was.

With a frisson of suspicion, I could not but cry out, "What is that – that manuscript that's almost burnt to a crisp?"

Amaury, furious, visibly not caring to say anything that I might find incriminating, at first took a long look at his manuscript – a manuscript that was now turning brown, and now black, and now shrinking and curling up – and finally sat down on a folding chair, pointing out a tall stool in front of it and proposing that I sit on that.

"Okay, Arthur, you want to talk. So talk."

"Now? In this stockroom?" I said, looking around doubtfully. "I . . . I was waiting for you in Augustus's smoking room."

"No," said Amaury, with an obstinacy that I was starting to find a bit irritating. "Start talking now."

"But why?"

"You can't say it's dark in this room – or cold – or . . ."

I stuck to my guns.

"Or what? What's wrong with you?"

"Nothing. Just sit down and talk. If not . . ."

"If not . . . what?"

"It's our only opportunity . . ."

Naturally, I found his conduct intriguing and, struck by his obstinacy, I had no option but to humour him. So I sat down, lit a cigar and got down to brass tacks:

"I'd always said that a day would dawn on which I'd inform you of my Saga – and this is it. You'll also find out that it's a story involving you as much as yours truly. That Damnation that's pursuing you is on my trail too. Its shadow is falling on both of us. My blood is yours, Amaury, for my papa is also yours!"

"What!" said Amaury, aghast. "You and I – siblings!"

"Just so. Siblings in a common affliction and a common fatality!"

224

"But how did you find this out?" said Amaury, now avid to know, to drink his poison to its last drop. "Who told you this thing of which I was told nothing?"

"Oh, I long had a faint intuition of it, of this baffling fact, this fact that nobody had any guts to talk about, this fact about which, in truth, nobody had any information at all, and it took much of my youth and adulthood to find out what I could about it, building supposition upon supposition, trying out idiotic assumptions, drawing hasty conclusions, computing, calculating, imagining, filling in bit by bit this mystifying jigsaw, this intimidating taboo, in which, as I was conscious, a solution was hiding.

"What a lot of work I put into building a circuit of possibly fruitful contacts – paying a bunch of lazy, parasitical informants on a monthly basis, bribing librarians to drag out any old and musty parish roll just as long as it might contain information about my family background, buttonholing all sorts of corrupt public officials, politicians, solicitors, councillors, diplomats, administrators, assistant administrators and assistant sub-administrators, right down to a city hall charlady and an account-ant's copyboy, all of whom, frankly, I paid a lot to obtain nothing much. I had finally to sift through a mountain of information, trying to distinguish what was important from what was insig-nificant, what was simply too fantastic from what was just poss-ibly so, racking my poor old brain to find, from fact to fact, from obscurity to obscurity, a point of global articulation, an organising factor, as you might say, that was always just slipping out of my grasp.

"I did find things out, though, I gradually got to know what it was all about, I got a hold of it at last. In a word, I hit upon a solution and I now know all I want to know about my upbringing, my past!

It is a story told by an idiot, full of sound and fury, signifying nothing.

*   *   *

"It's a long story, Amaury, an occasionally confusing, occasionally trivial and occasionally almost magical story – of that "I for an I", that's still, continuously, on my trail, on your trail. A story, too, of that man who originally thought it up and who put it into action all of 20 springs ago. That man who, right up to his dying day, would spit on any bid for compassion, any call for pity. That man who, again to his dying day, had but a solitary goal: that of winning tit for tat, an I for an I, a tooth for a tooth, vindicating his oath, satisfying his wrath – in Blood.

"And it was that man who would go out and kill off all our sons in turn!"

"Him . . . Him . . ." a haggard Amaury was murmuring.

"That's right, old man. You stuck a photograph of him up on your board but you had no information about him! That curious individual with his bushy chin and his wispy hair! My papa! Your papa!"

Amaury was sobbing now, clutching his stomach. "Oh, my papa! I was totally ignorant of all this! Such a ghastly man – and I'm his son! You too! Why?"

"Calm down, Amaury, control your passions. You'll soon know all about it."

Your papa, my papa (I don't know what to call him, or anyway I don't know its pronunciation), was born in Ankara.

His was an aristocratic family, of a particularly high rank locally, and colossally rich: it virtually had, so it was said, a Midas touch. But a fair distribution of its capital was difficult, for, consisting as it did of about 26 sons, cousins, aunts and so forth, all of whom had in turn, ordinarily, 5 or 6 offspring, it could count so many birthrights that it was thought, rightly, that its capital would gradually diminish until it was totally worn away, notwithstanding sporadic profits and windfalls.

Thus family tradition had it that almost all that capital should go to its firstborn son, whilst his young siblings had to subsist practically on scraps; thus that darling Firstborn would scoop it all up, mansions, villas, lands, woods, stocks, bonds, diamonds and gold ingots, and had no obligation to do any hard work, whilst his family had to labour away from morning to night.

Naturally, favouritism that flagrant, with a solitary son vacuuming up all his family's adoration, risks having a backlash. So, although our family sought to justify such discrimination as a way of upholding and prolonging its authority (and a primary mainstay of this authority was, as always, a substantial working capital – capital, that is, that couldn't sustain too much dissipation, in a cousin's dowry and so on), a custom was soon to grow up taking as its basis, by a bias that almost wilfully sought to instil guilt, not a *Sint ut sunt aut non sint*, but a *soi-disant* moral right which, grading an individual according to his rank, grants its firstborn all of its bounty, judging him good, virtuous, candid and kind, whilst justifying giving nothing to any of his siblings by painting portraits as foul as his was fair.

What was worst of all was that nobody was outwardly indignant or cynical about such a family law; nobody would simply say, *Summum Jus, summa Injuria*; nobody, firstborn or lastborn, thought of such an unjust division of his patrimony as anything but normal, anything but right; so nobody took a stand against so obvious a misappropriation of funds, so flagrant a corruption of authority.

In truth, as his only consolation in an unjust world, a victim of this law had but a solitary fantasy – of his firstborn sibling abruptly dying and his position passing to that son who had priority.

So what you had, and almost continuously, was sons without a sou, hard-up cousins and starving aunts uniting in imploration, praying for a fatal blow. And, surprisingly, Allah in his compassion occasionally did grant such a wish: a typhoon blowing up without warning, a spasmodic croup, would in fact kill him off (although a basic contradiction would subsist, with a gap narrowing bit by bit but not totally closing up).

227

At which point it was obvious that such a status quo, both too soft and too hard, couldn't go on for long as it was.

In fact, you might say that, for its motto, our family would gradually switch from that of Athos, Porthos, Aramis and d'Artagnan, *Un pour Tous, Tous pour Un*, to an opportunistic *I'm All Right Jack (You Scratch My Back, I'll Scratch Your Back)* that wasn't as sanguinary as you might think but that would last for only about six months, and finally to *Homo homini Lupus*, which was brought into play by such a dramatic stunt that all Ankara, and in particular its local aristocracy, was full of admiration for it.

A youth of about 18 had in front of him six prior claimants, a fact that, *a priori*, would disqualify him for good from arriving at firstborn status. And if Maximin (our prolific assassin) actually did attain such a status, it was by hatching, plotting, planning, polishing and finally, triumphantly, carrying out six killings in a row, six killings that in addition had nothing in common but a sort of paradoxical imagination.

His first victim was Nicias, a dwarf, a runt, towards whom, though a bit of a jackal, Maximin had no particular animosity. Nicias wasn't too bright, though, and killing him, by comparison with killing a jackal, was akin to taking candy from a baby.

Thus it was child's play for him to worm his way into Nicias's villa by proposing to instruct him how to draw a bow-and-arrow according to Buddhist philosophy. And whilst Nicias, who found such a proposal mystifying if also gratifying, was struggling with his books, Maximin, brandishing a pickax as hard as a rock and as slim as a rollmop stick, struck him down with a mortal blow, fracturing his ischium and provoking a constriction in his inguinal ganglion, which brought on a suffocating contraction and, almost instantly, a bout of dizzy fits that would soon turn into a total blackout, a blackout that was to last for as long as six days and that would at last kill him off in a local hospital, much to his country's sorrow, with crowds of curious, gawping Turks milling about in front of his hospital window, hoping to catch sight of him spinning around, an unusual kind of funfair attraction, you might think, but satisfying a local partiality to physical monstrosity, particularly as Ispahan had its famous "whirling" Fakir.

Optat's killing was just as tortuous.

Optat, a soft sort of individual, with a chronically pallid if not downright pasty skin and such a sickly body that it invariably had a contusion or a concussion or a dislocation, was fond only of alcohol, drinking jars and jars of it all night long. So what Maximin did was pay a postman to bring Optat a gigantic jug of 100% proof alcohol and inform him that it was from Hainault, as Optat had bought at Mons, by mail, a schnapps that aficion-ados said was out of this world. Naturally thinking that this was it, Optat would swallow a good third of his jug at a gulp, finding it so tasty that within half-an-hour not a drop was still undrunk.

But it had a fatal sting in its tail, so to say. In this jug Maximin had put an inflammatory product, which, innocuous if soaking in alcohol, would light up if brought into contact with air, so producing Optat's carbonisation. Optat, who, by his total satu-ration in alcohol, was a natural for such instant combustion, burnt as quickly as touchwood, diffusing a curious but savoury aroma of roast agouti all around him.

Maximin was passing by just at that instant – not, I should say, haphazardly – and, grasping a lasso, caught Optat, a living matchstick, a burning coal, a flaming twin of Joan of Arc, and sought to drag him off to a public fountain not far away.

And what Maximin did at that point was compound his iniquity by dunking his writhing rival as nonchalantly as you might dunk a toasty hot croissant in a cup of cappuccino – an iniquity, I might add, that was soon to profit his country (it's an ill wind that blows nobody good), as it was found within a month that an oddly acidic liquid, bubbling up from that fountain, had a strong antidotal quality, particularly against catarrh, but of application also to asthma, arthritis, bronchitis, gout, psoriasis, muscular dystrophy, malaria, lockjaw, syphilis, constipation and chilblains.

Following him was Parfait, with whom, though, Maximin saw a major difficulty looming up. For this Parfait was as tall as Goliath, as strong as a Turk and as malignant as a troll; was brutal, cunning, rascally and corrupt; and, to cap it all, was simply mad about fighting. If you hit him, Parfait hit you back, again and again and again: it was as basic as that.

Now Parfait had, in a souk, a shop which sold all kinds of candy – nougat, sugary almonds, lollipops, gumdrops, marshmallow, marzipan and mints – and in particular a yoghurt in syrup that Ankarans found so cooling on hot spring nights that it was quickly known, by a natural association, as a "Parfait".

Thus no day would dawn in Ankara without a Timariot or a Vizir or an Icoglan going to visit Parfait in his souk, asking, no doubt for a gala that night, for a marasquino "Parfait" or a blackcurrant "Parfait", two of his most scrumptious tidbits.

Thus, too, Maximin would call on Parfait in his turn, handing him thirty sous and asking for a gigantic banana "Parfait".

"*Parfait*," said Parfait, a born francophiliac.

But as soon as Parfait brought his concoction to him, Maximin took a spoonful, put on a wholly convincing show of throwing up, and told him, without mincing his words, that it was simply disgusting.

"What!" said Parfait, livid at such an affront, "You call my Parfait . . . *imparfait*!!!?"

Slap! Slap! Slap! Thus did Parfait attack Maximin and insist on satisfying his honour.

"As you wish," said Maximin coolly. "I'm willing to confront you in our family orchard tomorrow morning at dawn, but only if what you and I fight with is of my choosing – and what I say is not swords, not pistols, but soda siphons!"

For an instant Parfait was so put out by such a paradoxical form of ammunition as to look almost punch-drunk.

And, catching him off-guard, smartly profiting from this disarray, Maximin took up a thick, knobby club and struck his rival hard on his skull. Stumbling and groaning, Parfait was instantly cut down.

What Maximin did now was coat his moribund body with his own banana "Parfait", soaking it in syrup and adding, a blackly humorous finishing touch, a jarful of gumdrops, sprinkling it lavishly around his limbs.

At which point Maximin brought forth a dog that was champing at its bit, a gigantic, snarling Alsatian which for six months had had, for its daily chow, nothing but Parfait's "Parfaits". Not surprisingly, it sprang on Parfait's body, lapping it up and finally gulping it down.

Walking away, Maximin said with a sly grin, "Poor Parfait has just unwittingly thought up an original kind of candy: a Banana Split!"

Chuckling at his own wit, Maximin had to turn to his fourth victim, a claimant known as Quasimodo: a squat and dumpy guy, a bit simian in his gait, a drooling, burbling moron with, in fact, a strong hint of Victor Hugo's hunchback about him. Though approaching thirty, his IQ was that of a infant.

His constant occupation (or, if you wish, vocation) was talking to birds, holding forth, notably, to flocks of swallows, jays and sparrowhawks that would swoop around a small boat-pond in Ankara's public park foraging for crumbs – holding forth, I say, rambling on for hours about nothing in particular, waving his hands to and fro in a clumsy imitation of Saint Francis of Assisi. Finding this all highly comical, an occasional individual out strolling would fling him a ducat or a florin, with which Quasimodo would go off and buy food.

His killing was thus a cinch for Maximin, who on this occasion was totally in control – sinking a narrow crossbar into Quasimodo's pond, wiring it up to an accumulator, so producing on contact a strong flow of induction, and paying an urchin who was passing by, as Quasimodo was holding forth, to hurl a phony gold coin into it, a coin containing a tiny compass.

To cut a long story short, Quasimodo took a running jump into his pond, falling an instant victim to hydrocution.

It was Romuald who would follow Quasimodo. But just as Quasimodo was a snip, so Romuald was a tough nut to crack. For, cunning, wary and inquisitorial, this Romuald saw plots and plans constantly hatching around him and was suspicious of all his family.

Almost afraid of his own shadow, Romuald would finally withdraw into his villa for good, locking doors and windows, pacing back and forth with a gun in his hand, squinting with paranoid alarm at anybody chancing to pass by, starting up in fright if a postman, say, should look in at his window and, cautious to a fault, actually purchasing a hot air balloon, which would allow him, at long last, to pass a night without worrying about unknown assassins.

Maximin would first idly toy with a handful of solutions (causing Romuald's balloon to drift away out of sight by cutting a cord that was anchoring it to his villa roof; obstructing its auto-stabilisation pin or its gyroscopal joint; substituting for argon a gas such as krypton, thus provoking a gigantic blast inward or outward), but all in vain.

Finally, a lightbulb lit up in his brain. Hiring a small twin-prop aircraft, Maximin took off, flying around Romuald's balloon and abruptly swooping down upon it, brushing against it by only a yard or two, so producing a prodigious trough of air, suffocating its occupant and causing his balloon to spin skywards out of control.

Maximin's sixth and final victim was Sabin. But Sabin was a man who wouldn't allow anybody to approach him, Sabin who, having now just his aunt's husband in front of him as his family's patriarch, was afraid that his soon having all its capital at his disposal would risk provoking an attack on him from a rancorously grudging sibling or cousin.

So this Sabin simply wouldn't admit into his stronghold, without a pass (and occasionally two), a coalman, say, hauling in his monthly supply of coal or a pastrycook's boy bringing him his morning croissants.

A host of amusing rumours about him would buzz around Ankara. It was said that his army of thirty spahis, all as handy with yataghans as with swords or pistols, was paid a king's ransom to accompany him about town and would instantly, unpityingly, kill any man, woman or child coming within a yard of him. It was said that Sabin had a flunky who was first to savour his food, as any thought of poison put him in a funk. It was said, finally, that among his staff was a young man of an amazing physical similarity to Sabin who would withdraw to his couch at night whilst Sabin would pass *his* nights in his attic – an attic, it was also said, built by a craftsman (who was slain as soon as his job was at its conclusion) to withstand any intrusion, thanks to a combination lock on its thick iron door. In this attic, or so gossip had it, was a six-month supply of food and drink.

Such a strong rival, a rival unwilling to omit anything in his craving for total immunity from risk, was a stimulant for Maximin, who hadn't found much to stump him in his undiscriminatingly patchy job lot of killings up to that point. Born victims, his antagonists, just a bunch of stillborn duds! But taking on Sabin would finally justify his ambition, constituting its culminating point and putting his coruscating wits truly on trial.

It took him almost a month, though, to work out how to carry it off. Not that his brain was at all short of inspiration, but his rival's fortification struck him, at first sight, as wholly foolproof, with not a rusty link in its chain.

Until that day on which Maximin was idly making small talk to a local spiv who, in his own words, would "habitually supply

Sabin with an ass's foal, or should I say," this said with a salacious wink, "a foal's ass, for, you know, sir, and don't say I told you, it's only by balling a burro, and burrowing into its balls, that poor Sabin has . . . got it up."

"Aha," said Maximin, smiling slyly, "opportunity knocks at last. My sib has a major kink in his armour! I just know I can turn this information to good account."

And, following it up, Maximin found out from an administrator in Ankara's Municipal Zoo that, such was Sabin's voracity, a foal wouldn't usually satisfy him. At most it brought him an initial thrill; but, for his main dish, so to say, only a gigantic or, if not, a totally unfamiliar animal would turn him on.

Which was why Sabin had a habit of bribing this administrator to allow him to "borrow", for an occasional night of passion, an animal of truly substantial width and girth, a big ruminant, say, such as an ox or an orang-utan, a bison or a hippopotamus, or an unusual animal, a kangaroo or a cassowary, a capon or a boa constrictor, a platypus or a tapir, an opossum or an alligator, an albatross or a caiman, a dolphin or an aardvark.

But such a Cook's (or cock's) tour of Ankara's animalia still didn't satisfy Sabin, who, in sodomising so many curious animals, was trying to match a particularly vivid carnal frisson, that which his young loins had known, long ago, copulating with a lamantin (*Manatus inunguis* or *Manatus latirostris*) from Chad.

Now, just at that instant, a carnival from Halifax would turn up in Ankara, proposing to its townsfolk, among many similarly outlandish attractions (a pair of twins with linking hips, a hybrid hotchpotch of dwarfs, giants and albinos, a cow with a dachshund's body and a rabbit with two tails), a *soi-disant* "Loch Lomond Dragon" known as Rudolf. (In truth, it wasn't a dragon at all nor an aquatic python, but a dugong, an animal as mild as a lamb, that could, without risk of contradiction, pass for a lamantin, for it had, as do lamantins, a skin of shiny fur, an imposingly stocky trunk and a cordial disposition.)

It's obvious, is it not, what was about to occur. Sabin would start aching for Rudolf but, unwilling (and possibly also afraid) to go and look at him, would try to pay his way to borrowing, for a substantial sum, his darling dugong. Rudolf's groom, though, would initially turn down his proposal, and it was only by doubling, tripling and finally quintupling it that a cynical bargain was struck. Sabin could hardly contain his joy.

Vigilant as always, Maximin found out about this and was soon hatching a plan of his own, combining various sorts of TNT, building what you might call a tiny suppositorial bomb, managing, with typical aplomb, to worm his way into Rudolf's aquarium and, profiting from its lazily dozing in its bath, ramming in his fatal suppository and accompanying it with a fulmicotton priming cap which, on contact, would spark it all off.

His plot striking him as virtually airtight, and having nothing to do but hang around until nightfall, Maximin had a drink in a squalid pub not far from Sabin's mansion, hoping to sing, within four hours or so, a triumphant Hosanna.

Nor was our Maximin wrong. At 11.35 a young groom, that with whom Sabin had struck his bargain, did in fact turn up, drawing a bulky caravan in which, smiling as amiably as a cow watching a train go past, Rudolf was snoozing.

At 11.52 Ankara was abruptly lit up with a blinding flash, with a loud bang rattling its roofs and blowing out its windows, and a smoky, stifling, malodorous fug drifting about until morning.

And at 12.23, knowing now that his atrocity had no survivors, a radiantly victorious Maximin would swan into a chic local nightclub, although normally tight with his cash (but such a triumphant *coup* did in his opinion warrant a blowout), and drink two gigantic magnums of Cramant *brut*, jovially clinking his glass, toasting his companions and standing drinks all night long.

So, against fantastic odds, Maximin had at last brought it off. But alas, his Magnificat, his Hosanna, was sung too soon. Within just six days a half-cousin of his, suspicious of his abrupt promotion to firstborn status, would bump him off in his turn!

From that point on, killing was virtually a norm, killing turn and turn about: if our family had a law ruling its conduct, it was an uncompromising, proto-Darwinian law of survival. A young accountant, who was handling its capital, soon lost his sanity trying to control its multifarious ramifications. In just thirty-six months, rights to that capital would fan out to as many as thirty-two claimants, all of whom, without fail, would succumb to a fratricidal blow.

It was finally obvious that, with mutual killings continuing in such a ridiculous fashion, no family could last for long without at last dying out. It was painfully obvious, too, that only a third of our family at most was still intact. Panic stations! And, slowly, an artificial kind of harmony was brought about, with siblings and cousins and aunts all lining up to sign a pact – a shaky coalition which, not surprisingly, would fall apart within a month.

At which point, a law was laid down, imbuing this fratricidal war with an almost ritual quality.

What this draconian law primarily did was disallow any man from having two sons, so as to put no child at risk from his bloodthirsty sib. It also sought to limit similar rivalry among cousins, so that a day would dawn on which – by, as I say, a Darwinian distribution, winnowing out all non-survivors at birth – a solitary branch would grow from a strong family trunk.

To attain this ambitious goal, a trio of voluntary options was put at our family's disposal:

a) that, on giving birth, a woman was automatically slain;

b) that, just as soon as his first son was born, a man automatically had his balls cut off;

c) – and this option was most popular by far – that this man, although raising his firstborn in normal conditions, would do nothing to stop any following son from dying or would simply do away with him – notably, by abandoning him on a dunghill, drowning him in his bath or dishing him up for lunch to a British Lord, according to Jonathan Swift's famous Proposition, as a juicy joint of roast lamb or wild boar.

It was a law that would unblock an awkward situation and it was to last for six springs, during which transmission of our family's capital was not, thank God, an occasion for bloody squabbling.

Nobody now would kill just for fun; no patriarch would allow his branch to cast too long and dark a shadow across his rival's branch; a quorum was brought to pass that all found fairly satisfactory. And so this outwardly inhuman status quo wasn't actually as harsh as all that.

23

In which an anxious sibling turns a hoard of cash found
in a drum to fairly satisfactory account

But (says Savorgnan, continuing) a horrifying bit of bad luck
was to occur to this unhappy family of ours.

Flying into Acapulco's Good Samaritan hospital, a malicious
stork brought our mama not just an infant but a trio of infants
in its bulging bill. Luckily (for, if not, it was curtains for both
of us), our papa who, according to that family law I told you
about, would normally watch his son's birth, had had, just that
morning, to go to Washington, for, as his work was importing
goods from abroad, a toy company in that city was proposing a
major contract involving his buying up, at a discount, a gigantic
stock of harmonicas that it was manufacturing and that his own
company could offload at a profit without any difficulty, particularly in Ankara.

It was obvious to mama that, on signing his contract, papa
would instantly rush back down to Acapulco and, counting a trio
of sons, to two of which no man in his family had any right,
would do away with both of us.

In a spasm of instinctual passion, wishing to maintain our
survival at all costs, mama rang for a doctor and told him all
about our frightful situation. This doctor, a chivalrous and magnanimous young man who was still in thrall to his Hippocratic
oath, couldn't turn his back on so poignant a supplication and,
laying our sibling in mama's loving arms, quickly took flight with
us to snatch us away from our doom.

"And so," says Amaury, "if I follow you aright, my papa found just an only child on arriving back in Acapulco?"

"That's right. By falsifying our forms and giving us both an alias – profiting from a lucky opportunity involving a pair of stillborn twins occupying for an hour or so a corridor adjoining our incubation ward – nobody had to inform him of his two missing sons."

"But, if papa didn't know us, why harass us, why attack our sons?"

"About thirty springs ago poor mama caught a cold that was going around (*staphylococcus viridans*) and was visibly about to succumb. A Cardinal, in hospital for a minor malady, would grant absolution and unction but only following admission of all worldly sins. From such a man of God, such an august pastor, mama could hold nothing back.

"Now this pompous Cardinal, who was a bit of a crook, practising simony, trafficking in dubious shards from Christ's Cross or nails from his crucifixion, misappropriating church funds and blackmailing its faithful, would instantly think of mama's information as a kind of jackpot and start angling for bids. A distant cousin of ours, a cousin who, as it turns out, was acting for our family's Dauphin, got to know of this situation, accusing papa of going back on his family's law by hiding us from its quorum and, to punish him, killing his son, your sib, my sib!

"Alas, fanatically fond of this son, hoping to appoint him Dauphin and accusing us of conniving at his downfall (for, without us, in his opinion, nobody had any motivation for doing away with him), papa took his killing so badly that his family thought his mind was starting to crack up.

"Papa took an oath to kill us, to track us down until our dying day, and, first, to kill our sons – so that you and I would know in our turn how tragic it was for a man not to bask in filial adoration!"

"So papa did know us – did know our sons?"

"No. At first papa didn't know anything of us (in addition,

you *had* no son, nor had I), but took off, notwithstanding, with a solitary goal: to pick up our trail, to find out who had brought us up, and in what country you and I had grown up."

His first port of call was Acapulco, from which city, tracking us with a flair as cunning as that of a Huron or a Sioux, papa would laboriously follow, all of 20 springs on, in our path.

From Acapulco, now, to Guadalajara, a populous town in which I was taught my ABC and had my first communion along with you. But that young doctor, our saviour, was soon on to him, knowing, or probably just anticipating, his plan to follow us. So, on our 10th birthday, you and I hastily quit Guadalajara for Tiflis, Tiflis for Tobolsk, Tobolsk, finally, for Oslo. And it was in Oslo that our doctor would pass away without first informing us about that dark shadow that was cast across our path.

Now, at that point, I was split up from you. A circuitous path took you to a sanatorium in Uskub, from which you almost instantly ran away; but, run down by a truck whilst darting in and out of traffic on a busy highway, you totally forgot your past.

For my part, I got to Hull, a British port in which I was brought up by a drum-major, who, noting that I had a natural gift for studying and a passion for books, paid for my tuition at Oxford.

So it was that I lost contact with you. You didn't know anything about my way of living, including my alias; nor did I know anything about yours. But I did on occasion worry about you, thinking with nostalgia of our common past.

And, as soon as I was 25, and had my MA, I took a post as assistant in a Council for Propagating Low Latin, an organisation that had its HQ in Sofia. As I had only six hours of tuition a month, I had at my disposal a lot of days in which to find out what I could about you, profiting from this handy fact – that, by train, it was at most a day's outing from Sofia to Uskub.

In its sanatorium, though, nobody had any information about you. So I would go around Bulgaria, asking about you and carrying in my bag a charcoal drawing that I'd got a local artist, a skilful draughtsman if hardly a Goya, to do, following indications from a sanatorium doctor – a striking mug-shot it was too, though probably invalid, as it was so long ago that you'd run away.

Showing this drawing to anybody who was willing to look at it, to a farmhand, a sandwich boy, a fairground pitchman, a compositor, an accountant and a cop, I occasionally had a hunch of a forthcoming tip-off. But no, it was all to no avail.

Finally giving up my post as assistant, I quit Uskub without having had an inkling of information about you, without having had a hint of any kind.

But, moving at that point to Augsburg, a city in which I was paid a fabulous commission by its local Josiah Macy Jr. Foundation for my collaboration on Oskar Schärf-Hainisch von Schlussnig-Figl's study of Bororo's total lack of guttural sounds in its pronunciation – Bororo, a particularly rich and stimulating Parañan patois in which, as in Bantu, most nouns finish in a labial "*ll*" – I would go to Uskub on a trio of occasions, from 6 March to 20 April, from 28 July to 1 August, and again in mid-August, to carry on untiringly with my inquiry.

I had, at last, to draw this conclusion: I was 10, you too, naturally, at our splitting up. Now, if I was taking pains to find you again, I'd had no hint of you, for your part, trying to pick up my trail. So what could justify such a disturbing fact? I had to admit your vanishing act or, should I say, by postulating it *a priori*, to work out a motivation for it: (a) your dying as soon as you ran away from your sanatorium; (b) a gypsy carrying you off; (c) a brutal shock, an unknown trauma, fatally impairing your sanity or your instinct or your wisdom, cutting you off from all contact with a world of hard facts and truths!

Working my way through a mountain of inscriptions, immatriculation forms, almanacs, journals, logbooks and notarial

241

scripts, going from administration to administration, visiting stations and dockyards, harbours and airports, hospitals and shops, I took thirty-six months all told to find out that, 18 springs ago, a handful of local inhabitants had caught sight of a boy, a youthful vagabond with a moronic look about him, roaming through Mitrovitsa, a big industrial town not far from Uskub.

This youth didn't know any Bulgarian, had blood on his moccasins and was visibly starving.

I was instantly conscious, by both intuition and a kind of irrational conviction, that this was my first truly significant tip. I took a train to Mitrovitsa and a local man soon got in touch, corroborating my story and smiling fondly at my drawing. Long, long ago, taking pity on him, this man had found just such a lad, making him his goatboy, giving him a roof, a room and food.

So, having had six springs of worrying about you in vain, of not knowing who to turn to for information, I was at last starting to track you down!

I found out, as I said, that a truck had run into you during your flight from Uskub, its impact causing a concussion that was so total, so profound, that nobody had any notion what to call you or what your background was and so on.

But I was told by this man who took you in that you soon struck him as, basically, a bright young lad, not at all as stupid as you had at first. You gradually got to know how to talk again, and would display a gift for counting. Supplying you with an atlas, an assistant at a local school had a long talk with my man and got his grudging approval to prolong your tuition as far as it could possibly go.

In all you would pass thirty-six months in Mitrovitsa. Occasionally a bunch of snotty kids would attack you and spit on you and shout out, "Anônumos! Anônumos!", a callous, cutting word that was your local patois, naturally, for "anonymous". And, I was told, it was finally so familiar a catcall around town that it almost stuck to you for good. By quitting Mitrovitsa, though, you at last saw an opportunity of burning your boats,

throwing off your past and starting out again as "Amaury Conson", an alias you took from that assistant who taught you all
you know.

I was hoping to contact this original Amaury Conson. But on
my arrival in Mitrovitsa I couldn't find him at all. A cousin of
his, with whom I had a long chat, thought Conson was possibly
living in Zurich. And in six months I too was in Zurich, profiting
from a symposium in which I was giving a talk. I finally got in
touch with your tutor, who had no information about your situation but did pass on a crucial fact: that a man with a bushy chin
– outwardly, just a typically shabby old crackpot living from hand
to mouth but, inwardly, boiling with fury – was also asking about
you!

This, I thought, was curious. Who, apart from yours truly,
would want to contact you? And why?

Now, at that point, fairly constantly, I had an intuition of bad
luck pursuing both of us. In fact, waking up at night with a start,
I found I had, again and again, *pavor nocturnis*, a vision of a
killing.

It brought to my mind a day – but which day? – in our childhood, a day on which, whilst I was idly playing with a yo-yo and
you with a spinning top, our doctor saviour had sat us both on
his lap and told us, softly, almost inaudibly, that in a distant land
a man was looking for us, a man who had it in for us and would
probably try to harm us and that, on that far-off day on which
our own sons would start growing up, and run a similar risk,
you and I must vigilantly stand guard against him.

But this flashback, if I may call it that, was so hazy and confusing that I took about six days to work out just what it was trying
to signal from my unconscious.

And, abruptly, Acapulco was to pop into my mind – Acapulco,
that city in which I was born. I rang its municipal hospital and
found out about our birth, about how a young doctor had
thought to switch us about with a pair of stillborn twins, about
his adoption of us and our flight. And, chillingly, I also found

out that, oh, long, long ago, a man with a bushy chin had burst into our hospital rambling away about his poor lost son and shouting, "An I for an I, a truth for a truth!"

So, starting out with hardly a crumb of information, this man had by now got to know virtually all about us, had found out your alias and had actually got in touch with your homonym, that first Amaury Conson. It was a long haul, but today our arch-antagonist was swooping down upon us, was hot on our trail!

I was struck again by his untiring obstinacy, grasping instantly that this was a pursuit that would last right up to our dying day, that its instigator wouldn't think for an instant of pausing, that such a fanatic had but a solitary ambition driving him forward: that of having us at last within his grasp, of watching our sons writhing in agony, watching *us* writhing in agony!

I thought it vital that you in your turn should know of this man in whom such wrath was stoking up such fanaticism and who would go all out to find us. But I didn't know in what country to start looking for you. Or in what city. In a colonial bungalow? In Chicago, in a mansion by Frank Lloyd Wright, say, or an airy, glass, skyscraping condominium by Philip Johnson? In a Saint-Flour slum? In a villa with a balcony full of aspidistras in a provincial, almost pastoral suburb of Hamburg or Upsala? Did you know what risk you ran? And, most importantly, had you a son? All such points I quickly had to clarify.

Naturally, I had a possibility of communicating with you by radio or in a want ad. I did occasionally think of doing so, and I almost got round to it, finally changing my mind, though, as I was afraid that an unambiguous signal of that sort would also assist our Bushy Man.

Whilst, for his part, Amaury Conson, your tutor, was trying to obtain information as to your lot, my own papa, that charming British drum-major, sinking fast, and having no natural kin, had his solicitor add a codicil to his will according his only (if unnatural) son a gift of thirty diamonds, all of amazing proportion and purity, and including a particular rock that was practically worthy of a Koh-i-Noor or that Grand-Mogol for which Onassis was willing to fork out a cool million.

Having thus no financial worry of any kind, I quit my job to work only for you.

And, dying to know (if I may put it thus) from what was born that damnation pursuing us, my first act was to fly out to Ankara, in which city, I was told, our man was born.

So I alit at Ankara. But, at its airport, a customs and immigration official, who visibly had a high opinion of his own position, instantly sprang up, yapping, "I want to look at your arm!"

Though put out by such an offhand approach, I duly took off my parka. Adjusting his lorgnon, grasping my right arm, studying my wrist and giving out a loud cry of satisfaction, this official at last said that I should follow him into an adjoining room, a small back room in which sat a civil-looking chap who, though sporting not a uniform but an ordinary casual suit, was obviously his boss, for my man saw fit to bow to him and practically curtsy.

"What is it?" his boss said to him in a forthright way.

"Sahib," said my man (who couldn't know that, *au fait* with almost thirty subdivisions of Ponant patois, I had no particular difficulty with Turkish), "it's an individual from that . . . that Family, with . . . with that mark . . . you know what I'm talking about . . . on his right wrist. As soon as I saw him, I thought I'd find it – and I did. It was just a hunch, but, as you know, Sahib, my flair for this sort of thing is unfailing!"

It was a fact. I had, and had always had, on my right wrist, a livid, narrow furrow, forming a sort of parabola (just as did that Zahir that had so forcibly struck Augustus or that curious whitish scar that Albin would tattoo on all his gang of rascals and lascars) – a parabola that was, you might say, ajar, not joining up in any normal fashion but finishing with a straight inward dash. But, until that instant, I hadn't known that it was a family trait.

"You don't say?" said his boss. "I want to look at it."

245

His assistant, his "Chaouch", as Turks say, took my arm to show to his boss, who said to him, a bit grudgingly, I thought, "*Insh'Allah*, it *is* in truth what you said it was, Mahmoud Abd-ul-Aziz Ibn Osman Ibn Mustapha, and for this I'm going to put you up for promotion. But," now dismissing him with a nod, "not a word of it to anybody, or it'll all go wrong."

"Barakalla Oufik," was all that, on his way out, Mahmoud Abd-ul-Aziz Ibn Osman Ibn Mustapha said.

At that point his boss, not saying anything but pointing to a chair, on which I sat down, and lighting up a hookah that had a sharp, sultry aroma of Turkish tobacco, rang for a boy, commanding him to bring a jug of *kawa au jasmin*, a lurid Tahitian concoction which all Turks of distinction drink in gallons.

"You know Italian?"

"*Jawohl*," I said.

So, talking in Italian or, should I say, "spiking da Italianisch", this chap said that Ankara had had, that autumn, as many as thirty victims of coronary thrombosis. And, as my vaccination had long ago run out, I could not lawfully stay in his city.

This, I was conscious, was a totally phony claim, that wouldn't stand an instant's scrutiny in a court of law, but I was also conscious that, if such intimidation didn't work on its own, my man wouldn't stop at physical obstruction.

It was obvious that his instruction was to stop any individual with such a furrow on his wrist, any individual of "that ... Family", as his assistant, Mahmoud Abd-ul-Aziz, had curtly put it, from coming into Ankara. But what I didn't know, and had to find out, was what was prompting so unusual a form of discrimination. Why was Ankara so afraid of my arrival, of that of anybody of my "Family"?

Not daring to ask point-blank about that taboo that was clinging to my family, I took him in with a cunning trick.

Acting as panicky as though I truly thought I was running a mortal risk by coming to Ankara, I quickly got up, took off in my Lagonda-Bugatti and, driving to a small town not too far away, took a room in a B-and-B in which I was to stay put for about six days.

In that room I brought about an amazing physical transformation, staining my body a swarthy walnut colour, wrinkling my brow with a stick of charcoal, disguising my blond hair with a long black wig and putting on a brown burnous. And, casually mingling with a group of actors arriving in Ankara for a gala to launch its Municipal Casino, I got my visa, and an all-important pass, without any difficulty, finally making my way into town.

From a chum in London I had a card of introduction to a Turkish solicitor. So, continuing to sport my wig and adding a donnish-looking lorgnon, I took off my burnous and put on a chic Cardin suit.

In addition, afraid of an official coming up at random to study my wrist, I stuck a conspicuous Band-Aid on it and almost thought to put my arm in a sling as though I'd had a boil or a bad wasp sting and was just out of hospital.

I paid a visit to this solicitor that my chum had known at Oxford. Not daring to blurt out all my suspicions straightaway to a man with looks as sly and crafty as his, and so practically ad-libbing, I told him a long story about my passion for folk art and music and my coming to Ankara to draw up a vast Variorum of sayings, myths, sagas, amusing facts, songs and traditions.

Luckily, I'd hit upon his own particular hobby, for, grinning as broadly if I was actually tickling him, my man was to hold nothing back.

"Now . . . What should I start with? Do you know Ali Baba and his Tradition?"

"Uh, no . . . I'm afraid not."

"Oh, but you should. It's simply charming:

To a tinny ocarina playing a potpourri by Paganini, Ali Baba, tiny Pacha but as stocky as a buffalo, as a big fat tub of lard, now starts guzzling macaroni sizzling in a frying pan, guzzling pasta with a musty, fusty, rusty, dusty savour

247

to its flavour. Lying down on his divan, a cat starts licking its own down. Ali Baba burps and gulps down a joint. Good, says Ali, now I must go. Taking his gun, his arrows, his bazooka, his drum, mounting a darling stallion, Ali gallops through pampas, woods, mountains and canyons and, without knowing why, starts chasing a lion that was no doubt grazing on fruit and thinking it could lift up a rock and find alluvium. Ali Baba shouts: Oh, what good is it all? Did Ali know what it was all about, this thing, this thingamajig? For that you would want addition, subtraction, multiplication and division. Adding 3 to 5 is 8; adding 6 to 1 is 8 minus 1. What? says this moron, a calculation? It kills Ali Baba; as for our lion, it runs away so fast, so fatally fast, it croaks.

I said "Bis! Bis!" with as much animation as I could summon, causing him to bow and blush with obvious gratification. And I finally got down to brass tacks, hinting that in all this information at his disposal I'd no doubt find a handful of spicy notations on which I might draw for my work.

But, as soon as I'd said that, I saw him growing ominously broody, his brow furrowing. I was conscious of making a faux pas.

"In Ankara I know of a solitary spicy notation, as you would put it. But, and I'm not kidding, it's a thing that nobody's willing to talk about. I know of many a local guy with a big mouth who had no opportunity to finish his –"

And I didn't doubt that his claim had a grain of truth in it, for just at that point I saw an octagonal gash abruptly bloodying his brow and I saw him, almost instantly, slumping forward from its impact. It was a gunshot wound of pinpoint accuracy such as only a first-class marksman could pull off – a marksman who, firing from a balcony not far away, no doubt guiding his aim with a microvisual gunsight and smashing a fanlight window, had got him with his first shot.

"Good God!" I said inwardly, clutching at my mouth in horror.

I'd had a ghastly fright and was afraid to so much as touch him. And, in a flash, a brick was thrown in, a brick to which was stuck by a Band-Aid a stiff card on which I found this communication:

IF YOU KNOW WHAT'S GOOD FOR YOU, PAL,
DON'T STICK YOUR SNOUT IN OUR AFFAIRS!

Illustrating, or possibly signing, this ominous warning was a purplish stamp portraying an individual in a hood as arrogant and apocalyptic as a Ku-Klux-Klansman, an individual holding aloft a flag with a trio of flapping tails.

I initially thought that it was just a bit of bad luck on my part, that my informant was possibly part of a gang running guns or smuggling drugs and that this gang, thinking him about to spill it all out for hard cash, had shut him up by simply putting him out of commission, whilst handily intimidating his "confidant" – which is to say, yours truly – into giving up his mission.

But, studying his carcass, I saw that it too, on its right wrist, had that unpropitious sign singling out an individual as part of our Family. I'd unwittingly sought out a rival for my advisor!

I simply didn't what to do at that point, conscious as I was, without a shadow of a doubt, that I was running a risk just by staying in Ankara. But what I still hadn't found out was why? why? why?

What finally cast an illuminating ray of light on it all was, as almost always occurs, a miraculous combination of luck and confusion.

I was holing up in a room not far from Ankara's piano souk (it isn't commonly known that, globally, Ankara holds first position, in front of Osaka, in front of La Paz, in importing old pianos), a room I was hoping would function as a good port in a storm. And in that room I'd lurk and languish, constantly afraid of an assassin bursting in.

On my first night in it I was struck by a loud din rising up from an adjoining courtyard. Without at all panicking, I quickly ran out on to my balcony.

In that courtyard, huddling in a kind of plaza in front of Ankara's imposing Inns of Court, a building wholly without proportion, a vast, amorphous, granitic block, with walls of a particularly gaudy purplish colour, stood an incongruous group of musicians. I call it incongruous as what I saw was a trio of banjos, a cor anglais, a cithara, a bassoon, a bass drum and, capping it all, a soprano singing, in a monotonously droning fashion, as if in a clumsy imitation of plainsong, a fantastic, florid oratorio about a Blank King and his vanishing act – a King who, though in Abraham's bosom, would wolf down, in turn, 25 of his own vassals.

Wildly applauding, I cast a handful of kurus from my balcony, as I found this curious song most amusing, admiring it particularly for its humour, which was both sardonic and cryptic, both sly and difficult to grasp, admiring, too, its vividly Turkish quality, symbolising as it did a vital point of articulation for my assimilation of that country's racial and national unconscious.

At midnight, hungry, I thought to call out to Ali, a barman from a local snack bar, asking him to bring up to my room a tray of mutton pilaf, couscous and fruit.

Ali brought it up and I got to chatting with him for an instant, casually, about this and that, as you do in such a situation, and finally about that curious musical group, Ali asking what I'd thought of it and my giving him my opinion, a high opinion, of its gifts, adding, "I was particularly struck by that song about a Blank King, by its humour and its imagination."

"Its imagination, you say!" said Ali indignantly. "Huh! It hasn't got a grain, an atom, an iota of imagination! It's all factual, it's all God's truth! I, Ali, know all about this Family, all of us in Ankara do, a family that has as its main physical trait a narrow, livid furrow on its right wrist. I also know that, on top of its pyramid, so to say, is a king with a right to all its capital . . ."

Whilst Ali was rambling on in this fashion, my hand was clasping a poniard I had thought to tuck into a mackintosh that I'd just put on, mumbling about how frightfully cold it was on my balcony. For it was obvious that this was a provocation on his part, a provocation that was bound to finish with my dying at his hands.

In fact, I was wrong. Ali – *rara avis* – was totally impartial in this affair, candidly spilling it all out from A to Z, though not without lots of omissions, providing a succinct history of that wrath, and its origin, that, hounding our family, was playing havoc with my way of living – with yours, too, and that of all of us!

Putting scant trust in his capacity not to blab about it again, not to shoot off his mouth about this chat I was having with him now, which would, I didn't doubt, bring about my own instant liquidation, I had to do away with poor Ali, first allowing him, though, to say all that was on his mind.

Thus, having found out what I had to find out, and knowing what I was in for if I was to stay on, I quit Ankara, cursing it for always.

Within four days I was in Zurich. I took a taxi to Amaury Conson's flat, dying to fill him in on all I'd found out in Ankara, hoping, too, to know of his own inquiry into your situation.

But Amaury was kaput – shot at point-blank, again and again, whilst busy at his Aga making his morning cocoa.

His pyjamas had drunk up all his blood, and his iris had a twisting, curling spiral of crimson running through it that brought to mind nothing so much as a taw of that garish kind that boys roll back and forth in school playgrounds during lunch hour.

Thus I'd got to know all about that which was pursuing us, but I still didn't know in which country I might find you.

And, from that point on, I paid visits to city upon city, Ajaccio, Matifou, Pontchartrain, Joigny, Stockholm, Tunis, Casablanca, consulting thick parish rolls without picking up your tracks, haunting town halls and commissariats without coming away with a modicum of information from anybody . . .

24

*Which, starting with a downcast husband, will finish
with a furious sibling*

For six months my only goal was to find you – until, downcast,
worn out, I had to abandon it all.

And a glorious day would dawn on which, whilst cruising
aboard SS *Captain Crubovin*, a ship sailing from Toulon bound
for La Guaira (Caracas's port), I ran into Yolanda, its chaplain's
typist and all-round Girl Friday.

It was what you might call lust at first sight – a lust that nothing
but our instantly uniting in holy matrimony could satisfy.

Wishing to go on a world tour, I bought an ultrasonic aircraft
– and a day would dawn, too, during a flight across Africa, our
civil nuptials just 12 months old and Yolanda coyly announcing
a coming birth and in fact visibly filling out, a day on which, by
dint of an abrupt drop in its supply of gas, I had to bring my
craft down damn quickly. Not without difficulty I brought about
a bumpy but triumphant landing on a particularly grim spot in
Morocco, a sandy, Saharan hillock hardly as big as an old maid's
cotton hanky, with a crash, though, which split my right wing
in two.

Our stock of foodstuffs would hold out for a month, but it
took us an arduous and scorching four days' walk finally to find
our way to a tiny oasis at which local bands of nomads would
occasionally stock up on liquid, turn and turn about, according
to which month it was.

For our first six days I couldn't complain about our condition:
in truth, it wasn't all that bad. I had a go at hunting a dahu, an

amusing animal similar to a fawn but which, living on mountain foothills, had such a clumsy, squinting kind of body that, to catch it, what you had to do was approach it on all fours and mimic a goura's irritating chirp – a goura is a songbird that dahus simply cannot stand. Furious, caught short and, most importantly, with its guard down, our incautious dahu would try an abrupt U-turn and, wobbling, fall into a gully or a wadi, from which it wasn't difficult to pull it out. Yolanda would roast it on a spit and I'd tuck into it, finding it as scrumptious as I was now starting to find salt pork, our usual sort of food, monotonous.

Finally, thirst had us by our throats. Our oasis was almost dry and my aquavit would burn us without slaking our thirst.

This was my conclusion: that Yolanda and I had to light out again, on foot, moving only at nightfall, filling up our flasks at any oasis on our way, crossing Hoggar, surmounting arid tracts of sand and glacial mountains and, by going southwards, arriving at In Salah, Tindouf or Timbuctu, or, if striking out northwards, arriving at Igli, Aïn-Chaïr, Aïn-Taiba with its fort, Aïn-Aïachi with its oasis, Mac-Mahon with its garrison or Arouan with its Casbah.

But, at Hamada as at Tassili, at Adrar as at Iguidi, at Grand Atlas as at Borku, and at Djouf as at Touat, that inhuman Sahara brought so many hardships to any foolhardy individual daring to cross it on foot that I had difficulty making ground, particularly as poor Yolanda was visibly about to go into labour.

Finally, with Yolanda's sobbing supplications ringing in my brain, I had to abandon my darling to God and His compassion, striking out on my own, walking, jogging, almost running, clasping in my hand a compass with which I could quantify my position vis-à-vis Orion and Sirius, scrutinising my illimitably distant, illimitably sandy, illimitably starry horizon, following a caravan's worn-out tracks as far as it would go but also, occasionally, doubling back on my own trail, and constantly hoping, and in truth praying, that Lady Luck was in my camp.

And, I must say, it paid off, for within four days of my

starting out I saw a goum, an Arab military unit, on patrol.

Alas! How could I know that just as its commandant was cooling my burning throat with drops from his hip flask, an act that brought to mind Victor Hugo's famous hussar who

> *Parcourait à dada au soir d'un grand combat*
> *Un champ puant la Mort sur qui tombait la Nuit*
>
> *(His combat won, on foaming colt would cross*
> *That carcass-stinking camp on which Night falls),*

a hussar who brought comfort to a straggling Hidalgo by giving him a drop of rum and whom Hugo was fond of praising not just for his imposing bulk but also for his unfailing sang-froid – how could I know that, just at that instant, Yolanda was fading fast!

For, slaking my thirst, gulping down a mouthful of hot food, changing into dry clothing and strapping on my back an apparatus, minimal but functional, for honing my aircraft's cycloid (or cyclospiral) rotor fan, that which controls its admission circuit (what such a job actually calls for is a pruning hook or a gauging awl; but, making up for that, I had, for tools, a drill, a mattock, a picklock, a dipstick, a hacksaw, an adz and a nail-chuck that, to my dismay, had a tap with a missing partition, though its knob, thank God, was still intact), I got back to my aircraft to confront this harrowing sight: having just had six – six! – infants in a row, Yolanda lay dying.

Roaring in pain, I ran forward, giving my darling an invigorating drink from my flask. But, alas, with a last mournful cry, Yolanda sank away in my arms.

Oh, what words can I possibly find to portray my profound sorrow at Yolanda's passing away? How, to this day, can I talk calmly of my affliction? My sorry condition? Again and again I thought that I too would succumb, sacrificing our offspring, putting a pistol to my mouth and firing it, so painful was this loss.

Pitiful survivor as I was of a gloriously happy union, laid low,

255

cast down, my spirits in constant mourning, carrying my cross, mounting, oh, fifty Golgothas, all I sought, hoping for nothing now in this world, was to join Yolanda as quickly as I could. And I would longingly toy with my hacksaw, for such a sharp tool could cut through my skin with as scant difficulty as a fork prodding a soft runny gorgonzola and so accord that instant mortality that I was looking for!

But I thought of our six offspring, not any of whom I was blaming for my loss (how could I?), six squalling infants still squirming in bloody umbilical cords and probably running a risk of strangulation or asphyxiation.

I took pity on what was now my family. Infant by infant, I cut off that cord uniting my brood to a now arid womb that had brought it forth; and I did what I could to wash it, making all six snug and warm in my aircraft.

Now I had to fix its admission circuit, an arduous, frustrating job, for, try as I might, it would always light up too soon, without waiting for any propulsion of gas in its induction piping. Nor would honing its pivot joint do it on its own. I had to adjust it all, point by point, joystick and bolts, piping and pads, stuffing-box and pistons.

It took four days working on it nonstop till I got it functional again. And, taking off, I struck out for Agadir, hoping finally, in civilisation, to grant my brood that constant monitoring of which it was now so badly in want.

Whilst flying, though, what should pop into my mind but that warning that you and I had had in our childhood from our doctor saviour. And I thought about it, I thought about it long and hard, during my flight, arriving at last at this conclusion: if our family had drawn up so many codicils vis-à-vis its patrimony and its distribution, it was that it had a tradition of giving birth to too many offspring, a history of bi-, tri- or on occasion quadri-parturitions.

Thus that man who was pursuing us, who was trying to kill us, that man, our own papa, who had sworn to satisfy his thirst for our blood by first doing away with our sons, was no doubt particularly on watch for any hospital announcing a birth of an abnormal amount of infants.

If I took my six offspring to a clinic in Agadir, I could hardly stop it from making such a miraculous fact public. Nor could I stop my infanticidal antagonist from grasping his opportunity at last!

I was conscious, in fact, that what I couldn't do on any account was insist on raising my brood as a family. My only way of assuring that it wouldn't fall victim to this madman, this fanatic, was, cuckoo-fashion, to put my sons, all my sons, up for adoption . . .

"I'm with you now," murmurs Amaury, blanching, "I know how it's all coming out. Taking 'Tryphiodorus' as an alias, you put on a grubby smock, of a sort that a tramp might sport, and you had Augustus adopt Haig, Vowl adopt Anton . . ."

"That's right. But you still don't know it all. For think of this:

Hassan Ibn Abbou was also my son, whom I had to abandon as soon as I got to Agadir.

Parking my aircraft in a vacant hangar, and wishing to guard my offspring from any risk of association with our family, what I did first was to scratch off, with a crypto-coagulating nib, that tiny but singular wrist mark that, for any child, was damning proof of his background.

And, picking a baby out at random, according to an old song I'd known in my own childhood:

> 1 Potato, 2 Potato
> 3 Potato, 4
> 5 Potato, 6 Potato, and so on,

I took it to a hospital in Agadir. It was night. Groping along corridors by just as much light as a match would afford, I finally caught sight of a woman who had just had a stillborn child and who, visibly, was also not long for this world. It was an opportunity I couldn't miss. I insist that this poor woman was dying –

257

by finding a wad of cottonwool on a tray and soaking it in chloroform, I simply brought it all forward by a day or so. Placing this woman's baby in an adjoining cot, I had my own stand in for it.

At that point, scrawling what I thought was a suitably Arabic-sounding alias, Ibn Abbou (an alias which from that day forward would cling to my son), on a plastic tag and attaching it to his wrist, I took flight from Morocco, my goal that of finding vacant lots, if I may put it that way, for all of my offspring. You know now that Douglas was put into Augustus's hands at Arras; and that in Dublin, as Tryphiodorus, I thought to farm Anton out to Lady d'Antrim, who had as husband Lord Horatio Vowl, an Irish tobacco baron.

This Lord Vowl was famous for making for Dunhill, incorporating Latakia and Virginia tobacco in a combination known only to him, for it got its miraculously insinuating flavour not from its individual parts but from his cunning proportioning of such parts – was famous, I say, for making Balkan Sobrani, a brand familiar to all tobacco aficionados and which Davidoff would call a classic.

Alas! Within just thirty-six months, Lord Horatio, mounting a foal that was probably a bit too frisky for a man of his bulk, had a bad fall, so bad a fall, in fact, that it would instantly knock him out and put him in a fatal coma. With his last, dying gasp, Vowl was said to murmur to his assistant a formula, a formula as famous and also as unknown as Coca-Cola's, for manufacturing his tobacco, but its list of instructions would turn out so hard to follow that nobody, posthumously, so to say, has found a way of producing a tobacco with all its original purity and subtility of aroma. Which is why, nowadays, you'll find no such thing as good Balkan Sobrani; and which is also why a low-quality brand is now sold by tobacconists as a poor imitation, Squadron Four, which, combining a fairly uninspiring if not totally banal kind of Latakia with an insipid Virginia, a Virginia that's obviously not

258

a product of sunny Arlington, Fairfax, Richmond, Portsmouth, Chatham, Norfolk or any truly Virginian plantation, has a flavour that, candidly, you could only call so-so.

But if, thus, you know how I put half of my offspring out to adoption, you know nothing, if I'm not wrong, of my surviving trio.

First, I should say that it was my aim to bring up two out of six on my own. So, having a last infant to part with – it wasn't a boy but a girl, my only girl – I took a train for Davos . . .

"Davos?" said Amaury with curiosity.

"That's right. And you'll find out in your turn how *I* found out why any notion of salvation on my part was simply wishful thinking, why our family's Damnation was going to track us down till our dying day. For – oh, it was just damn bad luck! – in Davos, to part with that last child, I took it in my mind to go to a sanatorium."

"A sanatorium!" said Amaury, almost in a cry.

"Uh huh. A sanatorium," I said, in a singsong as mournful as an air-raid alarm, as a ship's foghorn in a storm, "right again, a sanatorium. I got into it, as was my wont, by night, walking at random along ill-lit corridors and at last, through a small, oblong window, spotting a dark cot in which was lying –"

Amaury dramatically cut in. "Anastasia!"

"Yup, Anastasia, Hollywood's most luminous, most numinous star. I saw, at my approach, that Anastasia, who now lay dying of TB, having but a solitary functioning lung and that lung now functioning so badly, so porous and spongy, so full of inflammation, palpitation, granulation and catarrh, you could almost wring it out, had brought into this world a baby as ugly as a bug, a baby that was also visibly on its way out of it, so allowing yours truly to act without that compunction, contrition and attrition that usually accompany a killing – for it would go with its mama into God's kingdom whilst I had a vacant cot for my last child!"

259

"What?" said Amaury. "So Douglas, Olga's husband . . ."

"And paramour!"

". . . was also Olga's sibling!"

"That's right."

"Oh calamity!" said Amaury, almost indistinctly; and, following an instant without saying a word, "But what of your two
sons – you know, whom you brought up on your own?"

For sixty months or so it wasn't all that bad. But (I was now
living in Ajaccio, that's in Corsica, you know) a day was to dawn
on which I took my two infants out to play in a small public
suburban park not too far from a wood. Thirsty, and imagining
I wasn't running any risk, I found my way to a bar to drink a
cold soda pop, a 7-Up, I think. Just as I was savouring it, and
chatting away to a bosomy young barmaid, a horrifying cry was
to jolt us both.

I quickly put down my glass and ran out, to find that that park
that I'd thought so ordinary, so innocuous, was now in total
confusion, full of sobbing matrons, swooning maids and livid
municipal guards. What was going on? Alas, I soon found out,
picking it up through an orgy of sniffling, blubbing, moaning,
groaning and hanky-wringing.

What I was told was that a tall, skinny man sporting an
amorphous sort of cap, playing a jaunty air on what I think you
call a kazoo, and coming out of that adjoining wood, had with
his music drawn a crowd of infants around him, including my
pair, and gradually, insidiously, drawn it away with him back
into it. Following a hiatus during which nobody had any notion
what to do, a hunt was got up, chasing him and sniffing him
out, scouring scrubland and shrubland, patrolling, raking soil and
looking for footprints. All, though, in vain. In addition, it was
said that this was a wood that had its own gang of bandits,
cutthroats notorious for holding infants to ransom or robbing
adults, so that, not surprisingly, nobody was willing to go all
that far into it.

Concurring with this opinion, my initial assumption was that it was a strictly random affair, that this atrocity, striking down all that's most virginal and incorrupt in our civilisation, had nothing to do with that horror that was pursuing us.

But, within four days, I found out from my *Figaro* that your firstborn son, Aignan, who was 20 and participating in a Martial Cantaral Foundation symposium on pathovocalisation, a symposium that (a fact by which I was also struck) had as its chairman my own boss, Gadsby V. Wright, was, how shall I say, kaput.

And I thought it all too obvious that, at Ajaccio as at Oxford, our Bushy Man was now moving into action . . .

Amaury abruptly cut in. "So you found out about Aignan and his . . . his dying in that awful fashion?"

"I did."

"But why didn't you go to Oxford for his burial? For it was your opportunity of making contact with your sibling, of our talking, of my finding out at last that this lunatic was pursuing us and possibly of our taking communal action against him."

"In fact, my original plan was instantly to fly to Britain. And, with that in mind, I rang up Lord Wright who, or so I was told by him, had caught sight of an unknown man accompanying Aignan to his symposium, a day prior to his vanishing act – a man, I should point out, with a bushy chin. I was conscious that, if I was to turn up at his burial, that man would know what I was doing in Oxford and so, obviously, who I was. As my incognito was, I thought, vital, I didn't go, hoping soon to contact you in privacy – probably by post."

For an instant I was struck by how unusually stiff Amaury was growing. Finally, in an faintly ominous pitch, this is what was said by him:

"You thought, you thought! You, you, always you! By not going to Oxford, by not risking your own skin, you simply forgot to pass on information about that shadow that was falling upon us. For you it was unimportant, it was trifling, it was trivial, it just wasn't worth talking about, that cross I had to carry! That son I had to carry – carry to his tomb! You had an opportunity to inform your own kith and kin – but, oh no, not you! Knowing all about it as you did, it didn't occur to you to say a word! Your sin by omission is, in my opinion, as shocking a sin, as mortal a sin, as our papa's sin by commission. But that blood that's flowing by your sin, by your omission, is now, and by my own hand, about to abandon your body, just as would a pack of rats from a sinking ship!"

It was obvious that poor Amaury was raving, half out of his mind, for I saw him pick up a thick black andiron and start walking forward with a low animal growl.

In my turn I took a pick, hoping to ward off his attack with it. But that attack didn't actually occur. For, during his approach, it was as though Amaury was abruptly drawn back by an almost inhuman compulsion – an aura of physical might that was pulling him down, down, down, into that gigantic basin of oil.

Giving out a bloodcurdling cry, slipping and falling, as though no laws of gravity could apply to him now, Amaury spun around and in a flash was out of sight . . .

VI

ARTHUR WILBURG
SAVORGNAN

25

Which contains, in its last paragraph, a highly significant blank

"And so," says Savorgnan, finally rounding off his account, "it was all up with Amaury Conson."

"By Baour Lormian, translator of Ossian," says Swann, using with obvious satisfaction a florid oath from his childhood, "that's a fascinating story all right. But I could point out a handful of contradictions in it."

"I know, I know," says Savorgnan. "For, if my chronology is right, Amaury's own fatality should not occur prior to that of Yvon, his lastborn son. But whilst, worn out, I was snoozing upstairs, am I right in thinking you told Squaw of Yvon's liquidation?"

"That I did," Swann admits. "You know your onions, Arthur, I must say. That wasn't what I was thinking of, though. What I found contradictory was that, if your lunatic dad did away with all six of your offspring – with Anton Vowl, Douglas Haig Clifford, Olga Clifford Mavrokhordatos, Hassan Ibn Abbou and that pair of sons that you brought up on your own and that your papa would spirit away from you in a distant past – why not you? By rights, your surviving such a holocaust is illogical."

"It's a fact that's also running through my own mind," says Savorgnan, visibly quaking. "I know, too, that it'll soon swoop down, thus putting a final point to all this horror that's blighting my family."

But Swann again contradicts him.

"No, it's a final point only if you all know your lot, your *fatum*, as in all good fiction."

With a look of contrition, Ottavio Ottaviani tugs at his chin.

"That's right, Ottavio," says Aloysius Swann. "It's your turn now to hold forth."

"But, boss," Ottaviani stubbornly insists, "my opinion isn't worth a sparrow's fart – so it's always said."

"Now now, don't go putting on airs," says his boss jovially. "I can't wait – and I know I'm talking for all of us – to find out what you plan to say to us."

Ottaviani sighs and starts talking.

"It was on my third birthday that, in Corsica, in a public park in Ajaccio, a tall, skinny chap cast a charm upon us, fascinating us, luring us away into a wood, kidnapping us –"

"Oh God, it's my son!" howls Savorgnan.

"Daddy!" sobs Ottaviani, taking him in his arms and hugging him.

"But, son," says Savorgnan, cuddling him in a spasm of patriarchal passion, "which of you is it – Ulrich or Yorick?"

"I'm Ulrich. That's to say, I was Ulrich at first. But I was caught, along with my sibling, by a bandit, who taught us how to snatch cocks and ducks from all kinds of country bumpkins, and I was finally sold, for an insultingly low sum, I must say, to a local infantryman from whom I think I got my vocation as cop. Yorick was sold, too, to a carnival showman known as Gribaldi."

"So my son Ulrich is still living," says Savorgnan with a loud sigh. "So you didn't fall victim to that Law, that 'I for an I'. But what of Yorick?"

"Yorick took off with his carnival for Bonifacio, whilst Ottaviani, by whom I was brought up, bought a small bungalow for us in Bastia. I didn't know in which city Yorick was living. And though, in my 20s, I occasionally had to go to Bonifacio for a job, I couldn't find any hint of Yorick or his carnival.

"All I found out about him was his studying music – drums, so I was told – and boarding a brig bound for Livorno, for that showman guy, an Albanian by birth, thus a Tuscan, had a wish, prior to cashing in his chips, for a last, nostalgic look at that district still so familiar to him from his youth . . ."

Swann laughs – abruptly, harshly.

"You want to know if Yorick is still living? You want him living, don't you, for that would imply your own survival. No such luck, I'm afraid! Yorick got his about 25 springs ago . . ."

"Alas, poor Yorick!" says Savorgnan, his vision misting up.

"Voilà," says Swann, brandishing a small black book. "Know what this is? It's my adjutant Pons's account of Yorick Gribaldi's dying:

Wasqu'lham: Today, Monday 28 July, a trio of conscripts is found missing from our battalion's barracks at morning roll call. Adjutant Boutz is furious:

"Six days!" Boutz shouts at his corporal. "I'm giving you just six days to put your hands, and your handcuffs, on that band of fucking good-for-nothings!"

But four days pass and our arrogant trio is still AWOL.

"It's Biribi for all of 'm!" growls Boutz.

Boutz informs Major Glupf, his commandant, who says in his forthright way that his garrison must do all it can to catch and bring back, a.s.a.p., living or not, hussars Pitchu, Folkoch and Worms, to stand trial in a court martial, on an accusation of disloyalty to Wasqu'lham's population.

Glupf consigns his garrison to barracks, mobilising six battalions, guns at hand, and promising thirty ducats to any man with vital information to supply. But this award brings in only a bit of salacious gossip that, frankly, has nothing to do with anything. Rummaging through a train and dragging a canal also fails to turn up trumps.

Now Boutz has to inform his major of an infantryman going AWOL in his turn: Ibrahim, a Roman by origin, 25, a corporal, a Military Cross and in addition Glupf's cousin! And, in 24 hours, a Tuscan drum-major, Gribaldi, follows suit, making 5 AWOLS in all, in just six days!

267

Boutz, running out of things to do, frowns. It's lucky that his nation is not at war and that its King's dying, with lots of public oratorios, has brought a modicum of calm and harmony to its population.

A furious Major Glupf insists on having a total blackout; and, his confining his garrison to barracks proving hard on local shops and bars, has to justify it publicly by giving out a rumour (phony, naturally) about an assassination of Lord Horatio. Mobilisation, it's said, is about to follow any day.

Glupf also craftily finds out, during his inquiry, that our skiving bastards had a point in common: about a day prior to going AWOL, all had drunk a glass of schnapps in a local bar, Conscript's Arms, *adjoining a municipal abattoir – a bar which has a barmaid, Rosa, with a notorious passion for dragoons.*

So, substituting civilian clothing for his uniform with its dazzling gold braid, Oskar Glupf thinks it worth having a look at this squaddy's hang-out. With a guard standing watch not too far off, Glupf sits down and has a bock, paying for it with a gold florin.

Noticing that Rosa is washing out cups and tankards in a sink, Glupf starts chatting about this and that, but, by Saint Stanislas, and notwithstanding all his cunning, gains nothing for his pains.

His suspicion, though, is still stuck on this barmaid, who (so common gossip has it), acting for a rival country trying hard to suck his own into an all-out war, is guilty of inciting his troops, doughboy and NCO, infantryman and dragoon, hussar and spahi, to turn traitor. But, with six battalions on constant patrol, with road blocks cutting off local highways, how could anybody possibly find a way out? So it's Glupf's opinion that his band of missing hussars is still lying doggo in Rosa's bar.

But how to find out? That day, without any obviously logical motivation, Glupf has Rosa's sink and its canalisation dug up. Nothing. And pays a visit to Rosa's upstairs room, tapping its walls, poking around on its roof. Nothing again.

At last Rosa is brought in front of a military tribunal.

Without wasting an instant, and without mincing words, an army solicitor shouts, "What did you do with our missing hussars? What did you do with Ibrahim, with Gribaldi and with Worms, all of whom hang out at your bar? And what, pray, did you do on Monday night, 28 July?"

But Rosa is a match for him.

"Worms? Gribaldi? Ibrahim? By all my holy saints, by my darling Virgin Mary, I don't know any Worms, Gribaldi or Ibrahim! Lots of troops hang out at my bar!"

"Harlot!" shouts out Glupf. "It's all around town!"

"I am? You liar! I got a boy of my own, a good boy, a dragoon, who'll kill anybody that puts a hand on my body."

"Who is it! Who!"

"I obj–" a solicitor starts to say, until Glupf shouts him down.

Finally an accusation of criminal disloyalty and incitation to kill is brought against Rosa.

But in his own summing-up Rosa's solicitor shows that this accusation has as its foundation not proof but only word-of-mouth, no convincing fact but only circumstantial supposition, no probing point but only Major Glupf's wish, at any cost, to vilify his antagonist.

So, to a standing ovation, with a host of "hurrahs" and "bravos" and "attababys" from an approving public, Rosa is found not guilty. Poor Glupf admits to losing – promising, though, that only a fight and not a war is lost, that a day will dawn, a day on which Rosa will find out who is truly in command, a day on which Auschwitz will turn up its gas – and strolls out whistling a military march.

Within six days of that trial, a commando attacks Rosa's bar with a bazooka. Body upon body, carcass upon carcass,

269

is found, including Rosa's, but not including Gribaldi's or Ibrahim's or that of any missing conscript . . .

"Now I'd call that totally unambiguous," says Swann, concluding his curious account.

"Why, not at all," says Savorgnan, instantly contradicting him. "I'm willing to go along with you on Yorick's going AWOL, but not on his dying."

"Arthur's right – not on his dying," says Ottaviani, parrot-fashion, hoping to sound brainy by imitating his dad.

"As Rosa's bar, not surprisingly, was blown to bits, with not a wall standing," says Swann, "Glupf and his troops had to start bulldozing away a mass of bricks and mortar and tiling and stuff, and a watch was found, a charming rococo watch with, on its dial, a ribbon of gold garlands of Arab origin – a watch, I might add, which Yorick Gribaldi had bought just that month."

"But who's to know it wasn't a gift from Yorick to Rosa?"

"That's right – a gift from Yorick to Rosa," parrots Ottaviani.

"Hmm, all right," admits Swann, "on its own it isn't implicit proof of Yorick's dying. But I'll furnish you now with a truly convincing proof. This, *ab absurdo*, is my postulation:

"Assuming that Yorick *is* in fact kaput, all anybody has to do is kill Ottavio Ottaviani, alias Ulrich Savorgnan, so that instantly, according to that old family law, Arthur Wilburg Savorgnan, having no son still living, will fall victim to it in his turn!"

"Cunning!" clucks Squaw.

"Inhuman!" shouts Savorgnan.

"Nazi!" spits out Ottaviani.

"And, in fact," says Swann almost nonchalantly, "I think I'll find out if my solution works. First of all, I'll kill Ottavio, who's starting to put my back up anyway."

"But why?" says Ottaviani imploringly. "I'm too young!"

"Now now, Ottavio, I want no grumbling from you," says his boss. "Wasn't it obvious to you that a climax was approaching fast?"

Ottaviani starts sobbing.

"But it's got nothing to do with – "

"Button your lip, you moron!" roars Swann, pounding him on his skull. "Why don't you look at this communication that was put into my hands not long ago?"

Swann unlocks his holdall, draws out a manuscript and hands it to Ottaviani.

"Why Ottaviani?" asks Squaw, who was obviously not *au fait* with Swann's tactics.

"You'll find out," murmurs Swann, smiling sardonically. "Aloud, Ottavio, *s'il vous plaît*."

Adjusting his lorgnon, coughing, swallowing, gargling, Ottaviani gulps and, with a slightly pompous intonation, starts:

> *"I'm going to rock this child in his cot," sighs Orgon, son of Ubu. "I'm going to wolf down mutton, broccoli, dumplings, rich plum pudding. I'm going to drink, not grog, but punch." Orgon drinks hock, too, rum, Scotch, plus two hot brimming mugs of Bovril to finish up with, which soon prompts him to nod off. Running brooks drown out his snoring. I stroll to rocks on which I too will nod off, with Orgon's dozing son, with Orgon, son of Ubu.*
>
> *Condors swoop down on us. Poor scrofulous lions slink out, scrutinising dingos with scornful looks. Chipmunks run wild. Opossums run, too, without stopping. North or south? I wouldn't know. Plunging off clifftops, bison split limbs in two. It hurts. Ivy grows on brick, rising up from stucco pots to shroud windows or roofs.*
>
> *From Ubu's bottom drops his own bulk in gold.*

"Hmm," says Savorgnan, having difficulty in disguising his confusion.

"What!" says Swann, as if furious at Savorgnan's stupidity, "isn't it obvious what's so fascinating about it?"

"Frankly, no."

"Look at it, Savorgnan – it hasn't got a solitary 'a'!"

"Good God!" says Savorgnan, snatching it out of Ottaviani's hands and staring at it. "It hasn't at that!"

"Mindblowing!" says Squaw.

"Fascinating," Savorgnan concurs, "just fascinating."

"And in addition," adds Swann, "I can find just a solitary 'y' in it – in 'ivy'!"

"Astonishing! Amazing! Astounding!"

Ottaviani finally asks for his manuscript back. Savorgnan hands it to him and, as though only now grasping its import, Ottaviani quickly scans it, moving his lips but not saying a word.

"So, Ottavio," says Swann sarcastically, "do you catch on now?"

Ottaviani looks ill, squirming in his chair, shaking uncontrollably, finding it impossibly difficult to say what's on his mind.

"I . . . I . . ."

"What?"

Crumpling up, Ottavio Ottaviani murmurs in a dying fall: "Nor has it got a solitary

26

Which, as you must know by now, is this book's last

"Pardon?" say his two companions, who hadn't caught that Omission of which only Ottaviani was conscious.

But Ottaviani says nothing, making only a short, sharp sound – a kind of pop or plop, a tiny bit grating, a tiny bit irritating, but so soft you almost instantly forgot it.

Squaw abruptly cuts in with a mournful cry.

"What is it?" asks Swann, blanching.

"Ottaviani! Ottaviani!" howls Squaw.

Crimson, florid, Ottaviani starts inflating. As imposing and plump as Buck Mulligan standing on top of a spiral stairway whilst intoning an "Introibo", his slowly magnifying body brings to mind a purplish balloon, of a sort that you might buy for your child in Parc Montsouris.

And, in a twinkling, just as such a balloon will combust if brought into contact with a sharp point, Ottaviani burst, his body ripping apart, making a din as loud as an aircraft attaining Mach III and outstripping sound with a mirror-smashing bang.

And, in an instant, not a nail, not a button – poor Ottaviani is nothing but a puny, chalky mass as small as a tiny turd of ash from a cigar but so oddly whitish in colour you might think it was talc.

Savorgnan stands dumbstruck, stiff and still. His two last sons dying in turn, two sons long thought in Abraham's bosom, abruptly brought back to him and now just as abruptly dying again – it was obviously too much for him. Sobbing, vainly trying to control his sorrow, this poor papa says to Swann:

"I'm right in thinking, am I not, that you did all his dirty work – you did just what that Bushy Man told you to do?"

"I wouldn't put it that way – but I *was* his faithful right hand, you know, his front, his proconsul . . ."

"No, I didn't know . . ."

"It was staring at you, though."

"I don't follow you."

"What is implicit in 'Aloysius Swann' if not 'a blank cygnal'?"

Savorgnan sighs, continuing, "As this is obviously my last call, my last hurrah, may I know how it is that I'm to quit this world of ours? For, if I know you, you won't disappoint your victim with any humdrum sort of killing!"

"*Oh là là*," says Swann, cackling, "I can think of about 5 amusingly roundabout ways of killing you.

"I could first of all, finding you caught up in a work of fiction, a book by Zola, say, from his Rougon-Macquart saga (but not *L'Assommoir*; possibly *Nana*) – I could hand you a fruit that had a bomb in it: an apricot, a cantaloup, or possibly an ananas, that sanguinary fruit that Lyndon B. Johnson, day in, day out, would drop on Hanoi, not giving a hoot for any notion of supranational rights, as many political symposia would forthrightly affirm. Anyway, my cunning apparatus would go off just as, hot and thirsty, you cut your ananas in two, so blowing you sky-high.

"Or I could also, using a nodal cord, submit to amputation, mutilation, incision, ablation, castration, abscission, scission, omission or division that most vital part of your body – your cock, your prick, your manly organ – or, possibly, by a kind of phallic symbolism, just your snout, an act that would kill you off within six months at most.

"Or, if I sought a truly outlandish solution, I could, in a country wood in which you had a habit of taking your constitutional, look, in an oak or a birch, for a good roosting spot for birds and submit its occupants to a fatal quantity of radioactivity (a milligram of uranium would do, its fission producing a strong gamma ray). In addition, not far from that oak or birch, I'd simply drop a big bag of fondants – I know how fond of fondants my old chum Arthur is. So, strolling to and fro, idly larking about, nibbling on cat's-tails and cowslips, you catch sight of this alluring bag of bonbons. Pouncing gluttonously on it, you sit down to stuff your gob and, just at that instant, from out of said oak or birch, birds start dropping on to you, birds full of radioactivity, irradiating your body with maximum impact.

"Or I could go about it this way.

"You'd fly out to Japan for a gala. In Tokyo, for I know your skill at Go, you'd no doubt want to watch a foolhardy tyro taking on a champion, Kaku Takagawa, a 'Kan Shu', if not actually a 'Kudan', in a local charity match – taking him on, as I say, but obviously with a strong handicap to assist him, not a 'furin' but a 'Naka yotsu'. Kaku Takagawa would start with a 'Moku had-zushi' and, his antagonist lost in a 'Ji dori Go' as clumsy as it was vain (what you should play is, as you know, Arthur, a 'Takamoku Kakari'), would triumphantly follow it up with an 'Ozaru' (or 'Grand Baboon's Gambit', as it's still known) and, rounding it off with a brilliant 'Oi Otoshi', win by a 'Naka oshi gatchi', to acclamation from an approving public.

"But, Takagawa having won his match, a production of a Noh play would follow, a play you'd find both long and mystifying. You'd want at first to go, but, out of tact to your hosts, you'd try to follow it for an act or so and, by constantly consulting a fitfully illuminating synopsis, try to grasp a word, a look, a sound, a hint of fury, of sorrow, of passion, that would allow you to know what it was all about, allow you to know what was going on not all that far from your fourth-row chair but what simply wasn't swimming into focus, just as a man who, rapt in a book, a work of fiction, constantly hoping for a solution, for a solution that's driving him crazy by lurking just out of his grasp, a solution that has had throughout, in fact from its first word, an infuriating habit of staring at him whilst continually avoiding his own scru-tiny, might find, advancing into its story, nothing but ambiguous mystification and rationalisation, obscurantism and obfuscation, all of it consigning to a dim and murky chiaroscuro that ambition, so to say, that lit its author's lamp.

"So at last, worn out by such taxing brainwork, you'd nod off, just as a dog would if Pavlov, stimulating it with a salivating aroma, didn't follow it up with a gift of a juicy chop, thus maximally inhibiting its cortico-subcortico-cortical circuit, that which controls its instincts, its 'arousal', as biologists say. And, at that instant, I'd find it child's play to bump you off.

"Or, finally (I told you, did I not, that I had 5 options), I could attack you whilst idly strolling in a public park admiring statuary by such as Girardon or Coustou, Gimond or, most particularly, Rodin. All I'd do is clutch in my fist a jack, a car jack, so that, as you stood in front of a Rodin, say, studying its imposing contours, I'd simply undo that bolt that maintains it upright, causing it to fall and crush you."

"Nobody, I think," says Arthur Wilburg Savorgnan, "could claim that I was lacking in humour. So I applaud your final spasm of imagination. But, if you want my opinion, I truly don't know how you could, at this instant, bring about my downfall in any such outlandish fashion. For, if I'm not wrong, this room contains nothing at all of what you want – no igniting fruit or nodal cord or radiating birds or Go board or Rodin statuary."

"Don't think I'm not conscious of that," says Swann icily. "But I'm carrying at my hip a plaything that I find is just as handy!"

So saying, Swann draws out a Smith-Corona pistol and, without pausing for an instant, shoots Savorgnan point-blank.

"Voilà," says Squaw, in a sort of monosyllabic singsong, "all kaput. All kaput. Who would think it? And, you know, I find this conclusion just a tiny bit anticlimactic, a tiny bit *Much Ado About Nothing*, a bit irritating, a bit discouraging, don't you think?"

"Oh, *chi va piano va sano*," says Swann, smiling. "All kaput, as you say. And all worthy of absolution; all, I pray, worthy of magnanimity and pardon. For, though guilty of many criminal acts, of many sins, our companions did, you must admit, furnish

276

a constant and unfailing collaboration. And I can think of many a protagonist, factual or fictional, who hasn't had to put up with so rigorous a constraint. In this story, though, our lot would confront it unflinchingly from start to finish . . ."

"Shut up," murmurs Squaw, to Swann's mortification, "you talk too much . . ."

"So now," says Squaw again, "is this actually our *Finis Coronat Opus*? Is this how our story must finish? Is this its last word?"

"It is," says Swann, "it is. This circuitous labyrinth, through which all of us would drift with a somnambulist's languorous gait, driving our plot forward with our contribution to it, our participation in it, moving on and on, braving its paralysing taboo, concocting out of that taboo, to a point of saturation, a story which, with all its manifold ramifications, would abolish what you might call its random factor only at a cost of our giving up any claim to a solution, similar to a lamp illuminating, and fitfully, only part of our path, according us only a hint, an inkling, of what is lying in front of us, of what is awaiting us – it is, I say, fast approaching its conclusion, its last word. But Franz Kafka said it first: you know what your goal is but you don't know of any path to that goal and what you call a path is only your own blind, groping doubt.

"All of us did, notwithstanding, go forward, slowly, haltingly, approaching a final point, for a final point was obligatory in a story such as ours, imagining, too, on occasion, that it was obvious what that final point was, confronting a 'What?' with a 'That', a 'Why' with a 'For', a 'How' with a 'This Way' or a 'That Way'.

"But an illusion was always lurking in such solutions, an illusion of wisdom, wisdom to which not any of us could truly lay claim, not our protagonists, not our author, and not I, Swann, his faithful right hand, and it was that lack of wisdom, that chronic inability of ours to grasp what was actually going on, that had us talking away, constructing our story, building up its idiotic plot, inflating all its intrinsic bombast, its absurd hocus-pocus, without at any instant attaining its cardinal point, its horizon, its infinity, that climactic coda of harmony out of which a solution would at long last loom,

but approaching, by an inch, by a micron, by an angstrom, that fatal point at which,

without that taboo constituting us and uniting us and drawing us apart,

a void,

a void with its brass hands,

a void with its cold, numb hands,

a void rubbing out its own inscription,

a void assuring this Book, of all Books, a truly singular purity and immaculation, notwithstanding all its markings in ink and paragraphs of print,

a void brings our story to its conclusion."

POSTSCRIPT

On that ambition, conspicuous throughout this tiring book
which you will soon shut, having had your fill of it without,
I trust, skipping too much – on that ambition, so to say,
which lit its author's lamp

My ambition, as Author, my point, I would go so far as to say my fixation, my constant fixation, was primarily to concoct an artifact as original as it was illuminating, an artifact that would, or just possibly might, act as a stimulant on notions of construction, of narration, of plotting, of action, a stimulant, in a word, on fiction-writing today.

Whilst, in my first books, writing principally about my situation, my psychology, my social background, my capacity (or incapacity) of adaptation, my mania for commodification (almost tantamount, as is said on occasion, to what you might call "thingification"), it was my wish, by drawing inspiration from a (modish) linguistic dogma claiming primacy for what Saussurian structuralists call a *signifiant* – it was my wish, I say, to polish up this tool that I had at my disposal, a tool that until now I would ply without pain or strain; not that it was my ambition to diminish any contradiction intrinsic to such a constraint nor, naturally, that I was wholly unconscious of it, but by contrast that I thought I might fulfil such an ambition by fully assuming that (as I say) modish structuralist dogma, which was, in my writing of this book, not a handicap, not a constriction, but, all in all, a spur to my imagination.

What was my purport in imposing this constraint? Offhand, with hindsight, I can think of many factors bubbling about in my brain, but I ought to admit right away that its origin was totally haphazard, touch and go, a flip of a coin. It all got out of hand with a companion calling my bluff (I said I could do it, this companion said I could not); and I should admit, too, that so inauspiciously shaky was that launching pad, I had no inkling at all that, as an acorn contains an oak, anything solid would grow out of it.

Initially I found such a constraint faintly amusing, if that; but I stuck to my guns. At which point, finding that it took my imagination down so many intriguing linguistic highways and byways, I couldn't stop thinking about it, plunging into it again and again, at last giving up all my ongoing work, much of which I was actually about to finish.

So was born, word by word, and paragraph by paragraph, a book caught within a formalist grid doubly arduous in that it would risk striking as insignificant anybody ignorant of its solution, a book that, crankily idiosyncratic as it no doubt is, I instantly found thoroughly satisfying:

a) I, as an author, having not an iota of inspiration (and, in addition, placing no faith at all in inspiration as a Platonic form!) was displaying in this book just as much imagination as a Ponson or a Paulhan; and (b) I was, most notably, and to my own total gratification, slaking a thirst as constant as it is callow (not to say childish): a soft spot on my part – what am I saying? a passion – for accumulation, saturation, imitation, quotation, translation and automatisation.

And soon, my faith in my ability to carry it off growing day by day, I thought I might start giving my plotting a symbolic turn, so that, by following my book's story hand in hand until totally coinciding with it, it would point up, without blatantly divulging, that Law that was its inspiration, that Law from which it would draw, not without occasional friction, and not without occasional vulgarity, but also not without occasional humour, nor, I think, without brio, a rich, fruitful narration, honing my writing skills in unthought-of ways.

282

I was thus to grasp a significant fact: that, just as, say, Frank Lloyd Wright built his own working and living conditions, so was I fashioning, *mutatis mutandis*, a prototypical product which – spurning that paradigm of articulation, organisation and imagination dominant in today's fiction, abandoning for good that rampant psychologisation which, along with a bias towards mawkish moralising (in fact, not so much mawk*ish* as downright *mawk*), is still for most critics a mainspring of our national gift for (or myth of?) "clarity" and "proportion" and "polish" – sought inspiration in a linguistic avant-gardism virtually unknown in this country, and for which no critic has a good word in so far as it's known at all, but which allows of a possibility of imitating, simulating and honouring a tradition that has brought forth a *Gargantua* and a *Tristram Shandy* and a *Mathias Sandorf* and a *Locus Solus* and (why not?) a *Bifur* or a *Fourbis*, books for which I had sworn undying admiration, without daring to harbour any illusions that I might possibly attain in any of my own works such jubilation and such fanciful humour, by dint of irony and wit, paradox and prodigality, by dint, in short, of an imagination knowing just how far to go too far.

So, as I think, in this work, for all that its origin was chaotic, I finally did satisfy most of my goals and obligations. Not only did I spin out a fairly straightforward story but I had a lot of fun with it (wasn't it Raymond Q. Knowall who said that it was hardly worth writing if it was simply as a soporific?), fun, principally (by locating and disclosing that contradiction in which all syntactic, structural or symbolic signification is bound up), in my ambition of participating, of collaborating, in a common policy to adopt a radical, wilfully conflictual position vis-à-vis fiction, a position that, implicitly critical as it is of a Troyat, a Mauriac, a Blondin or a Cau, of any Quai Conti, *Figaro* or Prix Goncourt hack, might still chart a path along which fiction could again find an inspiration, a charm, a stimulus, in narrational virtuosity of a sort thought lost for good.

METAGRAPHS

E SERVEM LEX EST, LEGEMQUE TENERE NECESSE EST?
 SPES CERTE NEC MENS, ME REFERENTE, DEEST;
 SED LEGE, ET ECCE EVEN NENTEMVE GREGEMVE
TENENTEM.
 PERLEGE, NEC ME RES EDERE RERE LEVES

LORD HOLLAND
Eve's Legend

The magic alphabet, the mysterious hieroglyph, come to us only in an incomplete and garbled form, garbled either by the passage of time or by those with a vested interest in our ignorance; should we retrieve the letter which has been lost or the sign which has been effaced, should we reconstruct the dissonant scale, we shall regain our authority in the world of the mind.

GÉRARD DE NERVAL
(quoted by Paul Eluard, *Poésie
involontaire et poésie intentionnelle*)

If one had a dictionary of primitive languages, one would find in it obvious vestiges of an earlier language spoken by an enlightened people, and even were these not to be found, it would mean only that the degradation had reached such a point that they had been wholly eradicated.

DE MAISTRE
Les Soirées de Saint-Pétersbourg
(quoted by Flaubert: *Brouillons de Bouvard*;
quoted by Geneviève Bollème)

The language of the Papuans is very impoverished; each tribe has its own language, and its vocabulary is ceaselessly diminished because, after every death, a few words are eliminated as a sign of mourning.

E. BARON
Géographie
(quoted by Roland Barthes: *Critique et Vérité*)

It is only in that instant when the laws are silent that great actions erupt.

SADE

Even for a word, we will not waste a vowel.

ANGLO-INDIAN PROVERB

"The unknown vowel". I have studied the phonemes of every language, past and present, in the world. Being principally interested in those vowels which are, as it were, the pure elements, the primitive cells, of language, I have followed vocalic sounds on their secular journeys, I have hearkened across the ages to the roar of the A, the whistle of the I, the bleat of the E, the hoot of the U and the snores of the O. The innumerable marriages that vowels have contracted with other sounds no longer hold any secrets for me. And yet, now almost at the end of my tareer, I realise that I still await, still anticipate, the unknown Vowel, the Vowel of Vowels that will contain all others, that will solve all proglems, a Vowel that is both beginning and end, that will take all of a man's breath to pronounce, by a monstrous distension of the jaws, as though combining in a single cry the yawn of boredom, the howl of hunger, the moan of love and the rattle of death. When I have found it, creation itself will be shallowed up and nothing will remain – nothing but the UNKNOWN NOWEL!

JEAN TARDIEU
Un mot pour un autre

Also by Georges Perec

LIFE A USER'S MANUAL
Translated by David Bellos

"One of the great novels of the century. . . a great book rather
than a merely brilliant one"   *TLS*

"A transcendent achievement, a book of world class"
                                    LEWIS JONES, *Daily Telegraph*

"The most enjoyable novel of the year"
                                    ADAM MARS-JONES, *Independent*

W or The Memory Childhood
Translated by David Bellos

"Haunting and compelling, chilling and totally effective.. Must
rank alongside the really crucial texts in the literature of the
Holocaust, the testimony of the survivors."
                                    NIGEL WILLIAMS, *Listener*

Things. A Story of the Sixties
Translated by David Bellos

"As a witty attack on consumerism *Things* is as much a parable of
the Nineties as it is a story of the Sixties."
                                    LINDA BRANDON, *Sunday Times*

A Man Asleep
Translated by Andrew Leak

"Grimly obsessing... one turns the pages with unlikely
fascination."   EUAN CAMERON, *Sunday Telegraph*

"53 Days"
Translated by David Bellos

"Can take its place at the beginning of a tradition of post-modern
and highly literary whodunits. Even in its unfinished state, it
makes a particularly dazzling addition to the canon."
                                    JONATHAN COE, *Sunday Times*